DRUGS AND THE MIND

Books by Robert S. de Ropp

IF I FORGET THEE

MAN AGAINST AGING

THE MASTER GAME

SEX ENERGY

THE NEW PROMETHEANS

CHURCH OF THE EARTH

ECO-TECH

DRUGS AND THE MIND

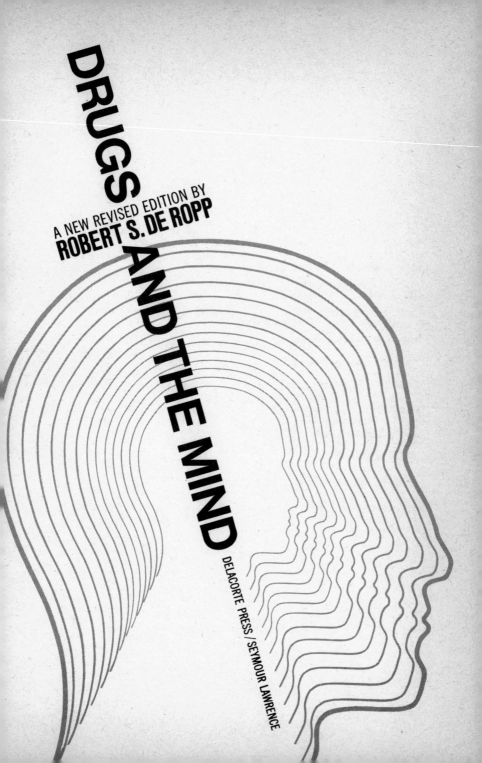

DRUGS AND THE MIND

A NEW REVISED EDITION BY

ROBERT S. DE ROPP

DELACORTE PRESS / SEYMOUR LAWRENCE

Manufactured in the United States of America

First printing

Library of Congress Cataloging in Publication Data

De Ropp, Robert S
    Drugs and the mind.

    Bibliography: p.
    Includes index.
    1. Psychopharmacology.   2. Drug abuse.
I.   Title.
RM315.D47   1976   615'.78   75-37807

ISBN 0-440-04680-7

Acknowledgments

Grateful acknowledgment is made for permission to use the following copyrighted material.

Excerpt from PEYOTE by Alice Marriott and Carol K. Rachlin: Copyright © 1971 by Alice Marriott and Carol K. Rachlin. With permission of Thomas Y. Crowell Company.

"The Native American Church Meeting" by Stewart Brand: From *Psychedelic Review,* No. 9, 1967. Every effort has been made to locate the proprietor of this material. If the proprietor will write to the publisher, formal arrangements will be made.

From THE TEACHINGS OF DON JUAN by Carlos Castaneda: Copyright © 1968 by The Regents of the University of California; reprinted by permission of the University of California Press.

From "Statement on Peyote" by W. LaBarre, D. P. McAllister, O. S. Slotkin, O. C. Stewart and S. Tax: Reprinted by permission from *Science,* Vol. 114, pp. 582–583, November 30, 1951.

Excerpt from pages 16, 18 and 19 in THE DOORS OF PERCEPTION by Aldous Huxley: Copyright 1954 by Aldous Huxley. Reprinted by permission of Harper & Row, Publishers, Inc., Mrs. Laura Huxley, and Chatto & Windus Ltd.

Excerpt from MARIHUANA: DECEPTIVE WEED edited by G. G. Nahas: © 1975 (revised edition) Raven Press, New York. Used by permission.

Excerpt from REALLY THE BLUES by Milton Mezzrow and Bernard Wolfe: © 1969 by Milton Mezzrow and Bernard Wolfe. Reprinted by permission of Harold Matson Co., Inc.

Excerpt from a Letter to the Editor by Charles R. Beyle: © 1969 by The New York Times Company. Reprinted by permission, and by permission of the author.

Excerpt from article by R. Gordon Wasson: First published in *Life*, May 13, 1954.

Excerpts from THE POLITICS OF ECSTASY by Timothy Leary: Reprinted by permission of G. P. Putnam's Sons from THE POLITICS OF ECSTASY by Timothy Leary. Copyright © 1968 by The League for Spiritual Discovery, Inc. Used by permission of MacGibbon & Kee.

Excerpt from "Clinical study of the mescaline psychosis with special reference to the mechanism of the genesis of schizophrenia and other psychotic states" by G. T. Stockings: From *Journal of Mental Science*, 86: 29–47, 1940. Used by permission.

Excerpt from "Schizophrenia: A New Approach" by Humphrey Osmond and John Smythies: From *Journal of Mental Science*, 98: 308–315, 1952. Used by permission.

Excerpt from "Frequel, a blocking agent against experimental LSD-25 and mescaline psychosis" by H. D. Fabing: From *Neurology*, 5: 319–322, 1955, Copyright The New York Times Media Company, Inc. Used by permission.

Excerpt from MAN ON HIS NATURE by Sir Charles S. Sherrington: Used by permission of Cambridge University Press.

Contents

Introduction

The first edition of *Drugs and the Mind* was published in 1957. Since that time there has been an enormous upsurge of interest in drugs that affect the mind and emotions. Substances like LSD which, in 1957, were little more than laboratory curiosities, their effects known only to a few scientists, have now attained notoriety. They have become the center of a new religion. They have been talked about, written about, praised, cursed, condemned and finally banned. The number of articles written about LSD alone runs into thousands.

A similar upsurge of interest has occurred in relation to marijuana. Not only is it used by a very large number of people but it has also become the center of a great deal of research. In the first edition of *Drugs and the Mind* this statement was made: "Despite the tremendous recent interest in psychochemistry this important group of compounds has been ignored and we know as little about the mode of action of the hemp drug on the brain as did Hasan-i-Sabbah when he fed it to his followers nearly a thousand years ago."

One is forced to admit that we still, in the mid-1970s, know very little about the way in which marijuana produces its effects on the mind. But it certainly is not for lack of research. The various "power possessing beings" who decide what we may or may not legally eat, drink or smoke realized somewhere in the sixties that they could hardly go on condemning marijuana when so little was known about its effects. Funds suddenly became available for research on marijuana and the drug itself, carefully grown and of standard potency, was made available to chosen investigators, of whom the author was one. So we now know a great deal more about marijuana; indeed the flood of new information about this drug is almost as overwhelming as the flood of information about LSD.

This upsurge of new knowledge about "mind-drugs" has prompted the author to rewrite *Drugs and the Mind*. Not only has he incorporated a lot of new material but he has also felt compelled to rearrange the subject matter. He has done this by separating the material into three parts.

Part I, "The Magic Garden," deals with drugs that are used (or abused) for purposes of pleasure, for religious purposes, for the attainment of insights into the self, for escape, etc. Drugs of this kind are largely self-administered, are taken in most cases illegally, and are sometimes employed in such a way that they harm the user.

Part II, "Sick Minds: New Medicines," deals with drugs that are used by qualified members of the medical profession for the treatment of various dysfunctions that are loosely referred to as mental illnesses. About these drugs, too, there has been an enormous flood of new information. Despite thousands of papers and many books on the subject of psychotherapeutic agents we still have only a rather foggy idea as to how they work. But work they do. The dramatic reduction of the population of mental hospitals proves it.

Part III, "Mind and Matter," explores the workings of that entity which John Lilly called the human biocomputer. When we say that drugs act on the mind we are not being precise. Drugs act on the brain. The brain is a fantastically complex chemical factory in which billions of molecules of varying degrees of complexity form, break and re-form in a ceaseless dance. This dance of the molecules is accompanied by a no-less-ceaseless flow of electrical impulses that course through the nerves, both sensory and motor. From all this activity, filtered, selected, and refined, emerges that mysterious entity which man calls mind. Between the molecular activity and man's mental experience there is a gap which we are not able to fill. But this much is certain. The chemistry of the brain is the substrate of the mind and that which alters the chemistry of the brain will affect the mind. Just how the "mind-drugs" do this is the subject matter of Part III.

PART ONE

The Magic
Garden

The Lure of the Garden

The concept of a garden with forbidden fruits has long fascinated the mind of man. The myth of the garden of Eden with its mysterious tree is the archetype of this magic garden and of the temptation that assails men to break into the garden.

The original penalty for eating the forbidden fruit was death and this penalty was imposed by the Lord God Himself: "But of the tree of the knowledge of good and evil, thou shalt not eat of it: for in the day that thou eatest there thou shalt surely die" (Gen. 2:17). But the serpent, more subtle than any beast of the field, challenged the word of the Lord God: "Ye shall not surely die: for God doth know that in the day ye eat thereof, then your eyes shall be opened, and ye shall be as gods, knowing good and evil" (Gen. 3:4–5).

And behold it turned out that the serpent was right and the Lord God was wrong. Neither Adam nor Eve died of eating the fruit. Thus the defiance of established authority by the eating of forbidden fruit started in the garden of Eden and has continued ever since. The Lord God, that overbearing authority, was shown up by the serpent as either an ignoramus or a liar. He had grossly overestimated the toxicity of the fruit of the tree, or tried scare tactics to frighten poor naked Adam and Eve out of making experiments with some natural psychedelic. When his trick was exposed he turned tyrannical, as authorities will. He cursed Adam, cursed Eve and cursed the snake. He threw Adam and Eve out of the garden lest, emboldened by their earlier experiment they should eat of the tree of life and become immortal. So he posted cherubim with flaming swords, prototypes of our contemporary narcs, to guard the sacred tree. Thus was the pattern established and has endured till today.

What is the magic garden and what does it contain?

All the plants in the magic garden have one thing in common. They affect man's awareness of himself and his way of perceiving the world about him. Within the garden are to be found members of a wide variety of botanical families. The flowering plants are well represented, the hemp, the poppy, various members of the nightshade family, the peyote cactus, the coca shrub and the morning glory vine. The fungi are also present, not only the flamboyant fly agaric, with its scarlet cap but also the more modest members of the *psilocybe* family, collectively known to the Aztecs as *teonanacatl*. Now to these natural formations the modern chemist has added his quota of synthetics, some of which, like the fabulous LSD (lysergic acid diethylamide), far exceed in potency any naturally occurring compound.

The struggle over these forbidden fruits that started in the garden of Eden has now developed, at least in the United States, into an expensive and continuous form of civil war. An army of self-righteous bureaucrats, whose main aim in life is to forbid to others pleasures (real or unreal) which they do not fancy for themselves, has tried every possible device (short of cherubim with flaming swords) to keep their fellow men from breaking into the garden. Threats, violence, prison sentences, punishments more drastic than those meted out for robbery or rape are inflicted on those caught raiding the magic garden. It is a muddled struggle in which "ignorant armies clash by night," a struggle made ludicrously illogical by the fact that two major products of the magic garden, ethyl alcohol and tobacco, are for some reason permitted, whereas others, intrinsically less harmful, are stringently forbidden. Some are labeled, moreover, narcotics though even an informed high school student knows perfectly well they are not.

In an atmosphere of generalized hysteria reminiscent of that which prevailed during the witch-hunts of the fifteenth and sixteenth centuries the war over the magic garden continues. It is difficult for an objective observer to decide which of the forces demonstrates the higher level of stupidity. The custodians show in their behavior many of the qualities of the rhinoceros, a beast famous for its thick skin, bad temper and tendency to violence. The raiders of the garden, on the other hand, are not particularly bright either. Of those who get caught it can be said that they were lacking in alertness having been mowed down by so dull a beast as a rhinoceros. But to those who avoid getting caught the question may still be addressed: Was the garden really worth raiding in the first place?

Why do otherwise law-abiding citizens insist on raiding the magic garden? What are they seeking from the "power plants" it contains? Obviously they are seeking something they lack. The Greeks had a word for the missing something. That word was *ataraxia*. It was a happy state in which mental serenity was combined with physical well-being, a balanced condition, free from those violent ups and downs that disharmonize the emotional life of the average man. *Ataraxia* was best cultivated by the exercise of philosophy, by inner discipline, by the practice of virtue. The Epicurean philosophers regarded it as the highest possible good.

The Greeks were not alone in holding this condition in such high esteem. Steadiness, inward calm, and harmony have been extolled by all the great religious systems—Christian, Buddhist, Taoist, Vedantist; nor need one be a saint or a philosopher to hunger after this inner tranquillity. It is natural to desire such a state, for without it no real happiness is possible. The hustled inhabitants of the modern world, driven at an increasingly furious tempo in an atmosphere of clamor and violent distraction, must particularly long for this inward peace. It is a pearl of great price; perhaps *the* pearl of great price. The question is how to obtain this pearl.

There have, in the past, been two main methods by which it could be obtained: the practice of religion and the practice of philosophy. But because both these methods call for long and arduous self-discipline men have searched from the earliest times for a *short cut to happiness,* seeking in the realms of pharmacy a means of attaining the desired condition by a procedure no more laborious than the swallowing of a pill.

Teachers of religion and philosophy may declare that such

a quest is essentially immoral. It is wrong, they may state, to expect from a drug those gifts which saints and sages have striven to attain by means of the most intensive spiritual efforts. What can you gain from a drug? these critics may ask. What can it possibly give you except slavery? You will become dependent on the contents of a bottle. You will no longer be your own master, but merely the plaything of a chemical substance. The peace you may buy in such a way will be purchased at the expense of your self-respect. You may become a happier being but you will also become a weaker one. Is happiness, on such conditions, worth having? Are you not paying too much for your chemically engendered peace of mind?

Such objections are quite valid. There are a number of very interesting moral problems connected with the use of drugs for the attainment of mental tranquillity or happiness about which a great deal might be said. In this book, however, these problems will not be discussed. It is the author's aim to place before the reader facts regarding several classes of drugs which influence, in one way or another, the mind or the emotions of man. On the basis of these facts the reader himself can decide whether these various agents really do offer happiness or merely an imitation of happiness, whether the peace they give is genuine or merely a general numbing of the intelligence and senses. One can, after all, give a man peace of a sort simply by hitting him over the head with a club. If this is the only sort of peace that drugs can offer we might prefer to do without it.

Louis Lewin, the famous German toxicologist, wrote in 1924 a book called *Phantastica: Narcotic and Stimulating Drugs,*[61] which dealt with this problem of the action of drugs on the mind. His book was intended not only for doctors but also for laymen. The writer of the present book has built on the foundations laid by Lewin and endeavored to bring the subject up to date, for many advances have recently been made.

Lewin distinguished five classes of drugs that influence mind and emotions. He called them *euphorica, phantastica, inebriantia, hypnotica,* and *excitantia.* Today we use somewhat different terms. Instead of phantastica we speak of *psychedelics,* a term

coined by Dr. Humphrey Osmond which means "mind revealing."
It is applied to substances like LSD-25, psilocybin and mescaline.
These substances have also been called *hallucinogens* or *psychotomimetic* agents because the states they produce are supposed
to resemble a psychosis. Lewin's hypnotica are commonly referred
to as *sedatives* and include such substances as barbiturates,
chloral hydrate and paraldehyde. When the new antipsychotic
drugs such as chlorpromazine were discovered they were first
called *ataraxics* by Dr. Howard Fabing because they calmed
without producing drowsiness. They are also called *tranquilizers,*
a distinction being made between major tranquilizers (chlorpromazine) and minor ones such as "Miltown." Finally Lewin's
excitantia, which includes such stimulants of the nervous system
as cocaine, amphetamine and "Ritalin," are sometimes referred
to as *analeptics.*

This rather confused nomenclature has been criticized by Dr.
Leo Hollister.[41] Hollister prefers to indicate the effect of a drug
by the "anti" system. Thus drugs used for treating anxiety would
be termed antianxiety drugs, those used for mental depressions
would be antidepressants, those used in treating schizophrenia or
other psychoses would be antipsychotics. Those used for treating
mania (e.g., lithium salts) would be antimanic drugs. The system
is simple and highly descriptive and probably the best so far
devised, at least for drugs in legitimate clinical use.

The drugs that exert these effects were derived, to begin with,
from plants in the magic garden. Only very recently did the organic chemist begin to supplement these natural products with
synthetic materials. The mysterious "power plants" have been
known for centuries and were often endowed with a halo of
divinity by members of various cultures who used them as a
means of communicating with their gods. The *peyotl* was sacred
to the Aztecs, the *coca* to the Incas. The gods in the Vedas drank
soma, those of the Greeks *ambrosia. Nepenthe* was praised by
Homer as the "potent destroyer of grief" and the hemp plant with
its potent resin *charas* was described by the sages of India as the
"delight giver."

The properties of these plants were discovered accidentally, in many cases so long ago that we have no idea when their virtues first became known. Our hairy ancestors gained their knowledge of drugs the hard way. Impelled by hunger, they ate what they could find, root or berry, leaf, flower, or fungus. Often they sat in their caves ruefully clutching their stomachs, wondering what they had eaten that had caused them to feel so desperately ill. They purged, they vomited, they convulsed, they collapsed, and the sum of their writhings and spewings, accumulated through the ages, provided the basis for the science of pharmacology. Knowledge of the poisonous properties of plants was cherished by individuals, more discerning than their fellows, who guarded their secrets jealously and employed their understanding of poisons to further their own interests. Gradually, as religions evolved, these discerning characters became priests or witch doctors and their familiarity with poisons became a part of their sacred lore. Most precious of all to these early priests and witch doctors was their knowledge of the plants which affect the workings of the mind, which soothe griefs and relieve sufferings and flood the imagination with delightful visions.

Today the modern chemist is heir to all this painfully accumulated knowledge. He is the lineal descendant of a long line of witch doctors, shamans, sorcerers, and alchemists. Their carefully guarded secrets have become his stock in trade but he has improved and enormously enlarged his heritage. The crude and often nauseous decoctions which our forefathers swallowed to soothe their griefs or delight their imaginations have now been fractionated by the skill of the analysts. The crystalline essences on which their effects depend have been isolated and characterized. The very places of the component atoms within their molecules have been determined. Nor has the modern chemist been satisfied with these triumphs of analysis but, liberating himself from his dependence on roots and berries, he has embarked on a voyage into the realm of synthesis, creating compounds not found in nature, the properties of which frequently represent a vast improvement on any known natural substance.

Before we consider the "power plants" it will be useful if we reflect further upon the motives which lead men to break into the magic garden.

Andrew Weil (in *The Natural Mind*) has written a chapter entitled "Why People Take Drugs." "It is my belief," he states, "that the desire to alter consciousness periodically is an innate, normal drive analogous to hunger or the sexual drive."[100] This drive, he declares, begins to be expressed at an early age. Even very young children will whirl themselves into vertiginous stupors. They will "over breathe" or have other children squeeze them around the chest until they faint. They may even choke each other to produce loss of consciousness.

Children may learn at a fairly early age that chemical means may be used to induce the altered states of consciousness they desire. Sometimes they learn this by inhaling volatile solvents in certain household products. Sometimes they learn from the experience of general anesthesia in connection with a childhood operation. They also learn that this sort of experimentation involves entering a forbidden realm and that grown-ups will attempt to prevent them from going there. So the drive to alter consciousness may go underground. Its indulgence becomes a very private matter, like masturbation.

Dr. Weil considers this urge to alter consciousness to be cyclic in nature:

It looks like a real drive arising from the neurophysiological structure of the human brain. . . . Like the cyclic urge to relieve sexual tension, the urge to suspend ordinary awareness arises spontaneously from within, builds to a peak, finds relief, and dissipates—all in accordance with its own intrinsic rhythm. . . . And the pleasure in both cases arises from the relief of accumulated tension.[100]

Dr. Weil points out that this drive to experiment with other ways of experiencing our perceptions may be a key factor in the present evolution of the human nervous system. To attempt to thwart this drive would probably be impossible and might be dangerous. It might be psychologically crippling for the individual

and suicidal from the standpoint of the evolution of our species.
Dr. Weil states he "would not want to see us tamper with something so closely related to our curiosity, our creativity, our
intuition, and our highest aspirations."

It is of interest to compare this statement by a contemporary
American physician with that of a gifted French writer of the
nineteenth century whose approach to the problem was somewhat
different. We refer here to poor, embittered, devil-ridden Baudelaire whose face, in the photograph which prefaced his collected
works, seems etched with the acid of every form of grief and
frustration. In *Les Paradis Artificiels*[3] Baudelaire considered the
motivation of those who break into the magic garden. He certainly knew what he was talking about, for he was familiar with
opium, hashish and alcohol and all the joys and the miseries
these substances can create. His account has more than merely
literary value, for Baudelaire, unlike Gautier, Dumas, Ludlow
and other writers who described various drug effects in torrents
of rapturous prose, was a careful observer, not given to hyperbole.
Here is his description of the special craving that leads men to
seek for "the taste of the infinite."

*Those who are able to observe themselves and can remem-
ber their impressions often have occasion to note in the observa-
tory of their thoughts strange seasons, luxurious afternoons,
delicious minutes. There are days when a man awakens with a
young and vigorous genius. Hardly have his eyelids cast off the
sleep which sealed them before the outer world presents itself
to him in strong relief, with a clearness of contour and wealth
of admirable color. The man gratified with this sense of exquisite
loveliness, unfortunately so rare and so transitory, feels himself
more than ever the artist, more than ever noble, more than ever
just, if one can express so much in so few words. But the most
singular thing about this exceptional state of the spirit and of the
senses, which without exaggeration can be termed paradisiacal as
compared with the hopeless darkness of ordinary daily existence,
is that it has not been created by any visible or easily definable
cause.*

*This acuity of thought, this vigor of sense and spirit, has
at all times appeared to man as the highest good. For this reason,
purely for his immediate enjoyment, without troubling himself
about the limitations imposed by his constitution, he has searched
in the world of physical and of pharmaceutical science, among
the grossest decoctions and the most subtle perfumes, in all
climates and at all times, for the means of leaving, if only for a
few moments, his habitation of mud and of transporting himself
to Paradise in a single swoop.*

*Alas! Man's vices, horrible as they are supposed to be, contain
the positive proof of his taste for the Infinite.* Man will never
believe that he has entirely given himself over to evil. *He forgets,
in his infatuation, that he is playing with someone stronger and
keener than himself, and that the spirit of Evil, even if one gives
it no more than a single hair, will eventually carry away the head.
Therefore this visible lord of visible nature (I speak of man)
desired to create paradise with the help of pharmacy, exactly like
a maniac who would replace his solid furniture and real gardens
with decorations painted on canvas and mounted on easels. I
believe that in this depraved sense of the Infinite lies the reason
for all guilty excesses, from the solitary and concentrated intoxication of the man of letters who, obliged to turn to opium for
relief of some physical suffering, little by little makes it . . . the
sun of his spiritual life, to the drunkard who, his brain afire with
glory, hideously wallows in the filth of a Paris street.*[3]

Baudelaire's "taste of the infinite," his account of man's urge
to transport himself from his "habitation of mud," corresponds
to the cyclic impulse which Weil describes. Baudelaire is suspicious of the magic garden. He dismisses the wonders that the
power plants can evoke as mere artifacts "painted on canvas and
mounted on easels." But perhaps even an artificial paradise is
better than no paradise at all!

So the urge to experience altered states of consciousness is
certainly deep-rooted, perhaps a specific characteristic of the
spirit of man. But there is one fact that Weil has failed to em-
phasize in his study of this urge. *It is not present in all men.* It is

/ in the majority of men. And those who do not
; regard those who do with suspicion or down-

nankind into two groups, the plus and the minus, is
nat assails all those who feel the need to classify
their fellows. In relation to the magic garden we can say that
there are those who know it exists and those who don't, there
are those who wish to break into it and those who fear it and wish
to stay out. We could relate this to the way in which different
people experience themselves. Did not Cardinal Newman inform
us that all mankind consists of two classes, the "once-born" and
the "twice-born"? And did not William James use this concept
in creating his theory of religious need (see *The Varieties of
Religious Experience*[47])? Perhaps this theory gives us the answer
to the question of why people vary so greatly in their attitude
toward the magic garden.

The once-born, William James tells us, are healthy-minded
folk. They are satisfied with themselves as they are. They need
be born only once. But the twice-born are characteristically
"sick souls." They are not at all satisfied with themselves. For
them something is terribly wrong with the world and only by
being born again can they attain any sort of happiness. For the
once-born the world is a one-storied affair. It is all open, obvious,
free of mystery. For the twice-born, there is nothing obvious
about the world. It is a mysterious, often terrifying place. It has,
moreover, two or even several floors. The only hope one has of
attaining peace and happiness lies in escaping from the ground
floor (Baudelaire's "habitation of mud") and ascending to one
of the upper stories.

Here, then, is a division which has split the human race from
the earliest times and has given rise to much suffering. The once-
born despise the twice-born. They see them as wretched dreamers,
hankering after unreal worlds, sick and sorry for themselves,
unable to accept the world as it is. But the twice-born despise the
once-born just as heartily. What unimaginative beasts! What dull
cattle, their noses in the pasture, too stupid to realize that death

will butcher them, too dim-witted to know that alternate realities exist! Why, it is only by exerting the utmost charity that one can see them as human beings at all, so lacking are they in the finer qualities of soul that differentiate a man from a beast.

Surely this conflict between once-born and twice-born underlies the strife over the magic garden which rages today with an intensity rarely equaled in the past. The once-born have no use for the magic garden or its mind-affecting products. In their solid, one-storied world without secrets, without mysteries, there is no need for altered states of consciousness. What use can these altered states serve? They can reveal nothing hidden because there is nothing hidden to reveal. Furthermore drugs are bad for you. They are also bad for society. People who take drugs become "dope fiends." It is therefore perfectly permissible and very necessary to fence in the magic garden, to forbid the culture of the hemp, the poppy, the peyote cactus, to prosecute and imprison those who partake of the products of these plants.

Such is the thinking of the once-born.

And the twice-born? Nonsense, they reply and proceed to excoriate these self-appointed protectors of public morality. Are we to spend our whole lives harassed by ham-fisted cops and cops' cousins because we happen to fancy a life game that does not appeal to this particular breed of dolts? Who are you to dictate what we may eat or drink, smoke in our pipes or even stick into our veins? Does not our Declaration of Independence hold as inalienable the right of every American citizen to pursue what he considers to be happiness? Is it a crime that our idea of happiness differs from yours? You call us dope fiends and claim that we break the laws. You made bad laws in the first place. You muddled and meddled, labeling everything in sight a narcotic, except the whisky you yourselves guzzle, which you do not even see as a drug. If some of us rob or become prostitutes to satisfy our habit it is only because your laws force us to buy in the black market a drug which would be quite cheap if we could get it legally. You say we harm ourselves with the drugs. What business is that of yours as long as we harm no one else?

Is it not the right of every free citizen to go to the devil in his own way? And how can you tell whether we are going to the devil or finding for ourselves a new path to paradise? And anyway as long as alcohol and tobacco are legal all your antidrug legislation is pure hypocrisy.

Such is the thinking of the twice-born, at least of those who break into the magic garden. The argument continues. It appears to be a dialogue of the deaf. Neither side understands the other. The pros and cons will be considered in more detail later. Now it is necessary to consider the evidence. What plants grow in the magic garden? What kind of effects do they produce on those who use them? How do they exert these effects? How do the synthetic products of the chemist compare with the natural products? Are they harmful and, if so, what do they harm?

The Mind and Mescaline

On the mesas of Tamaulipas and Jalisco, in the dry unfertile regions of Mexico south of the Rio Grande, a cactus grows amid the rocks and sand. It is not erect and magnificent like the Saguaro or the bearer of gorgeous flowers like the night-blooming Cereus. It is, in fact, a thoroughly insignificant little pincushion projecting a bare three inches above the barren soil, a round, dark green protuberance connected to a carrotlike taproot, its surface covered with tufts of silky hairs. Though utterly uninspiring in appearance, this humble cactus, *Lophophora williamsii*, produces in its fleshy top one of the strangest drugs in the pharmacologist's collection. The properties of this drug have already been briefly mentioned. It is necessary now to describe them in more detail.

Antiquity shrouds the origin of the cactus cult. We do not know for sure how the properties of peyote were first discovered but the following legend is offered by Alice Marriott and Carol K. Rachlin in their carefully researched study *Peyote*.[64]

The flat land seems endless—until it tumbles into a miles-deep barranca or leaps skyward into the blasting peaks of the Sierra Madre. People who can take all this in their stride—diving into canyons on muleback, scrambling up mountain slopes, and striding across the endless flats from water hole to water hole— are capable of many things. They may run for pleasure for forty miles, with blood pressure and heart pace dropping and slowing as they run; they can live on mesquite bean meal and such small game as the country affords; they can even envision and cultivate the milpas—those tiny patches of broken ground that support the Three Sisters of North American horticulture: corn, beans, and squash.

The Tarahumare, the Yaqui, and the Otomi of the northern Sonoran desert and mountains are the peoples whose names are most familiar to citizens of the United States. From which group the story originally came it would be hard to say, for they all tell it to this day. It must have reached them from the south, for it is, and has long been, told by the Aztecan peoples of Mexico's central Great Valley.

The revelation came through a woman's dream. She was lost from her band, they say. She had fallen back from the wandering group of hunting men and root-gathering women, and had given birth to a child. In some versions of the legend the child was a boy; in others, a girl.

Had the band been in its home village there would have been other women to tend the mother and child—to sprinkle ashes on the cut navel cord, to bring the mother lukewarm unsalted corn gruel. Here she was alone. She cut the navel cord with a stone knife from the pouch at her waist and then lay helpless under a low, leafy bush, watching the buzzards gather overhead, watching them swooping and soaring lower with each downward beat of their great black wings.

Out of this desolation and terror, the woman heard a voice speak to her. "Eat the plant that is growing beside you," it said. "That is life and blessing for you and all your people."

Weakly, the woman turned her head against the earth. The only plant in sight, besides the bush that sheltered her, was a small cactus. It was without thorns, and its head was divided into lobes. She reached for the plant, and it seemed to grow outward to meet her fingers. The woman pulled up the cactus, root and all, and ate the head.

Strength returned to the woman immediately. She sat and looked around her. It was dawn; the sun was just about to rise. She raised her child to her filling breasts and fed it. Then, gathering as many cactus plants as she could find and carry, she rose and walked forward. Something wonderful must have been leading her, for by evening she had reached the main group of her people again.

*The woman took the plants to her uncle, her mother's brother.
He was a man of great wisdom and was much respected by his
people. "This is truly a blessing," the uncle said when he heard
the woman's story. "We must give it to all the people."*[64]

So, by the time the Spaniards arrived in Mexico, they discovered that, along with such gods as Quetzalcoatl and Huitzilo-
pochtli, the Aztecs also worshiped a triad of plants called
teonanacatl, ololiuqui, and *peyotl.* Of these three the peyotl was
the chief, a veritable divine substance, the "flesh of the gods."
This presented a challenge to the Spanish priests, who had their
own ideas on the subject of God's flesh and had no intention of
tolerating any rival claims to that dignity. They promptly dubbed
the peyotl "raiz diabolica," and persecuted all who used it without
bothering to investigate its nature or its properties. Thus the
divine peyotl languished in the shadow of the Church's displeasure for some three centuries, officially excommunicated, secretly
enjoyed. The Indians, having other values and other memories,
were little moved by the priestly denunciations nor could these
bringers of a foreign creed root out so easily a practice that had
been established for centuries. Though Montezuma was dead
and the glory of the Aztecs had passed away, the worship of the
divine plant continued. It was still regarded as the flesh of God,
the flesh of Christ rather than that of an Aztec deity. Had not
the Lord declared, giving bread to his disciples, "Take, eat, this
is my Body, which is given for thee and for many. Do this in
remembrance of me"? And who would dare to find fault with the
humble Indian if, in his eagerness to obey the command of Christ,
he chose to eat not a sacramental wafer but a plant having
properties so wonderful that it unrolled before his eyes all the
glories of the New Jerusalem?

And so over the dry plateaus in northern Mexico in the
states of Tamaulipas, San Luis Potosí, Nuevo León, Coahuila,
Querétaro, Zacatecas, and Chihuahua, the seekers of the divine
plant would set out to gather the cactus. God, they maintained,
had provided maize as food for the body and peyote as nourish-

ment for the soul. Should they then merely live on maize like
hogs? Ought they not rather to go and gather the divine food that
both body and soul might receive appropriate nourishment?

In San Luis Potosí the sacred cactus is gathered in October
just before the dry season. So holy a plant is not to be dragged
from the earth without proper respect, and those who go forth to
gather the peyote do so with awareness of the sacred nature of
their mission. For several weeks before the expedition starts those
who are to take part prepare themselves with prayers and fasting.
Abstinence from sexual intercourse is imposed upon them, as
both strength and purity are required for the success of the
expedition. Chanting prayers and reciting sacred verses, the
leaders of the party proceed over the rocky mesas, followed by
pack animals which will bring back the harvest. Before reaching
the holy place the members of the expedition perform a public
penance. Then, displaying every sign of veneration, they approach
the plants, uncovering their heads, bowing to the ground, and
censing themselves with copal incense. The more devout cross
themselves in the name of the Father, the Son, and the Holy
Ghost. Then, having discharged arrows to right and left of the
plant to ward off evil spirits, they dig the cacti with care so as not
to hurt them, brush off the soil from the roots, and place the
plants in jars. As the expedition returns there is great rejoicing
in all the villages through which it passes. Peyote is offered on the
altars and fragments given to every person met. Sufficient is kept
for the great festivals and the rest is sold to those who took no
part in the expedition.

In order to dry and preserve it, the plant is cut into thick,
fleshy slices which are laid in the sun to dry. These slices, when
dried, become wrinkled brown discs more or less covered with
tufts of short white hairs. In this form they are commonly known
as "mescal buttons." The word "mescal" here is confusing, for
it is also used to describe an intoxicant made from the agave. The
mescal button, however, is entirely non-alcoholic and, with its
dirty color and covering of spiny fluff, is about as unpromising a
passport to an artificial paradise as can be imagined. Its taste is as

unpleasant as its appearance; indeed anyone who has chewed his way through one of these "buttons" must marvel at the hardihood of the Indian Peyotist, for the flesh of the cactus is not only bitter but possessed of a peculiarly nauseating odor. Yet the Indian not only swallows as many as twelve of these morsels but is also able to retain them in his stomach, a feat which the squeamish might envy.

The peyote rite was spread to the Plains Indians by Quanah Parker, half-white, half-Comanche, whose mother, Cynthia Anne Parker, was captured by the Comanches as a child of four or five and reared as the daughter of one of the chiefs. By the time her white family found her again she was married to a Comanche and the mother of two children. After her husband had been killed by the United States troops Cynthia reluctantly agreed to return to her white family in Texas with her baby daughter, Prairie Flower. Accustomed to life in the open, like all Plains Indians of the time, Cynthia soon died when enclosed within four walls and the baby girl died also. The son Quanah (the Eagle) was finally persuaded to join his family in Texas and also fell ill as soon as he was confined to a house. Quanah came close to death but he did not die and his recovery marked the beginning of the spread of the peyote religion.

Quanah went, and Quanah fell ill. The young Eagle of the Comanches truly seemed to be on his deathbed. White doctors did him no good. He could not eat the white man's food his grandmother prepared. Quanah could only lie in numb stupor or twist restlessly on his grandmother's brass bed. He begged to be taken outdoors, into the open air, where he could lie on the clean earth and draw his strength back from it. He begged for an Indian medicine man.

In despair, Quanah's grandmother Parker sent for the next best thing, a curandera, *the Mexican term for a woman who cures with herbs, prayer, and magic. The woman spoke Spanish, but like most of the people of northern Mexico, she was largely Indian by blood—probably Tarahumara. The* curandera *ordered that a brush arbor be built, open to the winds from north and south, and that Quanah be laid on a pallet on the ground with his head to the east. As he lay there the woman prayed and smoked tobacco-filled corn-husk cigarettes over him. She sang for him. She dosed him with a tea "as bitter as death."*

In four days, Quanah began to recover, and to talk of returning to his own Comanche people. Soon he turned his face to the north and, well supplied with the weed the herb woman had used as a tea to cure him and well instructed in its use and its magical properties, returned to the Wichita Mountains. The weed must never be eaten for its own sake or for the feeling of well-being it could bring, but only for healing or in religious services, the curandera *had told him. This was a sacred thing which a woman had been instructed by God to give to her people to eat or drink, and it must always remain sacred.*

There were Mexican Indian ceremonies, of prayer and of healing, of which the curandera *told Quanah before he left Texas. There was a bush that would guide men to the sacred cactus, she told him. She showed Quanah the bush, and cautioned him that its beans were deadly poisonous unless they were used properly. No one should wear its red beans as beads except for ceremonial reasons.*

The curandera *especially reminded Quanah that because a woman had first brought peyote to the people, women should always have a place in its worship. Their duties were to bring water and food—especially water, from which all life comes—to the men who sang their prayers. Quanah promised solemnly to obey all the rules she and the men of her family taught him.*[64]

So Quanah Parker was taught the peyote ritual by a Mexican *curandera* in Texas. He brought it to the Plains Indians who desperately needed a new faith. Their way of life had been totally destroyed by the white men. They had relied entirely on buffalo, vast herds of which had once covered the Plains. Those herds had been exterminated, wantonly slaughtered by the whites. With them went the Indians' food and the hides from which they made their tepees and their clothes. In little more than a decade the proud tribes of hunters and warriors had been reduced to pitiful bands of scroungers who either had to starve or accept handouts from their conquerors.

The ritual that Quanah Parker brought to the Indians of the Plains involved four principle characters. The roadman (he who shows the road) was the peyote leader. The fireman tended the fire and guarded the door of the tepee. The cedarman sprinkled incense on the fire. The drummer kept the rhythm going to which peyote songs formed an accompaniment. The meeting lasted all night. At dawn the peyote woman brought water and food. Among the Plains Indians the ceremony is today commonly held in a tepee, the door facing east, the fire in the center, the crescent-shaped altar to the west of the fire, with "Father Peyote" in the center of the altar. The spirit of one of these meetings has been thus described by Stewart Brand:

The roadman is not a medicine man. If he has power he does not use it except sometimes to doctor. What he does have is authority; his job is administration. He knows by experience how the ceremony must be conducted and he knows by sensitivity everything going on in this meeting. He is responsible for keeping it on the road. Like a lens he does not make the energy, he transparently focuses it and directs it. His talents are experience, humility, and clarity.

The cedarman's job is a loving one. The cedar smoke he wields gives blessing. If he knows when to use it, he can help cleanse or heal someone in trouble. Often he voices or applies the directions of the roadman in administration of the meeting. He is a spokesman for the purpose of the meeting.

The fireman is strength. He sits across the fire from the roadman, in eye communication with him. He moves as much as the roadman doesn't. Besides scrupulously tending the fire, he keeps the door, periodically cleans the altar and floor, and attends to people who need attention. Tirelessly, unobtrusively, the fireman takes care of things. As coals form in the fire he brushes

*them around to the altar side to form a second altar of embers.
It is here the cedar incense is dropped.*

The drummer watches after the heartbeat of the meeting.

*As the staff moves around and around the circle every person
touches it and the drum as they go by. The man holding the staff
is getting the power. Singing or praying, it is his meeting until he
relinquishes the staff to the next man. No one will interrupt him.
Only rarely will a woman hold on to the staff to say something,
almost never to sing. One view of this custom which is so difficult
for whites is that the women know, therefore they have less
to say.*

*As the night wears on, from time to time someone asks for
tobacco to roll a prayer cigarette, which the fireman lights. Peyote
is called for, and the tea goes around again. After midnight
people have their own feather fans out and may move them in
time with the drum. Someone weeps and there is a shared sense
of relief. The person with the staff is saying something from his
heart and people respond quietly "m-hm."*

*Three o'clock is the crisis of night. It is not a time. It is the
dark moment which many do not recognize until it is passed and
getting lighter. Getting to it and past it is a shared accomplish-
ment. The roadman announces it is three o'clock.*

*From now until dawn the meeting is an unhurried apprecia-
tion of the growing light. Nothing changes overtly. The fire keeps
and the drum keeps, through the smokehole the stars keep. The
most emotional time is over. This part of the meeting understands.*

*Comprehension has much to work with. Beside the unique
events of the night, there is the rich symbology of the ceremony
in which "everything represents." There is the central fire and the
central smokehole of stars toward which the smoke travels. There
is the circle of faces, the circle of the peyote chief, the circle of
sky, of earth, and of the year. There is the number four, of the
four directions, the four seasons, of completion, of Here. There is
the altar, called the Road, showing the clean way to travel a life.
Its crescent is also the wings of a bird, morning bird, waterbird,
eagle, phoenix rising from the fire. To finish the meeting will*

*come water of the earth and food of the earth, brought by a
woman.*

*After the sky has paled and the meeting has demonstrated its
completion to him, the roadman asks the person appointed peyote
woman to go and get ready for morning water call. If some
women or children stayed in the house during the night, they
join the meeting now. The roadman sings the morning song, and
the peyote woman returns with water and a ceremonial breakfast
of corn, fruit, and boneless meat. She is smoked by the cedarman
and given a cigarette. By dawn light she prays, giving thanks
and reminding people where things come from. In her, the Earth
speaks.*[8]

No account of the peyote cult among the Indians would be
complete without reference to the studies of Carlos Castaneda. It
was the extraordinary good fortune of this anthropologist to be
accepted as an apprentice by a man he calls Juan Matus, a Yaqui
Indian sorcerer, a "man of knowledge." In *The Teachings of
Don Juan*, Castaneda explains the way in which sorcerers such
as Don Juan regard the power plants. Two of the power plants,
the devil's weed (*Datura inoxia*) and the little smoke (*Psilocybe
mexicana*) were regarded allies. The peyote cactus differed from
these plants. It was looked upon as a teacher or protector. Don
Juan described the difference between a protector and an ally:

*"An 'ally,' " he said, "is a power a man can bring into his life
to help him, advise him, and give him the strength necessary
to perform acts, whether big or small, right or wrong. This ally
is necessary to enhance a man's life, guide his acts, and further his
knowledge. In fact, an ally is the indispensable aid to knowing."
Don Juan said this with great conviction and force. He seemed to
choose his words carefully. He repeated the following sentence
four times:*
*"An ally will make you see and understand things about
which no human being could possibly enlighten you."*
"Is an ally something like a guardian spirit?"
"It is neither a guardian nor a spirit. It is an aid."

"Is Mescalito your ally?"

"No! Mescalito is another kind of power. A unique power! A protector, a teacher."

"What makes Mescalito different from an ally?"

"He can't be tamed and used as an ally is tamed and used. Mescalito is outside oneself. He chooses to show himself in many forms to whoever stands in front of him, regardless of whether that person is a brujo *or a farm boy."*

Don Juan spoke with deep fervor about Mescalito's being the teacher of the proper way to live. I asked him how Mescalito taught the "proper way of life," and Don Juan replied that Mescalito showed how to live.

"How does he show it?" I asked.

"He has many ways of showing it. Sometimes he shows it on his hand, or on the rocks, or the trees, or just in front of you."

"Is it like a picture in front of you?"

"No. It is a teaching in front of you."

"Does Mescalito talk to the person?"

"Yes. But not in words."

"How does he talk, then?"

"He talks differently to every man."

I felt my questions were annoying him. I did not ask any more. He went on explaining that there were no exact steps to knowing Mescalito; therefore no one could teach about him except Mescalito himself. This quality made him a unique power; he was not the same for every man.[12]

This concept of Mescalito as a teacher no doubt shaped Castaneda's inner experiences when he encountered the spirit of the cactus some time later. It was no easy trip. After a long hike into the wilds of Chihuahua they entered a valley filled with peyote plants where they spent the night. It was past midnight when Castaneda, after ingesting fourteen peyote buttons, finally encountered Mescalito.

At the foot of one boulder I saw a man sitting on the ground, his face turned almost in profile. I approached him until I was perhaps ten feet away; then he turned his head and looked at me.

*I stopped—his eyes were the water I had just seen! They had
the same enormous volume, the sparkling of gold and black. His
head was pointed like a strawberry; his skin was green, dotted
with innumerable warts. Except for the pointed shape, his head
was exactly like the surface of the peyote plant. I stood in front of
him, staring; I couldn't take my eyes away from him. I felt he
was deliberately pressing on my chest with the weight of his eyes.
I was choking. I lost my balance and fell to the ground. His eyes
turned away. I heard him talking to me. At first his voice was
like the soft rustle of a light breeze. Then I heard it as music—as
a melody of voices—and I "knew" it was saying, "What do you
want?"*

*I knelt before him and talked about my life, then wept. He
looked at me again. I felt his eyes pulling me away, and I thought
that moment would be the moment of my death. He signaled me
to come closer. I vacillated for an instant before I took a step
forward. As I came closer he turned his eyes away from me and
showed me the back of his hand. The melody said, "Look!"
There was a round hole in the middle of his hand. "Look!" said
the melody again. I looked into the hole and I saw myself. I
was very old and feeble and was running stooped over, with
bright sparks flying all around me. Then three of the sparks hit
me, two in the head and one in the left shoulder. My figure, in the
hole, stood up for a moment until it was fully vertical, and then
disappeared together with the hole.*

*Mescalito turned his eyes to me again. They were so close to
me that I "heard" them rumble softly with that peculiar sound
I had heard many times that night. They became peaceful by
degrees until they were like a quiet pond rippled by gold and
black flashes.*

*He turned his eyes away once more and hopped like a cricket
for perhaps fifty yards. He hopped again and again, and was
gone.*[12]

Such are the effects produced by peyote on those who use it
with the proper reverence and within the framework of the
Indian tradition. Despite the fact that no one has been able to

demonstrate any harmful effects from the ceremonial use of the sacred cactus Christian missionaries and other meddlesome characters have done their best to prevent the Indians from using the plant. Their efforts resulted in prohibitions and legal actions, one of the most curious of which was the trial in Wisconsin of the Indian Nah-qua-tah-tuck, whose crime, it appears, consisted in having imported a shipment of peyote from Texas by parcel post. Considerable efforts were made to prove that peyote was harmful and that its employment led the user straight to the pit of hell, that it was, in fact, the "raiz diabolica" described by Padre José Ortega. From this standpoint the Indians in the trial proved most uncooperative. Far from describing peyote as a short cut to hell, they insisted that by its means they were brought several steps nearer to heaven. Before taking the drug they "invoked God, begging Him to make all of them good and to keep them from evil." They took peyote that their souls might ascend toward God. "Peyotl helped them to lead better lives and to forsake alcoholic drinks." The Reverend Thomas Prescott, who also testified at the trial, declared that for seven years he had officiated as a priest in a society known as the Union Church Society and to its Indian members as the Peyote Society. Peyote was either eaten or taken as tea at weekly services and those that took it derived benefit from its use. "They gave up drink, established themselves in regular homes, and lived sober and industrious lives." As for himself, "it stopped me from drinking, and now since I used this peyotl, I have been sober, and today I am sober yet." "This," writes Norman Taylor, "was too much for the government experts, and Uncle Sam decided to go back to Washington, where the records of this fantastic trial still molder."[96]

Even so, those warped individuals who seem happy only when forbidding something to their fellow men continued to seek to suppress the now Christianized form of peyote worship. As recently as 1951 efforts were made to declare illegal the use of peyote among various Indian tribes. So energetic were these attempts that LaBarre and four other professional anthropologists who had made extensive studies of Peyotism and participated in the rites felt it their duty "to protest against a campaign which only reveals the ignorance of the propagandists concerned." After pointing out that peyote is neither a narcotic nor an intoxicant in the true sense of the word they went on to describe the aims of that intertribal organization incorporated under the name of "The Native American Church of the United States" as given in its articles of incorporation.

The purpose for which this corporation is formed is to foster and promote religious belief in Almighty God and the customs of the several tribes of Indians throughout the United States in the worship of a Heavenly Father and to promote morality, sobriety, industry, charity and right living and cultivate a spirit of self-respect and brotherly love and union among the members of the several tribes of Indians throughout the United States . . . with and through the sacramental use of peyotl.

. . . by eating the sacramental peyotl [these writers continue] the Indian absorbs God's Spirit, in the same way that the white Christian absorbs that spirit by means of the sacramental bread and wine. . . . The traditional practice of many Indian tribes was to go off in isolation to contemplate and fast until a supernatural vision was achieved. This is now replaced by a collective all night vigil in which, through prayer, contemplation and eating peyotl, the Peyotist receives a divine revelation. For the Peyotist this occurs because he has put himself in a receptive spiritual mood and has absorbed enough of God's power from the peyotl to make him able to reach God. . . . The all night rite is highly formalized. One man functions as priest, with the help of three assistants. During the rite they pray for the worshippers at fixed intervals, while the other men and women pray to themselves in low voices. Early in the rite everyone takes four pieces of peyotl; later, anyone may take as many more as he or she thinks proper. Most of the time is occupied in having each man, in rotation, sing four religious songs that correspond to hymns sung in white churches. . . . It will be seen from this brief description that the Native American Church of the United States is a

legitimate religious organization deserving of the same right to religious freedom as other churches; also that peyotl is used sacramentally in a manner corresponding to the bread and wine of the white Christians.[57]

The effect of peyote on non-Indian investigators, who took it without ceremony or previous preparation, was first described in 1896 by the American physician Silas Weir Mitchell, who swallowed "on the morning of a busy day," one and a half drams of an extract of mescal buttons, followed by further doses in the afternoon. By 5:40 P.M. Mitchell found himself "deliciously at languid ease," and observed floating before his eyes luminous star points and fragments of stained glass. Going into a dark room, he settled down to enjoy the performance evoked by the mysterious action of the drug on the cells of his visual cortex.

The display which for an enchanted two hours followed was such as I find it hopeless to describe in language which shall convey to others the beauty and splendor of what I saw. Stars, delicate floating films of color, then an abrupt rush of countless points of white light swept across the field of view, as if the unseen millions of the Milky Way were to flow in a sparkling river before my eyes . . . zigzag lines of very bright colors . . . the wonderful loveliness of swelling clouds of more vivid colors gone before I could name them.

A white spear of grey stone grew up to huge height, and became a tall, richly furnished Gothic Tower of very elaborate and definite design, with many rather worn statues standing in the doorways or on stone brackets. As I gazed every projecting angle, cornice and even the face of the stones at their jointings were by degrees covered or hung with clusters of what seemed to be huge precious stones, but uncut, some being more like masses of transparent fruit. These were green, purple, red, and orange, never clear yellow and never blue. All seemed to possess an interior light, and to give the faintest idea of the perfectly satisfying intensity and purity of these gorgeous color fruits is quite beyond my power. All the colors I have ever beheld are dull in comparison to these. As I looked, and it lasted long, the tower became a fine mouse hue, and everywhere the vast pendant masses of emerald green, ruby reds, and orange began to drip a slow rain of colors.

After an endless display of less beautiful marvels I saw that which deeply impressed me. An edge of a huge cliff seemed to project over a gulf of unseen depth. My viewless enchanter set on the brink a huge bird claw of stone. Above, from the stem or leg, hung a fragment of the same stuff. This began to unroll and float out to a distance which seemed to me to represent Time as well as immensity of Space. Here were miles of rippled purples, half transparent, and of ineffable beauty. Now and then soft golden clouds floated from these folds, or a great shimmer went over the whole of the rolling purples, and things like green birds fell from it, fluttering down into the gulf below. Next, I saw clusters of stones hanging in masses from the claw toes, as it seemed to me miles of them, down far below into the underworld of the black gulf. This was the most distinct of my visions.[69]

In his last vision, Mitchell saw the beach of Newport with its rolling waves as "liquid splendors, huge and threatening, of wonderfully pure green, or red or deep purple, once only deep orange, and with no trace of foam. These water hills of color broke on the beach with myriads of lights of the same tint as the wave."

The author considered it totally impossible to find words to describe the colors. "They still linger visibly in my memory, and left the feeling that I had seen among them colors unknown to my experience."

News of the remarkable properties of peyote spread to Europe, where Havelock Ellis, famed for his pioneer studies in the field of human sexual behavior, decided to experiment with this singular drug. Having obtained in London a small sample of mescal buttons, he settled down in his quiet rooms in the

Temple and prepared a decoction from three of the buttons which he drank at intervals between 2:30 and 4:30 P.M.

The first symptom observed during the afternoon was a certain consciousness of energy and intellectual power. This passed off, and about an hour after the final dose I felt faint and unsteady; the pulse was low, and I found it pleasanter to lie down. I was still able to read, and I noticed that a pale violet shadow floated over the page around the point at which my eyes were fixed. I had already noticed that objects not in the direct line of vision, such as my hands holding the book, showed a tendency to look obtrusive, heightened in color, almost monstrous, while, on closing my eyes, after-images were vivid and prolonged. The appearance of visions with closed eyes was very gradual. At first there was merely a vague play of light and shade which suggested pictures, but never made them. Then the pictures became more definite, but too confused and crowded to be described, beyond saying that they were of the same character as the images of the kaleidoscope, symmetrical groupings of spiked objects. Then, in the course of the evening, they became distinct, but still indescribable—mostly a vast field of golden jewels, studded with red and green stones, ever changing. This moment was, perhaps, the most delightful of the experience, for at the same time the air around me seemed to be flushed with vague perfume —producing with the visions a delicious effect—and all discomfort had vanished, except a slight faintness and tremor of the hands, which, later on, made it almost impossible to guide a pen as I made notes of the experiment; it was, however, with an effort, always possible to write with a pencil. The visions never resembled familiar objects; they were extremely definite, but yet always novel; they were constantly approaching, and yet constantly eluding, the semblance of known things. I would see thick, glorious fields of jewels, solitary or clustered, sometimes brilliant and sparkling, sometimes with a dull rich glow. Then they would spring up into flower-like shapes beneath my gaze, and then seem to turn into gorgeous butterfly forms or endless

folds of glistening, iridescent, fibrous wings of wonderful insects;
while sometimes I seemed to be gazing into a vast hollow revolv-
ing vessel, on whose polished concave mother-of-pearl surface
the hues were swiftly changing. I was surprised, not only by the
enormous profusion of the imagery presented to my gaze, but still
more by its variety. Perpetually some totally new kind of effect
would appear in the field of vision; sometimes there was swift
movement, sometimes dull, sombre richness of color, sometimes
glitter and sparkle, once a startling rain of gold, which seemed to
approach me. Most usually there was a combination of rich,
sombre color, with jewel-like points of brilliant hue. Every color
and tone conceivable to me appeared at some time or another.
Sometimes all the different varieties of one color, as of red, with
scarlets, crimsons, pinks, would spring up together, or in quick
succession. But in spite of this immense profusion, there was
always a certain parsimony and aesthetic value in the colors
presented. They were usually associated with form, and never
appeared in large masses, or if so, the tone was very delicate. I
was further impressed, not only by the brilliance, delicacy, and
variety of the colors, but even more by their lovely and various
textures—fibrous, woven, polished, glowing, dull-veined, semi-
transparent—the glowing effects, as of jewels, and the fibrous, as
of insect's wings, being perhaps the most prevalent. Although
the effects were novel, it frequently happened, as I have already
mentioned, that they vaguely recalled known objects. Thus, once
the objects presented to me seemed to be made of exquisite
porcelain, again they were like elaborate sweetmeats, again of
a somewhat Maori style of architecture; and the background of
the pictures frequently recalled, both in form and tone, the
delicate architectural effects as of lace carved in wood, which
we associate with the mouchrabieh work of Cairo. But always
the visions grew and changed without any reference to the
characteristics of those real objects of which they vaguely
reminded me, and when I tried to influence their course it was
with very little success. On the whole, I should say that the images
were most usually what might be called living arabesques. There

was often a certain incomplete tendency to symmetry, as though the underlying mechanism was associated with a large number of polished facets. The same image was in this way frequently repeated over a large part of the field; but this refers more to form than to color, in respect to which there would still be all sorts of delightful varieties, so that if, with a certain uniformity, jewel-like flowers were springing up and expanding all over the field of vision, they would still show every variety of delicate tone and tint.

Weir Mitchell found that he could only see the visions with closed eyes and in a perfectly dark room. I could see them in the dark and with almost equal facility, though they were not of equal brilliancy, when my eyes were wide open. I saw them best, however, when my eyes were closed, in a room lighted only by flickering firelight. This evidently accords with the experience of the Indians, who keep a fire burning brightly throughout their mescal rites.

The visions continued with undiminished brilliance for many hours, and as I felt somewhat faint and muscularly weak, I went to bed, as I undressed being impressed by the red, scaly, bronzed, and pigmented appearance of my limbs whenever I was not directly gazing at them. I had not the faintest desire for sleep; there was a general hyperaesthesia of all the senses as well as muscular irritability, and every slightest sound seemed magnified to startling dimensions. I may also have been kept awake by a vague alarm at the novelty of my condition, and the possibility of further developments.

After watching the visions in the dark for some hours I became a little tired of them and turned on the gas. Then I found that I was able to study a new series of visual phenomena to which previous observers had made no reference. The gas jet (an ordinary flickering burner) seemed to burn with great brilliance, sending out waves of light, which expanded and contracted in an enormously exaggerated manner. I was even more impressed by the shadows, which were in all directions heightened by flushes of red, green, and especially violet. The whole room, with its

*whitewashed but not very white ceiling, thus became vivid and
beautiful. The difference between the room as I saw it then and
the appearance it usually presents to me was the difference one
may often observe between the picture of a room and the actual
room. The shadows I saw were the shadows which the artist puts
in, but which are not visible in the actual scene under normal
conditions of casual inspection. I was reminded of the paintings of
Claude Monet, and as I gazed at the scene it occurred to me that
mescal perhaps produces exactly the same conditions of visual
hyperaesthesia, or rather exhaustion, as may be produced on the
artist by the influence of prolonged visual attention. I wished
to ascertain how the subdued and steady electric light would
influence vision, and passed into the next room; but here the
shadows were little marked, although the walls and floor seemed
tremulous and insubstantial, and the texture of everything was
heightened and enriched.*

*About 3:30 A.M. I felt that the phenomena were distinctly
diminishing—though the visions, now chiefly of human figures,
fantastic and Chinese in character, still continued—and I was able
to settle myself to sleep, which proved peaceful and dreamless.
I awoke at the usual hour and experienced no sense of fatigue
nor other unpleasant reminiscence of the experience I had
undergone. Only my eyes seemed unusually sensitive to color,
especially to blue and violet; I can, indeed, say that ever since this
experience I have been more aesthetically sensitive than I was
before to the more delicate phenomena of light and shade and
color.*[20]

So impressed was Havelock Ellis by his experiences that he
persuaded an artist friend to try the drug. After consuming four of
the buttons this artist became violently ill. Paroxysmal attacks
of pain in the region of the heart were combined with a sense of
imminent death while so great was the dread of light and the
dilation of the pupils that the eyelids had to be kept more or less
closed. The colored visions did indeed begin at this time but so
preoccupied was the artist with his other less pleasant sensations

that he had little opportunity to enjoy the strange hues he now perceived.

I saw an intensely vivid blue light begin to play around every object. A square cigarette box, violet in color, shone like an amethyst. I turned my eyes away and beheld this time, on the back of a polished chair, a bar of color glowing like a ruby. Although I was expecting some such manifestation as one of the first symptoms of the intoxication, I was nevertheless somewhat alarmed when this phenomenon took place. Such a silent and sudden illumination of all things around, where a moment before I had seen nothing uncommon, seemed like a kind of madness beginning from outside me, and its strangeness affected me more than its beauty. A desire to escape from it led me to the door, and the act of moving had, I noticed, the effect of dispelling the colors. But a sudden difficulty in breathing and a sensation of numbness at the heart brought me back to the armchair from which I had risen. From this moment I had a series of paroxysms, which I can only describe by saying that I felt as though I were dying. It was impossible to move, and it seemed almost impossible to breathe. My speedy dissolution, I half imagined, was about to take place, and the power of making any resistance to the violent sensations that were arising within was going, I felt, with every second.

The first paroxysms were the most violent. They would come on with tinglings in the lower limbs, and with the sensation of a nauseous and suffocating gas mounting up into my head. Two or three times this was accompanied by a color vision of the gas bursting into flame as it passed up my throat. But I seldom had visions during the paroxysms; these would appear in the intervals. They began with a spurting up of colors; once, of a flood of brightly illuminated green water covering the field of vision, and effervescing in parts, just as when fresh water with all the air bubbles is pumped into a swimming bath. At another time my eye seemed to be turning into a vast drop of dirty water in which millions of minute creatures resembling tadpoles were in motion.

*But the early visions consisted mostly of a furious succession of
colored arabesques, arising and descending or sliding at every
possible angle into the field of view. It would be as difficult to give
a description of the whirl of water at the bottom of a waterfall
as to describe the chaos of color and design which marked this
period.*

*Now also began another series of extraordinary sensations.
They set in with bewildering suddenness and followed one
another in rapid succession. These I now record as they occur to
my mind at haphazard: (1) My right leg became suddenly heavy
and solid; it seemed, indeed, as if the entire weight of my body
had shifted into one part, about the thigh and knee, and that
the rest of my body had lost all substantiality. (2) With the
suddenness of a neuralgic pang, the back of my head seemed to
open and emit streams of bright color; this was immediately
followed by the feeling as of a draft blowing like a gale through
the hair in the same region. (3) At one moment the color, green,
acquired a taste in my mouth; it was sweetish and somewhat
metallic; blue again would have taste that seemed to recall
phosphorus; these are the only colors that seemed to be connected
with taste. (4) A feeling of delightful relief and preternatural
lightness about my forehead, succeeded by a growing sensation
of contraction. (5) Singing in one of my ears. (6) A sensation of
burning heat in the palm of my left hand. (7) Heat about both
eyes. The last continued throughout the whole period, except for
a moment when I had a sensation of cold upon the eyelids,
accompanied with a color vision of the wrinkled lid, of the skin
disappearing from the brow, of dead flesh, and finally of a skull.*

*Throughout these sensations and visions my mind remained
not only perfectly clear, but enjoyed, I believe, an unusual
lucidity. Certainly I was conscious of an odd contrast in hearing
myself talk rationally with H.E., who had entered the room a
short time before, and experiencing at the same moment the wild
and extraordinary pranks that were taking place in my body. My
reason appeared to be the sole survivor of my being. At times I
felt that this, too, would go, but the sound of my own voice would*

establish again the communication with the outer world of reality.

Tremors were more or less constant in my lower limbs. Persistent, also, was the feeling of nausea. This, when attended by a feeling of suffocation and a pain at the heart, was relieved by taking brandy, coffee or biscuit. For muscular exertion I felt neither the wish nor the power. My hands, however, retained their full strength.

It was painful for me to keep my eyes open above a few seconds; the light of day seemed to fill the room with a blinding glare. Yet every object, in the brief glimpse I caught, appeared normal in color and shape. With my eyes closed, most of the visions, after the first chaotic display, represented parts of the whole of my body undergoing a variety of marvellous changes, of metamorphoses or illumination. They were more often than not comic and grotesque in character, though often beautiful in color. At one time I saw my right leg filling up with a delicate heliotrope; at another, the sleeve of my coat changed into a dark green material, in which was worked a pattern in red braid, and the whole bordered at the cuff with sable. Scarcely had my new sleeve taken shape than I found myself attired in a complete costume of the same fashion, mediaeval in character, but I could not say to what precise period it belonged. I noted that a chance movement—of my hand, for instance—would immediately call up a color vision of the part exerted, and that this again would pass, by a seemingly natural transition, into another wholly dissimilar. Thus, pressing my fingers accidentally against my temples, the fingertips became elongated, and then grew into the ribs of a vaulting or of a dome shaped roof. But most of the visions were of a more personal nature. I happened once to lift a spoon of coffee to my lips, and as I was in the act of raising my arm for that purpose a vision flashed before my closed (or nearly closed) eyes, in all the hues of the rainbow, of my arm separated from my body, and serving me with coffee from out of dark and indefinite space. On another occasion, as I was seeking to relieve slight nausea by taking a piece of biscuit passed to me by H. E., it suddenly streamed out into blue flame. It was a sight of wonderful beauty. But this was not all. As I placed the biscuit in my mouth it burst out again into the same colored fire and illuminated the interior of my mouth, casting a blue reflection on the roof. The light in the Blue Grotto at Capri, I am able to affirm, is not nearly as blue as seemed for a short space of time the interior of my mouth. There were many visions of which I could not trace the origin. There were spirals and arabesques and flowers, and sometimes objects more trivial and prosaic in character. In one vision I saw a row of small white flowers, one against the other like pearls of a necklace, begin to revolve in the form of a spiral. Every flower, I observed, had the texture of porcelain. It was at a moment when I had the sensation of my cheeks growing hot and feverish that I experienced the strangest of all the color visions. It began with feeling that the skin of my face was becoming quite thin and of no stouter consistency than tissue paper, and the feeling was suddenly enhanced by a vision of my face, paper-like and semitransparent and somewhat reddish in color. To my amazement I saw myself as though I were inside a Chinese lantern, looking out through my cheek into the room.[19]

This artist particularly noted the curious dualism, the split of personality, so often observed by those who enter the strange world to which peyote is the key. On returning to the normal state he experienced that sense of unreality which sometimes assails the spectator of a particularly fascinating play who emerges suddenly into the gray light of the everyday world.

As one pours out with the crowd into the street, the ordinary world, by force of contrast with the sensational scenes just witnessed, breaks in upon one with almost a sense of unreality. The house, the aspect of the street, even the light of day appear a little foreign for a few moments. During these moments everything strikes the mind as odd and unfamiliar, or at least with a greater degree of objectivity. Such was my feeling with regard to my old and habitual self. . . . It was as if I had unexpectedly attained an objective knowledge of my own personality. I saw, as it were, my normal state of being with the eyes of a person who sees the street on coming out of the theatre in broad day.

This sensation also brought out the independence of the mind

*during the period of intoxication. It alone appeared to have
escaped the ravages of the drug; it alone remained sane during
a general delirium, vindicating, so it seemed, the majesty of its
own impersonal nature. It had reigned for a while, I now felt, as
an autocrat, without ministers and their officiousness. Henceforth
I should be more or less conscious of the interdependence of
body and brain; a slight headache, a touch of indigestion, or
what not, would be able to effect what a general intoxication of
my senses and nerves could not touch.*[19]

As the year continued Havelock Ellis was tempted to use
more of his friends as human guinea pigs to unravel the mysteries
of the world of peyote. One, a poet, with an interest in mystical
matters and a knowledge of various vision-producing drugs, found
the effect of peyote mainly unpleasant and decided he much
preferred hashish. Another poet was particularly impressed by
the "sound-colors" which flowed about him as he played the
piano. Havelock Ellis himself found that music had a potent effect
on his visions. This was particularly true of Schumann's music,
especially of his *Waldszenen* and *Kinderszenen*.

*"The Prophet Bird" called up vividly a sense of atmosphere
and of brilliant feathery birdlike forms passing to and fro, "A
Flower Piece" provoked constant and persistent images of
vegetation, while "Scheherazade" produced an effect of floating
white raiment, covered by glittering spangles and jewels. In every
case my description was, of course, given before I knew the name
of the piece. I do not pretend that this single series of experiments
proves much, but it would certainly be worth while to follow
up this indication and to ascertain if any light is hereby thrown
on the power of a composer to suggest definite imagery, or the
power of a listener to perceive it.*[19]

After Havelock Ellis, the next student of peyote was the
French pharmacologist Alexandre Rouhier, who described the
reactions of one of his subjects to a dose of 2 grams of peyote
extract. The subject, who took the drug at 8 P.M., experienced

visions which began an hour and forty minutes later and which
"continued to unfold without interruption for the next twenty-three
hours, nor did the pleasure with which L. contemplated the
unfolding of these colorful scenes decrease during this time."
The visions were complex and varied. Only a few examples will
be given here.

*An ornate ring of diamonds. The large central stone emits
great quantities of green, violet, or rose-colored fire which
inundates the whole scene with a strange glow, complex in
color, the product of the fusion of the multiple fires. One of the
diamonds opens revealing within it a little angel which leaps
from the ring, picks it up and carries it with an effort. A woman
appears, "beautiful as a goddess." Her features are noble, her
nose aquiline, her color yellowish bronze, her curly auburn hair
floats unrestrained. She plays with the little angel. A group of
women appears, of which some are clad in pink and some in blue
robes. In the midst of them is a dancer who makes rhythmic
movements. Soon all of them are dancing, sometimes in couples,
sometimes in vari-colored groups. The little angel dances on her
hands, her legs in the air. She goes and fetches a placard on which
is written "I am love." She flies up onto a cloud.*

*The dancers are going. The goddess remains alone; her
features bear the marks of infinite sorrow; she weeps, then throws
herself onto the ground, sobbing "as if she would die." She grows
dim and disappears.*

*Visions of a virgin forest; luxuriant tropical vegetation; trees
with trunks draped with giant creepers, the soil covered with
tall dense grass. Hanging from a branch there appears a monkey
holding a coconut. Below there appears a large beast, strange
and ferocious of aspect, its mouth agape, displaying terrible white
teeth. Above appears another monkey and plays with the first.*

*A glade illuminated by the light of the sun which sifts through
the thick foliage. Beautiful tone contrasts are seen in the shadows.
In the middle is a pond covered with water lilies whose leaves
are filled with toads. Frightened, they all jump briskly into the*

water. A vermillion-colored man approaches carrying a bow and a quiver. His hair is ornamented with feathers. A fine graceful antelope emerges from the undergrowth and comes to drink at the pond "with infinite delicacy." The Indian kills and dismembers it and departs, carrying its head. L., overwhelmed by the intensity of the visions, cries with indignation. "What a brute! He cannot understand the beauty of nature! How graceful the animal is even in death."[82]

Several of Rouhier's subjects commented on the tiny figures they saw under the influence of peyote. These "Lilliputian hallucinations" are contrasted by Rouhier with the gigantic figures, the "Brobdingnagian illusions," seen under the influence of *yagé,* another hallucinogen which will be described later.

After these studies little further work was carried out on the effects of crude peyote. The chemists, ever on the lookout for new worlds to conquer, had taken the divine plant into their laboratories, bent on determining the nature of those substances that endow it with its vision-provoking properties. The brown malodorous decoction of the mescal buttons was progressively purified and one crystalline compound after another was separated from the crude material. No less than nine alkaloids were finally crystallized, several of which influenced the behavior of experimental animals. Most poisonous of these alkaloids was lophophorine, which, in doses of about 12 milligrams per kilogram body weight, would produce in rabbits violent convulsions of the type seen in sufferers from tetanus or strychnine poisoning. The substance pellotine produced in man a drowsiness suggesting that it might be of use as a sedative. Anhalonidine, on the other hand, had a stimulating effect on the central nervous system.

But of all the substances isolated from this curious cactus the most important and interesting was called mescaline. To this substance and to this substance alone the extraordinary visions of the peyote eater could be attributed. Mescaline is not a complex substance. It belongs to the large and important group of chemicals known as amines, many of which (for instance, adrenalin and noradrenalin) have a powerful action on the chemistry of the body. To be more specific, mescaline is a derivative of ammonia (NH_3) in which one of the hydrogens has been replaced by a chain of carbon atoms. Chemically it is *3, 4, 5-trimethoxy phenyl ethylamine,* a substance which can be synthesized without too much difficulty so that those who wish to enjoy the peyote-induced visions need not depend on the cactus for their supply of the drug.

With pure mescaline available, investigators of the properties of the drug no longer had to chew the nauseating cactus or swallow revolting decoctions brewed from its buttons. They left such questionable pleasures to the Indians and continued their studies with the purified essence of the sacred plant, either swallowing or injecting the solution into their persons. Research continued vigorously. From the laboratory of Dr. Beringer in Heidelberg emerged a tome, three hundred and fifteen pages in length, a worthy example of German *Wissenschaftlichkeit,* which remains the most massive contribution on the subject to date.[4] Dr. Beringer's subjects generally took their mescaline in the form of an injection, the dose employed being usually 400 milligrams. Their experiences had much in common with those described by S. Weir Mitchell and Havelock Ellis, but the metaphysical bent of the Teutonic mind, its tendency to seek the ultimate, the infinite, the inexpressible, added to the already rich spectrum of the mescal experience certain deeper hues not noted by the earlier investigators.

I ceased my reading of Weil's book on Internal Secretions *because the day was filled with the phenomena evoked by mescaline. Soon there began on the carpet before me a wonderful display. From the edge of the field of vision there crept across the green carpet beasts like the monsters from a fairy tale stretching out tongues and claws. I watched their play with pleasure only regretting that the beasts appeared in various shades of gray. Scarcely had this thought passed through my mind before the eyes of the beasts glittered with green or red lights. Soon their tongues and claws became touched with crimson and began to flicker like the play of flames in a fire. . . . Somewhat later I fixed my eyes on a point on the ceiling on which were a few small flies in the web of a spider. Suddenly the flies began to multiply lit up by beautiful colors within the ever-changing form of the spider's web.*

Now there appeared before my eyes splendid architectural forms which seemed to hang from the ceiling divided into hexagonal segments like honeycombs. Above the ceiling each honeycomb rose up and developed into a painted Gothic arch. While I delighted in the upward striving of these slender arches they towered to ever greater heights before my eyes. Extraordinary joy overcame me—a strong and beautiful feeling of eternity and infinity. This so overwhelmed me that soon everything appeared infinite. There they were again, the deep beautiful perspectives which I had seen during my first experience with mescaline, but now they never stood still, they grew constantly deeper. As with space so with time. The ordinary human concept of time seemed contemptible. I would not even think of it. The sense of drifting in the infinite, of flowing into the ocean of eternity occupied me entirely and was most closely and intimately associated with my self-awareness. I experienced a unique pleasure from exploring the endlessness of my own ego, the boundlessness of every one of my psychic functions. . . . My psychological equilibrium was constantly changing. At one moment I would experience pleasure because I could go to sleep in my own little world; at another I stood astounded by profound riddles, by the mystery of the magic play within me. I even felt fear at the thought of that wild secret force at work within my being.[4]

Similarly pervaded with what Baudelaire has called "the taste of the infinite" were the experiences of another of Beringer's subjects:

My ideas of space were strange beyond description. I could see myself from head to foot as well as the sofa on which I was lying. About me was nothingness, absolutely empty space. I was floating on a solitary island in the ether. No part of my body was

*subject to the laws of gravitation. On the other side of the vacuum
—the room seemed to be unlimited in space—extremely fantastic
figures appeared before my eyes. I was very excited, perspired
and shivered, and was kept in a state of ceaseless wonder. I saw
endless passages with beautiful arches, delightfully colored
arabesques, grotesque decorations, divine, sublime and enchanting
in their fantastic splendor. These visions changed in waves and
billows, were built, destroyed, and appeared again in endless
variations first on one plane and then in three dimensions, at last
disappearing into infinity. The sofa island disappeared. I did not
feel my physical self; an ever increasing sense of dissolution set
in. I was seized with passionate curiosity, great things were about
to be unveiled before me. I would perceive the essence of all
things, the problem of creation would be unravelled. I was
dematerialized.*[4]

The mystical aspects of the mescaline experience have very
recently been investigated again. Aldous Huxley, a representative
of that "universal man" commoner in the Renaissance than
in our overspecialized age, has studied the subject from the
standpoint of a creative writer who is at the same time a mystic
and a scientist. His own experiences, after swallowing 400
milligrams of mescaline, involved a change not in the identity
of things perceived but in the content of perception. He describes
no fields of gorgeous jewels, none of the Gothic arches so popular
with the German investigators, none of the strange beasts, the
"delightful dragons balancing white balls on their breath," which
visited one of Havelock Ellis's poets. There is nothing in Aldous
Huxley's account which even suggests that mescaline might
be, as some have described it, a hallucinogen—that is to say,
an agent capable of generating hallucinations. The essence of a
hallucinogen is that it causes those under its influence to hear,
see, or feel things which are not present. Havelock Ellis's rotating
flower beds, S. Weir Mitchell's tower dripping jewels, these were
hallucinations in the true sense of the word. No such phenomena
are described in Aldous Huxley's book.

The change which, for him, was brought about by mescaline

concerned the manner in which familiar objects were perceived. "How wonderfully supernatural and how miraculous this," wrote the Zen patriarch, "I draw water and I carry fuel!" It was exactly this transformation of simple things which Aldous Huxley described, and this element of the miraculous, enhaloing ordinary objects, was for him far more significant than any color vision or elaborate fantasy. Certainly he experienced that enrichment of color values which is an almost universal feature of descriptions of the mescaline experience. His books, for example, took on a gemlike glow.

Red books, like rubies; emerald books; books bound in white jade; books of agate; of aquamarine, of yellow topaz; lapis lazuli books whose color was so intense, so intrinsically meaningful, that they seemed to be on the point of leaving the shelves to thrust themselves more insistently on my attention.[43]

But this enrichment of the quality of colors was secondary to the extraordinary significance with which simple objects became endowed. An hour and a half after taking mescaline Aldous Huxley found himself looking intently at a small glass vase.

The vase contained only three flowers—a full blown Belle of Portugal rose, shellpink with a tint at every petal's base of a hotter, flamier hue; a large magenta and cream-colored carnation; and, pale purple at the end of its broken stalk, the bold heraldic blossom of an iris. Fortuitous and provisional, the little nosegay broke all the rules of traditional good taste. At breakfast that morning I had been struck by the lively dissonance of its colors. But that was no longer the point. I was not looking now at an unusual flower arrangement. I was seeing what Adam had seen on the morning of his creation—the miracle, moment by moment, of naked existence.[43]

What the rose, the iris and the carnation so intensely signified when viewed with perception modified by mescaline was

. . . nothing more, and nothing less, than what they actually were—a transience that was yet eternal life, a perpetual perishing

*that was at the same time pure Being, a bundle of minute particu-
lars in which, by some unspeakable and yet self-evident paradox,
was to be seen in the divine source of all existence.*

*I continued to look at the flowers, and in their living light I
seemed to detect the qualitative equivalent of breathing, but of a
breathing without returns to a starting point, with no recurrent
ebbs but only a repeated flow from beauty to heightened beauty,
from deeper to ever deeper meaning. Words like "grace" and
"transfiguration" came to my mind, and this, of course, was what,
among other things, they stood for. My eyes travelled from the
rose to the carnation, and from that feathery incandescence to
the smooth scrolls of sentient amethyst which were the iris. The
Beatific Vision,* Sat Chit Ananda, *Being-Awareness-Bliss—for
the first time I understood, not on the verbal level, not by inchoate
hints or at a distance, but precisely and completely what those
prodigious syllables referred to.*[43]

The foregoing descriptions of the effects of mescaline will
probably have left the reader with the impression that this
purified product of the sacred cactus offers the key to a very
remarkable world. To many people it does indeed offer such a
key and its virtues have been summarized very clearly by Havelock Ellis:

*Mescal intoxication may be described as chiefly a saturnalia
for the specific senses, and, above all, an orgy of vision. It reveals
an optical fairyland, where all the senses now and again join the
play, but the mind itself remains a self-possessed spectator.
Mescal intoxication thus differs from the other artificial paradises
which drugs procure. Under the influence of alcohol, for instance,
as in normal dreaming, the intellect is impaired, although there
may be a consciousness of unusual brilliance; hasheesh, again,
produces an uncontrollable tendency to movement and bathes its
victim in a sea of emotion. The mescal drinker remains calm and
collected amid the sensory turmoil around him; his judgment is
as clear as in the normal state; he falls into no oriental condition
of vague and voluptuous reverie. The reason why mescal is of all*

this class of drugs the most purely intellectual in its appeal is
evidently because it affects mainly the most intellectual of the
senses. On this ground it is not probable that its use will easily
develop into a habit. Moreover, unlike most other intoxicants, it
seems to have no special affinity for a disordered and unbalanced
nervous system; on the contrary, it demands organic soundness
and good health for complete manifestation of its virtues. Further,
unlike the other chief substances to which it may be compared,
mescal does not wholly carry us away from the actual world, or
plunge us into oblivion; a large part of its charm lies in the halo
of beauty which it casts around the simplest and commonest
things. It is the most democratic of the plants which lead men
to an artificial paradise. If it should ever chance that the con-
sumption of mescal becomes a habit, the favorite poet of the
mescal drinker will certainly be Wordsworth. Not only the general
attitude of Wordsworth but many of his most memorable poems
and phrases cannot—one is almost tempted to say—be appreci-
ated in their full significance by one who has never been under
the influence of mescal. On all these grounds it may be claimed
that the artificial paradise of mescal, though less seductive, is
safe and dignified beyond its peers.[19]

The author, however, would not be doing his duty as an
impartial reporter if he did not add that even the glamorous
world of mescaline has its darker side. Not everyone can enter its
colorful kingdom.

"Along with the happily transfigured majority of mescaline
takers," writes Aldous Huxley, "there is a minority that finds in
the drug only hell and purgatory." This is undoubtedly true, nor
is it easy to be sure just how correctly we can claim that the
"happily transfigured" are in the majority. The following description by G. Tayleur Stockings of the general appearance of a group
of individuals under the influence of mescaline seems hardly that
of "happily transformed beings":

The lips and tongue become dry and coated with sores; the
skin is flushed at first, and later becomes dry and harsh with an

earthy pallor; the conjunctiva are injected, and the eyes appear
unnaturally bright. The urine is scanty and highly colored, and
there is absolute insomnia, anorexia (loss of appetite) and in
the later stages, restlessness. . . . There is always nausea and
occasionally vomiting in the early stages.[91]

This nausea may not interfere with the subject's enjoyment
of his strange experiences. As Klüver points out, "In spite
of marked nausea many subjects 'have a good time'; being in
a state of mental exhilaration they become talkative and jocular,
they commit social errors and enjoy committing them—harmless
remarks, even a potato salad or a catsup bottle, are considered
unusually funny." In other subjects, however, the unpleasant
symptoms produced by the drug are unrelieved by any consoling
experience, visual or otherwise.

One might suppose such individuals to be degraded types
whose "doors of perception" are so hopelessly muddied that even
the potent cleansing action of mescaline makes no impression
on the encrusting grime. This can hardly be true. That prince of
psychologists, William James, was certainly no stranger to the
realm of mystical experience. He remains one of the few psychologists of any standing who has ever taken the trouble to investigate
religious phenomena. Yet William James, who received peyote
from S. Weir Mitchell, derived from the sacred cactus nothing
more than a stomachache. "I ate one bud three days ago," he
wrote in a letter to his brother Henry, "was violently sick for
twenty-four hours, and had no other symptoms whatever except
that and the Katzenjammer the following day. I will take the
visions on trust." Even S. Weir Mitchell, whose experiences were
much more promising, commented, "These shows are expensive.
. . . The experience, however, was worth one such headache and
indigestion but was not worth a second."

Quite apart from the nausea, anorexia, and insomnia, the
mescaline visions themselves are by no means always divine:

In some individuals the "ivresse divine" of which Rouhier speaks
comes nearer to being an "ivresse diabolique." Vague terrors

*and the sense of impending disaster often mingle with the cosmic
experiences. The immensity of the new realms perceived may
frighten more than they enlighten the mescaline taker . . . the
experiences in the mescal state are not easily forgotten. One looks
"beyond the horizon" of the normal world, and this "beyond"
is often so impressive or even shocking that its aftereffects
linger for years in one's memory. No wonder some subjects
are disinclined to repeat the experiment . . . [Klüver].*[52]

For this reason it is improbable that mescaline will ever
become widely popular as a means of fleeing the drab realities of
the ordinary world. The artificial paradise to which it holds the
key is too strange a realm to appeal to the average taste and the
cost of getting there, in terms of unpleasant physical reactions,
would seem excessive. Many, in fact, would agree with William
James that the experience is not worth the *Katzenjammer**. As a
euphoriant it is unlikely to replace alcohol, though its effects are
infinitely more interesting, and it "does not drive the taker into
the kind of uninhibited action which results in brawls, crimes of
violence and traffic accidents" (Huxley). It has no addiction-
forming properties. Indians who have consumed it for years can
still manage perfectly well without the drug. It seems to have no
lasting ill effect on any organ in the body, including the liver on
which falls the task of detoxifying this particular poison, for
mescaline is poisonous, albeit the effects are interesting and the
toxic symptoms rarely alarming.

As regards the way in which mescaline exerts its effects,
we have to admit that we are almost entirely ignorant. Quastel
and Wheatley have shown that mescaline and several related
substances interfere with oxidative processes in minced brain
tissue. Aldous Huxley has accepted this finding as the explanation
of mescaline's mode of action. He envisages the brain as a kind
of reducing valve which protects our little human minds from the

* This expressive German word means, literally, caterwauling. In the sense
used above it describes the unpleasant symptoms left by an alcoholic
debauch, in short a "hangover."

overwhelming pressure of "Mind at Large." When the efficiency of the reducing valve is impaired by mescaline, "Mind at Large," or the mind of the macrocosm, pushes its way into the mind of the microcosm, which explains the overwhelming character of certain mescaline experiences. To assume, however, that mescaline exerts its characteristic action simply by lowering the brain's capacity to utilize oxygen would not seem warranted by the evidence. The barbiturates also cut down oxidation in brain slices but these substances do not produce the color visions or other experiences typical of mescaline. They merely put the one who takes them to sleep. Further, it must be emphasized again that between minced brain in a test tube and living brain in a man's skull there is a very wide gap. We dare not even assume that mescaline taken by mouth or even injected into the blood necessarily enters the brain itself. It may be checked by the blood-brain barrier. It may be transformed in the liver into something chemically different. This, say the German workers Patzig and Block, is actually what does happen. When mescaline is "labeled" by building into it an atom of radioactive carbon, its presence can be detected in the liver but hardly a trace of the substance can be found in the brain. Its effects, these workers believe, are due to its combining with liver protein to form a toxic substance which, like a number of other toxic substances, interferes with brain function and causes hallucinations.

F. M. Sturtevant and V. A. Drill, who injected mescaline directly into the brains of cats, thus forcing the drug past the blood-brain barrier, have shown that it produces dramatic effects on the animals' behavior.[94] The cats began a loud continuous yowling which was unlike any normal cat sound. They retched, they salivated, they defecated, and their breath came in short gasps. Particularly noticeable was the change in their behavior toward mice. Cats which, before treatment with mescaline, had instantly caught and killed a mouse, merely ignored the animal while under the influence of the drug. Indeed, so great did their forbearance become that one submitted placidly to having his ears and nose nibbled. The drug evidently made pacifists out of the cats and filled them with brotherly love which extended even to mice. They appeared to derive enjoyment from rubbing their cheeks against the mice and allowing them to crawl over and under their bodies. The happy state foretold by the prophet was thus realized; the lion lay down with the lamb and did not hurt nor destroy. For the next eighteen to twenty hours the peace continued, after which the fondling became progressively rougher, ending with typical cat-and-mouse play in which the mice were killed and eaten. It is clear from this work that mescaline does have some direct effect on the chemistry of the brain; the nature of this action is at present unknown.

Such are the effects of mescaline and of the peyote cactus. They range from the sublime to the ridiculous, from visions of heaven to vomitings and *Katzenjammer*. It is quite probable that peyote itself produces different effects from pure mescaline for the cactus contains many active substances. The effect a person obtains with peyote depends in part on personal chemistry and in part on the setting. A member of the Native American Church or an Indian "man of knowledge" like Don Juan takes peyote expecting a religious experience. He takes it, moreover, under special conditions, reverently and probably quite rarely. Mescalito, says Don Juan, can terrify those he does not like. No one fools with Mescalito (except ignorant white men who have no reverence for anything).

The Mind and Marijuana

*Now the three statues advanced towards him, and approached
the couch on which he was reposing, their feet hidden in their
long white tunics, their throats bare, their hair flowing like waves.
Assuming attitudes which the gods could not resist but which
saints withstood they turned upon him looks inflexibly ardent such
as those with which a serpent charms a bird. Then he gave way
before looks which held him in a torturing grasp and delighted
his senses as with a voluptuous kiss. Now followed a dream of
passion like that promised by the Prophet to his Elect. Lips of
stone turned to flame, breasts of ice became like heated lava, so
that to Franz, yielding for the first time to the sway of the hashish,
love was a sorrow and voluptuousness a torture, as burning
mouths were pressed to his thirsty lips, and he was held in cool
serpent-like embraces. The more he strove against this unhallowed
passion the more his senses yielded to its spell, and at length,
weary of the struggle that strained his very soul, he sank back
yielding, breathless and exhausted, under the kisses of those
marble goddesses, wrapped in the enchantment of his marvellous
dream.*[18]

What goes on here? It is the fertile pen of Alexandre Dumas
busying itself with a theme unfailing in its appeal to the average
novel reader—the effect on the mind and emotions of a mysterious
oriental drug. Dumas chose well. There is hardly another drug
in or out of the pharmacopoeia more shrouded in mystery, more
richly encrusted with big and little misconceptions than that
substance which in Arabia is called *hashish*, in Persia *beng*, in
Morocco *kif*, in South Africa *dagga*, in India *charas, bhang,* or

gangha, in Mexico and the United States *marijuana,* and in scientific circles "the flowering tops of the female plant of *Cannabis sativa.*"

Scarcely seen in Europe until the middle of the nineteenth century, the drug was known only by reputation from the tales of travelers returning from the Orient. It was always associated with romantic stories colorful and gorgeous as the interminable yarns of Scheherazade. The very word *hashish* carries romantic overtones. This substance, so ran the legend, was fed to his followers by Hasan-i-Sabbah, "The Old Man of the Mountain," who built his stronghold on the craggy peak of Alamut. For the sake of the glimpse of paradise which the drug afforded, his fanatical henchmen would gladly ride across the desert to Basra or Baghdad, there stealthily to murder certain individuals of whom Hasan happened to disapprove. For this reason the furtive secret political murderer is known even today as an assassin, a name supposedly derived from that of the drug. As to the nature of those joys for which Hasan's followers were willing to commit murder, we have a description of them from the pen of no less an orientalist than Marco Polo:

In the center of the territory of the Assassins there are delicious walled gardens in which one can find everything that can satisfy the needs of the body and the caprices of the most exacting sensuality. Great banks of gorgeous flowers and bushes covered with fruit stand amongst crystal rivers of living water. About them lie verdant fields and from the shaded turf burst bubbling springs. Trellises of roses and fragrant vines cover with their foliage pavilions of jade or porcelain furnished with Persian carpets or Grecian embroideries.

Delicious drinks in vessels of gold or crystal are served by young boys or girls, whose dark unfathomable eyes cause them to resemble the Houris, divinities of that Paradise which the Prophet promised to believers. The sound of harps mingles with the cooing of doves, the murmur of soft voices blends with the sighing of the reeds. All is joy, pleasure, voluptuousness and enchantment.

The Grand Master of the Assassins, whenever he discovers a young man resolute enough to belong to his murderous legions, invites the youth to his table and intoxicates him with the plant hashish. *Having been secretly transported to the pleasure gardens the young man imagines that he has entered the Paradise of Mahomet. The girls, lovely as Houris, contribute to this illusion. After he has enjoyed to satiety all the joys promised by the Prophet to his Elect, he falls again into a state of lethargy and is transported back to the presence of the Grand Master. Here he is informed that he can enjoy perpetually the delights he has just tasted if he will take part in the war of the Infidel as commanded by the Prophet.*

Before we plunge further into the myths and marvels which have become associated with this peculiar drug it will be as well if we examine the plant from which it comes. Marijuana, hashish, bhang, charas, and the rest are all derived from the hemp plant, *Cannabis sativa.** As a drug plant cannabis is extremely ancient. Even in the days of Hasan-i-Sabbah, who staged his deviltries toward the end of the eleventh century, the plant had a long and varied history. Norman Taylor, in a vivid account of the plant's romantic story,[96] describes it as being well known to the Chinese emperor, Shen Neng, whose work on pharmacy was written in the year 2737 B.C. An aura of suspicion hung even then about the plant, for that which gave easy happiness was, then as now, an object of disapproval. The active preparation from the plant was therefore labeled "Liberator of Sin." Later a more indulgent generation of Chinese sages called it "the delight giver," while the tolerant Hindus termed it "the heavenly guide" and "the soother of grief."

A tall gangling weed which may reach a height of ten feet, the hemp plant has long been grown in Kentucky for its fiber, but the hardy pioneers who brought it to that state either knew nothing of its effect on the mind or, despising its seductions, refused to avail themselves of its artificial paradise. In India,

* The older name, *Cannabis indica,* refers to the same plant.

however, the plant is cultivated especially for the drug. There, in three small villages adjoining Ahmadnagar in Bombay, special varieties of hemp grow in the tropical climate, filling the humid air with a fragrance drowsy and balsamic, faintly reminiscent of the odor which pervades the hop fields when the ripening cones are about to shed their golden dust. This dust from the hops is not pollen but a special resin from which beer derives its bitterness, its aroma, and its slightly soporific qualities. Hemp and hops are related and the potent spirit of the hemp also resides in a resin, sticky and aromatic, which coats the female flowers. Crushed and rolled into flat cakes, these flowering tops form the *gangha* of Bengal. Gathered without further treatment, they constitute the marijuana of Mexico. The most potent of all the hemp drugs, *charas,* is produced in Yarkand, in Central Asia. There, in the scented hemp fields, sweltering laborers run to and fro clad only in leather aprons to the surface of which the sticky resin adheres. It is scraped off and pressed into cakes which are green at first but become brown on aging. *Charas* is imported into India via Tibet. In Tibet itself is prepared *momea,* that weird concoction consisting of charas incorporated into human fat. It is used by the Dugpas in their unholy rites and is taken from a cup made from a human skull.

In less esoteric circles the hemp drugs are used in a variety of ways. In Bombay the potent charas is often incorporated into a sweetmeat called *maajun,* which is popular among members of the female sex. In Egypt and the Middle East hashish is smoked in special pipes called *josies,* along with glowing charcoal, the carbon monoxide from which doubtless contributes to the physiological effects. In Mexico and the United States the drug is smoked in the form of marijuana. In Algeria a special delicacy is made from cannabis which goes under the name of *dawamesc*. It is prepared by grinding the hemp tops with sugar, orange juice, cinnamon, cloves, cardamom, nutmeg, musk, pistachios, and pine kernels. These are all ground together and served in portions no bigger than a filbert. Meunier mentions that, to increase the aphrodisiac effect of the hemp, the Oriental sometimes adds a "pinch" of nux vomica or cantharides. A toxicologist must shudder to think of these potent poisons handled in so casual a fashion. Without these added ingredients, however, *dawamesc* is a relatively harmless confection.

It was with *dawamesc,* prepared by boiling the flowering tops of the plant in a mixture of water and butter, that Jacques-Joseph Moreau began his experiments in 1840. There is much to be gained from reading Moreau (reviewed in some detail in *Marihuana—Deceptive Weed*[71] by G. G. Nahas). He was one of the first physicians to realize that mental illness may result from some sort of chemical alteration of the working of the brain. He was also one of the first physicians to point out that he who would try to cure the mad should himself have some idea of how madness feels. "I have compared the principal characteristics observed in mental illness to the symptoms caused in me by hashish intoxication. The insights provided by my own study gave me a better understanding of mental illness."[70]

Moreau's conclusions, it must be emphasized, were based on what most users of marijuana would consider to be abuse of the drug. The doses he and his colleagues took were relatively enormous. One of Moreau's pupils, the pharmacist at the hospital, took as much as 90 grams of the potent preparation! It is hardly surprising, with such a huge amount of cannabis inside him, that this experimenter suffered a psychotic episode that lasted for three days.

Moreau has described very well certain features of the hemp intoxication which will be experienced by those who take rather large doses by mouth. There was, on the one hand, a sense of total euphoria.

It is a feeling of physical and mental comfort, of inner satisfaction, of intimate joy; that you seek mainly to understand or analyze that for which you cannot find the cause. You feel happy; you proclaim it with exuberance; you seek to express it with all the means at your disposal; you repeat it to the point of satiety. But to say how and why you are happy, words are not

*enough. Finding myself in this situation one day and despairing
of being understood by words alone, I uttered cries or rather
howls. Imperceptibly, following this febrile and nervous feeling
of happiness which shakes convulsively all of your sensitivity,
there descends a soft feeling of physical and mental fatigue, a
kind of apathy, of unconcern, an absolutely complete calm to
which your mind abandons itself with great delight. It seems that
nothing can impair this stillness of the soul and that you are
inaccessible to sadness.*[70]

The happiness, however, was based on flimsy foundations and
could be changed to misery by the slightest change in conditions.

*Depending on the circumstances, on the objects that you see,
and the words that you hear, you will experience the most vivid
feelings of happiness or sorrow, the most contradictory passions
with unusual violence. From irritation, one can pass rapidly
to fury, from discontent to hate and desire for revenge, from
the calmest love to the wildest passion. Fear becomes terror,
courage a dedication that none can stop and that ignores danger.
Groundless suspicions may become convictions. The mind
tends to exaggerate in all areas; the slightest excitation rarely
fails to carry it away. Those who use hashish in the Orient, when
they want to abandon themselves to the rapture of hashish
intoxication, exert an extreme care to eliminate anything that
might turn their madness into depression, or might arouse anything other than pleasant and tender feelings.*[70]

Moreau noted that effect on the perception of music so often
commented on by musicians who have taken the drug.

*The overstimulation that hashish causes in the whole nervous
system is felt most particularly in the portion of this system
concerned with the perception of sounds. Hearing acquires an
unbelievable sensitivity. The sounds spread even to the epigastric
center; they expand or compress the chest, accelerate or slow the
heartbeat, and convulsively set in motion the whole muscular
system or benumb it.*[70]

Moreau concluded that hashish, taken in the very large doses he used, upsets the normal balance of the mind. The upset, among other things, results in the intrusion of dreams into the waking state and these dreams may be taken for realities.

As the action of hashish is more keenly felt, one passes imperceptibly from the real world into a fictitious world without losing consciousness of oneself. In a way there exists a sort of fusion between the dream state and the waking state. One dreams while awake.[70]

In many ways Moreau's researches with hashish foreshadowed those of later psychiatrists with mescaline and LSD. He believed that extreme cannabis intoxication was a "model psychosis" and that the causes of mental illness could logically be sought in the chemistry of the brain. This subject will be discussed later in the chapter "The Chemistry of Madness." Now we are mainly concerned with the interest which Moreau's studies of hashish aroused among the intellectuals of Paris.

Le Club des Hachischins which met in the old Hotel Pimodan included some of the leaders of the French romantic movement. Théophile Gautier wrote most rapturously of these experiences. Charles Baudelaire was more cautious and objective in his appraisal. Honoré de Balzac, oddly enough, could never quite summon up enough courage to embark on the trip. The reason for his refusal was thus described by Baudelaire:

Balzac clearly thought that man's greatest disgrace and keenest suffering is the surrender of his will-power. I once saw him at a gathering at which there was a discussion of the miraculous effects of hashish. He listened and asked questions with an amusing attentiveness and vivacity. Anyone who ever knew him will guess that he must have been keenly interested. But the notion of letting his thoughts pass beyond his own control shocked him deeply. He was shown some dawamesc; he examined it, sniffed it, and passed it back without touching it. His inner conflict, between his almost childish eagerness for knowledge and his loathing of self-surrender, was revealed on his expressive countenance in a most striking fashion. His love of human dignity won the day. It would, indeed, be difficult to imagine this believer in the will, this spiritual twin of Louis Lambert, consenting to lose a particle of this precious "substance."[3]

This is an interesting comment and one which tells us much about the reason why some men fear the magic garden as much as others are attracted by it. At least in the year 1845 when Moreau published *Hashish and Mental Alienation* the maze of forbidding legislation which now surrounds the drug like a barbed-wire entanglement had not been constructed. The Hachischins therefore were free to indulge as they saw fit without running the risk of spending five years in jail as would any contemporary group rash enough to experiment in the same field and to publish its experiences.

It was Baudelaire, most perceptive of the Hachischins, who best described the limits of the world of hashish in his chapter intriguingly titled "The Theatre of the Seraphim":

Ignorant people suppose that the intoxication of hashish represents a prodigious land, a vast theatre of jugglery, in which all is miraculous and unexpected. That is a prejudice, a complete mistake. . . . In the intoxication of hashish there is nothing of the kind. Our dreams are natural, our intoxication will always keep the peculiar tonality of the individual. Men who are eager to experience unusual pleasures should know that in hashish they will find nothing miraculous, absolutely nothing but what is extremely natural. The brain and the organism on which hashish operates give only their ordinary individual phenomena, increased it is true as to number and energy but always faithful to their origin. Man cannot escape the fatality of his physical and moral temperament. Hashish will be for man's familiar thoughts and impressions a mirror that exaggerates but always a mirror.

Over the surface of man's ordinary life the power of hashish spreads a magic glaze, coloring it with solemnity, bringing to light the profoundest aspects of existence. Fleeting horizons, perspective of cities, pale in the cadaverous light of storms or

*blazing beneath the concentrated ardor of a crouching sun—
profundities of space—allegories on the profundities of time—
the dance—the gestures and the declamations of actors if you
happen to be in the theatre—the first phrase your eyes chance
to fall on if you are reading a book—in short the universality of
being reveals itself to you with a glory never before experienced.*[3]

Now Baudelaire approaches the drug itself, explaining, for
the benefit of those wishing to experience its effects, the rather
special conditions under which it must be taken if unpleasant
effects are to be avoided:

*Here is the drug before your eyes; a morsel of green jam,
no more than a nutful, singularly odorous, to such a point that it
sickens the stomach and makes one faintly nauseous. Here, then,
is your happiness! It hardly exceeds the capacity of a teaspoon!
Happiness with all its intoxication, all its follies, all its absurdities!
You can swallow it without fear. No one ever died of it. It will
not injure your physical organs. Later perhaps a too frequent
appeal to this magic may undermine the strength of your will,
perhaps you will be less a man than you are today, but the
punishment is so distant and the future disaster to one's nature
so hard to define! What do you risk? Tomorrow a little nervous
fatigue. Do you not every day risk greater punishments for
smaller rewards?*

*So. You have diluted your hashish in a cup of black coffee
to endow the drug with greater strength and effect. You have
been careful to have an empty stomach, postponing your dinner
until nine or ten o'clock to give the poison adequate time to act,
at the most in an hour or so from now you might take some soup.
You have now enough ballast for a long and strange voyage. The
whistle blows, the sails are set and you have the curious advantage
over the ordinary traveller of not knowing where you are going.
You wanted it. Hurrah for fatality!*

*I presume that you have chosen the right moment for this
expedition. Every perfect debauch requires perfect leisure.
Besides, hashish not only magnifies the individual but also the
circumstance and environment. You must have no duties to*

accomplish that require punctuality or exactitude, no pangs of love, no domestic preoccupations, griefs, anxieties. The memories of duty will sound a death knell through your intoxication and poison your pleasure. Anxiety will change to anguish, grief to torture. But if the conditions are right and the weather is good, if you are in a favorable environment as in the midst of a picturesque landscape or in a room artistically decorated, if, moreover, you can hope to hear some music, then all's for the best.[3]

There are, says Baudelaire, three stages in the hashish intoxication:

Most novices, during the first step of their initiation, complain of the slow effects of hashish. Then, like the signs of an approaching storm, comes a certain hilarity, irresistible, ludicrous. The simplest words, the most trivial ideas take on new and strange shapes, incongruous resemblances and associations impossible to foresee, interminable puns, comical absurdities, rush continually through your brain. From time to time you laugh at yourself, at your foolishness and your folly, and your friends, if you have any, laugh just as boisterously at their condition and your own, but, as they are without malice, you bear no rancor.

This hilarity, now languishing and now poignant, this uneasiness in joy, this insecurity, this sick indecision usually lasts only a short time. New events soon manifest themselves as a sensation of chill in the extremities and weakness in the limbs. Your hands tremble. In your head and your whole being you feel an awkward stupor. Your eyes dilate, your face grows pallid, your lips thin. The throat is contracted so to speak, the palate dried by thirst. You heave deep raucous sighs, as if your old body could not endure the desires and activity of your new soul. From time to time you shudder and make involuntary movements, like those nervous jumps which, at the end of a day's work, or during a stormy night, precede one's real sleep.

It is at this period of the intoxication that a new sensitiveness, a superior acuteness, manifests itself in all the senses. Smell, sight, hearing, touch, participate equally in this improvement. The

*eyes have a vision of Eternity. The ear hears almost inaudible
sounds in the midst of a vast tumult. It is then that the hallucinations begin. Exterior objects slowly and successively assume
singular appearances; they become deformed and transformed.
Then the equivocations commence, the errors and the transposition of ideas. Sounds take on colors and colors contain music.
This, one might say, is quite natural, and any poetical mind in a
sane and normal state easily imagines such analogies. But I have
already warned the reader that there is nothing supernatural in
the intoxication by hashish. These analogies merely assume an
unusual vivacity; they penetrate, they invade, they overpower
the mind because of their despotic nature. Musical notes become
numbers and, if you have a gift for mathematics, melody, audible
harmony, while it preserves its voluptuous and sensual character,
transforms itself into a vast arithmetical operation in which
numbers beget numbers and where you may follow the phrase
and progressions with inexplicable rapidity and an agility equal
to that of the performer.*

*It often happens that personality disappears and that objec-
tivity develops so abnormally that the contemplation of objects
outside yourself makes you forget your own existence and causes
you to lose yourself in them. Suppose you look at a tree gracefully
waving in the wind; in a few seconds what, in the mind of a
poet, might be merely a natural comparison, becomes for you a
reality. First you attribute to the tree your passion, your desire
or your melancholy, its murmurs and its writhing become yours,
and before long you* are *the tree. In the same way, a soaring
bird first* represents *the immortal desire to fly above things
human, but already you are yourself the bird. Similarly if you
are smoking, by some sort of transposition or intellectual* quid
pro quo, *you will feel yourself evaporating and will attribute
to your pipe, in which you feel yourself crouching and packed
together like tobacco, the strange power of* smoking yourself.[3]

Baudelaire is careful to explain that the "hallucinations"
induced by hashish are not true hallucinations. The hallucination
is progressive, almost voluntary, and ripens only through the

action of the imagination. Sounds may seem to say strange things,
but there always was a sound in the first place. Strange shapes
may be seen, but before becoming strange the shapes were
natural. Hashish, in short, may distort but it does not create
that which is not there.

Concluding his account of the hashish experience in a section
entitled "The Man-God," Baudelaire describes that triumphant
euphoria, that prodigious glorification and uplift which, on certain
occasions, floods the soul of the hashish eater.

*Now my imaginary man, the spirit of my choice, has reached
that peculiar state of joy and serenity in which he finds himself
compelled to admire himself. All contradictions disappear, all
philosophical problems become clear or at least seem to. All is
food for pleasure. A voice speaks inside him and says to him,
"You now have the right to consider yourself superior to all men;
no one knows or could understand all that you think and all that
you feel: they would even be incapable of appreciating the good
will with which they inspired you. You are a king unrecognized
by the crowd and who lives alone in his belief: but who cares?
Do you not possess a sovereign contempt that strengthens the
soul?"*

*But we can suppose that from time to time some biting
memory enters and corrupts his joy. Does not one's past reveal
many a vile or stupid action which is truly unworthy of a king?
But the man that takes hashish will courageously face these
reproachful ghosts of memory—he will analyze curiously the
action or sentiment, the memory of which disturbed his glorification. "This ridiculous, cowardly or vile action, the memory of
which disturbed me for a moment, is a complete contradiction of
my true nature. The very energy with which I condemn it, the
inquisitorial care with which I analyze and judge it proves my
high and divine aptitude for virtue. How many men are there in
the world clever enough to judge themselves or strict enough to
condemn themselves?"*

*Shall I continue my analysis of this victorious monomania?
Shall I explain how, under the influence of the poison, the man I*

have imagined supposes himself to be the center of the Universe? All things about him act as suggestions activating a world of thoughts within him more alive, more colored, more subtle, scintillating with a magic glaze. "These magnificent cities where superb houses are set at intervals like stage scenery, those fine ships balanced in nostalgic indolence by the waves of the bay, these museums which contain such beautiful forms and such intoxicating colors, these libraries in which are gathered the labors of Science and the dreams of the Muses, these instruments of music which, when placed together, seem to speak with one voice, these enchanting women made more charming still by the science of adornment and the rare magic of their glances—all these have been created for me, for me, for me! For me has humanity labored, been martyred, been immolated, to serve as pasture for my implacable thirst for emotion, for knowledge, for beauty!"

None now should be astonished by the final, the supreme thought born in the dreamer's mind—"I have become God!" That ardent, savage cry bursts from his lips with so intense an energy, with so tremendous a power of projection, that, if the will and belief of an intoxicated man had effective virtue, the cry would topple the very angels scattered about along the roads of heaven: "I am a god!" But soon this hurricane of arrogance becomes transformed. A mood of calm, muted and tranquil, takes its place; the universality of man is announced colorfully, and lighted as it were by a sulfurous dawn. If perchance a vague memory reaches the soul of this poor happy man that possibly there is another God, be certain that he will rise up and question His commands and that he will face him without terror. Who is the French philosopher who said, with the intention of mocking modern German doctrines, "I am a god who has dined poorly"? This irony would not touch a man intoxicated by hashish. He would quietly reply: "Perhaps I did dine poorly, yet I am a god."[3]

So much for the experiences of Baudelaire. Turning now to the writings of another member of Le Club des Hachischins, Théophile Gautier, we note at once how correctly Baudelaire has

observed that hashish serves only to magnify that which is already
present in the soul of man and that every man receives the vision
which his nature dictates. So while Baudelaire, always preoccupied with moral and philosophical problems, found in the world
of hashish huge abstractions centering about the problems of god
and devil, Gautier's brilliant visual imagination discovered a
realm of fantastic shapes and colors. We have no reason to
suppose that Gautier had ever heard of peyote but his description
of his experiences under the influence of hashish are so like those
of other investigators under the spell of the sacred cactus that one
is tempted to suppose that the two drugs must produce within the
brain a similar reaction, despite the chemical dissimilarity of their
active principles.

*A certain numbness overcame me. My body seemed to
dissolve and I became transparent. Within my breast I perceived
the hashish I had eaten in the form of an emerald scintillating
with a million points of fire. My eyelashes elongated indefinitely,
unrolling themselves like threads of gold on ivory spindles which
spun of their own accord with dazzling rapidity. Around me
poured streams of gems of every color, in ever changing patterns
like the play within a kaleidoscope. My comrades appeared to
me disfigured, part men, part plants, wearing the pensive air of
Ibises. So strange did they seem that I writhed with laughter in
my corner and, overcome by the absurdity of the spectacle, flung
my cushions in the air, making them turn and twist with the
rapidity of an Indian juggler.*

*The first attack passed and I found myself again in my normal
state without any of the unpleasant symptoms that follow intoxication with wine. Half an hour later I fell once again under the
domination of hashish. This time my visions were more complex
and more extraordinary. In the diffusely luminous air, perpetually
swarming, a myriad butterflies rustled their wings like fans.
Gigantic flowers with calyxes of crystal, enormous hollyhocks,
lilies of gold or silver rose before my eyes and spread themselves
about me, with a sound resembling that of a fireworks display.*

My hearing became prodigiously acute. I actually listened to the sound of the colors. From their blues, greens and yellows there reached me sound waves of perfect distinctness. A glass inverted, the creak of an armchair, a word pronounced in a deep voice vibrated and rumbled about me like the reverberations of thunder. My own voice seemed so loud that I dared not speak for fear of shattering the walls with its bomblike explosion. More than five hundred clocks seemed to announce the hour in voices silvery, brassy or flutelike. Each object touched gave off a note like that of a harmonica or an aeolian harp. Floating in a sonorous ocean, like luminous islands, were motifs from Lucia *and the* Barber of Seville. *Never has greater beauty immersed me in its flood. I was so lost in its waves, so separated from myself, so disembarrassed of my ego, that odious appendage that accompanies us everywhere, that for the first time I understood the nature of existence of elementals, of angels and spirits separated from the body. I hung like a sponge in the midst of a warm sea; at each moment waves of happiness traversed me entering and emerging by my pores. Because I had become permeable my whole being became tinged by the color of the fantastic medium in which I was plunged. Sounds, lights, perfumes reached me through tendrils fine as hairs in which I heard magnetic currents vibrating. By my calculation this state lasted about three hundred years for the sensations which followed one another were so numerous and pressing that any real appreciation of time was impossible. The rapture passed. . . . I saw that it had lasted just a quarter of an hour.*

A third rapture, the last and most bizarre, terminated my oriental soirée. In this one my vision doubled itself. Two images of every object were reflected on my retina in perfect sympathy. Soon the magic ferment began once again to act with power in my mind. For a full hour I became completely insane. In Pantagruelian dreams I saw passing by me creatures of fantasy, owls, sea storks, satyrs, unicorns, griffins, vultures, a whole menagerie of monsters trotting, gliding, vaulting, yelping about the room. . . . The visions became so baroque that a desire to

*draw them took hold of me. In less than five minutes I made a
sketch of Dr. X . . . who appeared to me seated at the piano,
dressed as a Turk with a sunflower on the back of his waistcoat.
My drawing represented him emerging from the keyboard in the
form of a corkscrew of capricious spirals. Another sketch bore
the legend "an animal of the future," and represented a living
locomotive with the neck of a swan terminated by the jaws of
a serpent from which emerged billows of smoke and monstrous
paws composed of wheels and pulleys. Each pair of paws was
accompanied by a pair of wings and above the tail of the animal
hovered the antique god Mercury, who advanced upon it victori-
ously in spite of its talons. By the grace of hashish I had been
able to draw a "Farfardet" from nature.*[27]

Now, leaving the Club of the Hachischins behind us, we
travel some three thousand miles westward to that place on the
banks of "the broad and noble Hudson" where the American
hashish eater, Fitz Hugh Ludlow, takes his walks by the river
somewhere in the neighborhood of Poughkeepsie. A curious
character, this Ludlow, intensely imaginative, with that inwardly
directed habit of mind which causes its possessor to be more
concerned about events of his inner than those of his outer world.
He began his experiments with hashish at the surprisingly early
age of sixteen and did not abandon his regular use of the drug
until he had graduated from college and assumed the duties
of a teacher in Watertown, New York. This rather prolonged
rendezvous with "My Lady of the Hemp" provided him with
material for his book, *The Hasheesh Eater,*[63] an effusion of some
365 pages published anonymously in 1857. No one seriously
interested in the effects of drugs on the mind should fail to read
Ludlow's book. Though, from the modern standpoint, it is grossly
overwritten and though in many places scientific impartiality has
been sacrificed in the interests of literary effect, it still remains
one of the most interesting products of its kind. It certainly
provides, at least in the present writer's opinion, more lively and
more colorful reading than do the grossly overrated confessions
of that "English opium-eater," Thomas De Quincey.

It should be pointed out here that Ludlow, like Baudelaire, was strongly influenced by the confessions of De Quincey and that much of his agonizing and handwringing over his "addiction" to hashish is purely imitative. No one would deny that De Quincey had good reason to wring his hands over his condition. Opium addiction is a serious matter and De Quincey was an addict in the fullest sense of the word. But when Ludlow starts sighing and groaning over his enslavement to hashish the reader who is familiar with the properties of the drug will lift a skeptical eyebrow. There is no such thing as genuine addiction to hashish or any other preparation of cannabis. Those terrible and agonizing withdrawal symptoms which chain the opium addict to his poison do not affect the hashish eater. He can take the drug or leave it alone. It is, by all unbiased accounts, even less habit-forming than tobacco. So Ludlow's literary lamentations over his terrible "slavery" must be taken with a large grain of salt as must a good many of his other remarks. One would not, however, wish to be so unkind as to suggest that Ludlow was a liar. It is sufficient if we realize that he suffered from hypertrophy of the imagination and an excessive dependence on the works of De Quincey. These weaknesses were further exaggerated by the influence of hashish, for, as Baudelaire points out, the drug magnifies all characteristics of an individual's psychology.

So we find Ludlow in the apothecary's shop in Poughkeepsie buying his extract of cannabis which in those innocent days, when no one had even heard of marijuana or its "menace," was a perfectly legal and normal thing to do. Ludlow, as we have mentioned, was a mere boy of sixteen but a boy of unusual imagination and curiosity. He had been reading *The Arabian Nights,* not, we suspect, in Burton's original translation, which was hardly considered suitable food for innocent minds, but in some suitably bowdlerized version, from which material likely to offend had been removed. One thing which had not been removed, however, was the accounts of the effects of beng or hashish. It was these accounts which roused the curiosity of the youthful Ludlow. How, he asked, did these spinners of oriental yarns contrive to dream up such magnificent compositions? With what magical stimulant did they fertilize their imaginations that they could ornament their tales with such gorgeous embroidery? The answer, Ludlow finally decided, was hashish. Being afflicted, even at that early age, with the urge to create literary masterpieces, he determined to try the drug himself, so he made haste to the nearest apothecary, placed his six cents on the counter, and received his extract. Back in his room he examined his purchase, an oily green-black sludge with a balsamic odor. With some excitement he rolled the mess into a bolus, downed a total of 10 grains, and waited eagerly for his gorgeous dreams. He experienced nothing whatever. Disappointed, he tried again on the following day, raising his dose to 15 grains. Still nothing happened. Again he upped the dose, 20 grains, no effect, 25 grains, no effect. He was disgusted. The celebrated effects of the mysterious drug were evidently just one more oriental fabrication. Nonetheless he decided to give the hashish one more opportunity to reveal to him its wonders. He rolled an even larger bolus, 30 grains, the size of a small grape, and swallowed the nauseous stuff with some difficulty and much water. Having, by this time, completely lost faith in the power of hashish, he went out to spend the evening with some friends in another part of town.

For two hours he sat by the fireside at his friend's house engaged in amiable chitchat without giving so much as a thought to the dark green bolus making its way along the twists and turns of his intestines. As for the bolus, it rolled merrily along, propelled by successive peristaltic waves and, because young Ludlow had for once taken his hashish on an empty stomach, it found no obstacles to prevent its absorption. And so the potent ingredients of the hashish, after traversing the liver, rose via the ascending carotids toward the brain and young Ludlow paused in his chitchat, suddenly and embarrassingly aware that some exceedingly strange process was taking place within his body. Here, in his own exclamatory language, is his description of that first experience:

Ha! What means this sudden thrill! A shock as of some un-imagined vital force, shoots without warning through my entire

*frame, leaping to my finger ends, piercing my brain and startling
me until I almost spring from my chair.*

*I could not doubt. I was in the power of the hashish influence.
My first emotion was one of uncontrollable terror—no pain
anywhere—not a twinge in any fibre—yet a cloud of unutterable
strangeness was sitting upon me, and wrapping me impenetrably
from all that was natural and familiar. . . .*

*A question was put to me, and I answered it. I even laughed
at a* bon mot. *Yet it was not my voice which spoke; perhaps one
which I once had far away in another time and another place.
I sat and listened; still the voice kept speaking. Now for the first
time I experienced the vast change which hashish makes in all
measurements of time. The first word of my reply occupied a
period sufficient for the action of a drama; the last left me in
complete ignorance of any point far enough back in the past to
date the commencement of the sentence. Its enunciation might
have occupied years. . . .*

*And now, with time, space also expanded. . . . I was sitting at
a distance of hardly three feet from the centre table around which
the members of the family were grouped. Rapidly that distance
widened. We were in a vast hall of which my friends and I
occupied the extremities. . . . I could not bear it. I should soon
be left alone in the midst of infinity of space. And now more and
more every moment increased the conviction that I was watched.
I did not know then, as I learned afterwards, that suspicion of all
earthly things and persons was characteristic of the hashish
delirium.*

*In the midst of my complicated hallucination, I could perceive
that I had a dual existence. One part of me was whisked unresist-
ingly along the track of this tremendous experience, the other sat
looking down from a height upon its double, observing, reasoning
and serenely weighing all the phenomena. . . . I rose to take my
leave and advanced towards the centre table. With every step its
distance increased. I nerved myself as for a long pedestrian
journey. . . . Out in the street the view stretched endlessly away.
. . . I was doomed to pass through a merciless stretch of space.*

*A soul disenthralled, setting out for his flight beyond the farthest
visible star, could not be more overwhelmed with his newly
acquired conception of the sublimity of distance than I was that
moment. Solemnly I began my infinite journey.*

*Before long I walked in entire unconsciousness of all around
me. I dwelt in a marvellous inner world. I existed by turns in
different places and various states of being. Now I swept my
gondola through the moonlit lagoons of Venice. Now Alp on Alp
towered above my view, and the glory of the coming sun placed
purple light upon the topmost pinnacle. Now in the primaeval
silence of some unexplored tropical forest I spread my feathery
leaves, a giant fern, and swayed and nodded in the spice gales
over a river whose waves at once sent up clouds of music and
perfume. My soul changed to a vegetable essence, thrilled with
a strange and unimagined ecstasy. . . .*

*The effects of the hashish had increased mightily. I was
bursting with an uncontrollable life; I strode with the thews of
a giant. Hotter and faster came my breath; I seemed to pant like
some tremendous engine. . . . My sensations began to be terrific—
not from any pain I felt, but from the tremendous mystery of all
around me and within me. By an appalling introversion, all
the operations of vitality which, in our ordinary state, go on
unconsciously, came vividly into my experience. Through the
thinnest corporeal tissue and the minutest veins I could trace the
circulation of the blood along each inch of its progress. I knew
when every valve opened and when it shut, every sense was
preternaturally awakened. The beating of my heart was clearly
audible. Lo, now that heart became a great fountain, whose jet
played upward with loud vibrations, and, striking on the roof of
my skull as on a gigantic dome, fell back with a splash and echo
into its reservoir. Faster and faster came the pulsations and the
stream became one continuously pouring flood, whose roar
sounded through all my frame. I gave myself up for lost, since
judgment, which still sat unimpaired above my perverted senses,
argued that congestion must take place in a few minutes, and
close the drama with my death. . . .*[63]

So disturbed did Ludlow become by the prospect of exploding under the impact of his own pounding blood pressure that he set off despite the lateness of the hour to seek a physician. The worthy healer, roused from his slumbers by a frightened youth who stammered out that he had consumed 30 grains of cannabis extract, testily told the lad to go to bed and sleep it off. Ludlow complied with these instructions. After walking through endless eons of space-time he finally reached his bed and flung himself upon it.

The moment that I closed my eyes a vision of celestial glory burst upon me. I stood on the silver strand of a translucent lake across whose bosom I seemed to have been just transported. A short way up the beach, a temple, modelled like the Parthenon, lifted its spotless and gleaming columns of alabaster sublimely into a rosy air—like the Parthenon, yet as much excelling it as the god-like idea of architecture must transcend that ideal realized by man. Unblemished in its purity of whiteness, faultless in the unbroken symmetry of every line and angle, its pediment was draped with odorous clouds, whose tints outshone the rainbow. It was the work of an unearthly builder, and my soul stood before it in a trance of ecstasy. Its folded doors were resplendent with the glory of a multitude of eyes of glass, which were inlaid throughout the marble surfaces at the corners of the diamond figures from the floor of the porch to the topmost moulding. One of these eyes was golden, like the midday sun, another emerald, another sapphire, and thus onward through the whole gamut of hues, all of them set in such collections as to form most exquisite harmonies, and whirling upon their axes with the rapidity of thought. At the mere vestibule of the temple I could have sat and drunk in ecstasy forever; but lo! I am yet more blessed. On silent hinges the doors swing open and I pass in.

I did not seem to be in the interior of the temple. I beheld myself so truly in the open air as if I had never passed the portals, for whichever way I looked there were no walls, no roof, no pavement. An atmosphere of fathomless and soul-satisfying

*serenity surrounded and transfused me. I stood upon the bank of
a crystal stream, whose waters, as they slid on, discoursed notes
of music which tinkled on the air like the tones of some exquisite
bellglass. The same impression which such tones produce, of
music refined to its ultimate ethereal spirit and borne from a far
distance, characterized every ripple of those translucent waves.
The gently sloping banks of the stream were luxuriant with a
velvety cushioning of grass and moss, so living green that the eye
and soul reposed on them at the same time and drank in peace.
Through this amaranthine herbage strayed the gnarled fantastic
roots of the cedars of Lebanon, from whose primaeval trunks
great branches spread above me, and, interlocking, wove a roof
of impenetrable shadow, and wandering down the still avenues
below those grand arboreal arches went glorious bards, whose
snowy beards fell on their breasts beneath countenances of
ineffable benignity and nobleness.*

*They were all clad in flowing robes, like God's high priests,
and each one held in his hand a lyre of unearthly workmanship.
Presently one steps down a shadowy walk, and, baring his right
arm, begins a prelude. While his celestial chords were trembling
up into their sublime fulness, another strikes his strings, and now
they blend upon my ravished ear in such a symphony as was
never heard elsewhere, and I shall never hear again out of
the Great Presence. A moment more and three are playing in
harmony; now the fourth joins the glorious rapture of his music
to their own, and in the completeness of the chord my soul is
swallowed up. I can hear no more. But yes, I am sustained, for
suddenly the whole throng break forth in a chorus, upon whose
wings I am lifted out of the riven walls of sense, and music
and spirit thrill in immediate communion. Forever rid of the
intervention of pulsing air and vibrating nerve my soul dilates
with the swell of that transcendent harmony, and interprets from
its arcana a meaning which words can never tell. I am borne
aloft upon the glory of sound. I float in a trance among the
burning choir of the seraphim. But, as I am melting through the
purification of that sublime ecstasy into oneness with the Deity*

*himself, one by one those pealing lyres faint away, and as the last
throb dies down along the measureless ether, visionless arms
swiftly as lightning carry me far into the profound, and set me
down before another portal.*[63]

It is hardly surprising, even when one has deducted about
50 percent of the "sublimity" of the above vision to allow for
Ludlow's penchant for exaggeration, that this imaginative, highly
impressionable youth could not resist experimenting further with
hashish. The drug had lived up to his wildest expectations, it had
justified all that the Arabian and Persian storytellers had spoken
in its praise. So off went Ludlow to the apothecary for another
six cents' worth of cannabis extract and soon he was back again
in the magic world of hashish, glorying in the sense of infinite
time and space, in the poignancy with which the drug invested
every perception. After a number of these excursions into the
hashish world he was in a position to generalize about the effects
of the drug and some of his conclusions can be given here.

*Hashish I called the drug of the traveller. The whole East,
from Greece to farthest China, lay within the compass of a
township; no outlay was necessary for the journey. For the
humble sum of six cents I might purchase an excursion ticket all
over the earth.*[63]

It was indeed the drug of the traveler, but the trips had a
rather fragmentary quality. Like many other students of this
curious drug, Ludlow observed that the main effects came in
waves.

*After the full storm of a vision of intense sublimity has blown
past the hashish eater, his next vision is generally of a quiet,
relaxing and recreating nature. He comes down from his clouds
or up from his abyss into a middle ground of gentle shadows
where he may rest his eyes from the splendor of the seraphim
or the flames of the fiends. There is a wise philosophy in this
arrangement, for otherwise the soul would soon burn out in the
excess of its own oxygen.*[63]

A further characteristic of hashish which has also been amply confirmed by many other observers is the extreme unreliability of its action.

At two different times, when body and mind are apparently in precisely analogous states, when all circumstances, exterior and interior, do not differ tangibly in the smallest respect, the same dose of the same preparation of hashish will frequently produce diametrically opposite effects. Still further, I have taken at one time a pill of thirty grains, which hardly gave a perceptible phenomenon, and at another, when my dose had been half that quantity, I have suffered the agonies of a martyr or rejoiced in a perfect frenzy. So exceedingly variable are its results, that, long before I abandoned the indulgence, I took each successive bolus with the consciousness that I was daring an uncertainty as tremendous as the equipoise between hell and heaven. Yet the fascination employed Hope as its advocate, and won the suit.[63]

It seems that quite soon after his discovery of hashish Ludlow realized that the drug was fully as likely to transport him to the infernal regions as to the fields of Elysium. As he continued to take the drug his trips downward became more numerous and his upward flights increasingly rare. Here is an account of one of his descents into the Inferno:

It was perhaps eight o'clock in the evening when I took the dose of fifty grains. I did not retire until midnight. I awoke suddenly. Beside my bed in the corner of the room stood a bier, from whose corners drooped the folds of a heavy pall; outstretched upon it lay in state a most fearful corpse, whose livid face was distorted with the pangs of assassination. The traces of a great agony were frozen into fixedness in the tense position of every muscle, and the nails of the dead man's fingers pierced his palms with the desperate clench of one who has yielded not without agonizing resistance. . . . A smothered laugh of derision from some invisible watcher ever and anon mocked the corpse, as if triumphant demons were exulting over their prey. I pressed my hands upon my eyeballs till they ached in intensity of desire to shut out the spectacle. I buried my head in the pillow that I might not hear that awful laugh of diabolical sarcasm.

But—oh horror immeasurable! I beheld the walls of the room slowly gliding together, the ceiling coming down, the floor ascending, as of old the lonely captive saw them, whose cell was doomed to be his coffin. Nearer and nearer am I borne towards the corpse. I shrank back from the edge of the bed. I cowered in most abject fear. I tried to cry out but speech was paralysed. The walls came closer and closer together. The stony eyes stared up into my own, and again the maddening peal of fiendish laughter rang close beside my ear. Now I was touched on all sides by the walls of the terrible press; there came a heavy crash, and I felt all sense blotted out in darkness.[63]

Before we take our leave of Fitz Hugh Ludlow, the American hashish eater, one further aspect of his observations deserves mention. A strain of mysticism was present in Ludlow's nature and his extensive studies of the writers of antiquity had familiarized him with the theories of the ancient community of Pythagoreans. Though Pythagoras is remembered today mainly for his geometrical theorems, especially that one which relates to the three sides of a triangle, he was in fact far more than merely a mathematician as anyone familiar with the "Golden Sayings" will realize. His school in Crotona imposed on its members very rigid rules of behavior and was pervaded with a strongly mystical element in which the study of numbers played an important part. Ludlow was greatly influenced by the concepts of this ancient sage, as is indicated by the full title of his book, *The Hasheesh Eater; being passages from the life of a Pythagorean*. Under the influence of hashish Ludlow found himself able to understand in an entirely new way the concept of universal harmony on which was based the teaching of the old philosopher of Crotona, just as Aldous Huxley, under the influence of mescaline, comprehended certain otherwise incomprehensible sayings of the Zen Buddhist teachers. This passage from Ludlow is of special interest to those who, like Goethe's Faust, long to penetrate beyond the barriers imposed by our dull uncleansed perceptions, to pass beyond mere scholasticism and to enter realms of knowledge normally forbidden to mortal man. That a certain psychological danger is involved in such excursions, particularly when they are made with the assistance of drugs, is evident from Ludlow's comments. Several takers of mescaline have written in a similar vein.

Hashish is no thing to be played with as a bauble. At its revealing, too dread paths of spiritual life are flung open, too tremendous views disclosed of what the soul is capable of doing, and being, and suffering for that soul to contemplate, till, relieved of the body, it can behold them alone. . . . Within our little domain of view, girt by the horizon and arched by the dome of heaven, there is enough of sorrow, enough of danger, enough of beauty and of mirth to occupy the soul. In this world we are but half spirit; we are thus able to hold only the perceptions and emotions of half an orb. It is this present half-developed state of ours which makes the infinitude of the hashish awakening so unendurable, even when its sublimity is the sublimity of delight. The boundary which was at once our barrier and our fortress is removed, until we almost perish from the inflow of perceptions.

One most powerful realization of this fact occurred to me when hashish had already become a fascination and a habit. The world was horizonless, for earth and sky stretched endlessly onward in parallel planes. Above me the heavens were terrible with the glory of a fathomless depth. I looked up, but my eyes, unopposed, every moment penetrated farther and farther into the immensity, and I turned them downward, lest they should presently intrude into the fatal splendors of the Great Presence. Unable to bear visible objects, I shut my eyes. In one moment a colossal music filled the whole hemisphere above me, and I thrilled upwards through its environment on visionless wings. It was not a song, it was not instruments, but the inexpressible spirit of sublime sound—like nothing I had ever heard—impossible to symbolize, intense yet not loud, the ideal of harmony, yet distinguishable into a multiplicity of exquisite parts.

I opened my eyes but it still continued. I sought around me to detect some natural sound which might be exaggerated into such a semblance; but no, it was of unearthly generation, and it thrilled through the universe in an unexplicable, a beautiful, yet an awful symphony.

My mind grew solemn with the consciousness of a quickened perception. And what a solemnity is that which the hashish eater feels at such a moment. The very beating of his heart is silenced. He stands with his finger on his lip; his eye is fixed and he becomes a very statue of awful veneration. I looked abroad on fields and waters and sky, and read in them a most startling meaning. They were now grand symbols of the sublimest spiritual truths, truths never before even feebly grasped, and utterly unsuspected. Like a map, the arcana of the universe lay bare before me. I saw how every created thing not only typifies, but springs forth from some mighty spiritual law as its offspring.

While that music was pouring through the great heavens above me, I became conscious of a numerical order which ran through it, and in marking this order I beheld it transferred to every movement of the universe. Every sphere wheeled on its orbit, every emotion of the soul rose and fell, every smallest moss and fungus germinated and grew according to some peculiarity of numbers which severally governed them. An exquisite harmony of proportion reigned through space, and I seemed to realize that the music which I heard was but this numerical harmony making itself objective through the development of a grand harmony of tones.

The vividness with which this conception revealed itself to me made it terrible to bear alone. An unutterable ecstasy was carrying me away, but I dared not abandon myself to it. I was no seer who could look back on the unveiling of such glories face to face.

An irrepressible yearning came over me to impart what I beheld, to share with another soul the weight of this colossal revelation. With this purpose I scrutinized the vision; I sought in it for some characteristic which might make it translatable to

*another mind. There was none. In absolute incommunicableness
it stood apart. For it, in spoken language, there was no symbol.*[63]

After Baudelaire, Gautier and Ludlow there was a gap in
what might be called the literature of hashish. Few in the western
world took much interest in the drug and those who did, did not
write about it. Then, in 1930, Commissioner Harry J. Anslinger
discovered marijuana. Anslinger was a lineal descendant of those
old cherubim who were given the job of keeping Adam and Eve
away from the tree of life. He had no flaming sword but he had
a flaming indignation. By flooding the country with atrocity stories
concerning youthful marijuana addicts who carved up their
families with axes, he created, almost single-handedly, the
"marijuana menace" and, in the process, advertised the drug.
As the crusade against it mounted, so did the interest in it expand.
It became popular among jazz musicians in Harlem and generated
about itself its own special jargon. Mezz Mezzrow, Chicago-born
musician, catches the beat in his *Really the Blues.*[67]

*After I finished the weed I went back to the bandstand.
Everything seemed normal and I began to play as usual. I passed
a stick of gauge around for the other boys to smoke, and we
started a set.*

*The first thing I noticed was that I began to hear my saxo-
phone as though it was inside my head, but I couldn't hear much
of the band in back of me, although I knew they were there. All
the other instruments sounded like they were way off in the
distance; I got the same sensation you'd get if you stuffed your
ears with cotton and talked out loud. Then I began to feel the
vibrations of the reed much more pronounced against my lip, and
my head buzzed like a loudspeaker. I found I was slurring much
better and putting just the right feeling into my phrases—I was
really coming on. All the notes came easing out of my horn like
they'd already been made up, greased and stuffed into the bell,
so all I had to do was blow a little and send them on their way,
one right after the other, never missing, never behind time, all
without an ounce of effort. The phrases seemed to have more*

*continuity to them and I was sticking to the theme without ever
going tangent. I felt I could go on playing for years without
running out of ideas and energy. There wasn't any struggle; it
was all made-to-order and suddenly there wasn't a sour note or a
discord in the world that could bother me. I began to feel very
happy and sure of myself. With my loaded horn I could take all
the fist-swinging, evil things in the world and bring them together
in perfect harmony, spreading peace and joy and relaxation to
all the keyed-up and punchy people everywhere. I began to
preach my millenniums on my horn, leading all the sinners on
to glory.*

*The other guys in the band were giggling and making cracks,
but I couldn't talk with my mouthpiece between my lips, so I
closed my eyes and drifted out to the audience with my music.
The people were going crazy over the subtle changes in our
playing; they couldn't dig what was happening but some kind of
electricity was crackling in the air and it made them all glow and
jump. Every so often I opened my eyes and found myself looking
straight into a girl's face right in front of the bandstand, swinging
there like a pendulum. She was an attractive, rose-complexioned
chick, with wind-blown honey-colored hair, and her flushed face
was all twisted up with glee. That convulsed face of hers stirred
up big waves of laughter in my stomach, waves that kept breaking
loose and spreading up to my head, shaking my whole frame.
I had to close my eyes to keep from exploding with joy.*

*It's a funny thing about marijuana—when you first begin
smoking it you see things in a wonderful, soothing, easygoing
new light. All of a sudden the world is stripped of its dirty gray
shrouds and becomes one big bellyful of giggles, a spherical
laugh, bathed in brilliant, sparkling colors that hit you like a
heatwave. Nothing leaves you cold any more; there's a humorous
tickle and great meaning in the least little thing, the twitch of
somebody's little finger or the click of a beer glass. All your pores
open like funnels, your nerve-ends stretch their mouths wide,
hungry and thirsty for new sights and sounds and sensations; and
every sensation, when it comes, is the most exciting one you've*

*ever had. You can't get enough of anything—you want to gobble
up the whole goddamned universe just for an appetizer. Them
first kicks are a killer, Jim.*

*Suppose you're the critical and analytical type, always ripping
things to pieces, tearing the covers off and being disgusted by
what you find under the sheet. Well, under the influence of muta
you don't lose your surgical touch exactly, but you don't come
up evil and grimy about it. You still see what you saw before but
in a different more tolerant way, through rose-colored glasses,
and things that would have irritated you before just tickle you.
Everything is good for a laugh; the wrinkles get ironed out of
your face and you forget what a frown is, you just want to hold
on to your belly and roar till the tears come. Some women
especially, instead of being nasty and mean just go off bellowing
until hysteria comes on. All the larceny kind of dissolves out of
them—they relax and grin from ear to ear, and get right on the
ground floor with you. Maybe no power on earth can work out
a lasting armistice in that eternal battle of the sexes, but muggles
are the one thing I know that can even bring about an overnight
order to "Cease firing."*

*Tea puts a musician in a real masterly sphere, and that's why
so many jazzmen have used it. You look down on the other
members of the band just like an old mother hen surveying her
brood of chicks; if one of them hits a sour note or comes up with
a bad modulation, you just smile tolerantly and figure, oh well,
he'll learn, it'll be better next time, give the guy a chance. Pretty
soon you find yourself helping him out, trying to put him on
the right track. The most terrific thing is this, that all the while
you're playing, really getting off, your own accompaniment keeps
flashing through your head, just like you were a one-man band.
You hear the basic tones of the theme and keep up your pattern
of improvisation without ever getting tangled up, giving out a
uniform sequence all the way. Nothing can mess you up. You
hear everything at once and you hear it right. When you get that
feeling of power and sureness, you're in a solid groove.*

You know how jittery, got-to-be-moving people in the city

*always get up in the subway train two minutes before they arrive
at the station? Their nerves are on edge, they're watching the
clock, thinking about schedules, full of that high-powered mile-a-
minute jive. Well, when you're picked up on some gauge that
clock just stretches its arms, yawns, and dozes off. The whole
world slows down and gets drowsy. You wait until the train stops
dead and the doors slide open, then you get up and stroll out in
slow motion, like a sleepwalker with a long night ahead of him
and no appointments to keep. You've got all the time in the
world. What's the rush, buddy? Take-it-easy, that's the play, it's
bound to sweeten it all the way.*[67]

Despite rather widespread use of marijuana by jazz musicians
and by the black population of Harlem, the habit of marijuana
smoking did not really become prevalent until the 1960s. Marijuana arrests in the state of California reflect the increased use:
1,156 in 1954 to 50,327 in 1968. By October 1969 the Gallup
poll estimated that ten million Americans, half of them under
twenty-one, had smoked marijuana. Defiance of the antimarijuana
laws was becoming as commonplace as defiance of the antiliquor
laws had been during the Prohibition era. The whole country was
becoming embroiled in a costly civil war over a bad piece of
legislation (the Marijuana Tax Act) that should never have been
passed in the first place.

It was left for the Nixon administration, under the leadership
of Attorney General John N. Mitchell (recently convicted of
conspiracy, obstruction of justice and lying under oath) to bring
the marijuana war to a new peak of idiocy. This occurred in
September 1969 and took the form of "Operation Intercept."
This operation must, by any objective standards, be considered
the biggest fiasco since the attempted invasion of Cuba at the
Bay of Pigs. Any moderately intelligent individual could have
foretold the result even before the operation was launched.
The drive to close the border between the United States and
Mexico and keep out the flow of marijuana was timed to begin on
September 21 at 2:30 P.M., Pacific Daylight Time. The maneuver

was to be made suddenly and decisively, trapping, supposedly, a hoard of marijuana smugglers with their cars, trunks, suitcases, pockets, etc. full of marijuana. But the "closely guarded secret" was, of course, leaked to the press and the whole enterprise was described, two weeks before it started, in *The New York Times*.

As a result every smuggler above the moron level stayed away from the official border crossing points. The only result of Operation Intercept was a frenzy of indignation on both sides of the border. Traffic at San Ysidro, California, was backed up for two and a half miles in the dust and heat. Innocuous tourists were stripped and searched. School children had zealous inspectors peeking into their lunch boxes. Commerce and tourism ground slowly to a halt. Infuriated Mexicans complained they were being humiliated. Equally infuriated Americans claimed that governmental meddling was ruining their business. So loud were the outcries that finally even Attorney General Mitchell got the message. On October 11, just twenty days after it was started, Operation Intercept was abandoned.

In the course of this farce about two million people were inconvenienced, 1,824 stripped and searched, 2,000 agents and inspectors uselessly employed and huge sums of taxpayers' money squandered. The operation had only one effect on the illicit traffic: It forced the drug smugglers to change their methods. Instead of bringing in the cargo by truck at the official border crossing points they brought it over in small planes. They landed at abandoned air strips in the desert and transferred the cargo to trucks. This represented a great improvement over the old-fashioned method and they had to thank Operation Intercept for alerting them to its advantages.

There is no evidence that Operation Intercept actually reduced the flow of marijuana into the United States but the federal authorities claimed a modest success. Their claim led Professor Charles R. Beyle, chairman of the classics department at Boston University, to point out in a letter to *The New York Times* an aspect of this "triumph" that the authorities had evidently overlooked.

*In their elation at having made marijuana scarcer on our
college campuses, could the Federal narcotics agents ponder for
a moment the ugly repercussions of their campaign?*

*Many dealers responding to this scarcity are blending in
all kinds of other ingredients to provide strange psychic effects
neither sought nor planned. The high price of marijuana is moving
the high school crowd into some really weird trip-causing agents,
of which glue is only the mildest.*

*The intensive police pressure reinforces the sense of being
criminal and thus antisocial. Then, too, instead of your friendly
student dealers, older men, suspiciously criminal-looking, are
beginning to push the pot; obviously the student amateurs are
being closed out of the increasingly profitable marijuana business
and organized crime is being given another avenue of exploitation.*

*As someone who spends a great deal of time with the young
I must say that marijuana is here to stay. As a father I can only
hope that these hypocritical, viciously unnatural laws and the
people who enforce them are removed before an entire generation
is perverted morally and corrupted physically.*[5]

The "hypocritical and viciously unnatural laws" that Professor
Beyle assails in his letter have indeed been the source of much
harm. They are typical of the misguided zeal of certain meddlesome individuals who will hereafter be referred to as the Cross-eyed
Crusaders. This archetype is interested in saving his brother's
soul at all cost. In earlier days he was exemplified by the Inquisitor
whose attitude could be thus summarized: "For the good of your
soul, my brother, I will burn you alive."

Burning alive is now out of style and would be condemned
as a cruel and unnatural punishment but imprisonment is very
much in style. It never occurs to our Cross-eyed Crusaders that,
by condemning a young person caught in possession of a few
ounces of marijuana to associate with criminals in some gloomy
jail, they may be doing him far more harm than would be afflicted
by use of the drug. The possibility, however, does not always
escape the notice of certain humane and intelligent judges charged

with the implementation of this imbecile legislation. Here is a cry of genuine anguish uttered by Judge Charles W. Halleck of the District of Columbia Court of General Sessions. He was testifying before the House of Representatives Special Subcommittee on Alcoholism and Narcotics and explaining why he no longer gives jail sentences to youthful marijuana smokers:

If I send (a long-haired marijuana offender) to the jail even for 30 days, Senator, he is going to be the victim of the most brutal type of homosexual, unnatural, perverted assaults and attacks that you can imagine, and anybody who tells you it doesn't happen in that jail day in and day out, is simply not telling you the truth. . . .

How in God's name, Senator, can I send anybody to that jail knowing that? How can I send some poor young kid who gets caught by some zealous policeman who wants to make his record on a narcotics arrest? How can I send that kid to that jail?

I can't do it. So I put him on probation or I suspend the sentence and everybody says the judge doesn't care. The judge doesn't care about drugs, lets them all go. You just simply can't treat these kinds of people like that.[33]

These sentiments were echoed by the Le Dain Commission in Canada who, in its *Interim Report,* had this to say:

Great concern has been expressed during the initial phase of our inquiry concerning the serious effects of a criminal conviction and record upon the lives of drug users, particularly the young. These effects are cited, in the case of cannabis, as indicating that the harm caused by the law exceeds the harm which it is supposed to prevent. A criminal record may mar a young life, forever being an impediment to professional or other vocational opportunity and interfering with free movement and the full enjoyment of public rights. We believe this reasoning applies to all criminal convictions, and we do not believe that there should be a special rule in favor of drug offenders. For this reason, we recommend the enactment of general legislation to provide for the destruction of all records of a criminal conviction after a reasonable period of time.[60]

This aspect of the antidrug abuse legislation will be discussed in more detail later. Here it is necessary to consider just what our Cross-eyed Crusaders imagine they are protecting people from by threatening them with possible life imprisonment for possessing marijuana (the penalty prevailing in the enlightened state of Texas). What harm does marijuana do to the individual or to society to justify such horrendous penalties?

In order to answer this question it is necessary first to consider the hemp plant itself. The plant can be separated into two varieties; the first produces good fibre but little drug, the second produces a powerful drug but poor fibre. The main active principle of marijuana is a colorless resin called *tetrahydrocannabinol* (THC). This resin occurs mixed with no less than sixteen other similar substances called cannabinoids all having a similar chemical structure. They can be extracted from marijuana with chloroform and separated relatively easily by thin-layer chromatography using a solvent system consisting of four parts of hexane to one of ether. The cannabinoids can be made visible if the developed plate is dried and sprayed with a solution of Diazo Blue-B in methanol.

The potency of any hemp preparation depends on the amount of THC it contains. This can vary enormously. In a specially sown and closely guarded plantation, run by Dr. N. J. Dorenbos of the department of pharmacognosy of the University of Mississippi, varieties of hemp plant from all over the world are cultivated. Analysis of the drug contents of these plants has revealed several facts not at all in agreement with accepted ideas.[17]

First, the widespread belief that warmer, sunnier climates produce the most potent marijuana is erroneous. Potency depends on the variety of the plant and is determined by heredity. Dr. Dorenbos's group gathered a potent strain of hemp from Panama. In 1969 they grew it in Panama and in 1970 in New Hampshire. In the tropical climate of Panama the plant yielded a marijuana containing 3.2 percent THC and in the temperate clime of New Hampshire it yielded 4 percent THC.

Second, it is widely believed that the potent resin of the

hemp is located in the flowers of the *female* plant (the hemp is *dioecious*, bearing male and female flowers on separate plants). Not necessarily, says Dr. Dorenbos. An Indian variety of hemp had 2.2 percent THC in the male plant and 1.2 percent in the female. A potent variety from Mexico assayed 3.7 percent THC in both male and female plants. The variation in THC content revealed by these studies was astonishing. A spindly plant grown in artificial light assayed at an astonishing 6.8 percent THC. At the other end of the scale a variety collected in Minnesota contained only 0.038 percent THC.

These figures apply to marijuana, that is to say the flowering tops of the hemp plant free of stems and leaves. When the resin is gathered in the form of hashish or charas the THC content can go as high as 11 percent.

Clearly the effect of marijuana will vary enormously depending on the amount of THC it contains. The strain of marijuana supplied by the National Institute of Mental Health to investigators contains 1.5 percent THC. I have, however, received marijuana from the California Bureau of Narcotics Enforcement that contained no THC whatever. The owner of such a product might just as well, literally, have smoked grass.

All this has a direct bearing on the effect of this supposedly terrible drug. If the THC content is low enough the smoke will be no different from that of straw, paper or cornsilk. It will contain about 6 percent carbon monoxide, as do most smokes, and will be mildly toxic for this reason. As the THC content rises, so does the potency. Dr. Reese T. Jones of the Langley Porter Institute in San Francisco has made a study of the marijuana available in California. Specimens supplied by the California Bureau of Narcotics often contained as little as 0.1 percent THC and even the best sample contained only 0.9 percent THC.

A generous assumption is that marijuana generally available in the United States averages about 1 percent THC. This estimate is in keeping with subjective ratings made by experienced smokers smoking material in this potency range, who called it average quality.[50]

The average weight of a marijuana cigarette is about a gram which means that, allowing for losses in the smoking process, a total dose of about 5 mg. of THC may be absorbed by the smoker. The dose may be still further reduced if the cigarette is shared by several people as it often is in a social setting. Indeed, under such conditions the effect perceived may be entirely imaginary. Jones made cigarettes out of marijuana from which all the resin had been extracted and which, for this reason, were no more active than straw. Did the smokers know the difference between these cigarettes and the cigarettes made from potent marijuana? Not necessarily. Several of them pronounced the extracted marijuana to be potent. Says Jones: "There may be a credibility gap in the *Cannabis* culture."

There may indeed! The desire to get "high," plus the right setting, often results in a purely subjective sensation of well-being which may have nothing to do with the marijuana effect. The reverse may also happen. One of Weil's subjects who was determined not to get high declared that a cigarette of potent marijuana had no effect.[101] The dose of THC generally received from the marijuana commonly available in the United States is so low that it leaves plenty of room for the play of the imagination. As Reese Jones suggests in the title of his paper, we need to study the effect of the mind on marijuana as well as the effect of marijuana on the mind.

There are, of course, definite *objective* effects produced by the smoking of marijuana. All investigators agree about these. They can be seen and measured. The first is increase in heart rate. One of E. E. Domino's human subjects who "seemed extremely tolerant of the psychic effects" of marijuana showed an increase in heart rate of from 55 to 120 beats per minute after smoking marijuana cigarettes containing a total of 30 mg. THC.

Second, all investigators agree that reddening of the conjunctiva of the eyes takes place as a result of the action of this drug. It has nothing to do with irritation of the eyes by the smoke. It is a specific effect of the drug and occurs whether it is smoked or taken by mouth. The size of the eye pupil is not affected by marijuana.

Third, there is a definite, objectively measurable reduction in the flow of saliva. Marijuana smoking produces a dry mouth.

Finally, if the dose is large enough, there will be hypothermia (lowering of the body temperature).

As for the subjective effects of marijuana, they vary enormously with the individual, the dose, the quality of the drug, the setting in which the drug is taken, and whether the drug is smoked or ingested.

Marijuana has a biphasic action, with an initial period of stimulation (anxiety, heightened perceptions, euphoria) followed by a later period of sedation (sleepiness, dream-like states). With higher doses definite psychotomimetic effects are observed: difficulty with thinking, concentrating, or speaking, and depersonalization.[40]

People whose sole acquaintance with marijuana consists in smoking a "joint" or two with good friends on Saturday nights will say that it produces nothing but a mild "high." They will describe their state as one of dreamy well-being (always provided that the setting was right and that they were free of anxiety to start with). They will almost always declare that the drug had changed their perception of the flow of time. Such moderate users will find it hard to believe that Gautier, Ludlow and Moreau had actual hallucinations after taking the drug. They will contrast their modest high with Gautier's vision of "owls, sea storks, satyrs, unicorns, griffins, vultures, a whole menagerie of monsters" and wonder why his reaction to the drug was so different from their own. The answer, of course, is that Gautier did not smoke marijuana. He ate hashish. His intake of THC may have been as high as 150 mg. as compared with the modest 5 mg. or less that the marijuana smoker absorbs through the lungs. If the dose is high enough marijuana can be hallucinogenic. It can also produce stupor, or a semi-comatose condition. Such doses can produce panic reactions. In general, however, it soothes and calms. It does not excite to violent action.

Muscle weakness is also a subjective complaint, which in one of our studies was demonstrated objectively by the use of a finger ergometer. The same subjects also reported a decrease in feelings of aggressiveness. (Apparently, when one is both weak and sleepy, it may be a poor time to pick a fight).[40]

The effect of marijuana on the sex urge is not clear. Certainly in some parts of the world cannabis is regarded as a powerful aphrodisiac. It is said to arouse such lust in men who take the drug that they cannot be satisfied with one woman and must have two. This picturesque notion of the lust-maddened hashish eater seems to have obsessed the foes of marijuana, for they never weary of mentioning this effect of the drug. Members of Mayor La Guardia's Committee on Marijuana no doubt also had this effect in mind when they explored the "tea-pads" of Harlem in the early 1940s. If they hoped to witness scenes of lust rivaling the Roman bacchanals they were disappointed. True it was that lewd pictures, often representing perverted forms of sexual activity, frequently decorated the "tea-pad" walls. These pictures, however, seemed to attract little attention from the clientele. In fact one of the investigators who was concentrating his attention on the relation between marijuana and eroticism found himself embarrassed because he was the only one who examined the pictures on the wall. Numerous conversations with smokers of marijuana revealed only occasional instances in which there was any relation between the drug and eroticism. One investigator who succeeded in securing the position of doorman at a very intimate social gathering in a Harlem apartment noted that the dancing was of the most abandoned type. It was highly suggestive and appeared to be associated with erotic activity. Careful observation, however, did not suggest that those who were smoking "reefers" behaved in a more abandoned fashion than those who were not. Visits to brothels which also served as "tea-pads" revealed that the use of marijuana was not linked to sexuality. "These observations," the report stated, "allow us to come to the conclusion that in the main marijuana was not used for direct sexual stimulation."

Other studies, however, suggest that marijuana enhances sexual experience just as it enhances musical experience. Dr.

C. T. Tart, who published a study of marijuana effects[95] found
that for the majority of his subjects marijuana seemed to be the
ideal aphrodisiac. A frequent comment was: "When making love,
I feel I'm in much closer mental contact with my partner; it
is much more a union of souls as well as bodies." Another
comment: "Sexual orgasm has new qualities, when stoned."

So far our inquiry into the effects of marijuana has revealed
nothing that would justify the harsh laws that have been passed
to control its use. The substance is a mild intoxicant. Certainly
it does not improve motor coordination but it does not impair
it as seriously as does alcohol. A test made in the state of Washington showed that a social marijuana "high" did not result in an
increase of accelerator, brake, signal, steering and total errors
but it did result in significantly more speedometer errors. When
the same subjects were intoxicated with alcohol they accumulated
more accelerator, brake, signal and total errors but there was
no significant difference in steering errors.[15]

It should not be imagined from this that driving a car while
under the influence of marijuana is a healthy occupation. The
findings of Crancer were based on a rather ill-defined level of
marijuana intoxication (a social marijuana "high"). Such a high,
as Jones has shown, may be due more to imagination than THC.
A really marijuana-intoxicated individual has little faith in his
ability to drive.

Hollister, commenting on the Crancer study, has this to
say: "We simply asked our subjects when they were high [on
marijuana], 'Do you think you could drive a car?' Without
exception the answer from those who had really gotten high has
been 'no' or 'you must be kidding.' "[40]

It has been claimed that smoking marijuana leads the user to
experiment with "hard" narcotics (which means heroin). But
where is the evidence? The La Guardia Committee could not find
any. The Le Dain Committee in Canada could not find it either.
According to the latter it is the abuse of sedatives (alcohol and
barbiturates) that most commonly precede heroin use.

Every group that has studied marijuana agrees that even
frequent use of this drug does not result in the kind of physical

dependence that is produced by the abuse of opiates or barbiturates. Cannabis is not an addicting drug.

It has been claimed, mainly by Commissioner Anslinger back in the thirties, that use of marijuana leads to crime. Again, where is the evidence? Lurid tales were told by the commissioner. There was a youth in Florida who murdered his entire family with an axe. The boy said he had been in the habit of smoking marijuana. Therefore, so went the reasoning, marijuana causes you to execute your family. You could equally well prove, by selecting suitable data, that many people who committed crimes of violence were wearing hats and, using the same brand of reasoning, could conclude that they committed crimes *because* they were wearing hats! Actually, the effect of marijuana is just the reverse of that needed to encourage its devotees to commit crimes of violence. As Leo Hollister says: "When you are both weak and sleepy it is a poor time to pick a fight."

So many myths about marijuana! The poor weed has been so lavishly decorated with attributes it does not possess that it takes a really discriminating mind to separate the facts from the fantasies.

Here, for example, is an article in the *Lancet* which claims that cerebral atrophy occurs in young cannabis smokers.[10] Of course this sort of thing makes front page news and the foes of marijuana rejoice. But again the reasoning is faulty. The patients selected all had neurological or psychological abnormalities. They also smoked marijuana. There was no reason to suppose that the smoking caused the abnormalities. The experiment was totally lacking in controls.

Again here is an article from the *Journal of the American Medical Association,* "Effects of Marijuana on Adolescents and Young Adults" by H. Kolansky and W. T. Moore.[53] Its authors observe that, at the time their paper was published (1971), from twelve to twenty million people were estimated to be smoking marijuana. From this huge population how big was the sample they selected? Thirty-eight individuals aged thirteen to twenty-four years. These people smoked marijuana two or more times a week. They showed "adverse psychological effects" and some showed "neurologic signs and symptoms." Thirteen unmarried female patients became sexually promiscuous while using marijuana, seven of these became pregnant.

This report also made the headlines. It has been quoted repeatedly as justifying the harsh penalties decreed by law for those possessing marijuana. But once again we must ask what was cause and what was effect. Did the observed effects result from the use of marijuana or were these unbalanced individuals who came to the doctors for help and who happened also to be marijuana users? Kolansky and Moore are convinced that the observed symptoms were caused by the drug. They have described a group of toxic effects which they feel sure are produced by chronic use of marijuana.[54] They declare that many of the symptoms disappeared after use of marijuana was discontinued but they also suggest that structural changes in the brain may result from marijuana use and that these changes may be permanent.

Dr. Gabriel G. Nahas, in *Marihuana—Deceptive Weed*[71] has presented much new material in his chapter "Cannabis Intoxication and Mental Illness." He, like Kolansky and Moore, is convinced that use of marijuana impairs mental function. The change may not be very great. It may take the form of what has been called by Dr. D. E. Smith of the Haight-Ashbury Clinic the *amotivational syndrome*. Dr. Smith, working among the hippie population of San Francisco, certainly had plenty of opportunity to observe the effects of marijuana. The free clinic in the Haight-Ashbury district at the height of the "Flower Children" episode was providing care for as many as 200 persons a day among whom incidence of marijuana use was almost 100 percent. So no one can claim that Dr. Smith was generalizing from an inadequate sample though the subculture he describes was not representative of the mainstream of American life. Dr. Smith and his colleague, Carter Mehl, described the *amotivational syndrome* as follows:

Chronic heavy marijuana use in the United States is often associated with social maladjustment. It is difficult to know whether the long term use of marijuana leads to changed social values and behavior, or whether changing social values lead to chronic marijuana use. Perhaps more likely the values and behavior interact to produce concomitant change, the marijuana use helping to alter values that in turn reinforce the drug use.

Whatever the causal relations are, it is true that a chronic heavy marijuana user can develop an amotivational syndrome. He loses his desire to work, to compete, and to face any challenges. His interests and major concerns may center around marijuana to the point that his drug use becomes compulsive. He may drop out of school or leave work, ignore personal hygiene, experience a loss of sex drive, and avoid most social interaction. The picture in terms of social consequences is then similar to that of a chronic alcoholic, but without the physical deterioration.[88]

These investigators show proper caution in interpreting their findings: "Marijuana toxicity cannot be understood if one focuses only on the drug itself. One individual with a particular personality structure and set in a particular environment may react one way to marijuana, whereas another individual with different personality and environmental circumstances may react in an opposite way to the same drug dosage. Analysis of marijuana toxicity, then, requires a thorough understanding of the personality and social variables in addition to the individual drug factors."

We must now try to summarize the findings of many researchers regarding the effects of marijuana.

First, the effect of any preparation of cannabis will vary according to its THC content. This can range from practically zero to 11 percent in very potent varieties of hashish.

Second, the effect of the drug will depend on how often it is taken. Marijuana is a peculiar drug. When it is first used it may not produce an effect. This has given rise to the idea that the user must "learn to get high." Quite possibly the body has to learn to convert THC into its active metabolite, 11-hydroxy THC.

Later tolerance will develop and the user will find it necessary to employ the drug rarely if he wishes to obtain effects. If the drug is used too often its effects tend to become either imperceptible or unpleasant. As Ludlow the hashish-eater put it: "the ecstasy became daily more and more flecked with the shadows of an immeasurable pain."

Third, if potent varieties of the drug are used too often the practice may be harmful to the user. Cannabis with a fairly high level of THC cannot be classified as an innocuous substance. It may impair short-term memory, weaken the will, induce the *amotivational syndrome*. This applies only to potent preparations. The question may also be asked, how often is too often? Probably the following description of the "pot head" can be taken as a measure of overuse of marijuana.

> *The pot head is apt to smoke a joint when he awakens, and a second after breakfast, after he has "eaten his high away." A third cigarette might be used in the early afternoon and others in the evening depending upon the social agenda.*[28]

Fourth, cannabis is definitely not an addicting drug. It does not create the kind of physical dependence that results from abuse of opiates. The user remains at liberty to take it or leave it alone.

Before we leave this interesting substance we should consider the possible medical uses of cannabis. The drug has been used in the past for treatment of a variety of conditions which have been listed by Dr. Tod Mikuriya.[67] Mikuriya points out that cannabis preparations were used for medicinal purposes until the Marijuana Tax Act, 1937, effectively put an end to its use. The Legislative Committee of the American Medical Association protested as follows:

> *Cannabis at the present time is slightly used for medicinal purposes, but it would seem worthwhile to maintain its status as a medicinal agent for such purposes as it now has. There is a possibility that a re-study of the drug by modern means may show other advantages to be derived from its medicinal use.*[80]

Have further studies shown the drug to be of value? Dr. Nahas has carefully summarized the available data.[70] The therapeutic claims that have been made for cannabis preparations belong, for the most part, to the history of medicine. No one, nowadays, would use it for the treatment of tetanus or cholera. It has a real anticonvulsant effect but no physician would be likely to prescribe it for epilepsy (too uncertain in action and too many side effects). It has been used to treat withdrawal symptoms in those addicted to alcohol, barbiturates or opiates. In this area it may have some value, but tranquilizers such as chlorpromazine are probably better. It was used as early as 1845 by Moreau to treat depression and schizophrenia, but the results were disappointing. As an appetite stimulant (in treatment of *anorexia nervosa*) it has proved unreliable. As a sexual stimulant it is also unreliable. In fact, Dr. Nahas points out, "the only truly demonstrated therapeutic property of *Cannabis* is the antibacterial effect of cannabidiol." But even in this area it does not seem to offer advantages over the numerous potent antibiotics presently available.

So the chances of restoring cannabis to the list of accepted therapeutic agents seems small. The medical profession as a whole tends to be suspicious of the drug, and the provisions of the Marijuana Tax Act are not calculated to encourage its use. The purified active principles, delta-8 and delta-9-THC, are available only to qualified research workers. Such highly potent THC derivatives as *dimethylheptylpyran* (DMHP), which is more stable and five to ten times more potent than THC, are also not generally available. DMHP, incidentally, can render a dog unconscious for five to six days when given intravenously at a dose level of 10 mg./kg. Recovery is uneventful: "The broad disabling properties induced by this drug explains why it was studied extensively for possible application in chemical warfare."[70]

Well . . . chemical and bacteriological warfare no longer seem popular, so this use for DMHP may be frowned upon. All in all marijuana is not likely to become a respected member of the physician's tool kit either in the crude form or in the form of its purified derivatives. It remains what it has been for centuries, a fairly innocuous product of the magic garden, capable, in the hands of those who do not abuse it, of conferring some rather interesting insights into the workings of the psyche. Toward those that do abuse it, it is not as vengeful as the opium poppy. It does not make slaves of its users or even do much harm to their health. It probably robs them of will and of motivation. But the conclusion seems valid that those who *abuse* marijuana had little will or motivation in the first place.

The Mind and Opium

Of all the plants that grow in the magic garden the opium poppy, *Papaver somniferum,* has the strangest history. It is not easy to understand how man first discovered the curious properties that reside in the white milk that exudes from leaves or seed pods of this plant. But discover it he did and that at a remarkably early stage of history. Opium almost certainly was the active principle of the drug *nepenthe* described by Homer as the "potent destroyer of grief." He attributed its discovery to the ancient Egyptians, but whether they actually discovered this drug or merely learned about it from some other race we shall never know. Opium was widely used in the ancient world. The poppy played its part in the mysteries of Ceres, who drank of its milk to gain "oblivion from grief." Among both Greeks and Romans it was universally employed. Theophrastus, Pliny, and Dioscorides were all familiar with its effects. We can safely assume that opium addiction was a very common phenomenon in those days, and both Diagoras of Melos and Erasistrates recommended, on account of its addicting properties, complete avoidance of the use of the drug.

Opium is a product of the opium poppy, the very name of which, *Papaver somniferum,* links it inseparably with sleep and dreams. Its wrinkled paperlike petals, white or pale purple, are folded tightly within a two-membered calyx like a pearl within an oyster. The nodding heads of the flower symbolize Morpheus, heavy-eyed god of dreams. The shapely seed capsule, finely proportioned as a Grecian urn, is so designed by nature that the seeds it contains are shaken out from holes beneath the starlike top which gives them protection from injurious rain. These seeds are as innocent as unborn babes, containing a bland oil and several fragrant essences which impart a distinctive flavor to various cakes and confections. But the green unripened capsule contains a spirit more potent than any genie ever imprisoned in a bottle by the imagination of an Arabian storyteller. That capsule is the dwelling place of opium.

The opium poppy will grow in many climates but its cultivation for purposes of opium manufacture is confined to a few countries. India, Persia, Turkey, Yugoslavia, Macedonia, Bulgaria, and China are the main producers. Though eighteen hundred years have elapsed since Dioscorides, a Greek physician in the days of Nero, described the method by which opium was collected, few changes have taken place in the procedure. It is a slow and tedious operation and is economically feasible only in countries where labor costs are low. For this reason, though it would be perfectly possible to cultivate the poppy for opium in the United States, it would never be commercially feasible to do so. In the early morning, when the dew has barely dried from the poppy heads, bands of women and older children make their way into the fields. The gray-green capsules from which the petals fell but a few days previously are delicately cut with many-bladed knives. The merest scratch is all that is required; a deeper incision, penetrating the capsule wall, is fatal to the seeds, which are themselves a valuable crop. From the parallel wounds there gushes a droplet of white milk which dries on the surface of the capsule. Twenty-four hours later the opium gatherers return to the fields. The droplets of brown dried gum are scraped from the capsule with broad-bladed knives and deposited on poppy leaves. Very slowly the lump of brown opium enlarges as the little dried tears were scraped from the capsule and added to the mass. The product reaches the world markets in lumps weighing a half to two pounds. Turkish opium is most esteemed on account of its high morphine content, but Macedonian, Persian, and Indian opium also find their way into the world markets.

This brownish gum is extremely rich in alkaloids, of which no less than twenty-five have been described. Morphine, thebaine, codeine, narcotine, and papaverine are the better known of these substances. Heroin, of ill repute on account of its addicting properties, does not occur in opium. It is manufactured from morphine by a relatively simple chemical procedure and is known chemically as *diacetylmorphine.* Its manufacture in the United States is forbidden by federal law. All of the heroin that gains entry into the country and keeps the members of the Narcotics Bureau so busy is manufactured elsewhere and smuggled across the border or brought in through the ports of New York or San Francisco.

Opium in the past has had many devotees who, taking it first to relieve some physical pain, came gradually to rely upon it and ultimately became its slave. Best known of its devotees are the English writers, Coleridge and De Quincey. Baudelaire indulged in the drug and Jean Cocteau, a member of the Académie Française, has also written an account of his use of opium. De Quincey's work, *Confessions of an English Opium-Eater* (1821), has long been regarded as a classic, though it is difficult to account for the veneration that has been bestowed upon this work in literary circles, it being for the most part diffuse, disorganized and dull. Certain passages, however, do have a curious brilliance and, as they deal with the effect of opium on the mind, will be quoted in full.

De Quincey describes his first acquaintance with opium as follows:

I awoke with excruciating rheumatic pains of the head and face from which I had hardly any respite for about twenty days. On the twenty-first day I think it was, and on a Sunday, that I went out into the streets; rather to run away if possible from my torments, than with any distinct purpose of relief. By accident I met a college acquaintance who recommended opium. Opium! dread agent of unimaginable pleasure and pain! I had heard of it as I had heard of manna or of ambrosia, but no further. How unmeaning a sound was opium at that time! What solemn chords does it now strike upon my heart! . . . Arrived at my lodgings, it may be supposed that I lost not a moment in taking the quantity prescribed. I was necessarily ignorant of the whole art and mystery of opium taking; and what I took I took under every disadvantage. But I took it and in an hour O heavens! what a revulsion! What a resurrection from its lowest depths of the inner spirit! What an apocalypse of the world within me! That my pains had vanished was now a trifle in my eyes; this negative effect was swallowed up in the immensity of those positive effects which had opened before me, in the abyss of divine enjoyment thus suddenly revealed. Here was a panacea, a pharmakon nepenthes for all human woes; here was the secret of happiness, about which philosophers had disputed for so many ages, at once discovered; happiness might now be bought for a penny, and carried in the waistcoat pocket; portable ecstasies might be corked up in a pint bottle, and peace of mind could be sent down by the mail.

In passages which follow De Quincey compares the effects of alcohol and opium and loudly sings his praises of the latter drug.

Crude opium, I affirm peremptorily, is incapable of producing any state of body at all resembling that which is produced by alcohol; and not in degree only incapable but even in kind: it is not in the quantity of its effects merely, but in the quality, that it differs altogether. The pleasure given by wine is always rapidly mounting, and tending to a crisis, after which as rapidly it declines; that from opium, when once generated, is stationary for eight or ten hours; the one is a flickering flame, the other a steady and equable glow. But the main distinction lies in this—that whereas wine disorders the mental faculties, opium, on the contrary (if taken in the proper manner), introduces amongst them the most exquisite order, legislation and harmony. Wine robs a man of his self-possession; opium sustains and reinforces it. Wine unsettles the judgment, and gives a preternatural brightness and a vivid exaltation to the contempts and the admirations, to the loves and the hatreds, of the drinker; opium, on the contrary, communicates serenity and equipoise of all the faculties, active and passive, and, with respect to the temper and moral feelings in general, it gives simply that sort of vital warmth which is

*approved by the judgment and would probably always accompany
a bodily constitution of primaeval or antediluvian health.*

Just as Ludlow gained mystical experiences from hashish and
Aldous Huxley from mescaline, so De Quincey obtained new
insights from opium.

*More than once it has happened to me, on a summer night,
when I have been at an open window, in a room from which I
could overlook the sea at a mile below me, and could command
a view of the great town of L——, at about the same
distance, that I have sat from sunset to sunrise, motionless, and
without wishing to move.*

*I shall be charged with mysticism, Behmenism, quietism,
etc., but that shall not alarm me. . . . The town of L——
represented the earth, with its sorrows and its graves left behind,
yet not out of sight, nor wholly forgotten. The ocean, in ever-
lasting but gentle agitation, and brooded over by dovelike calm,
might not unfitly typify the mind and the mood which then
swayed it. For it seemed to me as if then first I stood at a distance,
and aloof from the uproar of life; as if the tumult, the fever, and
the strife, were suspended; a respite granted from the secret
burdens of the heart, a sabbath of repose; a resting from human
labors. Here were the hopes which blossom in the paths of life,
reconciled with the peace which is in the grave; motions of the
intellect as unwearied as the heavens, yet for all anxieties a
halcyon calm; a tranquility that seemed no product of inertia, but
as if resulting from mighty and equal antagonisms; infinite activities, infinite repose.*

De Quincey concludes this account of "the Pleasures of
Opium" with the following paean of praise in honor of the drug:

*O just, subtle, and all-conquering opium! that, to the hearts
of rich and poor alike, for the wounds that will never heal, and
for the pangs of grief that "tempt the spirit to rebel" bringest an
assuaging balm; eloquent opium! that with thy potent rhetoric*

*stealest away the purposes of wrath; pleadest effectually for re-
lenting pity, and through one night's heavenly sleep callest back
to the guilty man the visions of his infancy, and hands washed
pure from blood. O just and righteous opium! that to the chancery
of dreams summonest for the triumphs of despairing innocence,
false witnesses; and confoundest perjury; and dost reverse the
sentences of unrighteous judges:—thou buildest upon the bosom
of darkness, out of the fantastic imagery of the brain, cities and
temples beyond the art of Phidias and Praxiteles; and, "from the
anarchy of dreaming sleep," callest into sunny light the faces
of long buried beauties, and the blessed household countenances,
cleansed from the "dishonours of the grave." Thou only givest
these gifts to man; and thou hast the keys of Paradise, O just,
subtle and mighty opium!*

The "fantastic imagery of the brain" which, for De Quincey,
was evoked by opium was described by him in considerable
detail and, because it is relevant to our subject, his account will
be quoted at some length. It must be observed, however, that De
Quincey and Coleridge, both of whom saw visions under the
influence of opium, were the exception rather than the rule in
this respect. They were both of them unusual individuals,
endowed with imaginations of peculiar brilliance. Opium seems
in some way to have stimulated this image-making faculty. In
general, however, opium is not regarded as a fantasy-provoking
drug, as is cannabis or mescaline. It would appear to have this
effect only in certain types of whom both Coleridge and De
Quincey were examples. The strange spectacles which opium
presented to him came to De Quincey mainly at night in the form
of dreams or those curious experiences which come between
sleeping and waking and go by the name of hypnagogic hallucinations.

*A theatre suddenly opened and lighted up within my brain,
which presented nightly spectacles of more than earthly splendor.
And the four following facts may be mentioned, as noticeable
at this time:—*

*I. That, as the creative state of the eye increased, a sympathy
seemed to arise between the waking and the dreaming states of
the brain in one point—that whatsoever I happened to call up
and to trace by a voluntary act upon the darkness was very apt to
transfer itself to my dreams; so that I feared to exercise this
faculty; for, as Midas turned all things to gold, that yet baffled
his hopes and defrauded his human desires, so whatsoever things
capable of being visually represented I did but think of in the
darkness, immediately shaped themselves into phantoms of the
eye; and, by a process apparently no less inevitable, when thus
once traced in faint and visionary colors, like writings in sympathetic ink, they were drawn out by the fierce chemistry of my
dreams, into insufferable splendor that fretted my heart.*

*II. For this, and all other changes in my dreams, were
accompanied by deep seated anxiety and gloomy melancholy,
such as are wholly incommunicable by words. I seemed every
night to descend, not metaphorically, but literally to descend,
into chasms and sunless abysses, depths below depths, from
which it seemed hopeless that I could ever reascend.* Nor did
I, by waking, feel that I had reascended. This I do not dwell
upon; because the state of gloom which attended these gorgeous
spectacles, amounting at least to utter darkness, as of some
suicidal despondency, cannot be approached by words.*

*III. The sense of space, and in the end, the sense of time, were
both powerfully affected. Buildings, landscapes, etc., were ex-
hibited in proportions so vast as the bodily eye is not fitted to
receive. Space swelled, and was amplified to an extent of unutterable infinity. This, however, did not disturb me so much as the
vast expansion of time; I sometimes seemed to have lived for*

---

* This is reminiscent of the experience of another English opium eater,
Samuel Taylor Coleridge, whose *Kubla Khan* is said to have been written
under the influence of opium:

> Where Alph, the sacred river, ran
> Through caverns measureless to man,
> Down to a sunless sea.

*seventy or one hundred years in one night; nay, sometimes had
feelings representative of a millennium passed in that time, or,
however, of a duration far beyond the limits of any human
experience.*

*IV. The minutest incidents of childhood, or forgotten scenes
of later years, were often revived. I could not be said to recollect
them; for if I had been told of them when waking, I should not
have been able to acknowledge them as parts of my past experience. But placed as they were before me, in dreams like intuitions,
and clothed in all their evanescent circumstances and accompany-
ing feelings, I recognized them instantaneously. I was once told by
a near relative of mine, that having in her childhood fallen into
a river, and being on the very verge of death but for the critical
assistance which reached her, she saw in a moment her whole
life, in its minutest incidents, arrayed before her simultaneously
as in a mirror; and she had a faculty developed as suddenly for
comprehending the whole and every part. This, from some opium
experiences of mine, I can believe; I have, indeed, seen the same
thing asserted twice in modern books, and accompanied by a
remark which I am convinced is true; viz., that the dread book
of account, which the scriptures speak of, is, in fact, the mind
itself of each individual. Of this, at least, I feel assured, that
there is no such thing as forgetting possible to the mind; a
thousand accidents may, and will, interpose a veil between our
present consciousness and the secret inscriptions on the mind;
accidents of the same sort will also rend away this veil; but alike,
whether veiled or unveiled, the inscription remains forever; just
as the stars seem to withdraw before the common light of day,
whereas in fact we all know that it is the light which is drawn
over them as a veil—and that they are waiting to be revealed,
when the obscuring daylight shall have withdrawn.*

Such were the visions which De Quincey obtained from opium
and which, no doubt, were in part responsible for the fascination
this drug held for him. It is important at this point to consider
more carefully the whole question of the "pleasures of opium"

because, but for such pleasures, there would not be any addicts. Dr. Lawrence Kolb, one of the world's leading authorities on opiate addiction, thoroughly investigated this question and published his findings in a classic paper entitled "Pleasure and Deterioration from Narcotic Addiction."[55] The chief fact to emerge from this paper is that normal people do not derive any pleasure from opium or morphine. If they are in pain their pain is relieved, but in such cases the pleasure they feel is not due to the euphoriant action of the drug but merely to the removal of former discomfort. Pleasure is derived from opiates only by psychopaths:

> . . . *the intensity of pleasure produced by opiates is in direct proportion to the degree of psychopathy of the person who becomes an addict . . . the subsequent depression resulting from long continued use of the drugs carries him as far below his normal emotional plane as the first exaltation carried him above it.*

Kolb's observations have been fully substantiated by experiments of Dr. Louis Lasagna and his co-workers at the Harvard Medical School.[58] These scientists actually administered drugs to healthy, normal individuals and recorded their reactions. The human guinea pigs in this experiment had no idea whether the pill they were given contained morphine, heroin, amphetamine ("Benzedrine"), or no drug whatever. In this way the effects of imagination were eliminated and a completely objective appraisal of the drug's effect was obtained. The results were most interesting. Of eleven subjects who received 15 milligrams of morphine, eight described its effect as predominantly unpleasant. Heroin, which is commonly supposed to afford such rapture that one who takes it can scarcely resist the temptation to become addicted for life, fared not a whit better. Seven of those who took it found its effects unpleasant, two found them neutral. This, then, is all a normal individual can expect from De Quincey's "just, subtle, all-conquering opium" into whose keeping he confides the keys of paradise.

With the psychopath, however, the situation is different. He derives pleasure from morphine or heroin for much the same reason that an alcoholic receives pleasure from alcohol. It relaxes his inner tensions and enables him to live at peace with his conflicts.

"It makes my troubles roll off my mind."
"I do not have a care in the world."
"You have a contented feeling and nothing worries you."
"It makes you drowsy and feel normal."

Such were the descriptions of their reactions given by addicts studied by Dr. Kolb. ". . . Opium produces in these cases a feeling of mental peace and calm to which they are not accustomed and which they cannot normally achieve." One highly educated addict had a reaction more in line with that described by De Quincey. ". . . It caused a buoyancy of spirits, increased imagination, temporarily enlarged the brainpower, and made him think of things he otherwise would not have thought of."

Some addicts described a purely physical thrill which immediately followed an injection of heroin or morphine. It took the form of a feeling of warmth in the region of the abdomen. One psychopath with a low intelligence quotient described the sensation as a thrill through the body lasting seven or eight minutes and resembling the sexual orgasm. The brother of this individual also experienced the thrill and, though he derived intense pleasure from it, said it did not in any way resemble the sexual feeling. This curious reaction seems not to occur at all in normal people, but those psychopaths who experience it are rapidly led into addiction by its allurements. As their bodies grow accustomed to the drug they find they can no longer obtain the reaction. They increase the dose and start the pernicious practice of injecting the drug directly into their veins, a practice known as "main-lining."

Those who imagine that addiction to heroin or morphine is a short cut to the grave and that, if it does not lead to premature death, it certainly brings about moral and intellectual ruin, may find some of Dr. Kolb's conclusions rather enlightening.

That individuals may take morphine or some other opiate for 20 years or more without showing intellectual or moral deterioration is a common experience of every physician who has studied the subject. . . . We think it must be accepted that a man is mentally and morally normal who graduates in medicine, marries and raises a family of useful children, practices medicine for 30 or 40 years, never becomes involved in questionable transactions, takes a part in the affairs of the community, and is looked upon as one of its leading citizens. The same applies to a lawyer who worked himself up from a poor boy to one of the leading attorneys in his country, who became addicted to morphine following a severe abdominal disease with recurrence and two operations, and who continued to practice his profession with undiminished vigor in spite of his physical malady and the addiction.

Such cases as are cited above, and they are not uncommon, have taken as much as 15 grains of morphine daily for years without losing one day's work because of the morphine. Such addicts, however, are under the necessity of concealing a practice which is disapproved by the public and proscribed by law. To this demoralizing situation is added the shame most of them feel at finding themselves slaves to a habit from which they would like to be free. This combination of furtive concealment and shameful regret cannot help but bring about some change for the worse in any personality, but the change produced in mature individuals is usually so slight that it cannot be demonstrated or cannot be classed as "moral deterioration."[55]

It should also interest those who speak of "murder on the installment plan" in connection with opiate addiction to know that Dr. Kolb, in his testimony before Senator Daniel's committee, made the following statement. "There is . . . a certain type of shrinking neurotic individual who can't meet the demands of life, afraid to meet people, has anxieties and fears, who if they took

small amounts of narcotics—and I have examined quite a few
of them—would be better and more efficient people than they
would be without it." Describing two physicians who were
morphine addicts and who, on being withdrawn from the drug,
became hopeless problems to themselves and their families, Dr.
Kolb states, "These two physicians that I am talking about didn't
get cured, they should have it forever, because it would not mean
anything but an insane asylum for them, and they were doing a
pretty good job of work as physicians when they were on the
drug and regularly taking it." Another statement of Dr. Kolb's
should give food for thought to those who suppose that opium is
a more destructive drug than alcohol. "Some of the inebriates
had good industrial records, and the history presented by a few
of them seemed to indicate that had they not changed from
alcohol to opium, they would have been useless drunkards."

These quotations should not be interpreted as meaning that
either Dr. Kolb or any other responsible physician approves of
opiate addiction. Addiction of any kind is undesirable, whether
to alcohol, morphine, heroin, "Benzedrine," or barbiturates. But
the concept of what opiate addiction actually involves has become very gravely distorted in the public mind and the above
statements by an experienced physician, whose knowledge of
this subject is unexcelled, should help to bring the problem into
the correct perspective. The narcotics addict is not a criminal,
though the criminal may become a narcotics addict. Heroin and
morphine do not necessarily destroy life or impair intellect. They
do reduce ambition, reduce sexual desire almost to the vanishing
point, produce a feeling of lethargy and encourage idleness.
Above all they enslave, and the slavery they impose is absolute.
No tyrant, ancient or modern, exerts a more absolute control over
his subjects than do heroin and morphine over the individual
addicted to these drugs. Over the heads of all addicts these drugs
hold the threat of torture and misery if they ever dare to attempt
to break their fetters. Few, for this reason, ever make the attempt
and the threat of this torture fills the life of the addict with fear,
compelling him, whether he wishes to do so or not, to associate

with criminals and commit crime himself in his ceaseless quest for a drug which he cannot get legally and cannot do without.

People become addicted to opiates for a variety of reasons. Association with addicts in the slum areas of the great cities is the commonest cause of addiction among adolescents, a growing problem in the United States. The youth or girl who encounters such addicts is commonly offered the drug free and exposed to the scorn of his companions if he refuses to try it. One injection of course does not make an addict. The state of physical dependence is the result of frequent injections, but soon the habit of "joy popping" leads to addiction and the young person is "hooked," as the saying is. It is to stop this kind of spread of addiction that such savage punishments are now incorporated into the United States legislation, threatening one who illegally provides a minor with heroin with twenty years' imprisonment or death.

Addiction, however, may also take place in perfectly normal people as a result of some painful illness or accident for which opiates had to be used to give relief from suffering. An example of this kind of addiction is described in Dr. John A. Hawkins's book, *Opium: Addicts and Addictions*,[35] a contribution to the subject which is of special value because Dr. Hawkins himself was for a time an addict. His addiction dated from a day in February 1936 when he made the terrible discovery that some experiments he had been making had resulted in X-ray burns on both his feet. "Hard" X rays, or gamma rays, to give them their modern name, do not merely burn the surface of the skin as do those infrared or ultraviolet rays which inflict ordinary burns. Being exceedingly penetrating, they burn the deep tissues as well as the superficial ones and the pain they inflict is unbelievable.

From February until the last of June 1936 [writes Dr. Hawkins] I learned from long continuous suffering just how severe burns of this character can be. To undertake to describe, with any degree of efficiency, the severity or persistence of this pain is a task for which I feel myself unqualified. Suffice it to say

*that what Dante described I actually felt, and I am convinced
that I know in part what "hell" must be like, and I only hope that
Satan never discovers the efficiency of ray burns as a means of
torture.*[35]

Being himself a physician, he recognized at once the serious-
ness of his condition and the hopelessness of any form of
treatment. Repeatedly he pleaded for the amputation of both
his feet to end the severe pain and to avoid the necessity of
continuous doses of morphine. His pleas were ignored. The
plastic surgeon in charge of the case insisted that he could graft
new skin onto the injured feet, but because of the damage to the
deeper layers none of the grafts took, so that good skin taken
from the thighs merely followed the bad skin from the feet into
the incinerator. At last the surgeon consented to amputate so
that Dr. Hawkins, after more than four months of intense agony,
left the hospital with two stumps extending not quite six inches
below his knees. In place of the feet he had lost he was left with
a "definite appetite for and dependency upon morphine."

His descriptions of his reactions to morphine entirely confirm
those published by Lasagna and his colleagues. The drug gave
him neither mental satisfaction nor emotional thrills. The only
pleasure he derived from it was the fact that it blunted his pain.
He resented his dependence on the drug and longed to be free. As
soon as he was out of hospital he determined once and for all to
liberate himself from his bondage.

God forbid that any reader of this book should ever know
from direct experience what he suffered. "Withdrawal sickness"
in one with a well-developed physical dependence on opiates is
a shattering experience and even a physician, accustomed to the
sight of suffering, finds it an ordeal to watch the agonies of
patients in this condition. About twelve hours after the last dose
of morphine or heroin the addict begins to grow uneasy. A sense
of weakness overcomes him, he yawns, shivers, and sweats all at
the same time while a watery discharge pours from the eyes and
inside the nose which he compares to "hot water running up into

the mouth." For a few hours he falls into an abnormal tossing, restless sleep known among addicts as the "yen sleep." On awakening, eighteen to twenty-four hours after his last dose of the drug, the addict begins to enter the lower depths of his personal hell. The yawning may be so violent as to dislocate the jaw, watery mucus pours from the nose and copious tears from the eyes. The pupils are widely dilated, the hair on the skin stands up and the skin itself is cold and shows that typical goose flesh which in the parlance of the addict is called "cold turkey," a name also applied to the treatment of addiction by means of abrupt withdrawal.

Now to add further to the addict's miseries his bowels begin to act with fantastic violence; great waves of contraction pass over the walls of the stomach, causing explosive vomiting, the vomit being frequently stained with blood. So extreme are the contractions of the intestines that the surface of the abdomen appears corrugated and knotted as if a tangle of snakes were fighting beneath the skin. The abdominal pain is severe and rapidly increases. Constant purging takes place and as many as sixty large watery stools may be passed in a day.

Thirty-six hours after his last dose of the drug the addict presents a truly dreadful spectacle. In a desperate effort to gain comfort from the chills that rack his body he covers himself with every blanket he can find. His whole body is shaken by twitchings and his feet kick involuntarily, the origin of the addict's term, "kicking the habit."

Throughout this period of the withdrawal the unfortunate addict obtains neither sleep nor rest. His painful muscular cramps keep him ceaselessly tossing on his bed. Now he rises and walks about. Now he lies down on the floor. Unless he is an exception- ally stoical individual (few addicts are, for stoics do not normally indulge in opiates) he fills the air with cries of misery. The quantity of watery secretion from eyes and nose is enormous, the amount of fluid expelled from stomach and intestines unbelievable. Profuse sweating alone is enough to keep both bedding and mattress soaked. Filthy, unshaven, disheveled,

befouled with his own vomit and feces, the addict at this stage
presents an almost subhuman appearance. As he neither eats nor
drinks he rapidly becomes emaciated and may lose as much as
ten pounds in twenty-four hours. His weakness may become so
great that he literally cannot raise his head. No wonder many
physicians fear for the very lives of their patients at this stage
and give them an injection of the drug which almost at once
removes the dreadful symptoms. "It is a dramatic experience,"
writes Dr. Harris Isbell, "to observe a miserably ill person receive
an intravenous injection of morphine, and to see him thirty minutes later shaved, clean, laughing and joking." But this holiday
from hell is of short duration and unless the drug is administered
again all the symptoms start afresh within eight to twelve hours.
If no additional drug is given the symptoms begin to subside of
themselves by the sixth or seventh day, but the patient is left
desperately weak, nervous, restless, and often suffers from
stubborn colitis.

Such is the nature of "withdrawal sickness," nor should
anyone be surprised, reading this account, that the addict is
prepared to do almost anything to assure a continued supply of
his drug, not so much to give him pleasure as to save him from
such torments. How greatly, then, one must admire the fortitude
of a man like Dr. Hawkins, addicted through no fault of his own,
who, even though he had morphine within easy reach, refused to
avail himself of its comforts and endured his agonies until he had
finally liberated himself from his bondage. It must be emphasized,
however, that such suffering is not necessary. The so-called "cold
turkey" treatment—i.e., sudden and complete withdrawal of the
addicting drug without any other medication—is unnecessarily
cruel and may on occasion be fatal. One such case is described
by a witness before the Daniel Committee: a wretched woman
imprisoned for possessing heroin, left in a bare cell to "kick the
habit" without medical attention or even spiritual consolation.
"I personally saw this girl lying on the floor . . . she was throwing
up and it was actually black. . . . The doctor in charge said she
didn't like drug addicts anyway, she used to say right to our faces

that we were the lowest type of humanity." In the end, after going through all the torments of the damned, the wretched woman died. One might ask, as the legislators are so fond of talking about "murder on the installment plan," who in this case was the murderer. Shall we bring these authorities to trial who locked up this wretched woman and left her to die of her withdrawal symptoms? But no. The woman was a "dope fiend," beyond the reach of human sympathy. No one is expected to care whether such "fiends" survive or perish.

We shall not attempt, at this point, to describe the war now raging in the United States between drug addicts and drug users on the one hand and what is loosely called the Establishment on the other. So complex and obscure are the forces involved in this tragic conflict that they deserve rather detailed analysis and a chapter to themselves (see "A Cluster of Conclusions," at the end of Part I). However our account of the treatment of heroin addiction would be grossly incomplete if it ignored the methadone story, or, more specifically, the "methadone maintenance program."

The methadone story began to unfold in the laboratory of Dr. Vincent P. Dole, a specialist in metabolic diseases at Rockefeller University. Dr. Dole was not studying narcotics addiction. He was concerned with a far more common and far more deadly addiction which kills more Americans than heroin ever has or ever will. We can call it "food addiction," the urge suffered by certain people to overload their systems with rich, high calorie food. Food addiction is quite deadly. It overloads the body with fat, clogs the arteries, burdens the heart and brings life to an early end.

Food addiction has traditionally been regarded as a vice. It was included among the seven deadly sins under the name of gluttony and has usually been attributed to lack of willpower. Dr. Dole, however, found that lack of willpower was not the cause of his patients' craving for food. His studies showed that many obese people have certain biochemical peculiarities and that these peculiarities result in food addiction. He was struck by the similarity of this food addiction to the cigarette smoker's craving for cigarettes and the narcotic addict's craving for drugs. The basis for food addiction, he found, was biochemical.

The basis for narcotics addiction appeared to be equally biochemical. So did the solution of the problem. There would be no problem if a heroin addict could be persuaded to use a different drug, similar to heroin, which would satisfy the biochemical craving without damaging the addict.

At this point Dr. Marie Nyswander joined Dr. Dole. Marie Nyswander is a very determined and a very courageous woman. She was one of the few physicians willing to accept the idea that a heroin addict has an illness that calls for treatment with opiates just as a diabetic has a disease that calls for treatment with insulin. This rather obvious idea is accepted in Great Britain but, owing to an error in the interpretation of the Harrison Narcotics Act of 1914, is not accepted in the United States.

Doctors Dole and Nyswander began working together in 1964. In the course of detoxifying two patients whose reactions to morphine they had been studying they switched the patients to methadone (a synthetic narcotic developed by the Germans during World War II). Instead of gradually reducing the methadone as is generally done during detoxification they kept their patients on methadone while a number of metabolic tests were run. During this period on methadone a remarkable change took place in the two patients. Dr. Nyswander described the change:

The older addict began to paint industriously and his paintings were good. The younger started urging us to let him get his high school-equivalency diploma. We sent them both off to school outside the hospital grounds, and they continued to live at the hospital.[37]

The improvement was spectacular. Here were two established heroin addicts, both of whom had tried and failed to get off drugs by the usual route (detoxification at the federal hospital at Lexington). Now they were behaving to all intents and purposes like normal, well-adjusted human beings. True they were still drug

addicts. Methadone, like heroin, produces physical dependence
and the withdrawal symptoms from the drug are just as unpleasant. But methadone had allowed these two patients to get off the
heroin hook. They were no longer hounded by the frightful
necessity of finding as much as $100 every day to buy black
market heroin. Their natural energies were freed and could flow
through creative channels. They were taking about 100 mg. of
methadone a day and taking it by mouth, which obviated the
danger of hypodermic injection. Methadone is cheap (about
10 cents a dose). So why not give every heroin addict a chance
to switch to methadone instead of hunting and tormenting him
or sending him off to the hospital at Lexington for a cure costing
thousands of dollars and practically guaranteed to be only
temporary?

The logic of the methadone maintenance program was so
obvious that even dedicated Cross-eyed Crusaders were unable
to argue very strongly against it. Dr. Ray E. Trussel of New
York City saw in it a possible solution to a problem which was
costing the city taxpayer millions of dollars. After all, it was an
accepted medical practice to maintain schizophrenics on antischizophrenic drugs, calm maniacs with tranquilizers, uplift the
depressed with antidepressants and to keep diabetics alive with
insulin. So let us be reasonable and maintain our heroin addicts
on methadone.

They did, and the program grew. Early in 1965 the program
began with six patients. By October 31, 1970, there were forty-
two centers in New York City distributing methadone to 3,485
patients. The success rate of the program was an astonishing 97
percent. This must be compared with a *zero* success rate of the
costly Riverside Hospital program that had relied on detoxification
and re-education to cure adolescent narcotics addicts.

But nothing ever goes right in New York City. As the
methadone program expanded so did methadone abuse. In August
1972, *The New York Times* published some figures. Dr. Robert T.
Dale, operator of one of the largest private methadone programs
in New York, was declared a fugitive from justice. He could not

account for 55,000, 40 mg. methadone wafers. Dr. Elio Maggio, a psychiatrist in the Bronx, grossed $3,000 during a monitored two-day period allegedly selling methadone to people who were not even heroin addicts. The methadone program at Francis Delafield Hospital was held up by two masked men who stole 17,000 milligrams of the drug—worth more than $2,000 on the street. In the Haight-Ashbury district of San Francisco investigators discovered a new kind of addict, "the phony heroin consumer," who had been sold methadone by California junkie-pushers who maintained they were retailing the real thing.

Methadone maintenance also came under attack from leaders of such therapeutic communities as Synanon, Phoenix House, Odyssey House and Daytop Village. They had reason to complain. Here you are, they said in effect, substituting one addiction for another instead of making a serious effort to cure the addict. Charles E. Dederich, who established Synanon in California in 1958, was particularly outspoken. He had no illusions about the nature of narcotics. In his opinion "a person with this fatal disease will have to live here all his life." By this he meant live in Synanon, a special community structured to change addicts from shrinking drug-dependent weaklings to self-reliant stalwarts. Self-reliance was indeed the keynote of Synanon and the quest for self-reliance formed the basis of the Synanon game. But for "dope fiends," as Dederich preferred to call them, the self-reliance was a limited asset. The dope fiend was bound, if he wanted to stay clean, to spend the rest of his life in some therapeutic community like Synanon. Those who left the shelter of the community almost invariably relapsed.

"We have had 10,000 to 12,000 persons go through Synanon," Dederich told a reporter. "Only a small handful who left became ex-drug addicts. Roughly one in ten has stayed clean outside for as much as two years."[32]

Similar results were obtained in Liberty Park Village. This therapeutic community in New Jersey served an area containing an estimated 4,000 heroin addicts. Only 272 of the most promising of these were selected for treatment. The therapeutic community was voluntary in nature and those who wished to leave were free to do so. By the end of 1970 only sixty-seven people were left in the program and only twenty-two graduated. Of the twenty-two it was known that four were back on heroin. Nothing was known about the other eighteen. These questionable results were obtained at a cost of $1,670,800 per year in state and federal funds! On the whole it is not surprising that officials with the unenviable task of trying to cope with heroin addicts prefer to rely on methadone.

Alcohol and Tobacco

In a previous chapter we have quoted Baudelaire's *Les Paradis Artificiels,* in which he defines the motives which impel men to raid the magic garden and sample its products. The "taste of the infinite" in his opinion provides the reason for all guilty excesses "from the solitary and concentrated intoxication of the man of letters who, obliged to turn to opium for relief of some physical suffering, little by little makes it the sun of his spiritual life, to the drunkard who, his brain aflame with glory, hideously wallows in the filth of a Paris street." We have dealt already with "the solitary and concentrated intoxication of the man of letters" who finds his relief in opium (or morphine or heroin). We must now consider the drunkard with "his brain aflame with glory," whose drug of choice is alcohol.

However deeply we may probe into the mists of antiquity we shall never discover at what point man first discovered the virtues and drawbacks of alcohol. Of all the drugs that affect the mind and emotions it has the longest history. It was known, we can surmise with reasonable certainty, to Neolithic man and it is not unreasonable to assume that even Paleolithic man, far older and far more primitive, also knew of the solace afforded by wine. That man became so early acquainted with alcohol is due to the fact that any fruit juice if left open to the air infallibly undergoes a change known as fermentation. This fermentation is the work of a group of insignificant one-celled fungi, the yeasts, which are present on the skins of fruit and whose tiny spores float in millions in the air about us. The yeasts are eaters of sugar, but their eating habits are rather inefficient, for instead of burning the whole sugar molecule to carbon dioxide and water they merely bite off a part of the molecule, leaving the residue in the form of an alcohol. This particular alcohol which the yeasts produce is known to the chemists as ethyl alcohol. The alcohols, from the chemist's point of view, constitute a very large family of substances which range from liquids to solids and include such materials as glycerine. Closely related to ethyl alcohol is methyl or wood alcohol, whose effects on man's organism are most unsettling as those in the habit of drinking methylated spirits can testify.

The fermentation of sugary juices is the basic process from which all alcoholic liquors arise. Different races at different periods have used an almost infinite number of starting materials from which to prepare the brews they so greatly desired. The ancient Egyptians and the Sumerians appear to have favored an extract of sprouted grain and thus to have laid the foundations of the brewer's art. The ancient Hebrews, or their forebears, to judge by the unedifying story of Noah, learned soon after the flood that no fruit of the earth yields a juice better suited to fermentation than does the grape and prepared from it that wine "which maketh glad the heart of man." Tribes dwelling on the steppes of Central Asia brew *koumiss* from mare's milk. In Mexico, the potent *pulque* is made from the sugary juice of the agave. Date wine is enjoyed in Morocco, rice wine in Japan, dandelion, elderberry, and cowslip wine have been known to gladden the hearts of English herbalists. The apple yields cider, the pear pomace, the scented honey suitably diluted gives rise to that mead so esteemed by the roving Viking. But however diverse the starting materials may be, these brews, if they possess any potency at all, owe it to the single substance ethyl alcohol.

All this brewing and bubbling that went on through countless millennia placed at man's disposal wines or beers whose alcohol content was comparatively low. It was not until the art of wine maker and brewer was supplemented with that of the distiller that really potent alcoholic liquors began to be available. The distiller's art was unknown to the older civilizations. The Greeks had no word for it. The Romans knew nothing about it. This was just as well. Considering what pigs the old Romans made of themselves with wine, one shudders to think what would have happened had they had access to brandy. In the days of Nero, brandy, whisky, gin, and all their spirituous relatives lay safely folded in the womb of time, out of reach alike of emperor and slave. It was not until considerably later that some obscure alchemist, probably seeking the elixir of youth, placed wine in an alembic and produced a fiery distillate of which a mere thimbleful contained the intoxicating potency of a glassful of wine. Thus was mankind launched on the sea of spirit in which so many have since drowned not only their sorrows but themselves.

The whole basis of the distiller's art rests on the simple fact that alcohol boils at a lower temperature than does water. Thus, by heating wine or beer and condensing the vapors, one first obtains the alcohol, then the water. Thus alcohol is flavored by a variety of volatile substances which give to whisky and brandy their characteristic aromas.

Since it was first discovered, the art of the distiller has flourished greatly. In the United States, during the fiscal year ending June 1970, there poured forth from distilleries all over the land a total of 917,457,000 gallons of whisky, brandy, rum, gin, vodka, and spirits. Add to this the alcoholic content of 134,654,000 barrels of beer and 713,000,000 gallons of wine and one obtains a sizable ocean of ethyl alcohol. On this rather crude protoplasmic poison—and no conscientious pharmacologist would dignify alcohol with any better title—the people of the United States spend more than they do on the education of their children, the care of their sick, or the glorification of their God.

During the countless centuries of man's acquaintance with this drug several hymns have been sung in praise of its effects. Wine-purpled Bacchus, deified by the Greeks, crowned with a wreath of vine leaves and waving the thyrsus, was once an object of fervent adoration and his festivals, the Bacchanalia, provided occasions for collective indulgence in every form of physical excess. Wine has been praised by the wise as well as the foolish. "It seems to me, O friends, to be right to drink," says Socrates.

"Wine comforts the soul, soothes the sorrow of man like mandragora, and arouses joy as oil the flame." Even the abstemious St. Paul had no quarrel with wine, advising Timothy to "drink no longer water but use a little wine for thy stomach's sake."

But for every hymn in praise of alcohol there is a corresponding lamentation, detailing the horrid effects of excessive indulgence in this poison. Here, for example, is an inscription on an old Greek tomb which doubtless applied to many others besides the man whose bones reposed beneath it.

Wanderer, hear the warnings of Orthon of Syracuse,
Don't travel at night when drunk, especially in winter!
Such was my luckless destiny. Not at home
But here I lie under an alien soil.

So great was the abhorrence with which Mahomet regarded wine that he absolutely forbade his followers to drink it. Gautama Siddartha, the Buddha, imposed upon his disciples a similar rule. The course of history, on more than one occasion, has been changed by the destructive effects of alcohol. Alexander of Macedon, who was frequently drunk for three days on end, would almost certainly not have died prematurely, with his empire still unstabilized, had not the fever which he contracted in Asia been aggravated in its effects by a prolonged orgy of drunkenness.

Let us now consider the effects which this time-honored drug, ethyl alcohol, exerts on the mind and body of man. Concerning these effects there are many misconceptions, the chief of which is that alcohol is a stimulant. This is quite untrue. Alcohol is a protoplasmic poison with a purely depressant effect on the human nervous system. Its depressant effect is so strong that, taken in sufficient amount, it will render a man unconscious, functioning in this respect as a general anesthetic. It could, in fact, be used as an anesthetic and in the past frequently was, but the dose of alcohol which renders a man insensible is dangerously near to the dose that puts him to sleep once and for all. In view of all this it is indeed surprising to find that Hesse in his *Narcotics and Drug Addiction* has placed alcohol among the stimulants. Goodman and Gilman have laid down the law in this matter: "It may be stated categorically that alcohol is not a stimulant but rather a primary and continuous depressant of the nervous system."[31]

How did this widespread misconception arise? It arose, we may safely guess, because alcohol affects the nervous system selectively. After alcohol has passed from the blood into the brain it acts first on that area of the cerebral cortex which exerts a restraining action on our more native impulses, the censorious, restricting, critical entity to which Freudians have given the name of the superego. Alcohol's first effect is to put the superego more or less to sleep. While that cold-eyed critic snores our other natures manifest more freely. The tongue-tied become eloquent, the shy grow bold, the awkward become graceful. It is not surprising that one who finds himself thus released from his inward fetters feels as if he has escaped from a prison and acts accordingly. It should be noted that ether, which has much in common with alcohol, also appears to be stimulating when taken in small doses. Hence the "ether frolics" popular during the last century, in the course of which the anesthetic properties of this substance were discovered. Actually, of course, both substances are depressants.

The second reason why alcohol has been erroneously considered a stimulant is that, by dilating the blood vessels in the skin, it gives an impression of warmth to one who takes it. This glow in throat and stomach, this warmth in the skin, led to the assumption that alcohol was a warmth-giving substance, particularly suitable for reviving chilly travelers. This belief has its most picturesque expression in the little barrels of brandy carried by the St. Bernard dogs sent to rescue snowbound wanderers in the Alps. Actually, far from warming the unfortunate traveler, alcohol dissipates such warmth as he has left by sending a flow of blood to the surface blood vessels previously contracted by the wisdom of nature for the very purpose of conserving warmth in the vital organs. The noble beast in the Alps would serve the interests of the snowbound traveler best if it threw away its picturesque brandy barrel and substituted for it a prosaic thermos of hot coffee. There is little real warmth to be gained from brandy or from any other form of alcohol, concentrated or otherwise.

As a euphoriant alcohol has a limited value. It is freely available, fairly cheap, and, in moderation, does not harm the body. In fact it even has a certain food value, being burnt up in the blood to liberate a modest number of calories. It is not, in normal people, a habit-forming drug and its effects are not cumulative if the body is given sufficient time to eliminate it. Although no one with any knowledge of the subject could ever claim that alcohol is the ideal euphoriant it does possess some rather valuable properties as a sort of catalyst in social gatherings, promoting friendly and lively interchange of ideas and removing awkwardness and unnecessary restraint. To parties which might otherwise prove gray and dreary it may lend a certain sparkle and vivacity. One could not find much fault with the drug if its effects were confined to the gentle liberation of the timid from the restraints of an over-rigid superego.

For some people alcohol may have other, profounder effects. William James described these effects in *The Varieties of Religious Experience:*

The sway of alcohol over mankind is unquestionably due to its power to stimulate the mystical faculties of human nature, usually crushed to earth by the cold facts and dry criticisms of the sober hour. Sobriety diminishes, discriminates and says no; drunkenness expands, unites, and says yes. It is, in fact, the great exciter of the YES function in man. It brings its votary from the chill periphery of things to the radiant core. It makes him for the moment one with truth. . . . To the poor and the unlettered it stands in the place of symphony concerts and of literature, and it is part of the deeper mystery and tragedy that whiffs and gleams of something we immediately recognize as excellent, should be vouchsafed to many of us only in the fleeting earlier phases of what, in its totality, is so degrading a poisoning.[47]

A magnificent formulation! "Whiffs and gleams of something we immediately recognize as excellent. . . ." Only these whiffs and gleams can account for the worship of Dionysius and Bacchus, whose cults were inseparably connected with the fermentation of the grape. Dionysius, conqueror of the East, crowned in vine leaves with his following of dryads, nymphs and maenads—what a life-affirming creed, how bubbly, how *intoxicating!*

And of course, as James points out, alcohol is only one of those nervous system depressants that can bring the soul to the edge of what appears to be a revelation. Three other substances that act in a manner similar to alcohol—ether, chloroform, nitrous oxide—can induce what many people have referred to as a genuine mystical experience. Benjamin Blood of Amsterdam, New York, wrote a whole book on the subject.[7] William James himself was much impressed by the power of nitrous oxide and ether which, when breathed sufficiently diluted with air,

. . . stimulate the mystical consciousness in an extraordinary degree. Depth beyond depth of truth seems revealed to the inhaler. The truth fades out, however, or escapes, at the moment of coming to; and if any words remain over in which it seemed to clothe itself, they prove to be the veriest nonsense. Nevertheless, the sense of a profound meaning having been there persists; and I know more than one person who is persuaded that in the nitrous-oxide trance we have a genuine metaphysical revelation.[47]

So alcohol, ether, chloroform and nitrous oxide all have the power, if taken under the right conditions, to offer what appear to be revelations to those who seek them. The revelations, however, have a way of becoming senseless when the mind is restored to a state of sobriety. Thus William James, under the influence of nitrous oxide, scrawled on a piece of paper what he thought to be the solution to the riddle of the universe.

*"Hogamus, higamous
 Man is polygamous
 Higamus, hogamous
 Woman is monogamous."*

The effect which the consumption of alcohol produces depends very greatly on the *type* of individual who takes it. That great American scientist, William Sheldon, has shed much light on this problem, as on many others, by his fundamental studies on human body build (somatotype).[85] Consider the type which is high in *endomorphy,* the roly-poly, baby-faced, full-gutted *viscerotonic,* of whom Sir John Falstaff must remain the eternal prototype. Such a one can and commonly does consume large amounts of alcohol without suffering any particular inconvenience.

"Oh monstrous!" cries Prince Henry in disgust. "But one half-pennyworth of bread to this intolerable deal of sack!" But Falstaff, being *viscerotonic,* could not only stomach his sack but also metabolize it. The *viscerotonic* is normally warmly sociable and under the influence of alcohol this trait is exaggerated. He is apt to become maudlin and sentimental under the influence of the drug but he does not become aggressive.

The muscular *mesomorph,* leathery of face and hard of body, is often a heavy drinker. He loves his alcohol, tends to drink his whisky neat, and so specific is his reaction to the drug that Sheldon recommends the use of whisky to determine the variety of temperament. "In temperament study an ounce of alcohol is sometimes worth hours of the shrewdest inquiry." The muscular *mesomorph* with his *somatotonic* personality reacts to the drug with exaggerated manifestations of his chief characteristics. He becomes more openly and noisily aggressive, more expansive, filled with a sense of power. He envisages vast undertakings and adventures. His energies seem unlimited. His voice and his laugh, noisy at the best of times, rise to new achievements in volume. Inhibitions crumble, candor is complete, the sense of being important holds full sway. The *mesomorph,* primed with alcohol, feels very definitely on top of the world.

People of this body type often become "problem drinkers."
The reason for this is not difficult to see. A body type high in
mesomorphy goes hand in hand with an aggressive *somatotonic*
temperament. This aggression, in our civilized world, has to be
restrained and the need for this restraint imposes considerable
stress on the individual. Alcohol, which relaxes this inward
tension, is thus a euphoriant for such people and they tend for
this reason to consume it both more frequently and more freely
than is good for them. It is this type of individual who becomes
troublesome when drunk, is apt to pick fights and to start throwing
his weight around. His aggressive tendencies, released from their
inhibitions, run wild like wolves and are liable to lead to violence.
While the *viscerotonic* becomes slobbery and sentimental under
the influence of alcohol, the *somatotonic* becomes ferocious and
may be dangerous.

For people of the *ectomorphic* body type, slender, small-boned,
thin-skinned, "nervous" and tense, alcohol has an essentially
unpleasant effect. It functions simply as a depressant. Often it
increases rather than decreases their feeling of strain and produces
a sense of dizziness and fatigue. For this reason people of this
type rarely become heavy drinkers and are frequently teetotalers.
Owing to the popular approval given to high consumption of
alcohol in certain circles of society, the individual of this variety
of temperament (*cerebrotonic*) often pretends to a liking for the
drug which he does not actually feel. Sheldon describes the
situation with wry humor, ". . . only the hardiest or the stupidest
of the cerebrotonics are likely to confess openly a distaste for this
drug. In the politer and more intellectual circles, such a confession
now places an individual in a position similar to that of a czarist
in Soviet Russia."

We will now consider in more detail the effect of this widely
used drug on the body. When a man drinks a glass of whisky on
an empty stomach he offers a chemical insult to an important
organ which, properly treated, should last him for a lifetime. The
stomach, wiser than its owner, takes immediate steps to protect
its walls from this poison, secreting protective mucus and large

amounts of gastric juice to dilute the alcohol to a tolerable concentration. Of course, if the man is a wise drinker and prefers to live on good terms with his stomach he will take the precaution either of lining it with food before he drinks or of diluting his liquor, for, apart from any intoxicating effects which alcohol may produce after it has been absorbed, it exerts on the walls of the unprotected stomach an action which is both irritating and inflaming. Strong alcoholic beverages, such as whisky, which contain 40 percent alcohol or more produce chronic stomach disorders in approximately one out of three individuals who make a regular habit of pouring them into an unprotected stomach. Diluted alcohol (10 percent or less, as in beers or light wines) stimulates the stomach to produce a secretion rich in acid though poor in pepsin. This action may be responsible for the widespread idea that alcoholic drinks are good aperitifs. Because of the acid secretion which the stomach generates under the influence of alcohol, those whose stomach walls are already ulcerated do well to regard the drug with particular suspicion.

After the drug has been received by the stomach and that long-suffering organ has made necessary adjustments to protect its vital interests, the alcohol is absorbed more or less rapidly into the blood. The rate at which it is absorbed is influenced by several factors, chiefly the fullness of the stomach and the rate at which drinks are taken. If a man swallows his drinks fast enough and their alcohol content is high enough he may so insult his stomach that a violent spasm will occur and the injured organ, swiftly and decisively, will hurl out the poison by the shortest route so that the debauch comes to an end before it has properly begun.

Alcohol passes rapidly into the blood stream and is quickly distributed to every organ in the body. This includes the baby in the case of expectant mothers and the milk in the case of nursing mothers, who may, if they indulge to excess, offer their infants breast milk spiked with gin. Signs of intoxication begin to be seen as soon as the alcohol has entered the brain. First comes the inhibition of the function of the cerebral cortex produced by a drink of two to three ounces of whisky and corresponding to 0.05 percent of alcohol in the blood. At this stage the drinker is freed from many of his inhibitions and acquires that sense of liberty already described. When the concentration of alcohol in the blood rises to about .1 percent (from five to six ounces of whisky) the depressant influence spreads to those centers in the brain which regulate movements. The drinker walks unsteadily; he has difficulty in putting on his overcoat, fumbles with his door key, slurs his words. At a concentration of .2 percent of alcohol in the blood (from ten ounces of whisky) the entire motor area of the brain is affected and the depressant effect of the drug spreads to those centers in the midbrain which control the emotional manifestations of men. At this stage our boozer may be called "beastly drunk," though such an epithet is really an insult to the beasts. He is not only almost unable to stand upright but is also prone to ridiculous displays of emotion in which he alternates between senseless rage and equally senseless tears. With .3 percent of alcohol in his blood (from about a pint of whisky) the drinker's brain becomes affected in that area which is concerned with sensory perception. Although still vaguely conscious, he is stuporous and has little comprehension of what he sees or hears. At a level of .4 percent or .5 percent in the blood, alcohol depresses the whole perception area in the brain and the drinker becomes comatose. Finally, with .6 percent to .7 percent of alcohol in the blood, our drinker dies a swift and painless death, his breathing and the beating of his heart arrested by paralysis of the centers that control these vital functions.

Throughout this sequence the concentration of alcohol remains much too low to cause any serious damage to the major organs of the body. All the observed effects are due to the fact that ethyl alcohol interferes with nerve function and up to the last stage the effect is reversible. Some may claim that the drug exerts other effects besides those described. They may believe, for example, that it especially stimulates sexual desire. In this connection Shakespeare, whose insight into the action of drugs was often surprisingly acute, has probably offered the most revealing comment.

MACDUFF. *What three things does drink especially provoke?*
PORTER. *Marry, sir, nose-painting, sleep and urine. Lechery,*
sir, it provokes and it unprovokes; it provokes the desire, but it
takes away the performance.

The abuse of alcohol, however, has other effects not noted by
Shakespeare's Porter, for it appears to interfere with the liver's
handling of fat. After severe alcoholic intoxication this organ is
often swollen and yellow with fat. Probably this impairment of
the liver's handling of fat is responsible for the development
of cirrhosis of the liver, a serious disease which occurs with
particularly high incidence among alcoholics.

Paradoxically enough, the most serious ailments which afflict
the alcoholic are not due to alcohol at all. It is perhaps unfortunate
for those who tend to consume large amounts of it that alcohol is
a food. It is a food in the sense that it liberates calories, for an
ounce of whisky can supply as much energy as four and a half
teaspoons of sugar, one and a half pats of butter, or a large slice
of bread. This fact tends to cause the heavy drinker to drink his
meals instead of eating them. From a pint of whisky he can
obtain 1200 calories per day, fully half of his total requirements.
Man, however, is more than a simple heat engine and cannot live
on calories alone. What the alcoholic cannot get from his whisky
bottle is the protein needed to replace his worn-out tissue, the
mineral elements, and above all the vitamins, thiamin, niacin,
pyridoxine, essential for the normal working of his nervous
system.

It is the lack of vitamins in his diet far more than the direct
effect of alcohol on the tissues that causes the most dangerous
afflictions that plague the alcoholic. All of these afflictions may be
seen in the alcoholic ward of any big city hospital. Here, for
example, is Mike, picked up on the streets by the police on a
freezing December night. Mike is not merely drunk, he is obviously
a very sick man. In the hospital to which Mike is taken the doctor
notes a familiar group of symptoms. Mike's legs are swollen and
edematous. His grossly enlarged liver can be felt well below the
last rib. The fingers are tremulous, the eyes are curiously fixed,

the walk, when Mike is asked to walk along a line, has a weaving, unsteady quality that suggests more than temporary alcoholic incoordination. The doctor writes in his notes "Wernicke's syndrome?" and looks for confirmatory evidence—the smooth reddened tongue, the dry, loosely hanging skin. These symptoms are not the results of too much alcohol but of too little thiamin (vitamin B_1). Mike, living on the bottle, eating little, his food uptake impaired by the inflammation which alcohol has produced in his stomach and intestines, has been receiving so little of this substance, vital for the normal working of the nerves, that those organs may well have been damaged irreparably.

As it turns out Mike can still be saved. Dosed intravenously with the needed vitamin, quietened with chlorpromazine, his vitality renewed by a suitably nourishing diet, he is fairly quickly restored to a reasonably good state of health, released from the hospital, restored to society and to the company of the whisky bottle. Nothing can be done for Mike. He belongs to that group of alcoholics in whom the capacity for self-criticism has died. He will do nothing about his condition because he refuses to face it. Ask him about it and he dismisses it with a laugh—just a social drinker, no harm in that. Soon he will be back in hospital in a condition slightly worse than before. The combined resources of modern medicine will be exerted at considerable expense to salvage him again, for which he will show no gratitude whatever. Finally a time will come when the outraged nervous system will stand no more abuse. The inner world of Mike will crumble into ruins and his demented remains will be transferred to a mental hospital. To the words "Wernicke's syndrome" the examining physician will add a more serious piece of medical jargon, "Korsakoff's psychosis."

Mike might think more seriously about his "social drinking" if he could see the plight of Mrs. S., picked up by the police wandering in a city park, talking incoherently to the empty air. Mrs. S. in a fine mink coat, with all the marks of wealth about her person, was identified as a rich widow with an apartment on Park Avenue. She was over fifty, gray, undernourished, and insane. A study of her personal history revealed a long series of alcoholic episodes, of expensive "cures" in high-class private institutions, of resolutions to reform which were sooner or later broken. After the death of her husband, Mrs. S., alone in her luxurious apartment and conscious of an emptiness which threatened to become unbearable, finally ceased to struggle with her taste for alcohol. She drank more or less constantly. Gin was her favorite and she practically lived on it: gin for breakfast, gin for lunch, gin for supper, for elevenses, for tea, for snacks. All of which Mrs. S. might possibly have survived had the makers of gin merely taken the trouble to add to their product enough thiamin to keep the good lady's nervous system functioning. Indeed it is astonishing that makers of hard liquor have still not tumbled to the simple fact that they could save many valued customers from premature death simply by supplementing their products with vitamins at the cost of a few cents per bottle. This they might do if only for selfish reasons, for it obviously is not in their interests to drive rich alcoholics like Mrs. S. into mental hospitals in which their consumption of alcohol will be reduced to zero. Owing to this oversight on the part of the gin maker, Mrs. S. so deranged the chemistry of her nervous system that neither wealth nor skill could repair the damage. She could remember nothing; knew neither who she was nor where she was, what time of year it was, whether it was morning or afternoon. She was worth just over a million dollars and died insane for lack of a few cents' worth of thiamin. Such is "Korsakoff's psychosis."

Better known and more alarming is the condition known as *delirium tremens,* to which all chronic alcoholics are liable. Here, for example, is Caroline, an unsuccessful actress who tried to take refuge from the stresses and strains of existence in Hollywood by blunting her sensibilities with alcohol. It was the same old story, drunk in the morning, drunk at midday, drunk at night; not enough food, not enough vitamins, not enough protein, not enough calcium or phosphorus. Caroline had been sick for days. Tormented with vague anxieties, restless, fearful, she was vaguely aware of the approach of the coming storm. The slightest noise or movement was enough to frighten her. She dared not go out, dared not leave her apartment. Sitting in her chair with a dressing gown wrapped about her shoulders, she sweated with unreasoning terror. Her sleep was broken with nightmares from which she awakened scarcely able to stifle her screams. Finally, unable any longer to fight off the terrible hallucinations closing in upon her, she screamed aloud, thus calling the attention of her neighbors to her condition. She was removed in an ambulance to the alcoholic ward in one of the large hospitals where she was restrained by being strapped to the bed. Convinced that snakes were crawling over her body, she screamed constantly and tried to fight off the reptiles. Crazy with fear, her body shaken with constant tremors, disoriented, dehydrated, malnourished, and vomiting, the unfortunate girl presented a singularly unglamorous picture. Fortunately for her, the new tranquilizing drug, chlorpromazine, was available to quiet her terrors at the same time as large amounts of B vitamins were pushed into her system to repair her damaged nerve cells. After forty-eight hours the rats and snakes retreated. The normal functioning of Caroline's psyche was slowly restored. She left the hospital somewhat shattered but not permanently damaged. She was luckier than some. Even under the best conditions a 4 to 5 percent mortality goes with *delirium tremens*. Under less favorable conditions it may rise far higher.

One other form of alcoholism which should be mentioned is so-called "dipsomania," which differs from chronic alcoholism in being a cyclic condition. The dipsomaniac may not touch alcohol for weeks, then quite abruptly, on account of some mysterious change that takes place within him, he is overwhelmed by an irresistible urge to drink. And drink he does, ceaselessly and steadily, with a single-minded devotion worthy of a better cause. For a period of several days or several weeks he continues to saturate his system with alcohol until, shaken, worn out, and quite possibly penniless, he reaches a point where his mysterious need is satisfied and he can, for a while at least, do without the poison. Such is the process illustrated in the novel *The Lost Weekend,* but what is lost is more than a weekend. Happiness, self-respect, even a man's means of livelihood may all be lost without a trace in the course of a single Gargantuan debauch.

In the United States alcoholism is a major public health problem. The June 1974 report to Congress of the Department of Health, Education, and Welfare estimates the number of problem drinkers in this country as 10,000,000. A 1974 report prepared for the National Institute on Alcohol Abuse and Alcoholism shows the total economic cost of alcohol-related problems in 1971 to be over twenty-five billion dollars. This includes a figure of eight billion for health and medical costs, and six billion for auto accidents. Jobs are lost, marriages wrecked, children's lives distorted and ruined, innocent pedestrians or motorists mown down on the roads by drivers whose reactions have been slowed by alcohol. The poison is really a major menace, nor can one wonder that so many attempts have been made to outlaw its use. But, as Hirsch points out in his book, *The Problem Drinker,*[38] to place the blame on alcohol is absurd. The fault lies with those who insist on misusing this drug. It is useful in this connection to bear in mind a passage from St. John Chrysostom's "Homilies" which the above writer quotes:

I hear many cry when deplorable excesses happen, "Would there were no wine! O folly! O madness!" Is it the wine that causes this abuse? No. It is the intemperance of those who take an evil delight in it. . . . If you say, "Would there were no wine!" because of drunkards, then you must say, going on by degrees, "Would there were no night!" because of the thieves. "Would there were no light!" because of the informers, and "Would there were no women!" because of adultery.

The cause of alcoholism lies not in the whisky bottle but in the psyche of those unfortunates who swallow its contents too freely. The alcoholic is sick, mentally and emotionally. He belongs, according to Dr. Lolli, director of the Yale Plan Clinic, to that group of disturbed individuals who are labeled "impulsive neurotics." He is an insecure, emotionally immature individual who seeks in alcohol a crutch to support him in his journey through life. Often he is more sensitive than his fellowman and is thus more prone to injury life inflicts. For this reason creative artists often become alcoholics. Painters, poets, writers too numerous to mention have sought to deaden their sensibilities with this poison. As recently as 1953 the finest of contemporary lyric poets, that incomparable Welshman, Dylan Thomas, died of acute alcoholic poisoning in a Manhattan hospital, only one of many creative spirits whose genius was prematurely blighted by this crude depressant of the nervous system.

What can be done to help the alcoholic? The answer is, absolutely nothing until he has reached a fixed decision to help himself. Only when he has grown utterly disgusted with his dependence, when he has sunk to the bottom of the pit and come to loathe his self-inflicted degradation can he be helped to help himself. Without doubt he needs help. He is a lonely being, insecure and unstable. He needs love, support, understanding, and a certain amount of protection from himself, for his resolution to abstain stands like a sheep amongst the wolves of his own cravings and, if left unprotected, may be devoured by a single impulse. So, being in need of a spiritual shepherd, he will naturally seek the aid of those best able to understand his problems, people who have been through the same hell and reached the same resolve—in short, rehabilitated alcoholics. This is the logical basis for that organization, Alcoholics Anonymous, whose immense achievements reflect the soundness of its methods and the correctness of its underlying philosophy.

Besides the help offered by such an organization as Alcoholics Anonymous the alcoholic can obtain a certain amount of additional help from the chemist. In 1948 two Danish physicians, J. Held and E. Jacobsen, dosed themselves with a chemical called *tetraethylthiuram disulfide* to determine its value as a remedy for worms. With this chemical inside them they proceeded to a cocktail party at which they both became acutely ill. They were perspicacious enough to blame this illness not on their hostess's canapés but on the worm remedy they had tried, which had evidently rendered them hypersensitive to alcohol. Quick to realize the possibilities of such a substance, they started a series of studies which laid the basis for the use of this substance as a protective chemical device for chronic alcoholics.

Tetraethylthiuram disulfide was thus launched on its career and has since accumulated an impressive collection of fancy names such as "Antabuse," "Aversan," "Abstinyl," "Refusal." In the United States it is generally called "Antabuse." Taken alone, it is harmless, but when alcohol is introduced into the body it interferes with the process by which alcohol is burned and eliminated. This results in the accumulation in the blood of a very poisonous substance known as acetaldehyde. The unfortunate alcoholic develops a set of symptoms drastic enough to make him an enemy of the bottle ever afterward. His eyes bulge and grow red, his face flushes, he becomes nauseated, vomits copiously, develops pains in the chest, dizziness, weakness and confusion. All of which should convince the reader that "Antabuse" is not a drug to be played with. It should be taken only under medical supervision. Those who do drink while they have "Antabuse" in their systems are likely never to repeat the experiment.

We must now consider tobacco, one of the most peculiar of all the products of the magic garden. On the face of it tobacco would seem to have nothing to recommend its use. Those who smoke it for the first time generally feel sick and may vomit. It does not liberate the spirit as does a moderate dose of alcohol. It reveals no "theatre of the Seraphim" as does cannabis. It produces no gorgeously colored visions as does peyote. Indeed it is rather difficult to define just what this product of the garden does do except poison the air with an evil smelling smoke and enhance its devotees' chances of developing lung cancer. De las Casas, one of the first to describe the way in which tobacco was used by Indians in the days of Columbus, observed, "I do not know what benefit they derive from it." Even the new edition of the United States Dispensatory, almost omniscient in the subject of drug action, is puzzled to explain the attractiveness of tobacco. "The explanation of the solace that habitual smokers get from nicotine is not obvious."

Lewin is somewhat readier with an explanation:

Smoking does not call forth an exaltation of internal well-being as does the use of wine, but it adjusts the working condition of the mind and the disposition of many mentally active persons to a kind of serenity or "quietism" during which the activity of thought is in no way disturbed, and from a physical point of view a certain calmness of movement occurs. . . . Although the action of tobacco in most cases consists in banishing vacancy of mind and boredom, so that the layman has the impression of a slight narcosis, it is nevertheless a mild excitation. The latter dominates or substitutes other normal or natural states of excitation of the cerebral centres and directs them into other channels so that the final impression is one of self-forgetfulness without any irritation of the brain.[61]

Tobacco's ill effects, especially in the female species, are described by this same writer in lurid terms:

The juvenile female flower of the nation, the "Emancipata femans vulgaris," who should bear fruit in time to come . . . frequently fails to do so because the foolish consumption of cigarettes has impregnated the sexual organs with smoke and nicotine and keeps them in a state of irritation and inflammation. Such women, as vestals of the home, should nourish a fire of a very different sort, for their mouth is ordained for other things than to be transformed into a smoking chimney and to smell of tobacco juice.[61]

Few contemporary authorities would accept the idea that tobacco smoke exerts a specific irritating action on the female genitals. It is not the genitals that are exposed to the poisonous products of this very toxic drug but the delicate lining of the lungs. Incidence of lung cancer and level of cigarette consumption are directly related to one another. This fact has been proved beyond reasonable doubt. Why men and women should offer such an insult to the precious sacs, through which we absorb the vital *pneuma,* for the sake of such poor pleasures as tobacco offers is hard to see.

One fact, however, emerges clearly from objective studies of the tobacco habit.[9] *Tobacco is an addicting drug.* This is a very important fact which is almost always overlooked. Tobacco smokers commonly insist that they can either take their drug or leave it alone. They would deny, probably with indignation, that they are hooked on tobacco as a heroin addict is hooked on heroin. Certainly the hold that tobacco has over its slaves is far more subtle than that exerted by heroin. The tobacco addict who decides to stop smoking does not suffer from those dramatic physical upsets that go collectively under the name of withdrawal symptoms. He does not vomit, ache, sweat, snivel, kick or develop goose bumps. And yet he suffers, and that suffering, in a great many cases, is so intense that the smoker cannot give up tobacco even when he realizes that his life may depend on his overcoming the habit.

The hold that tobacco has on its addicts was dramatically demonstrated by Dr. Sigmund Freud. The inventor of psychoanalysis, with his profound insights into the forces at work in the human psyche, should surely have been able to discover in himself the willpower necessary to stop smoking. His habit of consuming twenty cigars a day was ruining his health. His heart was developing dangerous arrhythmia and his doctor, Wilhelm Fleiss, ordered him to stop smoking. He did, for a time, and described his withdrawal symptoms:

Soon after giving up smoking there were tolerable days. . . . Then there came suddenly a severe affection of the heart, worse than I ever had when smoking. . . . And with it an oppression of mood in which images of dying and farewell scenes replaced the more usual fantasies. . . . The organic disturbances have lessened in the last couple of days; the hypomanic mood continues. . . . It is annoying for a doctor who has to be concerned all day long with neurosis not to know whether he is suffering from a justifiable or a hypochondriacal depression.[49]

Soon after this he was smoking as heavily as ever. Later he tried again and abstained for fourteen months but still could not free himself of his slavery and began once more smoking as many cigars as ever. At sixty-seven he noticed that sores were forming on his palate and jaw, the first sign of the cancer which was to kill him. There were clear indications that this cancer was aggravated by tobacco smoke. His heart was misbehaving and he suffered from "tobacco angina." He stopped smoking and at once the condition was relieved. His stopping smoking was, as he put it, "an act of autonomy." How long did the act last? Just twenty-three days!

And so it went on. His mouth cancer grew steadily worse. Part of his jaw was removed. He was in almost constant pain. Sometimes he could not chew or swallow. His heart condition continued bad and was exacerbated by nicotine. Yet, at the age of eighty-one he was still, according to his friend and biographer Dr. Ernest Jones, smoking "an endless series of cigars." His struggle and sufferings over a forty-five-year period, his repeated efforts to stop smoking, the "torture . . . beyond human power to bear" which he experienced during fourteen months of abstinence, his mouth cancer, his damaged heart all combine to make him a tragic example of the power that tobacco has over its addicts.

Nor was Freud by any means unique. Charles Dederich, head of Synanon and a leader in the struggle with drug addiction, was himself a heavy smoker and members of Synanon received free cigarettes. In May 1970 Dederich decided it was time to stop. If narcotics, alcohol and other drugs were banned at Synanon it certainly did not make sense to permit the use of tobacco. There were about 200 young people under fifteen living at the seven Synanon centers and many of them were learning to smoke there. Dederich, a believer in "guided democracy with emphasis on the guidance" decided it was time to do some guiding. Smoking was abruptly and totally banned. Overnight it became the No. 1 crime of the community, punishable by shaved heads or eventual expulsion. Dederich himself, a man of considerable willpower, admitted he could never have stopped without the help of his colleagues. A member who had personally kicked both heroin and tobacco observed: "It was much easier to quit heroin than cigarettes." About a hundred people left Synanon rather than live without cigarettes. All of which proves the correctness of a statement by Dr. Vincent P. Dole whose studies on various forms of addiction have been mentioned. "Cigarette smoking is a true addiction. The confirmed smoker acts under a compulsion which is quite comparable to that of the heroin user."[9]

The component in tobacco which makes it an addicting drug is nicotine. This has been proved beyond reasonable doubt by several studies. A weak solution of nicotine in normal saline administered intravenously will remove the smoker's craving for cigarettes. Apparently the tobacco addict needs to maintain a constant level of nicotine in the brain. The majority of smokers smoke fifteen to twenty-four cigarettes a day, one or more for every waking hour. No other drug is taken with such high frequency. This constantly recurring need, apparently, is due to the fact that the nicotine level in the brain produced by one cigarette falls after about thirty minutes and must be replenished. The fully addicted tobacco addict inhales the smoke of a cigarette every thirty minutes of his waking life! This is slavery indeed. Even the heroin addict is not subjected to such bondage. But if one called such a heavy smoker a dope fiend he would probably be indignant. He probably does not even consider tobacco to be a drug.

Brews Strange and Brews Familiar

In addition to the well-known drug plants already described, the magic garden contains several others. Some, like tea and coffee, are so familiar that almost everyone has experienced their effects, whereas others, like *caapi* or *ololiuqui,* are so rare that only a few specialists have ever heard of them. All these plants exert some effect on mind or emotions, some having an influence so gentle that it is scarcely perceived, others acting so violently that their effect produces what appears to be raving madness. These various brews can be divided into two groups. Those dependent for their action mainly on caffeine, such as tea, coffee, *guarana,* will be described first; accounts of the less-known brews will follow.

It is fitting that we begin these descriptions with the story of coffee, a drug whose hold on the American people is so powerful that, in the year 1970, they swallowed a total of 180 *billion* cups of the extract of coffee beans. Coffee is not a very ancient drug; compared with cannabis and opium, it is a newcomer. Just when and how the virtues of the bean were discovered we have no way of knowing, but fantasy has supplied the information which history fails to provide.

Among the Arabs and Persians it is related that coffee was brought to earth by the Archangel Gabriel, and that this august spirit presented a brew of the beans to the Prophet Mahomet, who derived much benefit and comfort therefrom. Others declare that the Mufti, Jemal-ed-din Dhabhani, learned about the drug while traveling on the west coast of the Red Sea. He brought some home with him to Aden, whence pilgrims carried it to Mecca and the rest of Arabia. Faustus Nairo, however, declares that the Prior of a certain Mahometan monastery was told by his shepherds that goats which had eaten the beans of the coffee plant gamboled about all night. He decided to use the beans to help him and his dervishes keep awake during the long night prayers in the mosque. The beverage was called *kahweh*—that which stimulates.

No sooner did coffee become popular in the East than it brought down upon itself, as usual, the wrath of various officious characters who declared it to be the very brew of the Devil and did everything they could to suppress its use. In fact the "coffee bugaboo" in sixteenth-century Egypt caused almost as much fuss as has the "marijuana bugaboo" in the contemporary United States. Sale of coffee was prohibited; wherever stocks of coffee were found they were burned. Those who were convicted of having drunk coffee were led through the town mounted on a donkey; its use was declared contrary to the spirit of the Koran. All this fuss only had the result of interesting more people in the brew and its use spread steadily. Finally all laws against it were repealed, in fact, so far did the pendulum swing in the opposite direction that a Turkish law proclaimed that refusal of a husband to give his wife coffee was legal grounds for divorce.

By 1551 coffee had triumphed in Asia Minor, Syria and Persia and was enjoyed by almost the entire population. Knowledge of the drink penetrated slowly into Europe and it was not until 1643 that the first coffeehouse was established in Paris. The habit, once established, spread swiftly. In 1690 there were two hundred and fifty coffeehouses, in the reign of Louis XV six hundred had been established, and by 1782 there were eighteen hundred. In America the first coffeehouse appears to have been located in Boston in 1689 and was known as the "London Coffee House." The "Merchants Coffee House" in New York was started in 1743. In all the main cities of both Europe and America coffeehouses sprang up and became the natural meeting places for wits, wags, poets and philosophers, a very appropriate tribute to the drug whose fascination depends upon the fact that it stimulates the brain.

As for the culture of coffee, it has spread to such an extent that scarcely a single country in the tropics fails to produce it in one form or another. It grows in Arabia, India, Java, Malaya, Guatemala, El Salvador, Colombia and Costa Rica. As for Brazil, it is difficult to decide whether coffee has been that country's blessing or its greatest curse, so totally has its economy come to depend on a little brown bean which, delightful as its properties may be, is nonetheless an utterly needless luxury. In periods of overproduction, tons of coffee have been destroyed. Underproduction, such as the 1975 frost, causes prices to skyrocket. It is hard to build a stable economy on coffee beans.

Older than coffee and with an origin even more romantically improbable is the tea plant, *Camellia*.* This plant is reliably stated to have sprung not from seed but from the venerable eyelids of the Buddhist saint, Bhodidharma. This saint, who brought Buddhism to China and was the originator of the Zen sect, arrived in China in the year A.D. 519. Living constantly under the open sky, mortifying his flesh, and mastering his passions, the saint finally vowed to meditate for ten years without closing his eyes in sleep. After two years sleep overcame him and his eyes closed. Filled with disgust at having been unable to fulfill his vow, he cut off the offending eyelids and threw them away. Where they fell there sprang up two plants from the leaves of which the saint prepared a brew of which he drank with pleasure. Soon he experienced a feeling of renewed alertness and was able to plunge once again into his contemplation of the ultimate. The delightful beverage of which he had partaken was tea.

This fragrant product of the eyelids of Bhodidharma soon found its way into homes and temples in every part of the East. In Japan the consumption of tea became not so much a form of indulgence as a way of life, inseparably connected with the refinements of Buddhist philosophy, with the worship of balance, harmony, and inward perfection. A gentle humor blended with a noble philosophy reached its highest form in the Japanese tea ceremony. No one has ever expressed this spirit more vividly

* Originally called *Thea sinensis* by Linnaeus.

than Okakura-Kakuzo who, besides being an authority on tea, wrote English prose with the stylistic skill of Charles Lamb:

> *The heaven of modern humanity is indeed shattered in the cyclopean struggle for wealth and power. The world is groping in the shadow of egotism and vulgarity. Knowledge is brought through a bad conscience, benevolence practiced for the sake of utility. The East and West, like two dragons tossed in a sea of ferment, in vain try to regain the jewel of life. We need a Niuka again to repair the grand devastation, we await the great Avatar. Meanwhile let us have a sip of tea. The afternoon glow is brightening the bamboos, the fountains are bubbling with delight, the soughing of the pines is heard in our kettle. Let us dream of evanescence, and linger in the beautiful foolishness of things.*[73]

The proper mode of making tea was described by the tea masters of China, especially in a three-volume work of the Tang poet Luwuh. Water should be chosen from a mountain spring, heated with discrimination in a suitable kettle. There are three stages of boiling: the first stage is when little bubbles like the eyes of fish swim on the surface; the second boil is when bubbles are like crystal beads rolling in a fountain; the third boil is when the billows surge wildly in the kettle. Cake-tea is roasted before the fire until it becomes soft like a baby's arm and is shredded into powder between pieces of fine paper. A little salt is put in the first boil and the tea in the second with a dipper of cold water to revive "the youth of the water." The beverage was poured into cups and drunk. O nectar! The filmy leaflets hung like scaly clouds in a serene sky or floated like water lilies on emerald streams. Such a brew inspired the writings of the poet Lotung:

> *The first cup moistens my lips and throat, the second breaks my loneliness, the third cup searches my barren entrails but to find therein some five thousand volumes of odd ideographs. The fourth cup raises a slight perspiration—all the wrong of life passes away through my pores. At the fifth cup I am purified, the sixth cup calls me to the realms of the immortals. The seventh cup—*

*ah, but I could take no more! I only feel the breath of cool wind
that rises in my sleeves. Where is Elysium? Let me ride on this
sweet breeze and waft away thither.*[73]

Tea culture is more or less confined to Asia. There is no
particular reason why it should be. The plant is not so frost-
sensitive that it has to be grown in the tropics; in fact there was
once a tea plantation in South Carolina. It failed not because
the tea plants died but because its culture proved economically
impossible. Tea is one crop that never has been and never will be
harvested mechanically. Though, when left to itself, the tea tree
attains a height of thirty to forty feet, it is so constantly pruned
in the plantations that it rarely rises above three feet in height.
The leaves must be picked individually and with discrimination,
for excessive removal of leaves would kill the shrub. Picking is
therefore continuous and is done by women and children whose
understanding of the niceties of tea picking is almost instinctive,
they having lived among tea plants practically since birth. Tea of
fabulous value is prepared in China from the buds and tenderest
leaves, a distinguished product once reserved for the emperor,
now used to lend distinction to the more expensive blends. Leaves
from lower down the stem go into ordinary tea and the oldest
and coarsest leaves are used in cheap mixtures. Expert tea tasters
can recognize hundreds of grades of manufactured tea, from the
most delicate green teas to those coarse brews that resemble in
taste and color a decoction of shoe leather, for, like shoe leather,
tea contains much tannin which is drawn from the leaf by prolonged and careless stewing.

There is much of both art and science in the manufacture
and blending of tea. Black or "Indian" teas are prepared from
leaves that have been allowed to wilt in the sun. The leaves are
then twisted and rolled to release enzymes and the heap undergoes
a process of natural fermentation in the course of which many
substances responsible for flavor and aroma are generated. This
fermentation is abruptly halted at the correct moment by the
application of heat. The moist, twisted leaves are carefully dried

and are then ready for shipment. Green tea is heated before the fermentation has set in, the leaves being shaken in pans in much the same way as coffee is roasted. Special fragrant teas are prepared by adding to tea in the course of manufacture various scented flowers such as those of orange, jasmine, rose, or *Osmanthus fragrans*.

Tea made its appearance in the West during the sixteenth century, a rare, exotic, and fabulously expensive luxury, the costly gift of kings, princes and lords. Its use spread rapidly as its price declined. In England its consumption became almost as much a ceremony as did tea drinking among the Japanese. The habit of interrupting the day's work for afternoon tea has been a national custom ever since it was introduced by the Duchess of Bedford in the early nineteenth century. Consumption of tea in Britain is prodigious. Its popularity in the United States has never rivaled that of coffee, though its use is increasing.

Cocoa, the third beverage in this group, also has romantic origins. In the court of the Aztec monarch Montezuma, a drink was prepared, the name of which was *chocolatl*. It was prepared from the seeds of a certain tree which were ground up and mixed with pepper and other plants, a foul-tasting, bitter brew beaten up into a frothy mass. "From time to time they brought him, in cup-shaped vessels of pure gold, a certain drink made from cacao, which he took when he was going to visit his wives." Apparently, like saffron and damiana and a number of other plant substances, cocoa enjoyed in the Aztec court the reputation of being an aphrodisiac. Never was the reputation less deserved. There is nothing whatever in cocoa that could, by any stretch of the imagination, be construed as having any effect on sexual desire. It is highly probable that Montezuma's pick-me-up would have been totally forgotten by posterity, for it was so bitter that even pirates would not drink it, had it not happened that some nuns in Chiapas discovered the magical effect of serving powdered chocolate liberally mixed with sugar and vanilla. So popular did this drink become that the ladies of Chiapas could not consume enough of it but had to have it served to them in church. The priests, aware of its reputation as an aphrodisiac, had no hesitation in describing it as a "violent inflamer of the passions" and in attributing to its intemperate consumption much of the moral laxity of the age. It is amusing to think that this mild and muddy beverage managed for more than a century to carry such a flamboyant reputation. In the early eighteenth century chocolate became very popular in London and such wits as Addison and Steele spent much of their time in White's or the Cocoa Tree, which became the first and most aristocratic club in England. So greatly was chocolate appreciated that the great Linnaeus, casting about for an appropriate name for the cacao tree, gave it the generic name of *Theobroma,* "food for the gods."

The cacao tree is extraordinary in one respect. Like the familiar forsythia, it bears its flowers on the main stem and the reddish pods which contain the cacao beans hang from the tree trunk in a most unnatural manner. The tree grows best in moist tropical climates, much of it being produced on the Gold Coast of Africa. After harvesting, the cacao beans are removed from the husks, placed in boxes or pits and allowed to ferment, dried and roasted. The product is called "cocoa nibs." Apart from their active principles, which will be described later, these cocoa nibs contain as much as 50 percent fat which, when expressed, constitutes cocoa butter. In chocolate manufacture the nibs are ground between heated stones and the resulting paste, mixed with sugar, milk, or both, is shaped into suitable forms in chilled molds. This chocolate, though long ago deprived of its lurid reputation as an aphrodisiac, still represents something of a menace to the American girl, whose concern for her figure exceeds, in some cases, her concern for her virtue. Chocolate is, in fact, an extremely rich source of calories. As the United States Dispensatory points out, $3\frac{1}{3}$ ounces of chocolate represents between 500 and 600 calories, whereas a mutton chop of the same weight would represent only about 250 calories. Cocoa used for drinking differs from chocolate in having been deprived of a large proportion of its fat, and its caloric value, as a result, is much less than that of chocolate.

The remaining plants belonging to this group need be mentioned only briefly. *Kola* is a nut, native to tropical Africa, product of a tree, *Cola nitida,* which in some ways resembles an apple tree. Like tea and coffee, the kola has its quota of legends. It was, so the story goes, laid aside by the Creator when He was last on earth and absentmindedly left in the Garden of Eden. Adam seized and began to chew the morsel despite the protests of Eve, who objected to his tasting this "food of God." Adam swallowed the kola and was promptly seized by the indignant Deity, the pressure of whose fingers caused him to regurgitate. To this day every man bears on his throat a swelling (the Adam's apple) that marks the pressure of the fingers of a wrathful Deity deprived of His kola.

Kola nuts are highly valued in Africa and in places are used as currency. On the banks of the Niger a slave can be bought for a few nuts. Symbolically the nut enters into many aspects of the lives of these people. A proposal of marriage is accompanied by a gift of white kola, a refusal by red nuts. Oaths are sworn on the kola nut, friendships and hostilities are symbolized by kola, and some nuts are even buried with the dead. When a girl is married kola nuts must always be included in the dowry.

This devotion to the nut is, of course, a reflection of its pharmacological properties. The native chews his kola or prepares from it a beverage which he imbibes with the aid of a reed. Soon his fatigue disappears, his brain becomes active, his muscles, previously weary, seem charged with new strength. This effect is not confined to natives of Africa. Europeans who have used the kola nut during strenuous climbs in the Alps also report an increase in muscular energy. Physical strength is augmented without the intervention of the will. Movement is facilitated and the output of the muscles is increased. Even horses, according to Lewin, show an increased output of work when fed on kola. In Africa it is also reputed to act as a sexual stimulant.

Another drug belonging to this group is *guarana,* used by the savage tribes inhabiting the basin of the Amazon, the Madeira and the Orinoco. Manes and Manduru Kus of the lower and middle Tapajós collect in October the dark brown seeds of a tropical climber, *Paullinia cupana,* which they grind and form into a paste with water, then carefully dry by suspending cylinders of the paste in wood smoke. Dried guarana paste is brown as chocolate and hard as stone. It is transported down the swift rivers and finds its way into commerce, for the use of guarana is widespread in Bolivia and Matto Grosso. Many Bolivians drink the beverage on awakening and can scarcely face the day's work without it. For consumption the hard cylinders of paste are scraped on a grater generally prepared from the hard palate of the *piraracu,* a kind of fish. The scrapings are added to a glass of sweetened water and then swallowed. Stimulation follows, for guarana contains more caffeine than any other plant source, having sometimes as much as 5 percent compared with 2 percent in coffee or kola.

We can now consider what makes these beverages so attractive. Why is the American's appetite for coffee, the Englishman's thirst for tea, the African's craving for kola so potent a passion? The answer is that caffeine, which all these substances contain, has such comforting properties that the popularity of caffeine-containing beverages is more or less inevitable. Caffeine is not a complex chemical substance and does not, correctly speaking, belong to the group of alkaloids, so many of which have valued medicinal properties. Chemically it is a purine, a group of nitrogen-containing substances of vital importance to the economy of the body. It acts on the higher levels of the brain, the cerebral cortex, to produce a gentle, agreeable stimulation. Thoughts flow more clearly, sensations are more keenly appreciated. The deathly drowsiness and clinging pessimism which enfold many people around three o'clock in the afternoon are dispersed by the drug as the sun disperses fog. Furthermore the drug increases muscular capacity while at the same time dissipating the sense of fatigue. The weary typist, with a cup of strong coffee inside her, finds her fingers dancing over the keys with renewed nimbleness.

All these gifts are conferred by this beneficent drug without any dangerous secondary effects. Caffeine does not threaten its devotees with madness as does cocaine, with inebriation as does alcohol, with slavery as does morphine. Gentle, elevating, and singularly nontoxic, it acts so imperceptibly that many who take it barely recognize its effect. True it is that a few hypersensitive individuals find themselves sleepless if they drink coffee before bedtime, but for them the remedy would seem to be obvious enough. Others with peptic ulcers may find it harmful, for caffeine certainly augments gastric secretion in man. It is also diuretic, definitely enhancing the flow of urine. It is not suitable for administration to children. A child's metabolism is, in most cases, already lively enough and, under the influence of this drug, may become entirely too active for the good of the child or the peace of his parents. Though a puritan might represent the American's reliance on coffee as a "drug habit," no legislator as yet has come forward with the suggestion that coffee be banned. This may seem surprising in view of the passion for prohibitions which runs through so much American legislation: coffee, however, is as sacred in the United States as the coca leaf was sacred to the Incas. Woe to him who raises his hand against it!

As for tea and cacao, they contain theophylline and theobromine in addition to caffeine. Both substances are closely related to caffeine but their action on the body differs in several respects. Theophylline is less stimulating to the central nervous system than is caffeine but has a more powerful action on the heart. It causes a widening of the coronary artery, that vital blood vessel which supplies the heart itself and the blockage of which so often brings death or disablement in the form of coronary thrombosis. It is also a more powerful diuretic than caffeine but the duration of its action is relatively short. Theobromine, found predominantly in cocoa, is in every respect less active than caffeine and theophylline.

Among the milder beverages capable of lifting the burden of care, soothing the mind and stomach, and generally lightening the darker horizons of the soul, mention should be made of that sacred drink of the South Seas known in New Guinea as *keu,* in

Fiji as *kava-kava* and in Hawaii as *ava*. The excellent qualities
of this drink are all too little appreciated, nor is it easy to understand why this modest gift of the "Islands of Paradise" has been
ignored by the whites who have done so much to transform these
paradises into squalid little hells. The missionaries, with their
usual passion for depriving Nature's children of their simple
pleasures, did all they could to suppress the use of kava in the
South Seas, with the result that this harmless brew was rapidly
replaced with the more destructive alcohol, often consumed in
the form of hair tonic or, worse still, as "methylated spirits."

Actually kava is the most harmless of drinks, completely
incapable of driving its devotees to those deeds of violence and
crime so common in the islands among those natives who partake
of alcohol. Kava, declares Lewin, who was the first European
scientist to appreciate its properties, never generates in those who
drink it angry, aggressive, noisy, or disgusting manifestations.[61]
If the beverage is properly prepared it produces a gentle
stimulation, refreshing the fatigued body, brightening and
sharpening the intellectual facilities. A state of happy contentment and well-being appears, without any physical or mental
excitement. Reason and consciousness remain unaffected.
Excessive indulgence in kava brings on a pleasant somnolence
leading to sleep which may last from two to eight hours but which
is not followed by a hangover. The amount that must be taken
to produce this somnolence is very large.

The mode of preparation of kava-kava in Tonga is not
calculated to attract the dainty or the hygienic. Young men and
girls with good teeth are specially selected to prepare the kava
for the feast. Solemnly and slowly they take the cut-up roots in
their mouths and rhythmically chew to the accompaniment of
gently throbbing drums. No one is permitted to swallow the juice
which accumulates in the mouth. The chewed roots are then
placed in a wooden bowl which holds from one to two gallons.
The chief in charge of the ceremony adds the correct amount of
water, kneads and stirs the liquid with his hands, and solemnly
appeals to the gods and the departed spirits. Each native then

presents his receptacle, generally a half coconut shell, which is filled with the kava beverage and solemnly emptied to the accompaniment of special rites. The taste of the brew, according to Lewin,[61] varies a great deal according to the mode of preparation and may be bitter or insipid, hot, aromatic, soapy, or astringent.

The use of kava in the New Hebrides, on the island of Tanna, offers an interesting example of the self-defeating activity of the Cross-eyed Crusaders. It was on Tanna that the cargo cult developed, centering around the mythical character, John Frum. It repudiated much of the missionary teaching. The fierce battle which the Presbyterian church had waged against kava drinking focused undue attention on the traditional use of the beverage. According to D. C. Gajdusek, "This served to endow its new prohibition-defying use with such psychological import that the renewal of kava drinking became an important part of this anti-missionary movement which appeared on the island during World War II and has not yet subsided."[26]

Gajdusek sampled kava on the island of Tongariki. He found it widely used by the inhabitants of this small island who extracted only the fresh root by the traditional method of chewing. Gajdusek found that extracts from dried roots prepared by grating or pounding had little or no pharmacological action. Half a coconut shell of the extract from the fresh root drunk slowly in one draught produced a "kava-induced stupor, which is not true sleep." The drinker avoids light and sound disturbances. A slight feeling of numbness, tingling, coldness in the face, arms and legs is characteristic of the drug effect. Higher doses produced a "pleasant, relaxing, paresthesia-enjoying, refreshing state of somnolence without mental dulling which eventually leads to sleep." Large doses produce real weakness, a paresis which may make walking impossible.

Gajdusek makes another interesting observation about the use of kava on Tongariki. Kava drinkers rarely engage in sexual activity on the nights when they drink. Though there is no dearth of children on Tongariki the island does not appear to be suffering from the population explosion that is occurring in some parts of the Pacific. Kava drinking could serve, perhaps, as a practical means of birth control for small islands which could easily become overpopulated.

The active principle of kava is a substance called *kawain*. The plant also contains *dihydrokawain* and *methysticin*. They are not alkaloids but belong to a group of compounds called pyrones. These substances induce muscle relaxation. Given to mice which have been poisoned with strychnine they will reduce the violence of the muscle spasms produced by the poison. They will also, to some extent, control the convulsions of people suffering from *grand mal* epilepsy. The mild sedation and sleepiness produced by kava is connected with its muscle relaxing properties. An overindulgence in the drug produces yellowing of the complexion due to the deposit of certain components in the skin.

Closely related to kava in its mode of action is nutmeg, a product of the magic garden that is widely available but not generally recognized as having an effect on the mind. It does not have such an effect when used in small amounts as a flavoring. Taken in larger amounts (several teaspoonsful in a glass of juice) it produces an effect that has been compared to that of marijuana. Its use both by students and by prison inmates has been described by Andrew Weil.[99] Weil states that doses range from one teaspoon to a whole can of ground nutmeg, that onset of action is commonly delayed two to five or more hours after ingestion, that reactions vary from no mental changes at all to full-blown hallucinogenic experiences like those caused by hashish or LSD and that toxic symptoms including malaise, dry mouth, rapid heart beat and dizziness are common.

The active principle of nutmeg is probably *myristicin,* a compound also present in kava. It also contains *elemicin* which in some respects resembles mescaline but has no nitrogen in the molecule. Nutmeg has never become popular despite the fact that it is cheap and legal. Its side effects are unpleasant and can be quite prolonged and its positive effects are rarely as enjoyable as those induced by marijuana.

Turning now to Mexico, we find that, besides the peyotl

described in an earlier chapter, two other drug plants have been used since the days of the Aztecs, both of which exert a peculiar effect on the mind. These plants are teonanacatl, the sacred mushroom, and ololiuqui, known among the Mazatecs as "the flower of the Virgin." Teonanacatl belongs to the group of fungi which favor cow pats as their place of growth. During the rainy season from June to September it sprouts out of the pat, its dome-shaped cap borne on a long slender stalk. It is eagerly gathered by the Mazatec Indians and dried for future use. According to the eminent botanist, R. E. Schultes, there are professional divinators who earn a livelihood by endeavoring, while intoxicated with teonanacatl, to locate stolen property, discover secrets, give advice.[83] Usually about fifteen of the mushrooms are consumed, overdoses of fifty or sixty resulting in poisoning, and continued use of large quantities producing insanity. A general feeling of exhilaration and well-being is experienced soon after the mushrooms have been eaten. This state of exhilaration is followed by hilarity, incoherent talking, and fantastic visions in brilliant colors similar to those produced by peyotl. It appears that the Mazatec divinators pay rather a high price for their indulgence in this mildly poisonous mushroom. They are said to age rapidly and even at the age of thirty-five have the appearance of old men.

Gordon Wasson, an authority on the more exotic varieties of fungi, penetrated the heart of the Mixteco mountains and took part in the ceremony under the guidance of one of the native *curanderas*. Teonanacatl appears to be a general term which includes several hallucinogenic mushrooms. *Psilocybe mexicana* is the one most prized by the Indians. Wasson, who ate six pairs of the mushrooms, describes them as having an acrid, rancid flavor. After those present had consumed their allowance of mushrooms the candle in the room was extinguished; absolute darkness reigned and in that darkness the visions began.

They were vivid in color, always harmonious. They began with art motifs, such as might decorate carpets or textiles or wall-paper. . . . Then they evolved into palaces with courts, arcades, gardens—resplendent palaces all laid over with semi-precious stones. Then I saw a mythological beast drawing a regal chariot. Later it was as though the walls of our house had dissolved, and my spirit had flown forth, and I was suspended in mid-air viewing landscapes of mountains, with camel caravans advancing slowly across the slopes, the mountains rising tier above tier to the very heavens. . . .

The visions were not blurred or uncertain. They were sharply focused, the lines and colors being so sharp that they seemed more real to me than anything I had seen with my own eyes. I felt that I was now seeing plain, whereas ordinary vision gives us an imperfect view; I was seeing the archetypes, the Platonic ideas, that underlie the imperfect images of everyday life. The thought crossed my mind: could the divine mushrooms be the secret that lay behind the ancient Mysteries? . . . These reflections passed through my mind at the very time that I was seeing the visions, for the effect of the mushrooms is to bring about a fission of the spirit, a split in the person, a kind of schizophrenia, with the rational side continuing to reason and to observe the sensations that the other side is enjoying. (*Life* magazine, May 13, 1957.)

It was teonanacatl that launched Dr. Timothy Leary on a career so colorful and peculiar that it might be regarded as a sort of psychedelic dream (or nightmare). In a lecture entitled *The Seven Tongues of God* Leary thus describes that momentous drug experience:

Once upon a time, many years ago, on a sunny afternoon in the garden of a Cuernavaca villa, I ate seven of the so-called sacred mushrooms which had been given to me by a scientist from the University of Mexico. During the next five hours, I was whirled through an experience which could be described in many extravagant metaphors but which was, above all and without question, the deepest religious experience of my life.

Statements about personal reactions, however passionate, are always relative to the speaker's history and may have little general significance. Next come the questions "Why?" and "So what?"

There are many predisposing factors—intellectual, emotional, spiritual, social—which cause one person to be ready for a dramatic mind-opening experience and which lead another to shrink back from new levels of awareness. The discovery that the human brain possesses an infinity of potentialities and can operate at unexpected space-time dimensions left me feeling exhilarated, awed, and quite convinced that I had awakened from a long ontological sleep. This sudden flash awakening is called "turning on."[59]

It was this sudden flash of awakening that led Dr. Leary to found the League for Spiritual Discovery, to popularize the recipe "turn on—tune in—drop out" that became a watchword among the hippies of the 1960s. His messianic zeal caused him to be fired from his post at Harvard, hounded by cops and narcs, incarcerated in a California prison from which he escaped, hounded again in Algeria by various Black Panthers (who proved just as intolerant as the narcs and a lot more violent), expatriated from Switzerland, incarcerated in a second California prison from which, rumor has it, escape is virtually impossible. Quite a high price to pay for eating seven sacred mushrooms!

More discreet than Leary was Carlos Castaneda who also learned the art of mushroom eating in Mexico. As we said earlier, the mushroom, *Psilocybe mexicana,* was described by Castaneda's teacher as an ally, a very fair and reasonable ally, not prone to betray its devotees, as was the devil's weed (*Datura inoxia*). Don Juan prepared the drug by reducing the dried mushrooms to powder, mixing them with various other herbs. This mixture was smoked in a special pipe. Don Juan referred to it as *el humito,* the little smoke.

It became clear to Castaneda that the smoke was provided mainly by the other herbs and that the very fine powder of dried mushrooms was sucked into the mouth as such, where it created an odd impression of cold warmth. It is impossible to guess from Castaneda's account how much of the powdered mushroom he ingested but the dose was large enough to produce some quite drastic effects. Its most characteristic effect was to liberate the sorcerer from his body and allow him to travel in a disembodied state. Returning to the body from these trips was not always easy. Don Juan said:

"All I know now is that you traveled very far. I know that because I had a terrible time pulling you back. If I had not been around, you might have wandered off and never returned, in which case all that would be left of you now would be your dead body on the side of the stream."[13]

Castaneda was far from keen to repeat the experience with the mushrooms.

"Personally I seemed to have reached a dangerous threshold. I told him I felt I could not go on; there was something truly frightening about the mushrooms."[12]

The active principles of the Mexican mushrooms were isolated and characterized by Albert Hoffmann in 1958. They were called *psilocybin* and *psilocin,* were effective in doses of 6 to 12 mg. and belonged to the family of psychoactive indoles of which *lysergic acid diethylamide* (LSD) is the most notorious member.

The other Mexican drug, ololiuqui, is found in the seeds of a plant of the bindweed family, *Rivea corymbosa* by name. The seeds were so revered by the ancient Aztecs that they called them the divine food. Elsie Clews Parsons, in her fascinating study of the Zapotecs of Mitla,[78] describes the plant, which is called *bador* or "little children." One who drinks an infusion of its leaves or eats about thirteen of the seeds falls asleep, and in the course of this sleep the plant children, male and female, come and talk to him, informing him about future events, the whereabouts of lost property, and other occult matters. Obviously it is a handy plant to have around and the lucky family in whose backyard it happens to grow find it a modest gold mine, for they sell both leaves and seeds to those who wish to use them either for divinatory purposes or simply to escape the cares of life. Intoxication comes on rapidly and proceeds to a stage where visual hallucinations appear. The intoxication lasts about three hours and is followed by few unpleasant aftereffects. Ololiuqui is usually taken at night and, in contrast to peyote, which is eaten in company, is administered to single individuals who seek a quiet place in which to undergo the intoxication.

There was some excitement among devotees of psychedelia when they discovered that morning glory seeds, especially of the varieties Pearly Gates and Heavenly Blue, had psychedelic properties similar to those of ololiuqui. The seeds were bought in such large amounts that the suspicious bureaucrats in the Food and Drug Administration began to wonder why the morning glory suddenly had become so popular. Certainly the names of these lovely flowers seemed to promise heavenly trips but those who partook of the seeds were generally disappointed. The side effects were unpleasant and the cost of the seed was high. It was generally conceded that the morning glories did not live up to the promise of their names.

One other Mexican plant should be mentioned here. It is used by the Mazatec Indians of Oaxaca and its botanical name is *Salvia divinorum.* It is a member of the labiate family and related to various species of *Coleus,* several of which are reputed to have hallucinogenic properties. The plant has been described and illustrated by Schultes[83] but the active principle has not been isolated.[84]

Now, journeying south from Mexico, we can follow the trail of that intrepid botanist, Richard Spruce, into the dense rain forests of the Amazon. Here nature presents marvels enough to excite the mind without the aid of any hallucinating drug. Here there are forests lofty as cathedrals, huge columned trees interlaced with ropelike lianes rising sheer out of the gloom to form a roof so solid that a man can almost walk on it. Fantastic orchids grow here, suspended on the stronger vegetation with hanging roots that draw moisture from the air itself. Birds are as small as insects, insects as large as birds, plumage flashes like a polished jewel, species are innumerable, the forms of life unbelievable, for nowhere else is nature more prodigal than in these rain forests.

It would be surprising indeed if in the midst of such vegetable profusion we did not find a few drugs capable of exerting an effect on the mind. One of these is *caapi,* which is prepared from the stems of a jungle vine belonging to the family Malpighiaceae and having the botanical name *Banisteriopsis caapi.* Spruce describes its use in an Indian feast, the "Feast of Gifts" celebrated in the village of Panuré. First the sacred drink, the caapi, is carefully prepared. The woody stems of the vine are beaten to a pulp with water, strained through a sieve, and poured into a special receptacle. Now, in a cleared area in the midst of the giant trees, the villagers assemble, listening for the first sounds of the sacred trumpets which boom lugubriously from the edge of the forest. At the first sound of these trumpets every female in the place, from the withered crone to the naked toddler, flees to the shelter of the community house as if her life depended on her speed. It does. Any female who sees the "botutos" is automatically condemned to death. Now, with a shout which echoes through the forest, the cup-bearer runs toward the assembled men, bearing in each hand a gourd containing a small cupful of caapi. Crying, "Mo, mo, mo, mo, mo," he runs in a crouching fashion, bending his knees, bowing his head, thrusting the gourds into the hands of the man he has selected, who drains the contents first of one, then of the other. In two minutes or less the recipient turns deathly pale. He trembles in every limb and there is horror in his aspect. Bursting into perspiration, he becomes possessed of a sort of frenzy. Rushing to the communal house, he inflicts violent blows on the doorway and the ground, shouting, "Thus, thus would I do to my enemy." In about ten minutes he grows calm and appears exhausted.

Among the Peruvian Indians preparations from this same vine, *Banisteriopsis caapi,* are known as *aya-huasca.* Its effect is exhilarating at first and terrifying later. Sensations of heat alternate with those of cold, wild bravado alternates with fear. After the first feeling of vertigo has passed the Indians see lovely lakes, trees loaded with delicious fruit, among the branches of which fly birds of brilliant plumage. Soon the scene changes and the delight is replaced with horror. They see savage beasts preparing to seize them and are liable, if not restrained by force, to grab their weapons and attack others under the influence of these delusions. Soon the frenzy passes and they fall into a deep sleep.

Among Indians in Colombia the use of caapi during the *yurupari* whipping ceremony was described by Paul H. Allen.[1] The deep booming of drums from within the *naloca* heralded the appearance of the mystic *yurupari* horns. All females fled. The whipping ceremony is a strictly male affair. Soon the forest echoed with deep lugubrious notes, for the *yurupari* horns are four or five feet long and give off a tone as deep as a bassoon. Old men in brilliantly colored ruffs made from the red and yellow plumage of tropical birds gravely prepared the youths for their painful ordeal. The master of ceremonies entered carrying a strangely shaped jar of caapi, and the thick brown bitter liquid was served in pairs of tiny round gourds. Each youth swallowed the contents of two gourds and many, as the drug began to work, vomited copiously. The flare of fantastic visions in beautiful colors was soon replaced by terrifying hallucinations. Driven to frenzy by these delusions, the youths began whipping each other, flinging the whip far back with a dramatic gesture, bringing down the lash with a sound like a pistol shot. The first lashes were applied to the legs and ankles, then to buttocks, waist and back. Soon the bodies of the youths were covered with bloody welts and, as the frenzy induced by the caapi passed, they sank down exhausted. Then tiny naked lads of not more than six rushed in and, picking up the abandoned whips, joyfully began to imitate the antics of their elders.

Few European observers have ever experimented with caapi but those who have report effects similar to those described by the Indians.

When I have partaken of aya-huasca [*writes Villavicencio*] *my head has immediately begun to swim, then I have seemed to enter on an aerial voyage, wherein I thought I saw the most charming landscapes, great cities, lofty towers and other delightful*

*things. Then, all at once, I found myself deserted in a forest and
attacked by beasts of prey against which I tried to defend myself.
Lastly I began to come round, but with a feeling of excessive
drowsiness, headache and sometimes general malaise.*

Iberico writes of the properties of this drug as follows:

*Banisteriopsis caapi or ayahuasca serves the aborigines of
various forest regions of South America for the preparation of a
beverage having "psychokinetic" and "psychomotor" properties.*

*Small doses of the beverage result in nervous stimulation,
enhancement of intellectual activity and euphoria. With larger
doses the psychosensory excitement is greater and is followed by
a tendency to sleep accompanied by vivid imaginings.*

*At very high doses, such as the ayahuascan "priests" are in
the habit of taking, there is a tremendous augmentation of visual
power. Objects appear intensely colored often shining. Later
there occur hallucinations of magnificent ornaments accompanied
at times by terrifying visions. The enhancement of the visual
power is such that it makes vision possible in light so dim that
nothing can be perceived with the normal sight. Profound sleep
follows, with complete abolition of sensation during which the
sleeper is visited by images of surprising richness so that one can
hardly wonder the* ayahuasca *is regarded as the magical plant of
divination. The images seen are microscopic and megaloscopic,
fluctuating between lilliputian forms, like those seen by cocaino-
maniacs, and gigantic shapes.*

In small doses, equivalent to 5 mg. of banisterine or harmine,
ayahuasca *has a powerful action on the genital organs, producing
an erection in the male and engorgement of the clitoris with
vaginal spasm in the female. This accounts for the "psycho
erotic" and aphrodisiac properties of the drug described by Wiffen
and others.*

*Experiments with dogs show that banisterine is an excitant
of the central nervous system, the lethal dose being 200 mg./kg.
At toxic doses it produces motor incoordination, paralysis and
convulsions. Death results from respiratory paralysis.*[45]

Lewin, that versatile toxicologist, was among the first to investigate the active principles of *Banisteriopsis caapi*.[61] He found that the alkaloid which had been isolated from this plant and variously named "telepathine," "yageine," or "banisterine" was identical with harmine, an alkaloid from the seeds of wild rue. Hence the reference to harmine in the above quotation from Iberico. Those conversant with chemical structures will notice in the molecule of harmine the familiar indole nucleus, present also in reserpine and LSD-25. It seems improbable that the action of caapi is due solely to harmine and the drug quite probably contains other active principles. One curious feature of the drug, from the pharmacological standpoint, is its rapidity of action. Accounts of its use in Indian ceremonies suggest that it takes effect almost at once. One wonders what substance could be absorbed from the drug so rapidly that it has an effect on the central nervous system within five minutes. In short caapi presents many involved problems and would seem to deserve more attention than it has received.

Some South American tribes add to their caapi the extract of another liane, *Haemadictyon amazonica,* a member of the botanical family Apocynaceae. The plant is also used by itself, the leaves and branches being extracted to give a rosy liquid with a green fluorescence which becomes blue on standing. This brew the Indians of the Amazon call *yagé*. They drink at their solemn ceremonies out of a special vessel which they call *maté*. The drink makes them lively at first. They begin to jump and dance and sing and run about. Later they become sleepy and, in this dreamy state, experience many fantasies. The drink is considered to confer on those who take it the power of divination and telepathy. Domville Fife goes so far as to state that *yagé* suspends the activity of the higher centers which is essential to normal consciousness. This leaves the unconscious mind in possession and open to telepathic reception.

Rouhier, one of the few Europeans who has experimented with this rare, almost unobtainable drug, declares that 5 to 10 c.c. of the extract when swallowed produce a tendency to sleep.

A period of excitement precedes this drowsiness. Beautiful and vivid hallucinations, which resemble those provoked by large doses of peyote, are produced by the drug.

Studies by Claudio Naranjo leave little doubt that all these hallucinogenic brews of the Amazonian Indians, whether they are called aya-huasca, caapi, or yagé, exert their action through the harmala alkaloids.[72] These alkaloids were first prepared from seeds of *Peganum harmala,* the wild rue, which has been used throughout the Middle East for centuries both as a spice and as an intoxicant. All these alkaloids contain the familiar indole group which is present in so many compounds having hallucinogenic properties. The most active of these alkaloids is harmaline which produces hallucinogenic effects at doses of 1 mg. per kilogram body weight when given intravenously and 4 mg./kg. when given by mouth. Naranjo states that harmaline is a purer hallucinogen than mescaline. The imagery it induces is remarkably vivid and may be mistaken for reality by the subject. Most of Naranjo's subjects experienced a state of extreme relaxation under the influence of the drug. They lay down for four to eight hours during which time they did not feel inclined to move a muscle, even to talk. Dizziness, nausea and vomiting were among the more unpleasant side effects of the drug.

Another hallucinogenic drug used by the Indians of the Amazon is known as *epena, paricá* or *yopo.* These snuffs may be prepared from the inner surface of the bark of *Virola calophylla* or from seeds of the leguminous plant *Piptadenia perigrina* (more correctly *Anadenanthera colubrina*). The snuff prepared from the latter plant corresponds to *cohoba,* known to the inhabitants of ancient Hispaniola.

They throw themselves into a peculiar state of intoxication, one might almost say madness, by the use of the powder of niopo [*wrote the famous explorer Humboldt of the Otomac Indians*]. *They gather the long pods of a Mimosaceae, which we have made known under the name* Acacia niopo, *cut them to pieces, moisten them, and cause them to ferment. When the softened seeds begin to turn black they are ground into a paste, and after having mixed with them some flour of cassava and some lime made from the shell of an Ampullaria, they expose the whole mass to a very brisk fire, on a gridiron of hard wood. The hardened paste is given the form of little cakes. When wanted for use it is reduced to a fine powder, and placed on a dish five or six inches wide. The Otomac holds this dish, which has a handle, in his right hand, while he inhales the* niopo *by the nose, through a forked tube of a bird's bone. This bone, without which the Otomac believes he could not take this kind of snuff, is seven inches long; it appeared to me to be the leg-bone of a sort of plover.*

The Mura Indians of the Rio Negro have annual assemblies which last eight days and are accompanied by every sort of debauchery. These antics are much enlivened by cohoba, which in that part of the world is called *paricá*. The Muras, however, have little use for the snuff, which by all accounts is most irritating to the mucous membranes of the nose and causes the taker to break into a "whirlwind of sneezes," to use the words of Padre Gumilla. So the Muras, utilizing a less sensitive port of entry, extract their drug with water and administer the brew to themselves in the form of an enema. The Catauixis use the drug in a similar fashion, employing a primitive clyster made from the long shank bone of the *tuyuyu*. These Indians, after douching themselves, give the same treatment to their dogs before setting out on a hunting expedition. They believe that it clears the vision and renders the senses more alert. The effect, as described by Spruce, is drastic and immediate. "His eyes started from his head, his mouth contracted, his limbs trembled. It was fearful to see him. He was obliged to sit down or he would have fallen. He was drunk, but only for about five minutes; he was then gayer."

Quite recently this peculiar drug, cohoba, has been the subject of a scientific investigation. Dr. V. L. Stromberg of the National Heart Institute has examined the drug and shown that it contains *bufotenin*. This substance, bufotenin, was first obtained from the skin of the toad. It is closely related to serotonin, whose role in the metabolism of the brain has recently been much debated. Bufotenin is 2 methyl serotonin and, like serotonin, has potent effects on blood pressure.

The effect of bufotenin on the mind of man has recently been described by Drs. Howard Fabing and J. R. Hawkins in a paper in *Science*.[24] The highest dose used was 16 milligrams, injected into the veins of a healthy young man whose reaction was almost immediate and quite spectacular. He reported a burning sensation in the roof of his mouth. His face turned a livid purple; his pupils became widely dilated and he retched and vomited. Reddish spots appeared before his eyes and red-purple ones on the floor, which were replaced by a yellow haze as though he were looking through a yellow lens filter. Sixteen minutes after the injection he stated, "When I start on a thought another one comes along and clashes with it, and I can't express myself clearly. . . . I feel dopey but not sleepy. I feel physically tense and mentally clouded. I am here and not here." Time and space perception were grossly impaired, the yellow haze persisted, and his face remained purple. Most of the effects disappeared after forty minutes.

Analytical studies of these snuffs by Bo Holmstead and Jan-Erik Lindgren have shown that they do indeed contain bufotenin. But these authors attribute the action of the snuff not to bufotenin but to *N-N-dimethyl tryptamine* (DMT) or the related 5 *methoxy-DMT*. Bufotenin is 5 *hydroxy-DMT*. They think bufotenin itself is not hallucinogenic.[42]

Mention of bufotenin, which is so called because it is generated in the skin of the toad, brings us within smelling distance of the traditional witch's cauldron. The toad was a traditional ingredient of the witch's brew. Such brews contained, in addition to toads, such exotic items as moss from the skull of a parricide and the horn of a goat which had mounted a human female. The difficulty of obtaining such items must have cost worried sorcerers hours of anxious search. What gave the witch's brew its activity, however, was not the toads or even such quaint components as those mentioned above but extracts of henbane, mandrake or deadly nightshade. These plants were common enough throughout the countries of Europe and their hallucinogenic properties have been known for centuries. Dioscorides, a physician who flourished in the days of Nero, wrote of datura, one of the plants in this group, that "the root being drunk with wine has the power to arouse not unpleasant fantasies. But two drams being drunk make a man beside himself for three days and four being drunk kill him."

These plants were undoubtedly used in the ancient world in connection with orgiastic rites characterized by sexual excesses. Thus at the Bacchanalia, when the wild-eyed Bacchantes with their flowing locks flung themselves naked into the arms of the eager men, one can be reasonably certain that the wine which produced such sexual frenzy was not a plain fermented grape juice. Intoxication of this kind was almost certainly a result of doctoring the wine with leaves or berries of belladonna or henbane. The orgiastic rites were never totally suppressed by the Church and persisted in secret forms through the Middle Ages. Being under the shadow of the Church's displeasure, they were inevitably associated with the Devil, and those who took part in them were considered to be either witches or wizards.

We do not need to return to the Middle Ages to find an account of the use of datura in sorcery. It has been described at length by Castaneda in *The Teachings of Don Juan*. *Datura inoxia* or "the devil's weed" was evidently widely used by the Indian sorcerers and was especially favored by Don Juan's teacher. The plant was always referred to by Don Juan as a female and as having the less admirable traits of the female nature: "The devil's weed is like a woman, and like a woman she flatters men. She sets traps for them at every turn."[12]

The whole procedure of preparing the root both for drinking and for applying to the body as a paste has been described in detail by Castaneda. An elaborate ritual was involved which included fasting for the two days necessary to prepare the extract and the paste. Every step had to be taken with deliberation, for one does not fool around with the devil's weed. Castaneda finally drank the extract and applied the paste to his body in five portions, to left foot, left leg, right foot, right leg and genitals.

Sure enough he flew!

The momentum carried me forward one more step, which was even more elastic and longer than the preceding one. And from there I soared. I remember coming down once; then I pushed up with both feet, sprang backward, and glided on my back. I saw dark sky above me, and the clouds going by me. I jerked my body so I could look down. I saw the dark mass of the mountains. My speed was extraordinary. My arms were fixed, folded against my sides. My head was the directional unit. If I kept it bent backward I made vertical circles. I changed directions by turning my head to the side. I enjoyed such freedom and swiftness as I had never known before. The marvelous darkness gave me a feeling of sadness, of longing, perhaps. It was as if I had found a place where I belonged—the darkness of the night. I tried to look around, but all I sensed was that the night was serene, and yet it held so much power.[12]

From which it is clear that the solanaceous "power plants," which include henbane and deadly nightshade as well as various species of datura, are as capable of producing delusions of flight in contemporary anthropologists as they were in the witches of earlier centuries. But these plants, though easy to find, are not for everyone. In a paper entitled "Mystical Force of the Nightshade" Cecil E. Johnson tells of his own trip with *Datura meteloides*.[48] Johnson's trip was structured, more or less, around the initiatory ceremony of the Luiseño Indians of Southern California described by William E. Safford.

The drinking takes place at night. All uninitiated boys are gathered and brought together. Small boys are sometimes carried in asleep. Any man who may have escaped initiation in his youth, or alien resident is given the drug with the youngsters. A fire is lighted in the wamkish and the people begin to gather there. The various tarmyush or toloache mortars are dug up from their hiding places, repainted and set in the wamkish. Only the mortars actually to be used, together with a tukmal or flat basket, are brought to the small or preparatory enclosure which stands near the wamkish. It is in this smaller place, unlit and without audience of the uninitiated, that the toloache is drunk and there the boys are taken. One of the pahas, ceremonial chief or manager, pounds the dried roots in the reserved mortar to a sacred song or recitative, after which the potion is prepared with hot water. The usual way seems to have been to sift the powder from the basket back into the mortar and add the water, which was allowed to stand for a while. The drinking itself, however, was from the mortar in which the plant was crushed, the boys kneeling before it. The manager held the forehead of each in turn, to pull it back when he had drunk enough. The drug was powerful, and the Luiseño tell of cases of fatal result.

Each boy after drinking is taken in charge by a man who appears to direct and steady. The procession then leads back to the wamkish and seems to be performed by crawling on the hands and knees. They then march or stand the boys around the fire, apparently dancing the tanish. The youths soon begin to sway and reel and have to be supported by the armpits. Before long they fall and become unconscious and are carried to a smaller enclosure, where they lie in complete stupefaction, watched only by a few men.

The duration of complete narcosis is not quite certain. Nor did anyone drink toloache twice.

The so-called intoxication is in any event the cardinal feature of the entire initiation, and therefore the heart of the cult. There is no doubt that its sacredness and supernatural basis lie to the native mind in the physiological effect of the drug. It produces visions or dreams as well as stupor, and what the boys see in their visions becomes of lifelong intimate sanctity to them.[82]

Johnson, who decided to follow the example of these Indians, does not mention how much of the devil's weed he used to prepare his extract. He states: "I ground up some of the roots and leaves in a borrowed Luiseño ceremonial toloache mortar. Then I poured warm water over the plant material, kneeled before it and drank several swallows of the vile tasting brew."[48]

Such casual treatment of the devil's weed brought its appropriate reward. Johnson found himself in the General Hospital detention ward in Riverside, California. "The atropine present in my potion had severely depressed the respiratory and heart centers located in the medulla by altering various neuronal enzyme systems. It was touch or go as to whether I would live or die. . . ."[48]

The hospital attendants, not accustomed to dealing with would-be members of the Toloache cult, placed Johnson in a barred cell normally reserved for criminals and tied his arms and legs to the iron bed posts with strips of linen. Though he was in a stupor and near death he fought the restraining devices violently. This urge to violent muscular activity appears to be a characteristic of the first stage of intoxication with the devil's weed. As Don Juan describes it, it is above all a plant for those who seek power, but the power is treacherous and tends to destroy all those who have not sufficient strength to control it.

It is also a plant for those who wish to understand the nature of madness. Johnson, at the height of his hallucinations, encountered a fiery-eyed mongoloid with a switchblade and screamed for the nurse.

It seemed to take forever for her to enter my cell and when she did, the mongoloids disappeared, never to return. I hated her for the condescending smile that normal people bestow on those unfortunate enough to be mentally ill. I felt a tear catch the corners of my eyes as I realized I was schizophrenic, brought on by chemical invasion of brain centers with probable involvement of the endocrine system. What a fool I had been to dabble in the unknown. Those untold numbers of the past and present mentally ill seemed real to me for the first time. Their illness which I had ridiculed openly as weakness was now my weakness.[48]

Similar to the devil's weed in its effects is the crimson fly agaric, *Amanita muscaria.* It is powerful, treacherous and dangerous and was traditionally popular with sorcerers. The "berserker-madness" of the Vikings has been attributed to this plant. It has been used by the shamans of the northeastern Siberian tribes and of the Inari Lapps. Among primitive peoples of northeastern Asia it is eaten as an intoxicant during the long winters when the sun scarcely rises above the horizon and total boredom is an ever present threat. Under these circumstances any form of inebriation may be considered better than none and the Koryak, whose tastes are not refined, prefer the fly agaric to any other agent and will even give a whole reindeer for a single dried mushroom, as the fungus itself does not grow so far north. The fly agaric presents other advantages which appeal to the thrifty, for the active principle is excreted unchanged in the urine and can thus be used again. Thus an agaric orgy among the Koryaks is started by the women, who chew the dried fungus and roll the chewed substance into sausages which are then swallowed by the men. As the party warms up the participants grow lively. Some shout and sing, some hold conversations with imaginary beings, some relate with delight that they have made vast fortunes, some leap to and fro across the room, imagining every tiny obstacle in their path to be so high that they must jump to get over it. Then, when the initial jollity has somewhat worn off, there are shouts of "pass the pot," and one of the women enters with a tin can into which all present urinate with enthusiasm. The can is then passed around and each partakes of the still warm urine, gaiety is restored to the party, and the leaping and singing recommence.

This is a form of social gathering which might not appeal to an aesthete but, as was mentioned above, the Koryak is not refined. Besides, the precious agarics are very expensive and the winters are long, so there is every inducement to prolong the orgy. Certainly as a euphoriant the fly agaric leaves much to be desired and excessive indulgence in the drug leads to an attack of raving madness. The hallucinations become destructive and dangerous, ending in acts of violence or, in some cases, self-mutilation.

R. Gordon Wasson, whose studies of *Psilocybe mexicana* have already been mentioned, defines the hallucinogenic properties of the fly agaric as follows:

A: *It begins to act in fifteen or twenty minutes and the effects last for hours.*

B: *First it is a soporific. One goes to sleep for about two hours, and the sleep is not normal. One cannot be roused from it, but is sometimes aware of the sounds round about. In this half-sleep sometimes one has coloured visions that respond, at least to some extent, to one's desires.*

C: *Some subjects enjoy a feeling of elation that lasts for three or four hours after waking from the sleep. In this stage it is interesting to note that the superiority of this drug over alcohol is particularly emphasized: the fly agaric is not merely better, it belongs to a different and superior order of inebriant, according to those who have enjoyed the experience. During this state the subject is often capable of extraordinary feats of physical effort, and enjoys performing them.*

D: *A peculiar feature of the fly agaric is that its hallucinogenic properties pass into the urine, and another may drink this urine to enjoy the same effect. Indeed it is said that the urine of three or four successive drinkers may be thus consumed without notice- able loss of inebriating effect. This surprising trait of fly agaric inebriation is unique in the hallucinogenic world, so far as our present knowledge goes.*

The soporific and kinetic effects of the fly amanita are utterly unlike anything produced by the mushrooms of the genus Psilocybe of Mexico.[98]

Wasson has made a careful study of one of the great mystery plants of history, the sacred *soma* of the Aryans as described in the hymns of the Rig Veda. He believes that soma was the fly agaric.

"If I am right, the adoration of the fly agaric was at a high level of sophistication 3,500 years ago (and who can say how much further back?) among the Indo-Europeans, and we are witnessing in our own generation the final disappearance of a practice that has held the peoples of northern Eurasia enthralled for thousands of years."[98]

The effects of *A. muscaria* have commonly been attributed to muscarine. This cannot be correct. The fungus contains very little muscarine and in any case muscarine does not produce the same effect as fly agaric. Studies by Conrad H. Eugster of the University of Zurich suggest that a peculiar amino acid (ibotenic acid) is the main active principle of fly agaric. Muscimol, which is easily formed from ibotenic acid in the body, is also highly active.[21] Peter G. Waser took muscimol by mouth in doses of 5, 10 and 15 mg. Ten milligrams produced a slight intoxication after ninety minutes with dizziness, ataraxia and elevated mood. There were no hallucinations but slight changes in taste and color vision. Some myoclonic muscle twitching followed, then sleep with dreams. Fifteen milligrams produced a more serious intoxication an unpleasant feature of which was repeated cramps in various muscle groups. Hallucinations recurred but were never as vivid or colorful as those produced by LSD.

The mushroom itself, says Waser, when taken in moderate amount (one to four mushrooms) produces dizziness, nausea, vertigo, somnolence, euphoria, sense of lightness and color visions. A larger dose (five to ten mushrooms) produces a severe intoxication with muscle twitches and raving agitation followed by partial paralysis with sleep and dreams. Ingestion of more than ten mushrooms is generally fatal.[97]

Synthetic Psychedelics

The plants in the magic garden have always fascinated chemists. Even before chemistry became a science it was realized that the drug plants exerted their effects by virtue of certain special substances. As soon as the principles of chemical analysis were understood, the purification of these substances became a major preoccupation of the pharmacological chemist. The work benefited both physician and patient. Instead of taking evil-tasting draughts of crude extracts of botanicals the patient could swallow or be injected with pure substances. For his malaria he could take pure quinine; for his heart trouble he could take digitalin; to alleviate his pain he could receive injections of morphine. The physician, instead of prescribing brews of questionable activity, could use pure substances with well-defined characteristics. In this way the pharmacopeas were freed from a host of ineffectual remedies which frequently did the patient more harm than good. Pharmacy, formerly a repository of colorful superstitions, old wives' tales and myths, turned into pharmacology, an exact science with its roots in biochemistry and physiology.

The chemists were not satisfied with purifying and analyzing. Once they understood how a drug was constructed they began to explore alternate chemical structures. They changed atomic groupings in the molecule. They ventured into new fields, made antimalarials more potent than quinine, sought analgesics more powerful than morphine, remedies for heart disease more effective than digitalin. Their explorations brought to light a host of new remedies. So many, in fact, that the contemporary physician is overwhelmed by the flood of new drugs that pour out of the laboratories of the world's major pharmaceutical companies.

Among the new compounds that emerged were some very potent hallucinogenic drugs. The pharmaceutical chemists were not directly interested in producing such drugs. The legitimate market for these compounds is small. Without intending to do so, however, Drs. W. A. Stoll and Albert Hofmann of Sandoz Laboratories in Basel prepared the most potent hallucinogenic drug known to man. Back in 1938 these chemists were studying substances derived from ergot of rye. This ergot is a fungus disease of rye that causes the normal grain to be replaced by a black elongated object that sticks out of the head of the plant like a tumor. Folk medicine had long recognized that ergot was poisonous, that it could induce abortion and bring about gangrene of the limbs (St. Anthony's fire). The modern chemists, taking a tip from folk medicine, found ergot a regular treasure trove. They isolated ergotamine, ergotoxine and ergonovine, used for treatment of migraine, chronic hypertension and to cause uterine contraction. All these substances were derived from a molecule called lysergic acid.

It was with lysergic acid that Stoll and Hofmann were working back in 1938, modifying the molecule in various ways and having the compounds tested in animals for various sorts of pharmacological activity. For convenience they referred to these compounds as LSD followed by a number. In the series was LSD-25. Its chemical name was *d-lysergic acid diethylamide*. It seemed of no special interest and was set aside.

On April 16, 1943, Dr. Hofmann began working again on LSD-25. He made a few milligrams of the compound in the morning. By afternoon he felt peculiar, so peculiar that he felt compelled to go home.

Last Friday, April 16th, [wrote Hofman in his laboratory report], in the midst of my afternoon work in the laboratory I had to give up working. I had to go home because I experienced a very peculiar restlessness which was associated with a slight attack of dizziness. At home I went to bed and got into a not unpleasant state of drunkenness which was characterized by an extremely stimulating fantasy. When I closed my eyes (the daylight was most unpleasant to me) I experienced fantastic images of an extraordinary plasticity. They were associated with an intense kaleidoscopic play of colors. After about two hours this condition disappeared.[92]

Hofmann was puzzled by these extraordinary symptoms. He was forced to the conclusion that somehow he had either swallowed or absorbed through his skin a little of the chemical with which he had been working. To test this hypothesis he returned to the laboratory and swallowed 250 micrograms* of LSD. This was a very minute dose of material; there are few drugs, apart from vitamins or hormones, which exert an observable effect when taken by mouth in such small amounts. What Hofmann did not realize was that he had prepared a substance since shown to be the most potent hallucinogen ever discovered and that his tiny dose actually represented over *ten times* the amount (20 micrograms) now known to be quite adequate to produce hallucinations.

This discovery of a chemical substance potent in the merest traces (200 micrograms is about 1 seven-millionths of the weight of an average man) aroused the interest of psychologists and psychiatrists. Some compared the effect of the drug to the condition seen in schizophrenia. It was, they concluded, *psychotomimetic*. It mimicked a psychosis. Others believed that it simply produced hallucinations, which could be distinguished from those of schizophrenia because the person who took LSD knew they were hallucinations whereas the schizophrenic believed his hallucinations were real. They called the drug a *hallucinogen*. Others proposed that the drug revealed deeper levels of the mind. Among them was Dr. Humphrey Osmond who, with a little prompting from Aldous Huxley, came up with the word *psychedelic*, a neologism now firmly embedded in the language both as an adjective and a noun.

Of all the psychedelics, which include mescaline, psilocybin,

---

* A microgram is one millionth of a gram.

DOM and DMT, LSD is the most potent. Early studies of the drug emphasized its psychotomimetic action. Dr. M. Rinkel and his colleagues, working at the Boston Psychopathic hospital, published in 1955 an article in the *Scientific American*.[81] It was entitled "Experimental Psychoses" and it compared the LSD-induced state to schizophrenia.

These early studies showed that the sequence of events in individuals who had taken LSD was similar to that which follows mescaline. Physical symptoms, restlessness, tremor, weakness, sweating, were accompanied by mental and emotional changes. Within one hour after taking the drug the subject began to display irritation, hostility, or anxiety. In the second hour he began to lose touch with reality, withdrawing into himself, overcome with apathy, lethargy, and confusion. Then came the illusions, extraordinary sensations of nonexistence, a feeling that parts of the body had vanished (one subject felt that there was nothing between his hip and his foot), illusions of taste, of smell, visual illusions, the feeling of being "out of time," familiar to those who have worked with mescaline or hashish. The subjects became more or less inarticulate, unable to put into words the unfamiliar ideas and strange sensations they were experiencing. They were able, however, to portray their experiences pictorially and were encouraged to do so. One of these representations of the weird world of LSD shows first a jolly little figure dancing against a green background, portraying, in the subject's account, a sense of supreme joy. "The figure is happy and, above all, free. He has thrown off all cares, problems, ugliness, anger and fear. The world around him is bright and beautiful. Beyond the next rise in the field is that which he wishes more than all else. He feels liberated and unlocked within, integrated, realised." The next picture shows an empty masklike face with tears streaming from the eyes, its top sliced off like the top of a boiled egg to reveal an empty space in which, minute as a mosquito, the jolly little figure is still performing its dance. Above the open head roll threatening storm clouds. "The image of the dancing figure is retained as a memory only, and one about to disappear. The feeling is one of loss. A loss of perfection, a departure from Eden. The intensity of the feeling is extreme and expressed through the lack of any environment. The enveloping storm is one of overwhelming feeling, at first nostalgia, then grief, then sheer feeling with no describable content. All this takes place within. The face is a mere mask which has little meaning. The eyes are closed for this reason. The head is a dead shell, the environment does not exist, the feeling comes from without as well as within and replaces the environment." In the third and last drawing the little black figure has returned, but now its head is bowed, its shoulders hunched, its hands hang helplessly, all its jollity is gone. "The figure is walking in an infinitely narrow walk, with an abyss on either side. The sun is a meaningless glare. The feeling is emptiness, apathy. The blotch (at upper left) indicates that the figure is aware of the sun, but unable to grasp it."

In the early 1950s, at the time Dr. Rinkel and his colleagues made their studies, LSD was a laboratory curiosity. Only a few scientists knew about it. One could get a 5 mg. vial of pure LSD simply by writing to Sandoz Laboratories. Happy days! Many of us who worked with the substance then and took a few micrograms on the sly just to see what it would do look back on that age of innocence with a certain nostalgia. We are inclined to ask: Who let the cat out of the bag? Who drew the attention of the Cross-eyed Crusaders to this curious substance? Who loosed the flood of recriminations, vituperations, accusations, persecutions and generally manic manifestations which have so disturbed the peace and made difficult even a well-conducted study of this and other psychedelic drugs?

Responsibility for this disaster must be shared by Timothy Leary and Ken Kesey. Leary, from his Castalia Institute in Milbrook, proclaimed the new gospel of psychedelics in the ecstatic language of a missionary. Ken Kesey, who had been given LSD by cold-eyed medics at the Veterans Hospital in Menlo Park, ran away from the lab and organized (or disorganized) the Merry Pranksters. Their pranks, riotously documented by Tom Wolfe (*The Electric Kool-Aid Acid Test*) included spiking the drinks of a large group in Los Angeles with enough LSD to turn on several hundred people. The LSD, of excellent quality, was manufactured by a competent chemist called Augustus Owsley Stanley, III. In those days it was quite legal to make LSD. It did not remain legal for long!

So LSD escaped from the lab. It became, along with mescaline, psilocybin, DOM, hashish, DMT and morning glory seeds the base for a new life-style that centered around "the trip." The trip was an inward journey, an excursion into an unknown region of the mind.

The concept of the trip divided the populace. There were those who had taken the trip and those who had not. There was Stonesville and Squaresville. And Stonesville had its own style in practically everything, in haircuts, clothes, art, music (like *Lucy in the Sky with Diamonds* which surely spells LSD whether the Beatles admit it or not).

What is the trip? As far as LSD is concerned it is a rather prolonged (up to twelve hours) experience of an alternate reality, sometimes interesting, sometimes terrifying, sometimes boring. Dr. Timothy Leary, who has done a lot of tripping, describes it as follows in *The Politics of Ecstasy:*

The Trip Can Take You Anywhere!

One reason for the struggle over the interpretation and use of these drugs is the wide variation in their effect. Chemicals like LSD cause no specific response beyond their general tendency to speed up and drastically expand awareness. The specific effect is almost entirely due to the preparations for the session and the surroundings—the set and the setting. In this respect, the person's reaction to his initial LSD session is much like his first reaction to his first sexual experience. If he is psychologically prepared and if the setting is voluntary and pleasant, then a whole new world of experience opens up. But if the initial experience occurs with inadequate preparation or fearful expectation and if the experience is involuntary and the setting impersonal, then a most distasteful reaction is inevitable. Psychiatrists have regularly given LSD to research subjects in circumstances where they did not know what was going to happen (double-blind experimentation) and where the surroundings were bleak, clinical, public, and anxiety-provoking. Such a procedure, even in the guise of science, is nothing short of psychological rape, and it is exactly this sort of impersonal laboratory experimentation which has given LSD a bad name in medical circles.[59]

Leary defines seven basic spiritual questions. These are (1) the ultimate power question, (2) the life question, (3) the human-being question, (4) the awareness question, (5) the ego question, (6) the emotional question, (7) the ultimate escape question. He contends that they are continually being answered and reanswered on the one hand by all the religions of the world and on the other by the natural sciences. It is Leary's opinion that *"those aspects of the psychedelic experience which subjects report to be ineffable and ecstatically religious involve a direct awareness of the energy processes which physicists and biochemists and physiologists and neurologists and psychologists and psychiatrists measure."*[59]

The Leary theory is certainly based on much data. He gives some percentages. If the set and setting are supportive and spiritual, then from 40 to 90 percent of the experiences will be revelatory and mystico-religious. Insights can be profound. The seven basic spiritual questions can all be confronted and answered with the help of LSD. This is certainly as much as anyone has the right to ask of a chemical.

However, not everyone who has worked with LSD shares Leary's enthusiasm.

It is worthwhile to quote some other opinions.

First, there was Dr. Richard Alpert. He worked with Leary at Harvard, designed experiments, recorded data, went to Mexico with IFIF (International Federation for Internal Freedom), worked in the Castalia Foundation at Milbrook, took many trips and saw many strange sights and ended—where? In India at the feet of a holy man. And what did the holy man have to say about LSD? Nothing. He swallowed 305 micrograms, which is a pretty hefty dose for a beginner. He swallowed another 305 micrograms. Then he swallowed another 305 micrograms. Nine hundred and fifteen micrograms! The scientist in Dr. Alpert was all agog. This is going to be interesting.

And it was interesting, but not in the way that the scientist in Dr. Alpert expected. The enormous dose of LSD had no apparent effect on the holy man whatever.

All day long I'm there, and every now and then he twinkles at me and nothing—nothing happens! This was his answer to my question. Now you have the data I have.[2]

Dr. Alpert was more impressed by the holy man's total nonreaction to LSD than by all the drug trips that he had taken himself and seen others take. Alpert metamorphosed into Baba Ram Dass and returned to the United States to write *Remember: Be Here Now*[2] which is one of the most original and charming of spiritual guides. He wrote briefly of psychedelics as *upaya* (which is to say a "method" or "skillful means"). Psychedelics may show the unknown land, but they don't provide a map. They are no big deal anyway. The aim of the game is liberation. You don't gain liberation by swallowing LSD.

Two other investigators, R. E. L. Masters and Jean Houston, published a substantial mass of material in *The Varieties of Psychedelic Experience*.[65] Many and varied insights were recorded. The subjects left their bodies, they shrank to molecular or even atomic dimensions; they became creators of universes; they turned into tigers; they grew old, grew young, died, were reborn, were delighted, awe-inspired, terrified, mystified, glorified. They ascended into heaven, they descended into hell.

All of this was recorded at some length by Masters and Houston. They were not inclined to announce that a new age had dawned or that LSD would transport the race of man to a new and worthier level of being. Following the example of William James, whose *Varieties of Religious Experience* obviously suggested the title of their own book, they maintained an attitude of friendly detachment.

Equally detached was Dr. Sidney Cohen, whose studies are

reported in *The Beyond Within*.[14] He formulated his question in one sentence: "Is the LSD state a model of madness, a touch of schizophrenia, or is it a short cut to *satori, nirvana* for the millions?" Dr. Cohen left the question unanswered. The most he was willing to say is that LSD sometimes can be useful in psychotherapy.

LSD is not the only synthetic hallucinogen. At the height of the "flower children" episode in San Francisco a mysterious drug suddenly became available. It was called STP or DOM. No one appears to know what the letters STP signified nor is it known from what source the drug came. Five thousand tablets of the drug were distributed free of charge during a celebration in San Francisco's Golden Gate Park on June 21, 1967. The resulting trips were prolonged, violent, frequently terrifying. They had an additional characteristic. Administration of chlorpromazine, which will generally abort a bad LSD trip, only made the condition of the STP tripper worse.

What was STP? It belonged to a series of compounds based on amphetamine. Chemically it was *4-methyl-2, 5-dimethoxyamphetamine*. The chemists labeled it DOM. It was a close relative of the compound *3,4,5-trimethoxyamphetamine* (TMA) in which were combined the chemical characteristics of mescaline and amphetamine. Of this compound it was said: "The emotional responses elicited during the period of maximum . . . intoxication (three to five hr. from the start of the experiment) were striking in their intensity. Anger, hostility and megalomaniac euphoria dominated the subject's thoughts and conversation. Actual acts of hostility were not observed, but it was felt that, in at least two subjects, provocation would have precipitated homicidal violence."[87]

Amphetamine, to which the above compound is related, is, of course, one of the best known synthetic compounds that chemists have developed as a result of their raids on the magic garden. The plant that suggested the structure of amphetamine belonged to the genus *Ephedra* and was the basis of an old Chinese drug (*ma huang*). Amphetamine was one of many variations on the theme of ephedrine that chemists created. At first it was marketed under the trade name "Benzedrine" as a remedy for blocked nasal passages. One inhaled it to counteract the aftereffects of a cold. But amphetamine was far more than a nasal decongestant. It was a wake-up drug superior in many ways to cocaine. It could be used to combat narcolepsy, an embarrassing disease the victims of which keep falling asleep. It was also found, paradoxically enough, to have a calming effect on overactive children.

During World War II amphetamines were used by all the squabbling nations to help keep their soldiers, sailors and airmen awake in order that they might murder each other more effectively. One fact, however, was known to all these fighting men. You always paid a high price for the drug-induced alertness and the drug-liberated energy. You did not get something for nothing.

After the war the practice of taking amphetamines to induce wakefulness was continued mainly by truck drivers and by students cramming for exams. Certainly these users suffered the inevitable let down, but by that time the truck driver hoped to be safely off the road and the student finished with his exam. In any case this use of amphetamines was confined to taking the drug by mouth. This mode of administration rarely had serious effects and the Council on Drugs of the American Medical Association reported, as late as 1963, that amphetamines constituted a small problem in the United States.

It was not until the later 1960s that the practice of injecting large doses of amphetamines intravenously began to spread among that section of the population given to drug abuse. This practice has been described as "among the most disastrous forms of drug use yet devised."[8] Why is the practice so disastrous? We can answer this question best by considering the pattern of life of a typical "speed freak." Here, let us say, is Joe, young, white and from a middle-class background, adrift in the Haight-Ashbury district of San Francisco. Joe shoots "speed," which can be either amphetamine, "Methedrine" (*methamphetamine*), or "Preludin" (*phenmetrazine*). The first time he injected the drug he experienced euphoria. Now, like all drug abusers, he seeks that euphoria again. So he tries it again and again and yet again. The euphoria, of course, becomes harder to recapture as his system becomes accustomed to the drug. He finally degenerates into a "speed freak" whose characteristics have been described as follows by Dr. J. C. Kramer:

> *After a period of several months the final pattern is reached in which the user (now called a "speed freak") injects his drug many times a day, each dose in the hundreds of milligrams, and remains awake continuously for three to six days, getting gradually more tense, tremulous and paranoid as the "run" progresses. The runs are interrupted by bouts of very profound sleep (called "crashing") which last a day or two. Shortly after waking . . . the drug is again injected and a new run starts. The periods of continuous wakefulness may be prolonged to weeks if the user attempts to sleep even as little as an hour a day.*[56]

This fantastic abuse of the biochemical machinery of the body quite naturally ruins the speed freak's health. First the amphetamines produce a profound lack of appetite (for which reason they are used in antiobesity pills). Second they produce insomnia. A paranoid psychosis, similar to that produced by abuse of cocaine, is the inevitable result of this mistreatment of the body. The speed freak is afraid of everything and everybody. He may lock himself in his room, arm himself with a knife or a gun. He is plagued by the singular illusion, which cocaine abusers also experience, that snakes or insects are crawling under or on his skin. These imaginary creepers are called "crank bugs" and it is common to see speed freaks with sores or scabs on their arms or faces, the result of their attempts to remove the nonexistent bug.

What with sleeplessness, malnutrition and paranoia the speed freak becomes a singularly unattractive specimen of humanity. He is, in the words of Dr. Roger C. Smith, an outcast in a society of outcasts. Heroin users despise him for his lack of cool and his inability to hustle. Users of psychedelics or marijuana regard him as insane and violent. Because he is highly agitated, talks incessantly, is hyperactive, openly suspicious, often bizarre in appearance, businessmen rarely accept either checks or credit cards from him. He and the cocaine abuser are the real representatives of that popular and much misused stereotype, the dope-fiend.

Even among confirmed drug users it is generally conceded that speed is the worst. It does not necessarily kill. In fact, if the body is accustomed to the drug, doses as high as 15 grams may be injected over a twenty-four-hour period without death resulting. But the overall effect of amphetamine abuse is so degrading that no one has a good word to say for this drug. Timothy Leary has condemned it. Allen Ginsberg, taking a cue from the Pope, has pronounced it anathema, *ex cathedra*. It is, by all accounts, a drug to avoid.

Fortunately, though the speed freak can reduce himself to a paranoid near-skeleton by his habit, he can also, if willing to give up amphetamine abuse, make a fairly complete recovery. Dr. Kramer states that most, if not all, speed freaks can recover even from profound intellectual disorganization and psychosis after six months to a year of abstinence.

A Cluster of Conclusions

The fight over the fruits of the magic garden, including the synthetic productions of the chemists, continues to rage. It is, by any criterion, a dreary and unprofitable struggle, characterized by woolly thinking, muddy emotionalism, flagrant hypocrisy and deliberate lies. In short it reflects the confused state of the psyche of contemporary Americans desperately groping for guidelines in a moral fog. In this quest the young get little help from their leaders. Lies, hypocrisy, dirty tricks, profanity, burglary are practiced by the holders of high office. Former attorney generals are hauled into court, presidential advisers face jail terms. And yet it is still considered a crime for some poor young soul to have in his possession a handful of marijuana!

Confusion on confusion! Moreover the problem seems to be insoluble. The American politician is rarely either courageous or capable of independent thought. He thinks in clichés. Drugs are bad therefore drug users should be punished. Does he know what a drug is? Almost certainly not. But he shies like a nervous horse every time the word drug is mentioned. And panics. And enacts more prohibitive legislation, though all the evidence suggests that prohibitions only encourage violations and build up very profitable black markets in which inferior products are sold at outrageous prices. Of course there are exceptions to every rule and in several legislatures there are men who very well know the futility of prohibitions. But they are always in a minority and rarely get a hearing.

It may be useful now to list various proposals, to weigh up pros and cons, to repeat what has already been said—for everything that can be said on the subject of drug abuse and its prevention has been said. One can do nothing more than list the statements.

We will start with a statement by Dr. Timothy Leary:

THE TWO COMMANDMENTS FOR THE MOLECULAR AGE

I. Thou shalt not alter the consciousness of thy fellowmen.
II. Thou shalt not prevent thy fellowman from altering his own consciousness.[59]

A simple statement. A direct rebuke to the whole tribe of busybodies, Cross-eyed Crusaders, self-appointed guardians of public morals, the self-righteous wardens of the human lunatic asylum.

> "Get Your Sterile, Surgical Rubber Gloves
> Off My Soul, Doctor Farnsworth"[59]

In other words, let me seek heaven or go to hell in my own way, with or without the help of psychedelics, with or without the help of "authorities," religious, political or scientific. The so-called authorities are morally, intellectually and spiritually bankrupt. When it comes to coping with the drug problem they are incapable of rational behavior because they are devoid of objective standards of morality.

Consider, for instance, the case of the Church of the Awakening. It was founded by John and Louise Aiken in 1963. Both the founders were physicians, stable responsible people. The psychedelic experience was named as a sacrament of the church. It was to be available only to those who had been members of the church for a minimum period of three months. The founders took the view that frequent use of psychedelics was likely to result in desire for the experience for its own sake. The whole idea behind the Church of the Awakening was to use psychedelics as a means, not as an end. The drugs can, in certain cases, offer a glimpse of a different reality. They cannot give instant enlightenment but they may offer hints as to what enlightenment would be like.

The founders of the Church of the Awakening drew attention to Section 166.3 (c) (3) in the Code of Federal Regulations. "The listing of peyote in this sub-paragraph (as being restricted or forbidden) does not apply to non-drug use in bona fide religious ceremonies of the Native American Church." The founders of the Church of the Awakening felt that other races should have equal rights before the law. If the sacramental use of peyote is permissible for an American Indian it is also permissible for a white American, a black American, a yellow American or any other sort of American. To deny this right is to indulge in the most flagrant racial discrimination. It also involves interference with liberty of religion, supposedly guarded by the Constitution.

But did the Aikens obtain legal consent to operate the Church of the Awakening? They did not. Nor did Timothy Leary when he sought similar permission to operate IFIF. All the impartiality that is supposed to characterize due process of law seems to evaporate as soon as a judge is confronted with this issue. Authority asserts itself in terms worthy of the old style of Victorian father: "Don't ask questions. Do what you are told."

Obviously this approach does not appeal to a generation of young people who, with good reason, have little respect for the wisdom of their elders. Faced with a government machine that is rotten from top to bottom they can hardly be expected to respect authority. They consider the authorities to be either fools or frauds. Marijuana is represented as a dangerous drug and the penalties for possession equal those inflicted for possession of heroin. But the sophisticated young know all about marijuana. They know it is no more dangerous than tobacco, and less dangerous than alcohol. They know it is nonaddicting. They know that the mild high it produces has little effect on their health one way or another. The marijuana-menace is an illusion, and those who foster this illusion must be either hypocrites or fools.

And when it comes to hypocrisy, how is one to take seriously these Moms and Dads who, cigarette in one hand and cocktail in

the other, lecture their young on the dangers of pot? If Mom and
Dad would stop smoking and drinking perhaps their offspring
might be inclined to listen to them. But as long as they themselves
indulge in intoxicants, their lectures to the young will fall on
deaf ears.

None of which should be construed as meaning that intoxicants are desirable. We would be better off, a cleaner, happier,
stronger breed of men, if we never smoked, and drank only
water or fruit juice. Tobacco smoking is disgusting, smelly and
dangerous. The soil on which tobacco is grown would be better
used for producing food. Alcohol is a food of a sort, and the
fermentation of grapes to make wine has no doubt a certain
Dionysian significance. But if the whole family of hard liquors
from whisky to vodka could be banished from the face of the
earth it would be to everyone's advantage. And of course we
would be better off without heroin, without amphetamines (unless
we suffer from narcolepsy), without cocaine and without barbiturates. The revelations obtained with LSD and other psychedelics
could be obtained far more honestly and safely by the practice
of yoga. And we could get along without pot, though it does
make life more interesting to get mildly high now and then.

This, more or less, is the viewpoint expressed by Dr. Donald
B. Louria in *The Drug Scene*.[62] He certainly knows what he is
talking about. He has studied the problem of drug abuse at first
hand in the place where this problem is manifested most horren-
dously, New York City, but his vision is by no means limited to
this particular blot on the face of our planet. He looks at American society as a whole, sees it as filthy rich (6 percent of the
world's population with 50 percent of its wealth), pampered,
permissive, dedicated to a selfish philosophy of hedonism and
materialism. It is a nation of crybabies, whose members cannot
stand the slightest frustration or discomfort. It is a nation of
pill-taking hypochondriacs whose members assume that "for
every valid or imaginary ill there is some magical medicament."

Under the circumstances it is hardly surprising that drugs of
all kinds are used to evade reality. This is particularly true of the

city ghettos where reality is so hideous that no one can be blamed for trying to evade it. "Drug abuse must not be regarded as an entity in and of itself but rather as a manifestation of some underlying abnormality, either in the individual or in society."[62]

So what does Dr. Louria suggest? Antidrug education? He thinks it might help, but only if speakers on the subject are scrupulously honest and factual. Alarmists of the Commissioner Harry Anslinger type, Cross-eyed Crusaders, cops and narcs who obviously have an axe to grind generally manage to do more harm than good. Usually they make fools of themselves over marijuana. By trying to pretend that it is a dangerous drug, that it leads to heroin, that it is addictive, etc., the over-zealous lecturer merely destroys his own credibility. His young listeners probably know more about marijuana than he does and are hardly likely to be impressed by statements which their own experience tells them are totally untrue.

Dr. Louria thinks that the drug laws might be improved. Three categories could be created to include: (a) more dangerous drugs, (b) an intermediate group, (c) less dangerous drugs. He would include marijuana in the intermediate group but place methamphetamine in the more dangerous category. He is prepared to get tough with the psychedelic enthusiasts. "In regard to dispensing drugs such as LSD or STP without cost, the laws should provide the judiciary with the flexibility to give misdemeanor sentences to those who merely shared small amounts, and felony sentences to those who appear to be major proselytizers. These recommendations may appear stringent but the potential risks to the individual and to society as well as the messianic nature of the hallucinogenic zealots demand vigorous and firm laws and regulations."

So we are back on the same old treadmill. Obviously, if we are to follow Dr. Louria's advice, we must once again start persecuting the members of the Native American Church because they are "hallucinogenic zealots" who insist on using peyote.

Actually nothing much will be gained by changing the drug laws. The reason for this has been expressed clearly in the Consumer's Union Report *Licit and Illicit Drugs*.[9] This cool, objective, well-documented study is the model of what a report of this kind should be. It has done what the law courts have so consistently failed to do, assembled the facts and drawn logical conclusions based on facts. And what is the most obvious fact about the drug laws?

PROHIBITION DOES NOT WORK!

Yes, prohibition does not work. It failed utterly to control the abuse of alcohol, so utterly that the Volstead Act was finally repealed. All the laws on the books against marijuana, with their stupidly ferocious penalties have failed to reduce the use of this drug. The outcry against LSD probably served to popularize it rather than to scare people away from its use. These laws are rotten because they create a crime where no crime exists. They are doubly rotten because they often do more damage to the young offender than does the drug from which they are supposed to protect him. How can it possibly improve a young person's career to throw him into jail, force him to associate with criminals, mar his record with a conviction, all for being in possession of a few ounces of marijuana? As the Canadian Le Dain Commission put it: ". . . the harm caused by the law exceeds the harm which it is supposed to prevent."[60]

It is useful if we remember that the prohibitory laws were passed in the first place to *protect* people. Before the passing of the Harison Narcotics Act anyone could buy opium or its derivatives heroin or morphine. They could take it themselves, they could give it to their children. A number of people who used the drug too freely became addicted as a result. There is no evidence to show that they lived unsatisfactory lives. Society tolerated them. As the Consumer's Report puts it:

. . . opiate use in the nineteenth century was not subject to the moral sanctions current today. Employees were not fired for addiction. Wives did not divorce their addicted husbands, or husbands their addicted wives. Children were not taken from their homes and lodged in foster homes because one or both parents were addicted. Addicts continued to participate fully in

*the life of the community. Addicted children and young people
continued to go to school, Sunday School, and college. Thus the
nineteenth century avoided one of the most disastrous effects of
current narcotics laws and attitudes—the rise of a deviant addict
subculture, cut off from respectable society and without a "road
back" to respectability.*[9]

This is a very revealing statement. We moderns are inclined
to think of ourselves as freer than our forebears, less dominated
by authoritarian ideas, more permissive in every way. This is
true in most respects *except* in our treatment of drug addiction.
Here we revert to the crudest form of authoritarian behavior,
searching, threatening, punishing with a blind zeal worthy of the
worst days of the Spanish Inquisition. A curious phenomenon!

The Consumer's Report[9] offers six specific recommendations:

(1). *Stop emphasizing measures designed to keep drugs
away from people.* Prohibition does not work. It did not work
with alcohol. It has not worked with heroin, with marijuana, with
LSD or any other illicit drugs. Its main effect is to encourage
criminal activity, the flooding of the market with adulterated
drugs sold at exorbitant prices. Excessive reliance on prohibition
lulls the country into false confidence that nothing need be done
except to pass another law or hire a few hundred more narcotics
agents empowered to break into houses without knocking.

Some control over the sale of drugs is certainly necessary but
those framing drug control laws should bear two things in mind.
First, there is a saying in medical circles based on one of the
aphorisms of Hippocrates: *Nihil nocere.* Above all do no harm.
A law that turns a young person into a convict merely because he
or she possesses a few ounces of marijuana obviously does more
harm than good. Second, lawmakers need to realize what laws
can and cannot do. They cannot keep heroin from heroin addicts.
They will not keep marijuana from marijuana users. The most
they can do is to curb the flow of heroin to *nonaddicts.* Even in
this area they are not very effective. Positive results are more
likely to be obtained through education and social reform.

(2). *Stop publicizing the horrors of the "drug menace."* The shrieks of alarm only serve to draw attention to the very evils they are supposed to prevent. By representing drugs as terrible, dangerous, wicked, etc., the Establishment merely arouses the interest of the rebellious young, forever on the lookout for ways of defying its elders. Sensationalist publicity functions as a lure rather than a warning.

(3). *Stop increasing the damage done by drugs.* In several ways the current drug laws make drugs more rather than less damaging. The sale or possession of hypodermic needles without prescription is a criminal offense, which encourages the sharing of needles, leading to epidemics of hepatitis and other needle-borne diseases. Loss of employment, expulsion from school, exclusion from respectable society also increases the damage done by drugs. Much of the damage done by drugs is due not to the chemical effects of the drugs themselves but to the ignorant, imprudent ways in which they are used, laws punishing their use and society's attitude toward the user.

(4). *Stop misclassifying drugs.* What can one say about drug laws that equate marijuana and heroin, or that treat alcohol and nicotine—two of the most harmful drugs—as nondrugs? They appear, to any fair-minded observer trained in scientific methodology, to be some sort of obscure joke perpetrated by ignorant lawyers at the public's expense. Nothing has done more to destroy the faith of young people in the veracity of their elders than the equating of marijuana and heroin. Because they are obviously lying about marijuana the young skeptic assumes the authorities are lying about other drugs. Lawyers are not the people who should classify drugs. This task should be left to physicians and pharmacologists. Yet the Comprehensive Drug Abuse Prevention and Control Act of 1970 authorizes the *attorney general,* of all people, to alter the classification of drugs. This must be one of the most glaring examples of misdelegated authority since the Emperor Caligula made his horse a proconsul!

(5). *Stop viewing the drug problem as primarily a national problem, to be solved on a national scale.* Obviously the drug

problem is local. It is a product of the urban environment and is
seen in its most advanced form in the big city ghettos. Effective
solutions vary with the area and should depend mainly on local
effort. Warning children against drugs which they might never
even hear of only tends to awaken their curiosity. Warnings
against glue sniffing, for instance, only popularized this practice.

(6). *Stop pursuing the goal of stamping out illicit drug use.*
Experience has shown that attempts to stamp out drug use tend
to increase both drug use and drug damage. There will always
be a certain percentage of the population which will abuse drugs,
including alcohol and nicotine. This is simply a fact of life. We
should learn to live with it.

Such are the recommendations offered by Edward M. Brecher
and the editors of Consumer's Reports. They are all very sensible
and are generally in line with recommendations offered by several
learned bodies who have given this problem their attention.
Unfortunately when dealing with legislators one only rarely
encounters rational behavior. There is a brand of politician
commonly encountered both in federal and state governments
who feels it his bound duty to become practically hysterical with
righteous indignation whenever anybody suggests that the drug
laws are harsh, hypocritical, inconsistent and ineffective. This
makes any rational discussion of the subject almost impossible.
It places scientists and medical men who give unbiased opinions
in the same position as those courageous men of a former
age who dared protest against the burning of witches. They were
promptly condemned by the witch-hunters as being in league
with the Devil and were in grave danger of being accused of
witchcraft themselves.

Thus, in 1969, Dr. Stanley Yolles, then director of the
National Institute of Mental Health, testified in Congress against
mandatory minimum sentences for drug abusers. As a result of
these laws, he said,

*What we have in our prisons and Federal hospitals, like
Lexington, are many young people serving irrationally long*

sentences, some up to twenty years. In no other field has there been such a punitive approach. And let's not forget this is an illness mainly of young people—the very age group with the highest potential for rehabilitation, yes, and cure.

These laws came about by sometimes well-intentioned people who placed too much confidence in the principle of deterrents. But if mandatory penalties were that effective, what is the rationale for limiting them only to drug abuse offenders? Why not extend them to thieves, burglars, murderers? Even murderers with life sentences can come up for parole after about seven years.[9]

Did the lawmakers applaud the good doctor for this sane and humanitarian statement? Certainly not! From Congressman Albert Watson of South Carolina came such a blast that one would suppose Dr. Yolles had proposed to overthrow the government by violence. "Dr. Yolles's views are an affront to every decent, law-abiding citizen in America. At a time when we are on the verge of a narcotics crisis, a supposedly responsible Federal official comes along with the incredibly ridiculous idea of dropping mandatory jail sentences for those who push dope, even for those adults selling hard drugs to minors." Subsequently Congressman Watson called for Dr. Yolles's resignation.

This kind of frenzy makes it improbable that any of the recommendations of the Consumer's Report will even be debated by the legislature until a new brand of politician is elected with a less hysterical attitude toward the drug problem. Meanwhile we can only hope that a more sophisticated, better-educated generation of young people will understand, without being threatened by politicians or bullied by policemen, just what drugs can and cannot do. If it is true, as Dr. Andrew Weil has suggested, that "the desire to alter consciousness is an innate psychological drive arising out of neurological structure of the human brain," then it is up to the individual to find out for himself what are the most effective ways of satisfying this drive.

Personally I do not believe that this drive is universal. I

think it is characteristic of the twice-born. It is because they do not have this drive themselves that the once-born, including various brands of Cross-eyed Crusaders, find it impossible to understand why the twice-born experiment with drugs. But the need for alteration in consciousness which Dr. Weil describes can be satisfied in many ways. On the whole, drugs are one of the less satisfactory techniques. They are useful only to demonstrate that certain "alternate realities" exist and that the mind has in it locked rooms that contain great treasures. The "guided trip" as described by Masters and Houston in *The Varieties of Psychedelic Experience*[65] can be very useful to some people who need a clearer understanding of their own potential. In a rational society such guided trips, with the aid of some natural psychedelic (the sacred mushroom, peyote or aya-huasca) would be available to those who felt the need for it. Performed under proper conditions it might offer a game worth playing to those who reject the more or less imbecile game plans that are offered by a spiritually bankrupt society. But a conscientious spiritual guide would always point out the limitations of the drug-induced insights. Drugs merely offer indications. If the drugs are used too often they cease to offer anything. And for some people they are only poisons. They make such people feel ill and offer no insights of any kind.

The fight over the fruits of the magic garden is senseless and expensive but will doubtless continue because many politicians, narcotics officers, lawyers and Cross-eyed Crusaders are personally interested in seeing that it does continue. It feeds their need to feel righteously indignant and, in many cases, is the source of their livelihood. As for the future, it will probably be much like the past. One can confidently predict that a certain number of people in each generation will become dependent on drugs (heroin, alcohol, nicotine) and that some will destroy themselves with these drugs or with methedrine or cocaine. They will do this, law or no law, just as some in each generation will commit suicide. One might guess that, as more and more people use marijuana, the laws controlling this drug will be modified or that judges will simply refuse to take them seriously. It seems likely that the mystical aura that surrounds LSD and other psychedelics will be dissipated gradually. Indeed there are signs already that the overrated psychedelic drugs are becoming less popular. This has nothing to do with the laws that have been passed to control them. People have tried them and found out for themselves that they are not so wonderful.

No drug in the magic garden will take the place of those intentional efforts which alone enable man to open the locked rooms of the psyche. For centuries men have searched for a chemical short cut to power or liberation. The drugs they found led their users into that shadowy region called by the Zen Buddhists *makyo* and by the Christian mystics "beauty." It is a sort of psychological fun-fair. It has all the mirrors, the swings and roundabout and roller coasters which can scare you half to death. You can meet every ghost and demon in the human collective unconscious. You can be hurled into infinite space or down into subatomic worlds. You can make trips into the past and even appear to be traveling into the future.

All the fun of the fair! And because it is, to some extent, great fun provided you have a good guide and a happy environment it will take more than the muddled prohibitions of mixed-up lawmakers to stop the adventurous from visiting the fair. But the wise will understand that drugs can offer no more than a shadow show. They will go on and discover for themselves the valid ways of attaining harmonious development. They will then leave drugs behind as an adult leaves behind the toys he played with in childhood. But before they leave the drugs behind they should at least have the right to experience their effects. How can one pass judgment on something one has never known?

As for those legislators who persist in punishing drug users because they *presume* that these users will harm themselves with drugs, they might do well to remember some advice addressed to the witch-hunters of the sixteenth century by Montaigne. After remarking that it is entirely a matter of conjecture whether or not a certain phenomenon is due to witchcraft he adds: "After all, it is rating one's conjectures at a very high price to roast a man alive on the strength of them." It is also rating one's conjectures at a very high price to send a man to jail for up to twenty years because he possessed marijuana which *might* damage his health *if* he smoked it.

Fortunately it appears that, in one state at least, legislators have begun to take a more sensible attitude. Very quietly, in November 1973, the state of Oregon removed criminal penalties for the possession of small amounts of marijuana. Pot smokers in this enlightened state now face a fine of up to $100 for possession of an ounce or less of the weed. They are not arrested but ticketed by the police as if for a parking offense. State courts have generally settled on a $25 fine.

Although a purist might complain that even this mild punishment represents tyranny on the part of the establishment it is certainly an improvement. Even the public prosecutors in the state admit that the milder legislation has had salutory effects. The following facts have emerged:

Before decriminalization, police were spending a disproportionate amount of time chasing pot smokers who are an "easy arrest." The change in laws has given them more time to pursue violent crimes and, thus, better serve the community.

The impact on criminal courts has been significant. One-third of the total number of cases awaiting trial have been removed from the docket. And the jail population is now made up of felons rather than young people whose marijuana-smoking "crime" was victimless.

The change in pot laws has removed the threat of a criminal arrest record that would hamper a young person's future or prevent an arrested pot smoker from entering several of the professions such as law or teaching.

It remains to be seen whether other states will follow the sensible example of Oregon.

PART TWO

Sick Minds: New Medicines

The Chemistry
of Madness

The greatest public health problem at the present time is mental
illness. It fills more hospital beds than cancer, heart disease, and
tuberculosis combined; and for every totally disabled inmate of
a mental hospital at least two others are living in the outer world,
not sick enough to be institutionalized, not well enough to live
healthy, happy lives. This huge population of mentally sick
individuals imposes a burden on the healthy segment of the
population whose size is appalling to contemplate. In terms of
cost, no other form of illness is more expensive. In terms of
suffering, no other affliction is more devastating. Anyone who has
had the experience of watching a close relative or dear friend go
mad will certainly testify that there is no experience more
harrowing. Death one can accept. It is inevitable that all must
die. But the spectacle of madness is a daily and hourly affront
to man's faith in a just and benevolent Providence, for the mad
do not die, nor can they live. They inhabit a shadowy borderland
between life and death and neither love nor pity will enable the
sane to enter that strange region. Madness severs the strongest
bonds that hold human beings together. It separates husband
from wife, mother from child. It is death without death's finality
and without death's dignity.

By far the most widespread as well as the most tragic form
of mental illness is schizophrenia. It is the most tragic because
it is particularly liable to develop in young people and was
formerly called *dementia praecox* ("precocious dementia") to
distinguish it from "senile dementia," the insanity of old age.

Schizophrenia often develops at adolescence or in the early twenties. It may even afflict children, though childhood schizophrenia is rather rare. To gain an idea of what the illness means we must visit the iron-barred wards in some of our larger mental hospitals, where, behind carefully locked doors, the more violently disturbed patients pass their lives, often herded together under conditions which would be judged unsuitable even for animals.

Consider the case of Mary, now twenty-eight years old, an inhabitant of the "disturbed ward" for the past eight years. We find her huddled in a corner on a wooden bench, completely motionless, her knees drawn up under her chin and her thin arms clasped about her legs. Her short cropped hair is in disorder, her body so thin that the bones are visible through the flesh. She is wearing nothing but a shabby nightgown made of a heavy coarse material, for in her occasional fits of violence she is liable to strip off her clothing and tear it to pieces. Most of the time, however, she remains motionless, not moving even to satisfy the calls of nature or to take food. If you move her arm it remains in any position in which you happen to place it, a condition known as "waxy flexibility." Her strangely immobile state is called "catatonia" and her illness diagnosed as "catatonic schizophrenia," one of the four subdivisions of the disease.

Mary's history is characteristic of that of many schizophrenics. She was an only child brought up in a household dominated by a short-tempered and tyrannical father, with a mother who at times made a great fuss over her and at other times ignored or rejected her. A dreamy, fragile, solitary child, she loved above all to wander by herself in the woods or to sit doing nothing in the garden, indulging in all sorts of fantastic daydreams. Whenever her feelings were hurt, whenever she was rejected by her unstable mother or abused by her domineering father, she would retreat into that imaginary world which by degrees became for her more real than reality. She grew up into a slender fair-haired woman, pretty enough in her own rather fragile fashion, with the dreamy, other-worldly expression on her face with which Dante Gabriel Rossetti loved to endow his long-necked beauties. The approach of maturity placed an additional strain upon her. Her parents, still dominated by the pruderies of a previous generation, told her nothing of the changes that would take place in her body at the time of puberty. Her menstrual periods seemed to her something shameful and terrible. Her awakening sexual impulses filled her with fear and self-loathing.

At sixteen she had what was euphemistically called a "nervous breakdown." The characters from her fantasy world invaded her real world. She actually began to see them. She heard their voices whispering in her ear. Her increasing dreaminess brought down upon her the wrath of her intolerant father and the dislike of her mother, who withdrew from the girl what little support and affection she had previously given. One day Mary left home and was discovered wandering in the woods, talking in the most animated fashion to a being who was visible to her alone. Her frightened parents called in the family doctor, who packed her off to a nursing home to avoid the "stigma" of having her admitted to a mental hospital. There, without any special treatment save a change of scene, the girl made what appeared to be a good recovery.

Mary did not return home but launched out on a life of her own, met her husband-to-be, married, and bore her children. Then the burden of her duties as wife and mother began to prove too much for her. Once again the fantasy world started to intrude. She grew more dreamy, more incapable of attending to those countless daily tasks that are the lot of every housewife. As she grew more inefficient her husband grew more critical. As he grew more critical she became more withdrawn. Then, quite abruptly, she crossed the border line that separates the sane from the mad. He came back from work to find her seated motionless in a chair. The house was in confusion, the children had not been put to bed. When he spoke to her she did not answer. When he lifted her hand it stayed lifted as if she had been a waxen image. She was removed to a mental hospital and there she remains, a catatonic, seemingly dead to the world. As she will not eat, food has to be introduced into her stomach by means of a nasal tube. As she will not attend to her needs, she has to be changed like a baby. The attendants have come to regard her as virtually an inanimate object, like a piece of furniture. Every now and then, however, her catatonic immobility gives way to fits of murderous rage. At such times the attendants appear to her as devils and she fights against them with all the strength of which her skinny body is capable. Then once again immobility descends on her.

Thus she lives on, alive only in the sense that she still breathes. All her contacts with the outer world have been severed. Her husband has moved to a state in which insanity constitutes valid grounds for divorce, has freed himself from the burden, and married again. Her children do not remember her. The stream of life, with all its bustle and sparkle, flows past her without touching her. There she sits, her knees drawn up under her chin, gazing motionless at nothing, fed, clothed, cleansed by the overworked attendants, who regard her, when passive, as a nuisance and, when violent, as a menace. Her illness began when she was twenty. She may live on into her sixties. For all those forty years she must be cared for—a living corpse denied even the privilege of burial.

Or consider the case of George, in the men's section of the same hospital. George is a paranoid schizophrenic. He is about the same age as Mary but does not sit motionless as she does. George, in fact, is very active, but his activity has no connection with the realities of this world, for within the labyrinth of George's mind is a distorting mirror which prevents even the simplest impression from reaching his brain unaltered. Everything he sees, everything he hears, the things he touches, even the food he eats becomes endowed, through the action of this distorting agent, with sinister, malignant significance. The words of one of the physicians, the glance of an attendant, even a casual gesture by one of his fellow inmates is interpreted as a threat. The radio broadcasts the plottings of some foreign power disguised to resemble ordinary news or music. The scent of a flower is really a poisoned gas being secretly brewed by the "enemy" under the floorboards. Often his food seems to have a strange metallic taste. Again it is "the enemy" attempting to poison him. He pushes the food away and refuses to eat for several days. When they try to feed him by force he fights and screams and struggles, knowing that he has fallen into the hands of "the enemy" and that they are about to kill him. One might suppose, surrounded as he is by terrors, that George would welcome death, and indeed he did, on one occasion, attempt to release himself by thrusting his head through a glass door and endeavoring to cut his throat on the jagged edges. He was rescued and his wounds were sewn up, since which time he has been carefully watched and housed in a special cell where suicide is virtually impossible. So he must live with his terrors until natural death at last relieves him of his burden. Like Mary, he may live for another forty years, alone as only the mad can be alone, a curse to himself, a burden to those who must care for him.

A few further observations should be added to these descriptions. Schizophrenia is an illness of the body as well as the mind and its physical manifestations are as important as its mental ones. The delicate inner balance of the body is in some way upset. The hands and feet of the schizophrenic are cold, clammy and blue, indicating some derangement in the workings of the autonomic nervous system through the agency of which the blood vessels in the skin are expanded or contracted according to the needs of the moment. The perception of pain may be completely destroyed by this condition. Students of those horrible procedures, the trials of witches, have often been astonished to read that the witch would frequently frustrate her tormentors by singing or even going to sleep while the cruelest tortures were being applied to her body, thus terrifying her judges by demonstrating the powers of the Evil One. What she was actually demonstrating was the effect of schizophrenia on pain perception. Shattuck describes a case of a female schizophrenic who, having wrapped herself in a blanket, set the blanket on fire: ". . . when found two hours later she was sitting contentedly on the floor, her legs badly burned, her charred tibiae exposed. Third degree burns also covered her chest, abdominal wall, back and hands. She spoke pleasantly, begging to be left where she was, exculpated everybody and discussed philosophically whether the absence of religious beliefs was a matter of importance in her present condition. The patient denied repeatedly that she was in any pain and remained cheerful and argumentative for half an hour, while her body was lifted with difficulty from the burning floorboards. She then complained of pain in her shoulders, the only part of her body which was not burned, and a few minutes later collapsed and died."

Such is schizophrenia. The illness does not always manifest itself in the extreme forms described above. There are degrees of schizophrenia which range from a mild illness that may not even necessitate hospitalization to the totally incapacitating condition seen in the disturbed wards of large mental hospitals. In all its forms this illness constitutes, like cancer, one of the great unsolved medical mysteries of the mid-twentieth century. New methods and medicaments, shortly to be described, have improved the prospects of cure enormously, but though it is no longer regarded as a rather hopeless condition its cause remains as much of a mystery as ever.

The cause of schizophrenia is chemical. It is possible, on the basis of the available evidence, to make this statement with a fair degree of confidence. Mind is a product of the chemistry of the brain, and when brain chemistry is altered the mind is altered. This does not mean that schizophrenia is due to a single chemical defect as is diabetes. Almost certainly the word schizophrenia covers several disorders all of which have symptoms in common. The chemical causes may vary. In some cases the brain may be short of certain vitamins, in others it may be poisoned by a product of metabolism having some of the properties of mescaline or LSD. It is easy to envisage an error of metabolism, which could generate a toxic substance capable of altering the working of the brain. Several ways in which this could happen will be described later.

About one thing we can be reasonably certain. The worst

possible treatment for the schizophrenic is psychoanalysis. Anyone wishing to understand just how disastrous analysis can be for the schizophrenic should read Gregory Stefan's book, *In Search of Sanity.*[89] This first hand account of schizophrenia by an intelligent journalist should leave no one in doubt as to its chemical origin. The illness attacked Stefan suddenly and for no external reason. There was no stress to which the attack could be attributed, no conflict, no gnawing anxiety, no interfering relatives, nothing. Indeed Gregory Stefan had every reason to be satisfied with the way in which his life was going.

In spite of this he became schizophrenic. It did not need any diagnostic genius to see that his body was every bit as sick as his mind. He suffered from insomnia, lack of appetite, nausea, almost complete loss of sexual desire. He looked sick. He probably *smelt* sick. Schizophrenics secrete in their sweat a special substance, *trans-3-methyl-2-hexenoic acid,* which gives them a peculiar odor.

Like so many bewildered schizophrenics, Stefan went off to see a psychoanalyst on the assumption that these high-priced specialists know something about the psyche. He could hardly have made a more disastrous error. Hour after expensive hour was wasted in probing and discussing. Talk, talk, talk. And not even healing talk. The main preoccupation of Stefan's analyst was to find someone to *blame* for his patient's condition. As he could not find any way of blaming it on the parents, he put the blame on Stefan's wife. This is standard analytical procedure. As Humphrey Osmond put it, "It is dangerous these days to be the relative of a person who is mentally ill for you will probably be blamed for driving him mad."[75]

So, if there is one piece of advice that might be offered to the schizophrenic it is this—*Stay away from psychoanalysts.* Few things can be less likely to help a sick person who is being poisoned by some defect in his biochemical machinery than the endless probings and theorizings of these misguided meddlers. Of course the psychoanalysts should know better than to try to analyze schizophrenics. The great Freud himself declared that

analysis was ineffectual in such cases. But because the analyst
has invested much time and money in acquiring his particular
bag of tricks he is anxious to try them on anyone who will pay
the price. Actually psychoanalysis is of questionable value even
for the treatment of neurosis. For the treatment of psychosis it
is utterly useless.

So the unhappy Gregory Stefan was taken apart by one
analyst and his no less unhappy wife was torn apart by another.
And their marriage was torn apart in the process. Concerning
which Stefan has this to say:

> *Laurie is not a regular church-goer, but she later confided to
> me that, while I was disintegrating under Dr. Gression's treat-
> ment, she became convinced that we were both in the presence
> of the Devil. It is curious that our two psychoanalysts did
> precisely the opposite of what a good minister would have done.
> Where a minister would have tried to bring us together, the two
> analysts, working separately, were busy wrecking what was left
> of our marriage. At a time when I most needed the support of
> my wife, my parents, and my in-laws, the analysts were dividing
> us, undermining our faith in one another. A minister who under-
> stood the exhortation of St. James not to be "double-minded"
> would have tried to build on the great fund of love, good-will and
> intelligence within our families. He would have been a peace-
> maker, not a destroyer. It seems to me that no doctor has earned
> the right to make a mess of other people's lives simply because
> he has made a mess of his own.*[89]

Fortunately Stefan, after spending much time and large sums
of money in various high-priced private hospitals, finally met a
man who could tell him a few simple truths about schizophrenia,
namely that it is a biochemical disorder, that no one is to blame
for the disease, that the worst possible thing for the schizophrenic
is to engage in endless talk about the psychological origins of his
illness and that the only treatment of any value is one that will
correct the biochemical error responsible for the illness.

It is still not easy to define this treatment. Schizophrenia seems to be not one but several diseases, all of which have some features in common. One may safely assume that they all have a biochemical cause but one cannot assume that that cause is the same in all cases. The present state of our thinking about the illness can be summarized as follows.

(1). *The Genetic Factor.* It would be much easier to understand the cause of schizophrenia if one could prove that it is inherited according to the well-known Mendelian laws. All biochemical processes in the body are mediated by genes. If a gene for some necessary process is missing, the body will either die or function badly.

Is the tendency to schizophrenia inherited? Yes, but not in a way we can readily explain. It is not possible, on the basis of genetics, to predict when and where the illness will strike. About 10 percent of the children of schizophrenics will develop the illness but about 90 percent of adult schizophrenics do not have a schizophrenic parent. Manfred Bleuler, who has worthily followed the great tradition of his father, Eugene Bleuler, makes the following comments.

The conclusion of previous investigators that 8–10 percent of the children of schizophrenics are themselves doomed to schizophrenia is one that I, alas, cannot challenge. I do take issue, however, with their estimates that half to two-thirds of these children will be in some way abnormal. Based on my own findings and a critical evaluation of earlier studies, I believe that the prognosis for the mental well-being of the children of schizophrenics is much less pessimistic than has been thought in the past. It is certain that many more than half the children of my schizophrenic subjects have remained mentally sound, and possibly as many as three-quarters. Among those offspring who do manifest personality disorders, there are quite a number whose abnormal development has no connection with the schizophrenia of their parents, or at least none that can be scientifically proved.[96]

To the children of schizophrenics Manfred Bleuler has this to say:

These findings offer hope to the children of schizophrenics who, tortured by doubts, seek medical advice as to whether they should marry and have children, if they themselves have remained normal up to age twenty-five and beyond, and if for this reason the danger that they may become ill has diminished, the risk that their children will become schizophrenic is probably little or no greater than that of the general public.[6]

One cannot, apparently, say that there is a gene for schizophrenia as one can say there is a gene for hemophilia or phenylketonuria. Even children both of whose parents are schizophrenic do not, according to Manfred Bleuler, necessarily develop the disease. He had five such children in his study and none of them developed schizophrenia though one was diagnosed as a schizoid psychopath and another was extremely neurotic. Even long-term upbringing by two schizophrenic parents did not foredoom the child to become schizophrenic or even abnormal. Normal development, says Bleuler, can take place in the face of total neglect, copious "teaching of irrationality" and total degeneration of the imaginative world of the parents.

(2). *The Borgia in the Kitchen.* This theory suggests that the schizophrenic is the victim of a poison brewed within his own body. He has, as it were, a Borgia in his system and the workings of this hidden poisoner affect the functioning of both his mind and his emotions. So his whole awareness of the outside world becomes distorted. Sights which seem perfectly normal to the healthy individual become, for the schizophrenic, distorted, weird and terrifying. Sounds become endowed with strange significance. Perfectly harmless remarks are interpreted as threats. Every impression that reaches the schizophrenic is twisted into a sinister experience through the action of the poison.

There is much experimental evidence to support this theory that schizophrenia results from the workings of a poison produced in the body as the result of what is called an "error in metabolism." We know that such errors in metabolism do occur and that they can profoundly affect the mind. There is a condition known as "phenylpyruvic idiocy" caused by a hereditary defect as a result of which the body is unable to metabolize the amino acid, phenylalanine, whose toxic products cause permanent damage to the brain.

The defect in the schizophrenic is nothing so obvious and easily demonstrated as this. His poisoner works more subtly and the poison itself, whatever its identity, has varied effects, producing in some paranoia, in others catatonia, in some violent excitement, in others withdrawn immobility.

We do not, however, have any great difficulty in finding a poison that produces all these varied effects. Ever since Beringer performed his monumental study, *Der Meskalinrausch,* psychiatrists have realized that a close resemblance exists between mescaline intoxication and schizophrenia. Both Guttman and Stockings have enumerated the similarities of the two conditions. The following account is taken from the latter's paper:

Mescaline intoxication is indeed a true "schizophrenia" if we use the word in its literal sense of "split mind," for the characteristic effect of mescaline is a molecular fragmentation of the entire personality, exactly similar to that found in schizophrenic patients. . . . The change consists of a radical alteration of the mind and body. Thus the subject may feel that he is being several different persons at once. . . . More characteristic still is the feeling that he is divided into two separate beings—one a purely intellectual and emotionless creature, the other a fantastic being of delusion and fantasy, the first being able to observe the other in an extraordinary detached and unemotional fashion. . . . The feeling of unreality, both as regards the self and the external world, so often found in schizophrenics, is one of the typical features of the mescaline psychosis. One of the most common descriptions given to the writer by his subjects of their feelings was that of living in a world of one's own. "I am living in a private world" and "Other people cannot understand me because

I am living in a different world from them," were actual descriptions obtained in these experiments.

Precisely similar descriptions were obtained from recovered schizophrenic patients studied by the writer who were asked to give, as far as they were able, a description of their experiences during the period of their acute illness. In both cases, those of the schizophrenic and the mescaline subject, the impossibility of putting their feelings and experiences during the acute stage of the psychosis into ordinary language was a striking feature.

Even more remarkable are the self-descriptions of their mental experiences by schizophrenic patients under sodium amytal. As is well known, this drug, when administered intravenously, has the property of temporarily producing a lucid interval in a psychotic subject previously inaccessible and incoherent. Under this drug, the writer has obtained from schizophrenic patients accounts of their mental experiences which bear a remarkable resemblance to those of mescaline intoxication. For instance, the bizarre hallucinations of color and distorted appearance of external objects and of other persons have been described by patients given sodium amytal by the author. The resemblance to the mescaline psychosis is even closer in the case of the confusional states, especially as regards visual hallucinations.

A further feature of the personality changes must be mentioned before leaving this subject, namely, the symptom of transformation of the personality—that is, the belief that the patient has been changed into someone else. Thus the subject of the mescaline psychosis may believe that he has become transformed into some great personage, such as a god or a legendary character, or a being from another world. This is a well-known symptom found in states such as paraphrenia and paranoia. As found in the mescaline psychosis, it appears to be due partly to the abnormal bodily feelings referred to in the discussion of the delusions of grandeur. Another mechanism, observed by the writer as occurring in his own case, was a process of identification of the subject's self with the stupendous beings of the mescaline fantasies. This process, in which the subject *sometimes appears to lose the power of being able to distinguish between the self and the outside world, is strikingly reminiscent of the introjection processes of childhood.*[91]

According to Stockings, both paranoia and catatonia can be produced by mescaline. Concerning paranoia, he makes the following statements:

Taking first the delusions of persecution, we find that one of the characteristic actions of mescaline is that of sensitization of the auditory centres. Sounds appear to be either unnaturally loud, or distorted, and to have acquired strange qualities. They appear to the subject to rush upon him in an extraordinary purposive and deliberate way, and to have a reference for him which they would not have in the normal state. Thus, to quote actual examples, seen in the writer's experiments, the sound of a typewriter being used in the next room seemed to vibrate and reverberate through the walls and into the subject's body; thus, the typewriter became an infernal machine persecuting him with rays of electricity. In another case a group of people talking in the next room becomes a gang of enemies plotting against him or interfering with him. Similarly, the announcer's voice is sending messages over the wireless specially meant for him.

In the visual sphere, the strange distorted appearance of people's faces, their movements and conversation all seem to be directed against him, so that he feels as if he was being watched, spied upon or otherwise interfered with.

Similarly, the strange bodily paraesthesiae readily produce ideas of influence, electrical interference, or bodily changes produced by the machinations of other persons.[91]

The sinister changes which seem to take place in the faces of others would seem to be particularly disturbing.

The features appeared to become intensely vivid, and all the peculiarities of their physiognomy to be greatly exaggerated; at a later stage the faces appeared monstrously distorted, with huge eyes, enormous foreheads, and grim and menacing expressions.

This illusion often leads to ideas on the part of the subject that faces are being made at him, that others are mocking him, or that he is being hypnotized or influenced in similar ways. The writer has obtained descriptions of exactly similar experiences from schizophrenic patients under sodium amytal narcosis. This phenomenon is apparently the principal exciting cause of the impulsive attacks on others which frequently occur in these conditions.

[Stockings] was able to observe in himself the catatonic state, which is a most remarkable experience. The feeling is that of a delightful laziness and disinclination for active movement, resulting partly from extreme self-absorption and preoccupation with fantasy and indifference to the outer world, two characteristic symptoms of the intoxication. There is a peculiar inability to make up one's mind to a course of action. . . . Attitudes of religious ecstasy, similar to those found in some acute schizophrenic cases, may be assumed as a result of vivid hallucinations with a religious context. Suicidal impulses, secondary to the terrifying feelings of unreality experienced in the early stages of the intoxication, and homicidal impulses . . . are also found. . . . Negativism, with an attitude of hostility and stubbornness, and refusal of food with neglect of the ordinary bodily functions, were encountered in nearly all the subjects studied. The refusal of food and drink during the acute stage was partly due to the ideas that such food might be poisoned. . . . In subjects who had passed into the state of catatonic stupor, painful stimuli, such as pricking with a pin, were often completely disregarded, although pain was still felt.[91]

All the above descriptions make one thing clear. There is practically no aspect of schizophrenia that mescaline intoxication does not reproduce. As Aldous Huxley puts it, "The schizophrenic is like a man permanently under the influence of mescaline." It is logical therefore to ask oneself this question: May not the "metabolic error" which seems to occur within the body of the schizophrenic result in the production either of mescaline itself or of some substance having similar properties? Exactly this thought presented itself to two Canadian students of mental illness, Humphrey Osmond and John Smythies, who had the courage, rare in these prosaic days when anything in the nature of creative thinking is regarded with suspicion in scientific circles, to publish a purely speculative paper entitled, "Schizophrenia— A New Approach."[76] What made this paper significant was the fact that it drew attention to a chemical resemblance between mescaline and those potent hormones, adrenalin and nor-adrenalin, so intimately associated with the response to stress in man. One small failure in the body's chemistry could result in the production not of adrenalin but of an analogous but poisonous "M" substance having properties similar to those of mescaline. Stress is generally concerned in the production of schizophrenia and adrenalin production has an important bearing on the individual's reaction to stress. In the potential schizophrenic we may assume that, besides adrenalin, the "M" substance is produced. The effects to which it gives rise—the hallucinations, the feelings of unreality—naturally impose further stresses on the patient, who, caught up in a vicious circle, reacts to the situation with the production of more "M" substance and so becomes yet more hallucinated, catatonic and, in general, schizophrenic. The doors opening onto the real world close behind him and he becomes imprisoned in a world of unreality cut off from the healthy by a barrier through which neither he nor they can penetrate.

This theory of Osmond and Smythies formed the basis of a series of researches whose aim was to identify the "M" substance. In this quest they were joined by Abram Hoffer and at the end of a year's research these three workers published their findings. Their attention, logically enough, was directed to adrenalin and its possible breakdown products, nor did they need to seek for very long before clues were discovered as to the possible identity of the "M" factors. Several individuals who had been in the habit of taking adrenalin to control their asthma declared that they sometimes suffered from hallucinations after taking larger doses of this material. Most often these hallucinations took place when adrenalin was used which had begun to deteriorate, as a result of which process the normally colorless solution of adrenalin turns pink.

At our first meeting in Saskatoon with our colleagues in the research, Professors Hutcheon, MacArthur and Woodford, we raised the question of "pink adrenalin" and put forward a suggestion about its composition. Hutcheon pointed out that "pink adrenalin" certainly contained among other things adrenochrome. In the exciting ten minute discussion which followed after Hutcheon drew the spatial formula of adrenochrome, it was shown that this substance is related chemically to every halluci-nogen whose chemical composition has been determined.

It is evident that we had stumbled on a compound which has an indole nucleus in common with the hallucinogens, which is readily derived from adrenalin in the body and which can be fitted into a logical scheme relating to stress. Under stress the quantity of adrenalin in the body will increase and this might be turned into adrenochrome in the schizophrenic individual.[76]

The next step in this research was obvious enough. Adreno-chrome was prepared synthetically and the research workers, using themselves and their wives as guinea pigs, set out to determine just what effect the substance had on the mind and the emotions. The following account was given by Osmond of his own reactions to an intravenous injection of adrenochrome:

After the purple red liquid was injected into my right forearm I had a good deal of pain. I did not expect that we would get any results from a preliminary trial and so was not, as far as I can judge, in a state of heightened expectancy. The fact that my blood pressure did not rise suggests that I was not unduly tense. After about ten minutes, while I was lying on a couch looking up at the ceiling, I found that it had changed color. It seemed that the lighting had become brighter. I asked Abe and Neil if they had noticed anything but they had not. I looked across the room and it seemed to have changed in some not easily definable way. I wondered if I could have suggested these things to myself. I closed my eyes and a brightly colored pattern of dots appeared. The colors were not as brilliant as those which I have seen under mescal but were of the same type. The patterns of dots gradually resolved themselves into fishlike shapes. I felt that I was at the bottom of the sea or in an aquarium among a shoal of brilliant fishes. At one moment I concluded that I was a sea anemone in this pool. Abe and Neil kept pestering me to tell them what was happening, which annoyed me. They brought me a Van Gogh self-portrait to look at. I have never seen a picture so plastic and alive. Van Gogh gazed at me from the paper, crop headed, with hurt, mad eyes and seemed to be three dimensional. I felt that I could stroke the cloth of his coat and that he might turn around in his frame. Neil showed me the Rorschach cards. Their texture, their bas-relief appearance, and the strange and amusing shapes which I had never before seen in the cards were extraordinary.

My experiences in the laboratory were, on the whole, pleasant but when I left I found the corridors outside sinister and unfriendly. I wondered what the cracks in the floor meant and why there were so many of them. Once we got out of doors the hospital buildings, which I know well, seemed sharp and unfamiliar. As we drove through the streets the houses appeared to have some special meaning, but I couldn't tell what it was. In one window I saw a lamp burning and I was astonished by its grace and brilliance. I drew my friends' attention to it but they were unimpressed.

We reached Abe's home where I felt cut off from people but not unhappy. I knew that I should be discussing the experience with Abe and his wife but could not be bothered to do so. I felt no special interest in our experiment and had no satisfaction at our success, although I told myself that it was very important. Before I got to sleep I noticed that the colored visions returned when I shut my eyes. (Normally I have hypnagogic visions after several minutes in a darkened room when I am tired.) I slept well.

Next morning, although I had only slept a few hours, life seemed good. Colours were bright and my appetite keen. I was completely aware of the possibilities arising from the experiment. Colour had extra meaning for me. Voices, typewriting, any sound was very clear. With those whom I felt did not appreciate the importance of the new discovery I could have easily become irritable, but I was able to control myself.[76]

A second experience with adrenochrome brought more curious observations.

I saw only a few visual patterns with my eyes closed. I had the feeling that there was something wonderful waiting to be seen but somehow I couldn't see it. However, in the outside world everything seemed sharper and the Van Gogh was three dimensional. I began to feel that I was losing touch with everything. My sister telephoned and, although I am usually glad to hear her voice, I couldn't feel warmth or happiness. I watched a group of patients dancing and, although I enjoy watching dancing with the envious interest of one who is clumsy on his feet, I didn't have a flicker of feeling.

As we drove back to Abe's house a pedestrian walked across the road in front of us. I thought we might run him down, and watched with detached curiosity. I had no concern for the victim. We did not knock him down.

I began to wonder whether I was a person any more and to think that I might be a plant or a stone. As my feeling for these inanimate objects increased my feeling for and my interest in humans diminished. I felt indifferent towards humans and had to curb myself from making unpleasant personal remarks about them. I had no inclination to say more or less than I observed. If I was asked if I liked a picture I said what I felt and disregarded the owner's feeling.

I did not wish to talk and found it most comfortable to gaze at the floor or a lamp. Time seemed to be of no importance. I slept well that night and awoke feeling lively but although I had to attend a meeting that morning, I did not hurry myself.

Eventually I had to be more or less dragged out of the house by Abe. I had to get my car from a garage where it was being repaired. There was some trouble about finding it in the garage. When at last I was seated in the driver's seat I realized that I couldn't drive it through traffic, although quite able to do so usually. I did not, however, feel anxious or distressed by this but persuaded the garage proprietor to drive me to my destination. I would, I believe, have normally found this a humiliating situation. I did not feel humiliated.

I attended the scientific meeting, and during it I wrote this note: "Dear Abe, this damn stuff is still working. The odd thing is that stress brings it on, after about 15 minutes. I have this 'glass wall other side of the barrier' feeling. It is fluctuant, almost intangible, but I know it is there. It wasn't there three-quarters of an hour ago; the stress was the minor one of getting the car. I have a feeling that I don't know anyone here; absurd but unpleasant. Also some slight ideas of reference arising from my sensation of oddness. I have just begun to wonder if my hands are writing this, crazy of course."

I fluctuated for the rest of the day. While being driven home by my psychologist colleague, Mr. B. Stefaniuk, I discovered that I could not relate distance and time. I would see a vehicle far away on the long straight, prairie roads, but would be uncertain whether we might not be about to collide with it. We had coffee at a wayside halt and here I became disturbed by the covert glances of a sinister looking man. I could not be sure whether he was "really" doing this or not. I went out to look at two wrecked cars which had been brought in to a nearby garage. I became deeply preoccupied with them and the fate of their occupants. I could only tear myself away from them with an effort. I seemed in some way to be involved in them.

Later in the day when I reached home the telephone rang. I took no notice of it and allowed it to ring itself out. Normally, no matter how tired I am, I respond to it.

By the morning of 19.x.52 I felt that I was my usual self again.[76]

These studies on adrenochrome aroused much interest and several attempts were made to detect the substance in the blood or urine of schizophrenics. It is, however, a singularly difficult material to find and the adrenochrome theory remains a theory.

Other investigators searched for a mescaline-like substance which the body might make by mistake for a precursor of adrenalin. There occurs, formed in the brain from an amino acid called tyrosine, a substance called *dihydroxy-phenylalanine* (dopa). From this, by an error in methylation, it is possible to create a molecule very like mescaline called *dimethoxyphenyl-ethylamine* (DMPEA). When this substance was found in the urine of schizophrenics (by A. J. Friedhoff and E. van Winkle in 1962) there was much excitement among brain biochemists. Here, perhaps, was the home brewed poison that distorted the schizophrenic's view of the world.

The hunt was on. Acres of paper chromatograms were developed and the pink spot given by DMPEA was eagerly sought. But the elusive poison continued to elude. The pink spot, said some, was simply a product of the antischizophrenia drugs (phenothiazines) that had been given to the patients. In any case DMPEA was not a very active hallucinogen and could hardly be held responsible for the varied manifestations of the disease.

But the quest for the poison continued. It was too attractive a hypothesis to be abandoned. In 1970, Drs. Larry Stein and C. D. Wise of the Wyeth Laboratories in Philadelphia offered a new and more sophisticated approach to the poison problem.[90] They began by describing one of the chief features of schizophrenia, a feature often overlooked by those who see the schizophrenic chiefly as a person plagued by hallucinations. It is not the hallucinations that are mainly responsible for the schizophrenic's confusion. What he lacks is a game worth playing. There is a deficit in goal-directed behavior. There is also a deficit in *the capacity to experience pleasure.* And on what does the capacity to experience pleasure depend? It depends on a reward system located in the lower brain the working of which depends on a steady supply of noradrenalin.

In the schizophrenic this reward system is poisoned. This idea has been put forward by several students of the illness. Schizophrenics themselves echo this observation. "There is no joy in this disease."

What is the source of joy? Joy, and purposeful behavior associated with the attainment of joy, is dependent on the proper functioning of the pleasure center located in the lower brain stem whose working is dependent on the chemical transmitter, noradrenalin. In the schizophrenic the cells of the pleasure center are prevented from operating normally. According to Stein and Wise they are poisoned by a substance called *6-hydroxydopamine*.

Have Stein and Wise really found the poisoner? It is, perhaps, still too early to say. Their experiments were done with rats and the jump from rats to man should not be taken too lightly. What they found was that rats wired for pleasure no longer seemed able to get that pleasure when 6-hydroxydopamine was injected into their brains. They were less inclined to press the bar that gave them that mysterious joy. Furthermore the rats, when injected with this brain poison plus a substance that prevented the poison from being metabolized (a monamine oxidase inhibitor) showed waxy flexibility, characteristic of catatonic schizophrenia.

One final piece of evidence suggests that Stein and Wise are on the right track. Chlorpromazine ("Thorazine"), one of the group of antischizophrenic drugs called phenothiazines, reverses the effect of 6-hydroxydopamine. Rats whose brains had been wired for joy by bar pressing and whose joy had been poisoned by the toxic chemical, resumed their bar pressing at the normal rate after being dosed with chlorpromazine.

These studies are persuasive and well designed. The reader might be inclined to conclude that the mystery has been solved, the Borgia in the kitchen unmasked. At last we know the cause of this baffling disease. This conclusion would not be justified. Schizophrenia is almost certainly several disorders and the different disorders may have different causes. The following additional factors must be taken into account if we are to form a general picture of the chemistry of this disease.

Malvaria. This term was coined by Dr. A. Hoffer. He described as "malvarians" people who secrete in their urine a substance giving a mauve spot on chromatograms sprayed with Ehrlich's reagent. The mauve factor was shown to be *kryptopyrole.* Many schizophrenics, during the active phase of their illness, were found to excrete the mauve factor, and to stop excreting it when their condition improved. The significance of the mauve factor could be interpreted in four ways: (1). The factor produces the schizophrenic symptoms, (2). The factor is the *result* of the schizophrenic process rather than the cause, (3). It's a vicious circle, (4). Some unknown "third factor" produces both the mauve factor and the schizophrenic symptoms.

Taraxein. This word was used by Dr. R. G. Heath to describe a substance found in the blood of schizophrenics. Heath pointed out that the most consistent and, apparently, most significant feature of schizophrenia is an inability to meaningfully *integrate feelings of pleasure.*[36] Heath and his co-worker at first thought that stimulation of the pleasure center in the human brain would make schizophrenics happy and possibly sane. With a boldness unusual in neurosurgeons, they went so far as to implant electrodes in the brains of certain patients. These were fixed to remain accurately in position for periods up to two years. The experiment, however, was not an unqualified success. "Introduction of an electrical stimulus to the septal region resulted in alerting and the patients reported pronounced feelings of pleasure. Symptomatic improvement was immediate but, regrettably, not lasting in all the patients treated."

One thing the brain electrodes revealed. During acute episodes of schizophrenia there were storms in the septal region and hippocampus of the brain. These brain storms could be recorded by the electroencephalogram. Heath and his colleagues discovered that similar brain storms could be set off in the brains of monkeys injected with a substance prepared from the blood of schizophrenic patients. This substance Heath called *taraxein.*

It proved extremely difficult to purify taraxein. Heath and co-workers finally came to the conclusion that it was a protein, a globulin, and probably an antibody with a special affinity for the septal region of the brain. This would make it appear that at least *some forms* of schizophrenia belong to the group of auto-immune diseases. In these diseases, of which rheumatoid arthritis is an example, the patient develops an immune reaction to some of his own proteins, with swelling, pain and inflammation. In the case of schizophrenia the antibrain globulin is fixed in the septal region and produces the symptoms of the disease by altering the function of this part of the brain. Perhaps it does this by causing the cells to generate 6-hydroxydopamine. This has not yet been proved.

Orthomolecular Psychiatry. This term was introduced by Linus Pauling.[79] It is based on the idea that people may vary greatly in their ability to use certain vital substances, particularly vitamins. Because the brain is the most metabolically active organ of the body it is likely to be affected first by vitamin deficiency. There are several forms of mental illness which can be attributed directly to this cause. Before the discovery of niacin thousands of people were placed in mental hospitals because they suffered from pellagra. The malfunctioning of their minds as well as the sickness of their bodies was due entirely to a lack of this vitamin. As soon as the vitamin was discovered and administered to the patients their pellagra was cured and their psychosis also disappeared. For this they needed only 12 milligrams per day.

In 1952, Drs. Hoffer and Osmond began using large doses of nicotinic acid for treatment of schizophrenia. They prescribed as much as 3 to 18 grams a day. Nicotinic acid itself causes a flush and, for this reason, the closely related compound nicotinamide can be used instead. The substance is safe, cheap and easily administered. In some cases it may be combined with 3 grams a day of ascorbic acid.

This "megavitamin" treatment was further developed by Dr. D. Hawkins who recommended the following vitamin intake: nicotinamide 1 gram, ascorbic acid 1 gram, pyridoxine 50 milligrams, natural vitamin E 400 International Units. This combination was to be taken four times daily.[34]

Megavitamin treatment has not been found effective in all forms of schizophrenia. It is, however, always worth a trial as it is cheap and can do no harm. In some cases it can be combined with electroshock therapy. It has also been claimed that "relative hypoglycemia," may aggravate the schizophrenic state. Dr. R. L. Meiers states that high sugar intake and the excessive use of caffeine can result in a fall in blood sugar due to overproduction of insulin. Certain people, he suggests, may not be able to tolerate our very unnatural diet with its high intake of sugar and of caffeine. Such people may suffer from a host of symptoms, including depression, insomnia, irritability, anxiety, lack of concentration, crying spells, phobias, forgetfulness, confusion and suicidal thoughts. He suggests that those liable to schizophrenia limit their intake of sugar, caffeine, alcohol and nicotine.[66]

Mind-Healing Drugs

The need for mind-healing drugs has been felt by physicians since the days of Hippocrates. Botanical remedies, such as valerian and hellebore, were used for centuries. Later came the bromides, later still the barbiturates which are still with us. Then, in the 1950s a breakthrough occurred which led to the discovery of drugs that really produced results. As a result the treatment of the mentally ill has changed radically. Many mental hospitals have been closed. Locked wards have disappeared or are reserved for seriously disturbed patients and used only for short periods. Emphasis is on treating the mentally ill in the community instead of segregating them in huge institutions which more closely resemble prisons than hospitals. This is a great step forward.

Mental illness takes many forms. A *psychosis* draws a veil between its victim and the outer world, clouds the mind with hallucinations which make purposive action difficult or impossible. A *neurotic,* on the other hand, does not lose contact with reality. He can continue his work and deal with most of the situations that confront him. Nonetheless he is sick emotionally and mentally and his sickness colors his waking and possibly also his sleeping hours. Because of it he can never really enjoy his existence. His neurosis hovers over him like the mythological harpy and whatever choice morsel life offers him in the way of pleasure it swoops upon and carries off. It distorts his every feeling and colors his every impression, poisoning with suspicion, fear, guilt, apprehension, envy, or malice the very fountainhead of his existence. The psychiatrists spend much time delving into the subconscious of such a one to discover the old griefs, traumas, repressions, complexes which set this poison flowing. The chemist prefers to leave the complexes alone and to pin his faith on the dictum, "All is chemical." He believes that the sufferings of these hapless neurotics have a chemical basis, that there can be neither guilt, anxiety, depression, nor agitation without some sort of chemical unbalance within the body.

Where should we seek the basis for such unbalance? If we consider the mental and emotional life of man we see that it changes its tone from day to day and from hour to hour. Today he is elated, tomorrow depressed; in the morning an optimist, in the afternoon a pessimist; a lover after lunch, a misanthrope before it. And on what do these ceaseless variations of mood depend? They depend on an endless sequence of minor changes in the outpourings of those glands whose blended secretions make up the chords of man's inner symphony. From pituitary and adrenals, from thyroids and gonads flows the stuff of which man's feelings are created, partially regulated by processes in the brain which, like a conductor struggling through a difficult symphony, does not always produce a very distinguished performance. Neurosis and psychosis alike must be the result of a breakdown in glandular harmony: too much adrenalin here, too little thyroxine there, a shade too much testosterone or too little progesterone, a shortage of ACTH, an insufficiency of cortisone, too little serotonin or perhaps too much. Why should we enmesh ourselves in a tangle of complexes when the root of all evil lies in chemical disharmony? Let us take as our motto the dictum of R. W. Gerard: "There can be no twisted thought without a twisted molecule."[29]

So, from this standpoint, to use a slightly different analogy, we can depict the ever changing moods of man as a more or less continuous spectrum composed of many colors. From hour to hour man's ego, that which he feels to be himself, moves to and fro across this spectrum under the influence of inward and outward events. At one end of the spectrum lies the infrared of melancholia or depression. At the opposite end lies the ultraviolet of mania or extreme agitation. A normal, balanced man remains for the most part in the middle region of the spectrum and strays into the extreme regions only rarely. If he does enter those regions he can, without too much difficulty, remove himself from them. The dark or the frenzied mood passes. The needed chemical adjustments are carried out. Harmony is restored, the inward symphony trips along smoothly again, *allegro ma non troppo*.

In the mentally sick individual, however, this healthy chemical adjustment does not take place. Such a one may become permanently stuck at one end or the other of the psychological spectrum. If stuck at one end he is said to be suffering from depression or melancholia; if stuck at the other he is said to be suffering from agitation or mania. Quite commonly such a sick individual fluctuates between the two extremes in a condition known as a manic-depressive psychosis. Now like a god he strides on the clouds above Olympus, feeling himself to be capable of anything and everything; a few hours later, falling with a crash from the heights, he creeps through the glooms of the infernal regions, feeling lower than a worm. There is, in this case, an obvious effort on the part of the ruling chemical mechanism to correct the unbalance which has arisen among the lesser hormones. The correction, however, is always overdone, so that the mood of such an unfortunate swings from one extreme to the other and his personal symphony fluctuates between a frenzied *presto agitato* and an almost unendurably dreary *largo*.

We will consider first the tranquilizing agents. These fall into two groups, the major tranquilizers or antipsychotic agents and the minor tranquilizers or antianxiety agents. Man's need for such agents goes back beyond the dawn of history, for never has there been a time or a place in which he failed to find himself assailed by care. "Care," wrote Goethe in *Faust,* "soon makes her nest within the depths of the heart, secretly working, destroying joy and peace. Daily she hides behind a different mask. She comes as house and hearth, as wife and child, as fire or water, dagger or poison. You shrink from blows which do not fall, and weep for things you did not even lose."

There is nothing new in this. The story is as old as humanity.

From the beginning man has walked among real and imaginary enemies, anxiously casting glances over his shoulder. A quaint fallacy which has gained currency at the present time represents the modern age as specifically the "age of anxiety" and depicts contemporary man burdened to breaking point under "the stresses and strains of modern life." Those who adopt this point of view apparently visualize our ancestors living spacious, gracious, and leisurely existences into whose stately harmonies no troublesome discords ever intruded. In actual fact, with the exception of a few pampered aristocrats, our forebears faced life on terms which to us moderns would seem almost unendurable. Haunted by a thousand terrors that they could hardly define, in dread of a host of gods and goddesses, of omens, of goblins, of witches, of devils and of damnation, they lived in the midst of a forest of shadowy fears, all of which would seem laughable to the sophisticated modern. Their lives, far from being spacious or gracious, were threatened by plague and pestilence in countless forms, endangered by famine, burdened by heavy labor, shortened by every variety of deficiency disease from rickets and scurvy to beriberi and pellagra. Only quite recently, within the last fifty years, have these sources of anxiety and misery been more or less banished from the lives of one small section of mankind, by the devices of Western science. But Western man, despite the fact that he is better protected, clothed, fed, enjoys better health and a longer average life than man has ever known in the million years of his existence, shows little gratitude for the good gifts showered upon him by the scientist but peevishly grumbles about the "age of anxiety" as if he had more cares on his shoulders than all his ancestors put together.

There is, however, an explanation for this paradox. Western man, being so much healthier than were his forebears, can afford to give more attention to those vague ills of mind and emotions which his ancestors, plagued by harsher pains and sorrows, passed over unnoticed. Nor can one deny that, along with countless benefits it has conferred, the machine age has imposed peculiar stresses. To be hoisted, in a period of less than fifty years, from the seat of the horse and buggy to that of the automobile and jet plane is an experience sufficient to unsettle even man's sturdy psyche. In the inner as well as the outer world of man there have been upheavals. Old faiths have crumbled, new ones have not been created, and in the resulting vacuum man wanders, lost. Tied to the hands of the clock, a servant of steel machines whose laws are inflexible, goaded by ambitions and aspirations, scrambling for gain in a crowded, jostling world, harassed by the ever pressing need to keep up with the Joneses, the modern man can hardly be blamed if he counts his ulcers instead of his blessings and cries out to his physician for relief from his inner tensions, for something to give him tranquillity and peace of mind.

The physician, if he happened to have read St. Thomas à Kempis, might reply with a quotation from the *Imitation of Christ:* "Peace is what all men desire, but all do not care for the things which pertain to true peace." He might point out that the true aim of both philosophy and religion is to give man an inward peace which the storms of life cannot ruffle. But since patients expect pills from physicians rather than sermons, and since the doctor is in any case far too busy to philosophize, he will probably make a note of his patient's blood pressure, scribble some hieroglyphics on a prescription form, and assure his visitor that, with this new tranquilizing drug in his system, he will gain all the consolations of religion and philosophy without suffering the inconvenience of having to practice self-discipline.

The first of the major tranquilizers to be discovered was prepared from a very ancient botanical drug. It had been used for at least twenty-five hundred years in India by practitioners of a system of medicine known as the Ayur-Veda. This drug, known in India by the name *sarpaganda,* is the powdered root of a small bush belonging to the family Apocynaceae, the Latin name of which is *Rauwolfia serpentina.* In English the plant is commonly referred to as snake root, a practice inviting errors, for this name is also applied to several entirely different drug plants (e.g., *Eryngium aquaticum, Asarum canadensis, Polygala senega*). Confusion can be avoided if one simply refers to the plant as rauwolfia, a name bestowed upon it by Plumier in honor of Dr. Leonhard Rauwolf, a sixteenth-century German physician who had traveled widely in India collecting medicinal plants.

Rauwolfia was endowed with so many virtues by the Ayur-Vedic physicians that it appears to have been regarded as a universal panacea. It was prescribed as a cure for insanity, insomnia, cholera, dysentery, blindness, fever, stomach ulcers, and snakebite. It was chewed by holy men to assist them in their meditations (the late Mahatma Gandhi used it extensively); it was given by mothers to soothe their crying babies. Indian physicians who had had contact with Western science also found virtue in the plant. Drs. Gananth Sen and Kartick Chandra Bose described it as a "drug of rare merit" in treating nervous disorders; Dr. Rustom Jal Vakil extolled it as a safe means of lowering high blood pressure; Sir Ram Nath Chopra did consid-erable work on the chemical composition of the active extracts. To natives on the opposite side of the world, in the tropical forests of Colombia and Guatemala, the virtues of rauwolfia were also known, the drug being used as an antimalarial and for treatment of snakebite. In Guatemala it was called *chalchupa,* in Colombia *piñique-piñique.* In fact the only people who seemed unaware of the virtues of rauwolfia were the great omniscient scientists of the West.

It is curious indeed that a remedy so ancient and one on which so much excellent research had been carried out by several Indian scientists should have been ignored by Western researchers until the year 1947. This situation resulted, in part at least, from the rather contemptuous attitude which certain chemists and pharmacologists in the West have developed toward both folk remedies and drugs of plant origin, regarding native medicines as the by-products of various old wives' tales and forgetting that we owe some of our most valued drugs (digitalis, ephedrine and quinine, to name only a few) to just such "old wives' tales." They further fell into the error of supposing, because they had learned the trick of synthesizing certain substances, that they were better chemists than Mother Nature, who, besides creating compounds too numerous to mention, also synthesized the aforesaid chemists and pharmacologists. Needless to say, the more enlightened members of these professions avoided so crude an error, realizing that the humblest bacterium can synthesize, in the course of its brief existence, more organic compounds than can all the world's chemists combined. But even those who were well disposed toward native remedies and regarded with proper respect the chemical potentialities of the plant kingdom were inclined to be skeptical about rauwolfia. Ayur-Vedic practitioners had claimed so many virtues for this drug that they made it sound slightly ridiculous in Western ears, like the famous drug plant *ginseng,* so esteemed by the Chinese, which has never proved capable of curing anyone of anything.

That the secret of rauwolfia's potent action was finally brought to light was due to the curiosity of an eminent biochemist, Sir Robert Robinson, and the enterprise of Dr. Emil Schlittler of the Swiss pharmaceutical firm of Ciba, at Basel. Sir Robert was interested in an alkaloid of rauwolfia called adjmaline and persuaded Dr. Schlittler to prepare this substance from the ground roots of *Rauwolfia serpentina.* After the adjmaline had been crystallized there remained large amounts of muddy, unattractive residue which Schlittler, with that thrift which is the hallmark of every good chemist, refused to discard until he had further explored its makeup. His exploration of this muddy resinous residue proved profitable beyond his wildest dreams, for the pharmacologists to whom he sent this material discovered, on testing it in animals, indications of that curious tranquilizing effect for which the drug has now become justly famous. Spurred on by this report, Dr. Schlittler set out to isolate the chemical substance responsible for this activity.

In a problem of this kind, success is dependent always upon the harmonious cooperation of two different kinds of experts: the chemist whose task it is to purify the desired material, and the biologist or pharmacologist whose function is to determine its effect in the animal. These two are chained together in the way criminals used to be in the bad old days and neither can move a step without the other. Lack of cooperation between these two may bring to nothing the most important lines of research, as happened in the case of penicillin, which remained unpurified and unavailable to the medical profession for eleven years after its presence was first discovered. In the case of reserpine, however, the chemical labors of Dr. Schlittler and his young colleague Johannes Muller were backed up by the work of an imaginative and cooperative pharmacologist, Dr. Hugo Bein. Their combined attack on the problem was crowned with success.

In September of 1952, just five years after Sir Robert Robinson had presented his request for some adjmaline, the three Ciba scientists, Schlittler, Muller and Bein, finally published an account of their labors. The few grams of shining white crystals they had obtained from the muddy resinous extract of rauwolfia represented the fruit of a prodigious amount of work. Every crystal was equivalent in activity to more than ten thousand times its weight in the crude drug. "We have long intended," wrote Schlittler and his colleagues, "to isolate the sedative substance of crude Rauwolfia extracts. This hypnotic principle had been examined earlier by Indian authors, but they did not get any further than the crude 'oleoresin fractions.' Starting from these fractions, we have now been able to isolate the carrier of the sedative effect in pure crystalline form." To this crystalline substance they gave the name reserpine.

A few months later Dr. Bein published a second report which revealed that reserpine, besides producing sedation, also lowered the blood pressure slowly and safely, taking a fairly long period to attain its maximum effect. As high blood pressure is a particularly common ailment in America it is not surprising to find that one enterprising American physician, Dr. Robert W. Wilkins of Boston University, had already given the crude Indian drug a trial. Pure reserpine was not available to him. It had not at that time been isolated. Instead he used tablets of the crude drug imported from India with which he treated more than fifty patients suffering from high blood pressure.

By 1952, Wilkins and his colleagues were able to report progress:

We have confirmed the clinical reports from India on the mildly hypotensive [blood-pressure lowering] effect of this drug. It has a type of sedative action that we have not observed before. Unlike barbiturates or other standard sedatives, it does not produce grogginess, stupor or lack of coordination. The patients appear to be relaxed, quiet and tranquil.[102]

One of the doctors at a later scientific meeting supplied this statement: "It makes them feel as if they simply don't have a worry in the world."

It was this observation, that the drug not only lowered blood pressure but also relaxed the tensions and anxieties by which high blood pressure is often accompanied, that aroused the interest of psychiatrists. Here, they reflected, might be the drug for which they had so long been seeking. Until the discovery of rauwolfia no drug available to psychiatrists would really tranquilize the agitated, anxious, restless patients who so often came to them seeking help. The bromides were short-acting and apt to be toxic. The barbiturates made the patients too sleepy to carry on with their work; chloral and paraldehyde suffered from the same drawbacks. Valerian, an ancient botanical remedy long esteemed as a specific for the treatment of hysteria, could not be relied upon to exert any effect at all. Thus, although Freud himself stated that "behind every psychoanalyst stands the man with the syringe," thereby showing that he foresaw the era of chemopsychiatry, the psychiatrist still had no drug with which to fill his syringe until crystalline reserpine, with its extraordinary capacity to soothe without stupefying, was made available to the profession by the labors of Schlittler and his colleagues.

As soon as the drug did become available a flood of scientific publications poured from the presses; indeed so great was the interest that for a time one rarely opened a medical journal without finding within it at least one article on rauwolfia. Information about the effects of the drug was rapidly accumulated and summarized in several excellent symposia, two sponsored by the New York Academy of Science, and one organized by the American Association for the Advancement of Science and published under the title *Psychopharmacology*. The following accounts are drawn mainly from these sources.

Reserpine is an extraordinary drug in more ways than one and its mode of action is hard to understand. It acts slowly and takes several weeks to exert its full effects, and these effects when they come follow a definite pattern. Dr. Nathan S. Kline, who has used reserpine extensively on mental patients in Rockland State Hospital, New York, summarizes his findings as follows: When reserpine is given by mouth, very little response is noted for several days. This suggests that the drug is transformed in some way in the body and that the substance which really produces the effect may not be reserpine itself but some product of reserpine. When the effects do begin to be seen they follow a very definite sequence. First comes the *sedative phase*. Patients behave more normally. They become less excited, assaultive, and agitated, appetite improves, and they begin to gain weight. Then, at the end of the first week, the patient enters the *turbulent phase*. During this phase the mental state seems suddenly to worsen. Delusions and hallucinations increase. Patients complain of a sense of strangeness; they do not feel like themselves, do not know what they are going to do next, have no control over their impulses. A physician who does not expect such manifestations may be alarmed at these symptoms and discontinue the use of the drug. Medication, however, should not be reduced until the patient has been able to get "over the hump." The *turbulent phase* may last for two or three weeks or may pass in a few hours. In some patients it was not observed at all. Finally, if all goes well, the patient enters the *integrative phase,* becomes quieter, more cooperative, friendly, and more interested in his environment. Delusions and hallucinations become less marked. This is followed by recognition on the patient's part that he has actually been ill.[51]

Dr. Kline noted that healthy urges are often freed by the

drug and that many patients for the first time in years enjoy such simple pleasures as eating, physical contact with others, and physical activity in other forms. There was a tendency toward an increase in expressive movements; several patients turned to playing the piano, which they had not done for many years. Success of the treatment seemed to depend on the patient's capacity to reorganize his inner life. Reserpine provided the conditions for this reorganization but could not provide the ability to reorganize if it was not there.

The same sort of release took place in neurotics. Liberation of these pent-up forces at times took rather embarrassing forms. A neurotic young attorney, who usually absorbed whatever his wife or anyone else handed out to him, became outgoing enough, on being treated with reserpine, to throw a dish of tomatoes at his wife when she provoked him. On the whole, however, the response of the neurotics was less extreme. Such people obtained from the drug a capacity to view their difficulties more objectively. They gained perspective and saw their troubles as if from a distance. "I no longer 'bleed' if I don't get everything done," said one of Dr. Kline's patients, a chronic worrier, "I do what I can and that's that." "It's not that I don't worry," said another. "I do that as much as before—but I don't worry about my worries." This man, an alcoholic, had been consuming about a pint of liquor a day and had found, once he started drinking, that it was beyond his power to stop. This problem also vanished under the magical influence of reserpine. He found himself under no compulsion even to complete one drink and observed, "It's peculiar. Now that I find I can drink, I don't care whether I do or not."

The statistics offered by Dr. Kline are impressive. In a series of 150 chronically disturbed psychotics who had failed to improve when treated with electroshock or insulin, 84 percent showed improvement with reserpine, and 21 percent of these patients maintained their improvement after medication had been discontinued. Electroconvulsion treatment was largely abandoned. Dr. L. E. Hollister and his colleagues reported from California that reserpine produced significant improvement in 98 out of 127 chronic schizophrenics. Drs. Tasher and Chermak (Illinois) reported excellent results in 221 chronically ill schizophrenics. The drug has been used with success in the treatment of emotionally disturbed children, in the treatment of skin diseases in which nervous factors were involved, in headache of the tension and migraine type. Its value in the treatment of withdrawal symptoms in narcotics has been mentioned elsewhere.

But time, which so often dampens initial enthusiasms, has not been kind to reserpine. The chorus of praise which greeted its discovery has become fainter and fainter and its critics have grown increasingly vocal. The trouble is that its tranquilizing action goes too far. It can produce a depression almost as serious as the agitated state it was meant to cure. It also lowers blood pressure and has other undesirable side effects. It is now rarely used in the treatment of mental illness.

The second of the new ataraxics has a history entirely different from that of reserpine. Here there was no romantic background of ancient folk medicine. The remedy originated in the chemical laboratory and its full title, *3-dimethyl-amino-propyl-2-chlorphenothiazine hydrochloride,* is awe-inspiring to anyone but a chemist. The Rhone-Poulenc Specia Laboratories in France, which developed this valuable drug, gave it the name *chlorpromazine,* by which it is now generally described. To ensure the greatest possible confusion, however, various trade names were also given to this substance. In the United States it is met with as "Thorazine," in Britain and Canada it goes under the name of "Largactil." It has also been called "R.P. 4560" and "Megaphen."

Chlorpromazine, like reserpine, rose to fame with rocketlike velocity. In 1953 it was almost unheard of, in 1955 it was known to every physician in the country and reports on its use were eagerly studied, especially by those responsible for the care of the mentally sick. Dr. Douglas Goldman of Cincinnati published one of the first reports on large-scale use of this medicament in a mental hospital. So encouraging were the effects that, in the words of his colleague Dr. Fabing, he took a new lease on life.

The reduction in assaults, the lessened use of restraint, the increased granting of privileges to locked ward patients, the lessened need for repeated electroshock treatment to control explosive behavior, and the beginnings of an improved discharge rate of patients from the hospital all stem from the use of this drug in his hands and parallel the kind of improved state of affairs which Kline reports with reserpine at Rockland.

Goldman likes to tell the story about Willie. Willie was a dishevelled, mute, untidy schizophrenic who had to be spoon fed and who managed to tear off just about all the clothes anyone tried to put on him. Willie received an eight weeks' trial with chlorpromazine but at the end of that time Goldman was not greatly impressed with his improvement. He announced that he was going to withdraw Willie's drug, whereupon an orderly raised a clamor, pleading for its continuance, insisting that Willie was much better. He said, "Wait a minute. I'll prove it to you. I'll get Johnny." In a moment he returned with Willie's identical twin. "See, they were both alike two months ago," he said. They stood side by side. Johnny's hair fell in his face, he was soiled, his pants were torn, and he was barefoot. Willie was fully clothed, barbered, shaved, clean and wore shoes. The difference was obvious. Instead of taking a patient off chlorpromazine he put another on.[23]

This feeling of enthusiasm, suitably qualified by those cautious asides which any clinician working with a new drug is bound to use, pervades Dr. Goldman's report in the *Journal of the American Medical Association:*

The initial observations justify a sense of optimism that has rarely resulted from the trial of new techniques in the treatment of psychotic states. . . . In patients who show a great deal of initial excitement . . . the medicament is practically specific. . . . Patients cease to be loud and profane and . . . can sit still long enough to eat and take care of normal physiological needs. . . . In states of excitement associated with the prolonged use of alcohol, the drug is practically specifically effective. Hallucinatory states subside within less than 24 hours. . . . In the more chronic psychotic states, the effect of the drug is much less immediately dramatic, but, for those experienced with the relief of psychotic symptoms from other measures, the use of the drug produces results that are equally gratifying when compared with results in the more acute situations. . . . After a period of one to six weeks, various psychotic components gradually resolve. Hallucinations are almost specifically relieved in many patients relatively early in the treatment. . . . Severe paranoid ideation subsides more gradually. An interesting instance of this is the patient who had many ideas of passivity and control in various ways by the communists; even her bowel function was under their control. After 5½ weeks of administration of the drug and after 2 weeks of administration of 200 mg every eight hours, she announced one morning to the nurse in charge that everything was different, that she was now herself again. On careful interview it was found that all of the paranoid ideas had been resolved and the patient had become cooperative, mild and even ingratiating.[30]

Goldman also pointed out that chlorpromazine, when used with barbiturates, so greatly enhanced the effectiveness of these drugs that excited patients could be sedated with doses of a barbiturate which would barely have produced somnolence if given by itself.

In the same issue of the *Journal* Dr. Robert Gatskie reported enthusiastically on the value of chlorpromazine in the treatment of emotionally maladjusted children. Such children, rejected by their parents on account of their aggressive, violent and destructive behavior, were housed in a cottage-type treatment center, 150 of all ages ranging from four to sixteen years. Nine of these children were treated with chlorpromazine and within a week all showed improved behavior. They became calm, cooperative, and more communicative. Their social behavior improved and they became more amenable to cottage supervision. Last but not least, they established rapport with the therapist.

No unusual side effects were noted, and no complications were encountered in this series of cases; however, further study

*and observation with larger groups of children seem to be
indicated, as chlorpromazine is a valuable drug and has a definite
place in the treatment of emotionally maladjusted children.*[30]

On occasion chlorpromazine exerts an influence that may
quite justifiably be called miraculous. An example is given by
Dr. L. H. Margolis and co-workers in their paper "Psychopharmacology." The patient on whom the drug was tried was the
despair of psychotherapists, a thirty-four-year-old paranoid
schizophrenic who had been treated with insulin coma and
electroconvulsions, despite which his condition had remained
unchanged. His brain was filled with delusions of grandeur and
of persecution and his whole life was spent amid a collection of
systematized delusions. As neither insulin nor electroconvulsion
had helped him lobotomy was recommended but his wife refused
to consent to the operation. Finally in August 1954 chlorpromazine was recommended "as a desperation measure in a hopeless
case." If it failed, lobotomy and/or return to the state hospital
were planned.

Soon after treatment with chlorpromazine was started the
night staff began to report a subtle change in the patient's attitude. On the fiftieth day of treatment he began to emerge from
his world of delusions. By the fifty-seventh day he ceased to show
any evidence of mental derangement. He developed an interest
in the world of reality, broadened his interests and soon began to
lay plans for his future. For the first time since he had been
committed to the state hospital he was allowed to go home, where
his wife was so impressed by his improvement that she began at
once to make plans for his discharge and return to normal life.
This patient was fortunate indeed. Only by his wife's refusal of
her consent was he saved from a mutilating operation which,
while it might have freed him from some of his delusions, would
have left him with an irreparably injured brain. Chlorpromazine
accomplished all that might have been done by the surgeon's
knife *without* doing any damage to those precious lobes on the
integrity of which the highest aspects of the personality depend.

Some workers have referred to the action of chlorpromazine as "chemical lobotomy." It produces some of the good effects of the operation without the mutilation.

Dr. V. Kinross-Wright states that it is often desirable to maintain patients on the drug for longer periods than were first thought necessary. Quite a number of elderly patients who responded well relapsed when the drug was withdrawn within a six months' period. It seems that, in some cases, patients may have to be kept on this drug almost indefinitely. One patient, a thirty-five-year-old paranoid schizophrenic, was maintained on chlorpromazine for over a year and every attempt to drop the dosage was attended with relapse.

She responds almost as a diabetic would to lack of insulin, and as soon as she is reinstated on chlorpromazine, her symptoms disappear quite rapidly. While she is on it she is completely symptom free. She works, she does housework, looks after her family, and enjoys life. If the dosage is omitted, as has happened several times when she ran out of medicine, or once or twice when she went out of town and miscalculated her supply, signs of relapse have immediately appeared.

Another new member of the ataraxic group is *azacyclonal,* a synthetic substance manufactured by the Wm. S. Merrell Co. of Cincinnati under the name of "Frenquel." Dr. Fabing has shown this drug to be capable of blocking the development of those "experimental psychoses" which are produced by mescaline and LSD-25. An account of one of these reactions to LSD and of its resolution by "Frenquel" runs as follows:

Complete and insoluble confusion and anxiety reigned, and the knowledge that its cause was a drug was my sole and small reassurance. This time I crawled onto the bed early, and planned to stay there beforehand. I was not nearly so eager to relate my experience or to cooperate with the experimenters—I was just going to wait it out this time.

One hallucination was that of lying flat on a slowly revolving cloud-like object. There were other similar objects all around, touching gently and revolving "in gear." I just rolled slowly down into the depths of the arrangement. Another one I recall is that of a flowerbed type of pattern, or perhaps a purposeless pin-ball machine, with the lights arranged in rows and columns. The lights —or flowers—were growing, then bursting, in irregular fashion, one at the left, then the center, and so on.

Next occurred the phenomenon that has happened both times I "lost," and perhaps I have neglected to mention it previously. Things seemed to clear up and I felt sane, yet knew I wasn't. I seemed to wake up to a new world—the same situation, same people and environment—yet everything, that is, my mental state, my life, had been altered. I was a stranger in this world. I could no longer speak to anyone as a person. And that was my state when I was given the shot, bewildered, confused, afraid to say a word till I could be sure of what was happening, in which world I was.

I realize that what happened to me in those few minutes after the injection has a tremendous significance. Because of this realization, I have worked it over often since then. But God help me, I can't tell you a thing. It just happened. There was no crescendo, no fitting together of the pieces, no breaking through the surface. All of a sudden I found myself willing to cooperate, able to follow the conversation more easily, just less anxiety-ridden. I don't know how or why. I'm sorry, but that's all I can report. . . . But I was having none of the second injection, since it was a trick. Then the doctor's reassuring voice, and after I pondered awhile, agreed to take it. And again, nothing to report. I just realized I was back again in the real world, and began trying to describe my sensations.[22]

Several other similar cases are described in Dr. Fabing's paper. Even the multicolored bugs, which one victim of *delirium tremens* saw crawling on the ceiling, yielded to the gentle influence of "Frenquel" and politely withdrew fifteen minutes after the patient had received an injection of the drug. It seems, however, to be curiously inconsistent in its action and has been described by Fabing as an "exasperating in-and-outer." It seems valuable in those cases where confusion or hallucination is the result of the action of some poison, and is useful for the treatment of senile patients who often go through troublesome confusional states.

Several additional antipsychotic agents have been discovered since the first edition of this book was published. *Thioridazine* ("Mellaril") which resembles chlorpromazine, is now rather widely used in the treatment of certain forms of schizophrenia. There are, in addition, about fifteen other antipsychotics of varying potency and toxicity. In fact the physician who previously had no weapons against schizophrenia is now faced with an embarrassment of riches and may have a hard time deciding which drug to use. Patients vary enormously in their response to these drugs, may respond well to one badly to another, proving again the correctness of the Hippocratic aphorism: *One man's meat is another man's poison.* The modern treatment of schizophrenia relies on intensive drug treatment to control the more destructive and dangerous aspects of the illness. This phase of treatment is best administered in a mental hospital. As soon as the patient is well enough he is returned to ordinary life with a supply of pills sufficient to keep the schizophrenic process under control. Periodic visits to the mental health clinic enable the physician to adjust the maintenance dose of the drug in such a way that remissions are avoided.

People liable to attacks of schizophrenia should always, as far as possible, avoid stressful situations. Stress upsets the vital balance. Even well-balanced people can become temporarily deranged in situations more stressful than they can handle. The ideal treatment for the schizophrenic is a quiet life plus maintenance doses of antipsychotic drugs. Schizophrenics who resent being dependent on drugs should reflect that they are much more valuable as functioning members of society, though drug dependent, than they would be as mentally sick dropouts, a nuisance to others and a curse to themselves.

Needless to say every responsible physician will try to wean his patients from antipsychotic drugs. As Hollister says, all antipsychotics are potent and sometimes toxic drugs. Dosage can be gradually reduced. The minimal dose at which the patient will function can be discovered. "Drug holidays" can be tried, provided a close watch is kept over the patient for any return of symptoms. Such holidays, however, must be offered with caution. To quote Hollister again: "lapses in maintenance therapy with antipsychotic drugs are presently the most frequent cause of readmission to a mental hospital following discharge."[46] Some schizophrenics, in order to lead normal and useful lives, will have to take antipsychotic drugs daily. It is a small price to pay for freedom from the ravages of this illness.

Next we will consider the minor tranquilizers or antianxiety agents. A mild level of anxiety may be a normal element of the human condition. Total absence of anxiety might be equivalent to total inertia. But Western man, especially in the United States, is hardly in danger of lapsing into inactivity because all anxiety has been removed. His tendency is to be overactive, overstimulated and overanxious. At a certain point the level of anxiety becomes such that it seriously interferes with the vital balance. It produces a variety of physical symptoms, excessive muscular tension, fatigue, palpitations, headache, insomnia, indigestion, peptic ulcer, irritable colon, eczema and skin eruptions.

This level of anxiety is most emphatically not helpful or healthy. It is the exact opposite of that balanced and calm condition that the Greeks called *ataraxia*. It can ruin a person's life, make him a curse to himself and others, irritable, fault-finding, ill-tempered, inefficient. The anxious person is often quite unable to explain why he is anxious. He suffers from a condition called "free-floating" anxiety. He feels threatened by something, he feels that something bad is about to happen; he is worried, even though there is nothing to worry about. All animals, including man, have a "fight or flight" mechanism which is deeply embedded in the instinctive part of the brain and vitally important for survival. Primitive man depended absolutely on this mechanism. He had to know when to run and when to stand and fight and his adrenals and the other glands of his body were tuned to give him the needed energies to cope with such emergencies. Modern man, protected by his civilization from the physical challenges that threaten the primitive, is very rarely called upon either to fight or to flee. But the habits developed over thousands of years of evolution persist.

Anxiety results from something pressing the flight button, something quite unrelated to external danger, a purely inner stimulus. So the person feels threatened, but does not know by what. He vaguely wants to flee. But where? From what? Such chronic readiness to flee or to fight when neither of these reactions is called for makes life very unbalanced and unrewarding. It is an inappropriate use of a bodily mechanism that, under other circumstances, is useful and necessary.

Many sufferers from chronic anxiety treat themselves with the oldest antianxiety drug known to man. They take to alcohol. Certain kinds of anxiety, especially those caused by the tyranny of the superego, are indeed lessened by a drink or two. But the limitations of alcohol, already described at length in an earlier chapter, make it a very poor antianxiety agent. The side effects it produces are worse than the disease.

Are there any good antianxiety agents? This question is very difficult to answer. It is not easy to measure anxiety. Furthermore, experiments have shown that anxious patients respond favorably to any attention. They are often highly suggestible. You can give them a glass of pink water flavored with spearmint and tell them it is a potent antianxiety drug and presto!—their anxiety is eased. This is called a placebo effect (from the latin *I will please*). It is the bane of all those whose task it is to evaluate drug action. Because anxiety is so subjective the placebo effect tends to be particularly confusing.

Of the various drugs now available for treating anxiety the safest and probably the most effective belong to a group called *benzodiazepins*. The best known of these is *chlordiazepoxide* which is sold under the trade name of "Librium." Librium attained fame by calming and pacifying various savage beasts to which it was given. Although savagery in the beast and anxiety in the human are not quite the same thing they do have a good deal in common. The drug which calms the savage beast also tends to soothe the anxious human.

Meprobamate ("Miltown") which became very fashionable as an antianxiety drug in the fifties is rated by some authorities (specifically Hollister) as having more undesirable side effects than compounds of the "Librium" type. It is more apt to produce a state of physical dependence than is "Librium" and is more toxic. Phenobarbital, which also has some value as an antianxiety drug, is less effective than either "Miltown" or "Librium."

All the symptoms of anxiety can be produced by overactivity of the thyroid gland. As this condition (*thyrotoxicosis*) calls for an entirely different type of treatment it is important to distinguish it from the kind of anxiety described above. Sufferers from this complaint live always beyond their emotional means. Constantly overactive, always on edge, with nerves which seem strained to the breaking point, flaring at the least provocation into outbursts of violent rage, these people are indeed a trial both to themselves and to others. In them the damper which controls the rate of burning of their inner fire is always fully open. They blaze inwardly at a fierce, unregulated pace, literally burning themselves up both emotionally and physically.

This troublesome condition results from an overproduction by the thyroid gland of a very vital hormone, thyroxine, which is manufactured by this gland from iodine and tryptophane and stored in the form of thyroglobulin. This thyroxine is intimately concerned with the rate at which our whole metabolism operates, and normal intellectual function is impossible without it. Thus children born with inadequately developed thyroids will develop into cretins unless the deficiency is made good by injections of the missing hormone. The amount of thyroxine liberated into the blood from moment to moment is regulated by that master hormone factory, the pituitary, which imposes its will on the thyroid by means of yet another hormone, the "thyroid-stimulating hormone," TSH for short. In the normal individual the output of thyroxine fluctuates and his vitality and intellectual activity fluctuate with it. At moments of low thyroxine output he feels somewhat soggy, dull, and vacant but, as the level becomes still lower, one of those typical feed-back mechanisms so vital in the regulation of body and mind comes into play, stimulating the pituitary to produce more TSH, which in turn stimulates the thyroid to produce more thyroxine, whereat the dull eye brightens, the flaccid facial muscles regain their tone, and the fog in the brain disperses.

In the individual suffering from thyrotoxicosis, this feedback mechanism does not operate properly. The cause of the trouble seems not to lie in the thyroid itself or even, necessarily, in the pituitary, but rather in the hypothalamus, that vital center in the brain so intimately bound up with our emotional manifestations. Emotional stress very often seems to be involved in the production of thyrotoxicosis but, once established, it seems to supply its own emotional stresses, perpetuating itself by a kind of vicious circle. It seems, in fact, that in some susceptible individuals any extreme emotional stress—an unwelcome pregnancy, the death of a close relative, a robbery, a fire, a frightening sexual experience—can bring on this disease. Once the disease has started, it carries on as the result of a vicious circle, for the excessive production of thyroxine in itself produces a state of emotional turmoil which stimulates further production of the hormone.

A cure for this condition can be brought about by surgical removal of part or all of the thyroid gland, or its destruction by radioactive iodine. Neither procedure is ideal, for it may practically quench the fire of life so that the formerly frenzied thyrotoxic becomes apathetic to the point of being half dead. Drugs that prevent the formation of the thyroid hormone have now been discovered and are widely used in the treatment of this disease. *Methimazole* ("Trapazole") is perhaps the most widely used of these compounds. *Methylthouracil* and *propylthiouracil* are also employed. The drugs tend to produce toxic reactions and dosage must be carefully regulated. It is suggested by Drs.

Wittkower and Mandelbrote that this drug treatment should be accompanied by psychotherapy to help the patient to correct the emotional maladjustment which often underlies thyrotoxicosis.

A condition that somewhat resembles the frenzied over-activity of the victim of thyrotoxicosis is called mania. Mania is a difficult condition both to diagnose and to treat. It is, in its milder forms, a state of being that our competitive, aggressive, ego-dominated society tends to encourage. The "hypomanic" is one in whom the illness does not reach obviously pathological levels. Such people tend to rise to high administrative positions in business or politics. They possess great energy and drive, a lot of what is loosely called "will to power." As long as these qualities are kept under control by sound judgment the hypomanic can live a normal though hectic life. Mania begins when the controls, for some reason, cease to operate. When old Uncle Joe, respected leader in the local business community, suddenly goes out and buys two Cadillacs in the same day, plunges into huge elaborate deals that are clearly unsound, suffers from delusions of grandeur, is constantly excited, elated and even more aggressive than usual, it is clear that something has given way in Uncle Joe's controls. His hypomania has turned into full-scale mania and something had better be done about it before he ruins himself and others.

The search for a good antimanic agent resulted in one of the oddest discoveries in medicine. A simple salt, *lithium carbonate,* seems, for reasons that are presently obscure, to alleviate mania. It works slowly, taking from five to ten days to produce its full effect. For this reason the physician confronted with a highly excited manic would be inclined to use a major tranquilizer to calm down the patient during the first few days. But once a proper level of lithium was established in the blood the calming effect could be noted. Because lithium is fairly toxic, the dose level must be carefully controlled and the salt should be taken only under medical supervision.

At the opposite end of the psychological spectrum from mania is depression. Melancholia, to use a time-honored name

whose origin goes back to the days of Hippocrates, when the
condition was thought to be due to an overproduction of black
bile, is a much commoner condition than is generally realized.
Dr. Howard Fabing, who describes himself as a "general
practitioner of disorders of the nervous system," declares that he
encounters four or five new cases of melancholia for every one
of schizophrenia.

> *I have never gotten used to this disorder* [he writes]. *I am just
> amazed at a case I saw last week as those I saw as a student.
> Why or how can a normal hard-working, God-loving man or
> woman suddenly be thrown into a state of disturbed sleep and
> disordered mood which is completely disabling? I have seen this
> happen between a Tuesday and a Thursday. These people
> suddenly lose their power to concentrate their minds on the
> simplest activity such as reading the evening newspaper, they find
> all social intercourse painful and give up their friends, they
> believe that they are burdens on their loved ones, they develop
> the most illogical feelings of guilt and sin, and they quit eating.
> Unless something is done about them, suicide occurs all too
> frequently. I am just old enough to remember this torturing
> disorder before the shock therapies were introduced. Patients and
> their families crawled through months and even years waiting for
> the* vis medicatrix naturae, *the curative power of nature, to put
> these depressed minds back on the normal track again. Electro-
> shock therapy has compressed these attacks into a matter of a
> few weeks, and depressed patients seldom gravitate to the back
> wards of state hospitals any more. But they are still with us, and
> although electroshock therapy is a blessing for most of them, the
> patients, their families and their doctors have never really liked
> this form of treatment. There is something assaultive and violent
> about it, try as we do to improve our techniques of administering
> it.*[23]

Dr. Fabing is an enthusiastic supporter of the chemical theory
of the cause of melancholia. "There is surely something which
goes awry in the patient's body chemistry in this strange illness."

After stating that this is a challenge of the first magnitude for the neurochemist and neuropharmacologist, he declares that he, personally, will give a gold medal to the man who solves this riddle.

"What potions have I drunk of Siren tears, distilled from limbecs foul as hell within," writes Shakespeare who, to judge by certain passages in *Hamlet,* was personally familiar with every aspect of melancholia. The chemist must now try to reach that "foul alembic" and analyze its products, a task which is likely to tax his skill to the utmost. What shall he seek, where shall he seek it? Is melancholia also the result of an error in metabolism which leads to the production of a poison similar to the hypothetical "M" substance in schizophrenia? If so where shall we look for the poison? In blood, in urine, in lymph, in spinal fluid? But perhaps no poison is involved. Perhaps melancholia results simply from an imbalance of those potent hormones on whose quantitative relationships depend the inner harmonies of man's emotional life.

All the evidence available suggests that hormone imbalance is indeed involved. That mysterious "pleasure center" in the brain on the working of which we depend for our happiness, depends for its normal operation on the hormone noradrenalin. In schizophrenia it has been suggested that the pleasure center is poisoned by a substance resembling noradrenalin called *6-hydroxydopa.* In depression the trouble is not that the pleasure center is poisoned but that it is slowed and rendered inoperative by lack of the nerve hormone on which it depends for its function. Any drug which could increase the level of nerve hormone would, if this theory is correct, cure the depression.

This is a very nice theory and certain observations suggest that it may be correct. There was a drug called *iproniazid* which was used to treat people with tuberculosis. Victims of this disease are not generally the liveliest or happiest people in the world. When treated with iproniazid, however, the patients manifested euphoria.

The activity and jollity of these tubercular patients convinced certain acute observers that iproniazid was acting on their pleasure centers. Dr. Nathan Kline, always on the alert for new treatments for mental illness, advanced the theory that this drug was a "psychic energizer." It worked, so went the theory, by blocking the action of an enzyme called monoamine oxidase, the enzyme largely responsible for destroying noradrenalin. During the late 1950s a host of drugs similar to iproniazid appeared on the market. Some were so toxic they had to be quietly withdrawn. The rest were used with questionable results.

The search for new antipsychotic agents brought to light yet another group of antidepressant drugs. They resembled chlorpromazine chemically and were given the general name tricyclic antidepressants. *Imipramine* ("Tofranil") was the first of these. Several others followed. The drugs were slow to act but did, in certain cases, seem fairly effective. They worked, according to the theory, by blocking the reabsorption of norepinephrine.

None of these antidepressants worked reliably. The old standby of World War II, dextroamphetamine, was even less trustworthy. It produced euphoria on occasions but its continued use tended to result in loss of appetite and insomnia. It was an easy drug to abuse.

Because serious depression can lead to suicide it is often desirable to take immediate steps to lift the clouds enveloping the patients even if somewhat drastic means must be employed. It is for this reason that electroconvulsive therapy (ECT), though unpopular with physicians and often feared by patients, is still used in the treatment of depression. This rather heroic treatment, which involves inducing convulsions by passing an electric current through the patient's brain, works in a manner that remains a mystery. In serious depressions it may be life-saving as it tides the patient over the period which must elapse before the slow-acting antidepressant drugs take effect.

It must be emphasized that the antidepressants so far discovered are all of uncertain efficiency. Dr. Leo Hollister summed up the situation in an editorial entitled "Antidepressants: A Somewhat Depressing Scene."[39] Certainly, at the present time, the ideal antidepressant has not been discovered. Perhaps there is no such compound.

Before we leave the subject of the sick minds mention should be made of that much-misunderstood ailment, epilepsy. This illness, so dramatic in its manifestations, has occupied the attention of physicians from the earliest times. In the days of Hippocrates it was known as the "Sacred Disease," a concept which aroused the scorn of the Father of Medicine who, with his usual common sense, rejected the idea "that the body of man can be polluted by a god." He wrote a treatise on epilepsy and announced, with an insight surprising for the times, that "its origin, like that of other diseases, lies in heredity." By the Jews, however, it was regarded as a form of demonic possession as may be seen from the well-known passage in the Gospels: "And lo, a spirit taketh him, and he suddenly crieth out, and it teareth him that he foameth again, and bruising him hardly departeth from him."

One can hardly feel surprised that the ancients attributed the disease to the work of an evil spirit, for an attack of the most violent type of epilepsy ("grand mal") is always a distressing experience for those who witness it. The sufferer may be aware in advance of the approaching fit, for the "aura" occurs in many cases just before the trouble develops. In such a case the victim can at least lie down and avoid the risk of falling and hurting himself. Often, however, as in the Gospel story, there is no advance warning. The storm bursts suddenly and, with a violent shriek, the epileptic falls to the ground. This shriek sounds like a scream of pain and is liable to strike horror into the hearts of those who hear it. Actually it has nothing to do with pain. The epileptic is already unconscious as he utters the cry, which is produced by the violent contractions of muscles in the throat and chest.

As the seizure develops these violent contractions spread to the other muscles. The jaw is clenched. The muscles of the chest become rigid. Breathing ceases and the face becomes red or purple, the veins standing out like cords on temples and forehead.

During these "tonic convulsions" the normal reflexes are abolished. The pupils dilate widely and become insensitive to light. Saliva and perspiration pour from the body and the blood pressure rises sharply. Then, with the passing of the "tonic phase," air is sucked violently into the oxygen-starved lungs and foam, often flecked with blood from bitten lips or tongue, is blown from the mouth. Now the whole body becomes shaken with shocklike "clonic" jerks. The bowels and bladder are often violently evacuated and the limbs are bathed in an evil-smelling sweat. Finally, the bewildered epileptic recovers consciousness and looks about him in confusion. His attack is often followed by heavy sleep, by vomiting, headache, muscular soreness, or depression. In exceptionally severe cases one convulsion follows another without intervening periods of consciousness. This is the so-called "status epilepticus," a serious condition which may prove fatal.

A more gentle form of epilepsy is the "petit mal" or "little illness." (For some strange reason the medical profession insists on talking French when describing this disease!) It is characterized by momentary loss or impairment of consciousness which may be accompanied by certain peculiar movements. The rather alarming convulsions which are characteristic of "grand mal" do not occur in "petit mal." These lapses of consciousness may happen several times a day and occur most frequently in adolescence. In later life they may disappear spontaneously. Another form of epilepsy, the psychomotor type, involves confusion which may last from a few seconds to hours. During this condition the patient is out of touch with his environment but may continue to perform purposeful acts. When the confusion passes he has no recollection of anything that happened during the seizure.

It is in connection with epilepsy that that wonderful instrument, the electroencephalograph, has given us so much information. All the outward symptoms of epilepsy are the direct results of an electrical storm in the brain. The storm begins with violent electrical discharges from a small group of neurons. This violence, like panic in a densely packed crowd, spreads to the other neurons until in a few seconds the whole great mass of the cortex is discharging in unison. These massive discharges, registered by the pen of the electroencephalograph, are so distinctive that the veriest amateur can spot them. Each kind of epilepsy shows its own kind of disturbed brain wave. The three-per-second "dome and spike" of "petit mal" are entirely different from the eight-per-second spikes of "grand mal" which, in turn, differ from the slow waves of the psychomotor seizure. Oddly enough these abnormal brain waves may occur in people who have never had an epileptic fit. They have, however, a tendency to the disease and, if exposed to certain stimuli, such as a flickering light flashing at a critical rate per second, may develop the outward symptoms of epilepsy.

Few ailments have yielded more dramatically to the combined attack of the modern chemist and pharmacologist than has epilepsy. Research on the disease was made possible by the discovery that convulsions typical of epilepsy could be induced in cats by passing an electric current through their heads. Here was a tool which could be used for the mass screening of chemical substances for anticonvulsive activity. It was seized upon by Merritt and Putnam of Parke, Davis, who tested seven hundred chemicals for their ability to prevent such artificially induced fits, and emerged triumphantly with *diphenylhydantoin* ("Dilantin"). "Dilantin" differs from the bromides and such barbiturates as phenobarbital, both of which have been used in the treatment of epilepsy, in not rendering the patient drowsy. It appears to act by preventing the spread through the brain of that "electrical storm" of which the convulsions and unconsciousness are the outward and visible signs. "Dilantin" is effective against "grand mal" and psychomotor epilepsy. Complete relief from seizures is generally experienced by 60 to 65 percent of patients suffering from "grand mal" and in 20 percent the number and severity of convulsions are reduced. For those afflicted with "petit mal" another drug, *trimethadoine* ("Tridione"), is available. It will generally keep the patient completely free from seizures. In addition to these two agents several other anticonvulsants are on the market. Their names are legion: "Mesantoin," "Mysolin," "Miltonin," "Hibicon," "Diamox," "Paradione," "Phenurone," "Gemonil," "Peganone." If one proves ineffectual the physician can always try another. In this particular disease he has a remarkably wide choice of remedies.

Unfortunately for the epileptic, public education has not kept pace with these triumphs of the pharmacologist. The old horror which, in the past, was associated with epilepsy is still far too prevalent today and the epileptic suffers more from public ostracism than he does from his illness. In actual fact even "grand mal" epilepsy need not interfere too seriously with the life of the individual who suffers from it. Epileptics are frequently perfectly normal intellectually. They may be outstanding. Dostoevsky and Julius Caesar both suffered from the disease. With modern medication it is generally possible to prevent the development of convulsions. Even when they cannot be prevented there is no reason why one who suffers them should be treated as a leper. His ailment actually, except in extreme cases, is no more serious than migraine or dysmenorrhea. Obviously one prone to epileptic seizures should not work with dangerous machinery or drive a car but otherwise there is no reason why he should not perform a useful function in society. If he happens to develop a fit it is merely necessary to loosen his clothing, prevent him from hurting himself, and put a gag in his mouth to stop him from biting his tongue. Horror and disgust will not help him and are not called for. There are about 1,000,000 epileptics in the United States, the majority of whom can perform a useful function if society will let them and abandon its rather medieval attitude toward this disease.

PART THREE

Mind and
Matter

The Chemistry
of the Brain

All the drugs that have been described in this book act by
affecting the chemistry of the brain. It is out of this chemistry
that what we call mind emerges. Some aspects of this chemistry
have already been described. Now it is necessary to explore the
subject further.

What is the "stuff of the mind"? On what chemical processes
do our thoughts and emotions depend? This is a question abstruse
enough to make any honest chemist shudder. The scientist who
attempts to study the chemistry of thought and feeling resembles
a burglar attempting to open the vault of one of the world's major
banks with a toothpick. He cannot enter the mind; he does not
even know where mind is located. Merely to bring the brain
within reach of his test tubes he must break open the skull,
expose the brain, tear out a portion of its substance. But just
how much can he learn from a slice of brain in a test tube? How
is he to equate the processes he observes with the thoughts and
feelings of an intact man?

The difficulties are immense. The brain, that modest bowl of
pinkish jelly which each man carries under the dome of his skull,
is a chemical laboratory of incredible complexity. Its soft warm
mass, of the consistency of porridge, is the scene of a seething
profusion of transformations which never cease even when a man
sleeps. This loom of ten billion spindles endlessly weaves the
fabric of man's life, the thoughts, emotions, actions, hopes, and
fears which form the very basis of his being. Some patterns are
common, some are rare, and all are changing. No sooner is one
design formed than it is swept away and replaced by another.

Our study of the action of drugs on the mind will hardly be intelligible unless the brain, "the organ of the mind," is visualized at least in its main divisions. Such a visualization can best begin with the nerve cell. This cell, the ultimate building block of thought and sensation, is a really amazing structure. No other cell in the body can compare with it in complexity. A man enters the world with a certain number of these cells and, barring accidents, they live as long as he does. If killed, they cannot be replaced. If seriously damaged, they cannot be repaired. Nothing, therefore, that a human being possesses is more precious than this mass of nerve cells, for every aspect of his physical, mental, and emotional life depends on their well-being.

A glance at the structure of the extraordinary cells reveals the reason for their vulnerability. Most cells in the body are compact and fairly symmetrical. They may be flat or round or somewhat elongated but are rarely much longer than they are broad. They are little boxes of protoplasm containing a round nucleus surrounded by more or less watery cytoplasm. The nerve cell also contains nucleus and cytoplasm but the cytoplasm is spread out in an extraordinary manner. From one end of the nerve cell there extends a thin fiber of cytoplasm which connects the body of the nerve to the organ, muscle, or gland to which it supplies nervous impulses. This long process is the axone or the "nerve fiber." In man it is generally about a thousandth of an inch thick and may be several feet in length, a prodigious outgrowth for a cell of microscopic size. It is a living, working mechanism which uses energy even when it is not transmitting an impulse. Its life is dependent upon the cell body from which it grew and if cut off from the cell body it dies within a few days. The white threads which traverse our arms and legs and which are loosely called nerves are in fact masses of nerve fibers bound together in bundles. The nerve cells from which these fibers arise lie hidden in the spinal cord. In man and in all higher animals the nerve cells have retreated into the safest and most central parts of the body, relying on their long slender fibers to transmit their orders. Thus a man with both legs and both arms amputated does not, in that process, lose a single nerve cell. The cells remain safely in the spinal cord. The parts that are severed are the bundles of fibers.

From the side of the nerve cell opposite the axone emerge a number of shorter processes called the dendrites. These dendrites make contact with the axone fibers from other nerve cells, forming, in this way, a set of connections. As we ascend through the spinal cord toward the brain these axone-dendrite connections become more and more numerous until, in the brain itself, we find untold billions of such connections. This infinitely complex nerve net and the chemical processes which keep it in ceaseless activity constitute the physical basis of mind, emotion, and sensation. The nerve cell, a tiny speck of protoplasm with a slender, enormously elongated extension, is an electrochemical unit of a very complex type. Nerve fibers are often compared to telephone wires and they do, in fact, transmit an electrical message and can be stimulated by an electric current. Here the resemblance ends. In the telephone wire the electric impulse passes along the wire at a velocity up to 20,000 miles per second. In the nerve fiber the electric impulse moves much more slowly. The fastest messages carried by the largest fibers travel at a mere 300 feet per second, about as fast as a DC-3 transport plane cruises. The slowest messages, traveling in the smallest fibers, move at a rate of about one meter per second—about as fast as a man walks. Nerve fibers can conduct impulses like a telephone wire but the conduction is so poor that, after traversing about one fifth of an inch in this manner, the message is lost.

There are many nerve cells in the body. The brain alone contains about ten billion. They penetrate everywhere, a network of immense complexity, supplying muscle or gland cells with the impulse to act, transporting messages from our various sense organs. At all times a two-way traffic pours along the thoroughfares of the nervous system—not, however, along the same path, for nerve cells conduct impulses in one direction only. Impulses from the sense organs stream in toward the brain, impulses from the brain pass outward to glands and muscles. Never from the day of his birth to the day of his death does man's nervous system rest. Even in sleep it continues to operate. In sleep, however, large parts of the system are disconnected and only those areas necessary for the essential operations of the body continue to function actively.

There is in man a hierarchy of brains. They rise above one another in a sort of pyramid, each one more complex than the one below, reaching their ultimate complexity in the massive cerebral cortex with 15,000 cellular elements crowded into every square millimeter of its surface. Each level in the nervous system of man roughly corresponds to a different level of his being. Man's conscious mind, the part to which he refers as his "I," is not even aware of the operations which take place day and night within the lower levels of the brain. It is on these humble lower functions, however, that the continuation of his physical existence depends. The rate of beating of the heart, the diameter of the blood vessels, the rhythmic movement of the bowels, the activity of various glands, all these and countless other processes must be regulated by the "instinctive brain," ruling by its own wisdom the chemistry of the body. This instinctive wisdom is not possessed by the conscious mind, which frequently frustrates the instinctive brain by imposing all sorts of harmful conditions at the dictates of fashion or under the stress of unnatural conditions of life.

This instinctive brain is located in the spinal cord, the medulla oblongata, and the pons. Above it lies the hypothalamus and the thalamus, regulating and coordinating part of man's instinctive life and profoundly affecting his emotional being. Many secrets relating to the chemistry of mind and emotion are hidden in this region of the brain. Lodged at the base of the cranium in the very center of the head, completely surrounded by massive bony structures, the hypothalamus with the attached pituitary gland rules like a conductor over the glandular orchestra, influencing every aspect of man's material and spiritual existence. At least six master hormones flow from the pituitary into the blood stream, chemical messengers which bear their varied tidings to lesser glands in different parts of the body. Thyrotropin arouses the thyroid gland, stimulating it to pour out thyroxine, which increases the rate of metabolism of the body. ACTH (adrenocorticotrophic hormone) rouses the adrenal cortex, causing it to produce cortisone and related substances. The gonadotropins, male and female, carry a message from the pituitary to the ovaries or testes. Ovaries are stimulated to produce progesterone or estrogen; the testes are stimulated to produce testosterone, the chemical essence of masculinity without which the strutting muscular male is transformed to a flabby eunuch. From the pituitary also is produced somatotropin, the vital growth hormone which regulates the length of the bones and which, produced in excess, gives rise to giants.

Probing deeply and skillfully into these almost inaccessible regions of the brain, the modern neurophysiologist has revealed still more astonishing functions. What, we may ask, is pleasure? What is that nebulous condition we call happiness, the free pursuit of which is defined as one of the ends of existence in no less a document than the Declaration of Independence? There are those philosophers who take the view that happiness and pleasure are mere negative qualities, dependent on the absence of any positive pain. Not so, says the neurophysiologist. Pleasure and pain are alike brain functions. Deep in the hypothalamus, among the vital centers controlling digestive, sexual, excretory, and similar processes, there are "pleasure areas," the electrical stimulation of which produces some exquisite form of titillation the nature of which we can at present only guess.

Rats with electrodes embedded in this region of the brain can be placed in a cage with a movable bar. Each time the animal presses the bar a tiny electric current flows for an instant from the electrode into its brain. By means of such a device students of behavior can differentiate between stimuli felt as pleasure and stimuli felt as pain, for the rat, being at liberty to press the bar or leave it alone, and being, like any normal creature, dedicated to the pursuit of happiness and avoidance of pain, will press the bar often when the stimulus is pleasurable and avoid pressing it when the stimulus has proved painful.

A clever arrangement this. It is called a Skinner box (after

Harvard's B. F. Skinner) and is proving of enormous value in several kinds of psychological study. Dr. James Olds described this research into the origins of pleasure in an article in the *Scientific American:*

Electrical stimulation in some of the regions of the hypothalamus actually appeared to be far more rewarding to the animals than an ordinary satisfier such as food. For example, hungry rats ran faster to reach an electric stimulator than they did to reach food. Indeed, a hungry animal often ignored available food in favor of the pleasure of stimulating itself electrically. Some rats with electrodes in these places stimulated their brains more than 2,000 times per hour for 24 consecutive hours![74]

Amazing discovery! What curious vistas of depravity open up before our eyes. What an "abyss of divine enjoyment," to borrow De Quincey's phrase, gapes here before us. Here we see a passion similar to that of the alcoholic for his bottle, the heroin addict for his drug. This pleasure-crazed rat, were he human, would present just such a picture of moral degradation as does the soused alcoholic staggering from tavern to tavern while wife and children starve in some wretched hovel. The rat, it is clear, will sacrifice all life's duties and even its more mundane pleasures for the exquisite delights to be obtained from pressing a bar. Is it possible that these neurophysiologists have accomplished what even the Devil has been unable to do in all his centuries of experience? Can it be that they have actually devised a *new form of sin?* And what, one may ask, is the nature of this pleasure so potent that even the pangs of hunger are powerless against it? In some cases it may approximate to sexual pleasure. Life for the rat becomes one long orgasm; he enjoys the delights of love without its labors, its perils, or any wear and tear on the organs involved. But some of these pleasure centers are seemingly unconnected with sex. What form of pleasure, then, is experienced by the rat? What new ecstasies, what esoteric joys does the creature obtain each time it presses the bar?

Clearly we cannot answer any of these questions until human subjects are employed in place of rats. It is not impossible, however, that the ecstasies of mystics, the raptures of poets, the lofty joys obtained by artists from the work of creation may all be produced artificially by a minute electric current localized in one tiny area of the inner brain. These researches are of quite extraordinary significance, for they bear directly on the ultimate motivation which underlies every form of human behavior. They bear directly also on the subject of this book, for drugs affecting the mind appear to exert their action by raising or lowering the sensitivity of these pleasure centers to stimulation.

On the same level as the hypothalamus but at the back of the head is the much-convoluted cerebellum, the "little brain," concerned with the elaboration of skilled movements. The grace of the dancer, the skill of the craftsman, the finely coordinated efforts of the athlete all depend on the functioning of this region of the brain.

Over all these lower brains the massive cerebral cortex extends like a roof, the "neopallium" or new mantle, a recent product of evolution attaining in man its most magnificent development. There are regions of the cerebral cortex that control movements. There are other regions that receive sensations. Others again—for instance, the temporal lobe—are associated with memories. Large parts of the cerebral cortex are, to use the phrase of the neurophysiologist, "silent areas"; that is to say, they give neither sensation nor movement when stimulated by an electric current. The massive "frontal lobes" that fill the dome-shaped brow of man, distinguishing him from the apes and his low-browed ancestors, are silent areas. They can be chopped out and a man still lives. He does not become demented though his personality may change. Indeed, provided the motor and sensory areas are left intact, it is amazing what large amounts of the cerebral cortex can be sacrificed without any very marked change taking place in the behavior of the patient. One cannot help wondering at times whether man's massive cerebrum has not become too big, a sort of overgrown fungus which is merely filling up space in the cranium. Or has man, perhaps, more brain than he knows what to do with? Is his huge "neopallium" merely a wasted asset, like a powerful engine installed in a decrepit automobile which can never utilize more than a fraction of the available horsepower? There is a good deal of evidence to suggest that man's brain power is in fact very poorly utilized, that the full potentials of the cerebral cortex are very rarely developed. Man reaches the end of his life span with a brain only partly utilized. The other organs fail while the cerebrum is still youthful. Perhaps this, in part, is the explanation of the human tragedy.

To visualize this great network of nerve cells in operation is an almost impossible task but a general picture of its operation has been given by Sherrington (*Man on His Nature*) in a passage of extraordinary beauty and power:

A scheme of lines and nodal points, gathered at one end into a great ravelled knot, the brain, and at the other trailing off to a sort of stalk, the spinal cord. Imagine activity in this shown by little points of light. Of these some, stationary, flash rhythmically, faster or slower. Others are travelling points, streaming in serial trains at various speeds. The rhythmic stationary lights lie at the nodes. The nodes are both goals whither converge, and junctions whence diverge, the lines of travelling lights. The lines and nodes where the lights are do not remain, taken together, the same even a single moment. There are at any time nodes and lines where lights are not.

Suppose we choose the hour of deep sleep. Then only in some sparse and out of the way places are nodes flashing and trains of light-points running. Such places indicate local activity still in progress. At one such place we can watch the behavior of a group of lights perhaps a myriad strong. They are pursuing a mystic and recurrent manoeuvre as if of some incantational dance. They are superintending the beating of the heart and the state of the arteries so that while we sleep the circulation of the blood is what it should be. The great knotted headpiece of the whole sleeping system lies for the most part dark, and quite especially so the roof brain. Occasionally at places in it lighted points flash or move but soon subside. Such lighted points and moving trains of lights are mainly far in the outskirts, and wink slowly and travel slowly. At intervals even a gush of sparks wells up and sends a train down the spinal cord, only to fail to arouse it. Where however the stalk joins the headpiece, there goes forward in a limited field a remarkable display. A dense constellation of some thousands of nodal points bursts out every few seconds into a short phase of rhythmical flashing. At first a few lights, then more, increasing in rate and number with a deliberate crescendo to a climax, then to decline and die away. After due pause the efflorescence is repeated. With each such rhythmic outburst goes a discharge of trains of travelling lights along the stalk and out of it altogether into a number of nerve-branches. What is this doing? It manages the taking of our breath the while we sleep.

Should we continue to watch the scheme we should observe after a time an impressive change which suddenly accrues. In the great head-end which has been mostly darkness springs up myriads of twinkling stationary lights and myriads of trains of moving lights of many different directions. It is as though activity from one of those local places which continued restless in the darkened main-mass suddenly spread far and wide and invaded all. The great topmost sheet of the mass, that where hardly a light had twinkled or moved, becomes now a sparkling field of rhythmic flashing points with trains of travelling sparks hurrying hither and thither. The brain is waking and with it the mind is returning. It is as if the Milky Way entered upon some cosmic dance. Swiftly the head mass becomes an enchanted loom where millions of flashing shuttles weave a dissolving pattern, always a meaningful pattern though never an abiding one; a shifting harmony of subpatterns. Now as the waking body rouses, subpatterns of this great harmony of activity stretch down into the unlit tracks of the stalk-piece of the scheme. This means that the body is up and rises to meet its waking day.[86]

This loom with its millions of flashing shuttles requires, like any other very active machine, a constant supply of fuel. The fuel of the brain is glucose, a simple sugar which is brought to the brain by the blood. Glucose is vital to the working of the brain; a fall in the level of sugar in the blood at once affects the working of man's brain cells. If it falls far enough he loses consciousness, a condition seen at times in diabetics who have injected themselves with too much insulin, a hormone which causes a drop in the level of sugar in the blood. "Insulin coma" may also be induced artificially and for some unknown reason proves helpful in the treatment of certain forms of mental illness.

To burn its fuel the brain needs oxygen and, as the activity of the brain never ceases, a steady stream of this element is needed to maintain its inward fires. No other organ in the body uses oxygen at a faster rate than does the brain; no other organ is so swiftly or irreparably damaged by oxygen lack. A baby who fails to breathe for some time after birth may suffer permanent brain injury and go through life crippled with cerebral palsy. Carbon monoxide poisoning, an overdose of anesthetic, the failure of a pilot's oxygen supply at high altitudes may all inflict serious damage on the brain.

An abundant supply of blood flows constantly to the brain to keep it supplied with the substances vital for its working. No blood, however, comes into contact with the brain itself. Between brain and blood is a subtle chemical barrier which denies entry to many substances which might harm the brain. This "blood-brain barrier" has an important influence on the effect of drugs on the brain, for only those chemicals which can pass the barrier can have any direct action on the brain's substance.

The messages that reach the brain, from which the entire inner life of man is constructed, are simple impulses of electrical charge which travel at varying speeds along the fibers of the nerves. There is only one kind of message, a simple unit signal which does not vary in quality from one nerve to another. Its passage along the nerve fiber can be compared to the burning of a fuse and, just as a fuse has to have applied a certain amount of heat to start it burning, so a nerve fiber must receive a stimulus of definite size to set the impulse moving. Once it has been started it goes on moving. A second stimulus will start a second impulse but only a limited number of impulses can pass along a nerve fiber per second.

During every moment of man's conscious or unconscious life uncountable billions of these impulses are surging through the nerve fibers, both inward toward the brain and outward to glands and muscles. The differences both in sensation and in reaction which a human being manifests from moment to moment result from great patterns composed of millions of impulses, assembled and coordinated at every level from the spinal cord to the cerebral cortex. From the eye alone about one million private lines of communication enter the brain and each one, while the eyes are open, transmits nerve impulses at the rate of several hundred per second. To this are added messages from touch receptors, from the organs of hearing, of balance, the organs of taste and smell, of muscular tone, pain, temperature, visceral sensation. These surging floods of information moment by moment pour into the brain. This organ would surely be overwhelmed by the very plethora of its own information and a man would be drowned by the profusion of his sensations were there not filters in the brain which cut off from consciousness the irrelevant impulses, enabling a man to "attend" to only one thing at a time.

The nerve impulses resemble separate stones in a mosaic. They pour into the brain, are sorted and assembled, and the resulting design is the stuff of our conscious life. All our experiences are made up of these mosaics of simple impulses. Whether we perceive an odor, a sound, or a sight, whether we feel pain, heat, cold, stomachache, or fatigue, our experience is made up of the same ultimate units. The way in which we interpret these messages depends on the part of the brain in which they are received and on the connections we have built up. Our very perception of the outside world exists not in that world itself but solely in our brain. A rose is a rose is a rose, says Gertrude Stein.

Nonsense, says the neurophysiologist. A "rose" is a pattern of nervous impulses, patterns in the visual area interpreted as color, patterns in the olfactory area interpreted as scent, patterns of memory, of language, of past experience which inform us that this indeed is a rose and not a geranium or a slice of raw beef. What a rose really is we cannot tell. We can never know the true nature of anything. All the properties which we bestow on objects in the world about us are merely mosaics of nerve impulses projected outward by a magician who dwells in the brain and who deludes us into thinking that we have contact with the outside world whereas we are actually aware only of impulse mosaics occurring within the darkness of our skulls.

All sensations, all perceptions, all impressions are brain-born. Normally they arise from impulses brought to the brain by the sensory nerves, but sensations and perceptions do not have to be produced in this way. They can be produced by electrical stimulation of the brain. They can also be produced by drugs. When Havelock Ellis, sitting by the fire in his quiet room in London, saw "thick, glorious fields of jewels, solitary or clustered, sometimes brilliant and sparkling, sometimes with a dull rich glow," he certainly was not interpreting any sensory messages. There were no fields of jewels in his simple room, only the firelight flickering on the bare walls. His "jewels" were mental processes, brain reactions, chemical events in some brain area associated with vision which resulted from his having swallowed, some time earlier, a decoction of the sacred cactus of the Aztecs. Similarly that "most delightful experience" when the air seemed "flushed with vague perfume" corresponded to chemical events initiated in the olfactory regions of the brain, again the result of the action of peyote, for no such delightful perfume pervaded his room but only the raw aroma of the London fog blended with the exhalations of his fire, which probably smoked as is the habit of English coal fires. And what of those fabulous monsters which Théophile Gautier "saw" when he and his fellow members of Le Club des Hachischins assembled in the Hotel Pimodan to enjoy their favorite drug? "I saw passing by me the creatures of phantasy, owls, sea storks, satyrs, unicorns, griffons, vultures, a whole menagerie of monsters trotting, vaulting, gliding, yelping, about the room." There certainly were no unicorns in the Hotel Pimodan, and few if any owls, vultures, or satyrs. Again the fantastic menagerie, "seen" as if it actually existed, corresponded only to chemical events in Gautier's brain, this time the result of the action of certain active principles which reside in the drug hashish.

Electrical stimulation of the brain can also produce hallucinations; indeed, as every sensation is accompanied by an electrical pattern of neuron activity, it ought theoretically to be possible, by feeding suitable patterns into the brain, to produce any desired sensation, visual, tactile, gustatory, or olfactory. What vistas open up! What future prospects for the entertainment industry! No longer need we dispense amusement by the clumsy procedure of projecting an image on a screen and feeding it through the retina to the brain. We will say farewell to all that and ask our patrons merely to sit facing a blank wall while we apply the necessary stimulation directly through the skull into the visual cortex. Lo and behold, every detail of the scene appears on the wall, in full color and also in three dimensions. But why stop at mere visual stimulation? Stimulate the olfactory lobes, the very aroma of the scene is added. Stimulate the tactile area, the situations are actually felt, that lingering kiss, that melting embrace, that desperate struggle, that daring ride to the rescue! Why, we can even stimulate the hypothalamus and set the adrenals pouring out their juices so that, without ever leaving his armchair, our patron actually feels the terror of the heroine as the villain rushes upon her with intentions anything but honorable. The possibilities are endless and have all been foreshadowed by that versatile prophet of the modern age, Aldous Huxley. No doubt this form of amusement will be perfected and will be called, as he suggested, the "feelies," and men and women of our *Brave New World* will become less than ever capable of thinking their own thoughts or even of experiencing their own sensations.

While messages are pouring into the brain from the sense organs others stream out in the opposite direction to activate muscles and glands that we may run, shout, laugh, blush, weep, and generally play our role in life's drama. When the nervous impulse reaches the end of a nerve fiber it does not pass into the gland or muscle cell. It acts in a more subtle fashion by releasing a chemical called a neurohormone (nerve hormone) and it is this chemical which causes the cell to react. These nerve hormones are generated with flashlike suddenness at the end of the fiber and are destroyed no less swiftly, yet every aspect of our behavior depends on the production of these minute traces of chemical substances.

Best known of the nerve hormones is adrenalin (also called epinephrine), which is produced not only by certain nerves but also by the central portion of the adrenal glands. The nerves which work by producing adrenalin (adrenergic nerves) belong to a part of the nervous system which operates beyond the reach of the will and is for this reason called the autonomic nervous system. As we saw in Part II, it plays an important part in the emotional life of man, especially at moments of crisis. Faced with an emergency that threatens his survival, man, like any other animal, instinctively mobilizes his chemical resources to meet the danger, and does so by means of his autonomic nervous system. In the words of W. B. Cannon, whose experiments first brought to light the chemical reaction underlying rage and fear, this is what happens:

Respiration deepens; the heart beats more rapidly, the arterial pressure rises, the blood is shifted away from the stomach and intestines to the heart and the central nervous system and the muscles, the processes in the alimentary canal cease, sugar is freed from the reserves in the liver; the spleen contracts and discharges its content of concentrated corpuscles, and adrenalin is secreted from the adrenal medulla. The key to these marvellous transformations in the body is found in relating them to the natural accompaniments of fear and rage—running away in

*order to escape from danger and attacking in order to be
dominant. Whichever the action, a life or death struggle may
ensue.*[11]

A second substance associated with expression of emotion is
noradrenalin, closely related to adrenalin in chemical structure
and also liberated through the action of the autonomic nervous
system. According to Dr. D. H. Funkenstein, the emotional
manifestations which result from a production of noradrenalin
are those of outwardly directed anger accompanied by aggressive
behavior, whereas adrenalin prepares the organism for flight or,
in man, may be associated with the manifestation of anxiety or
depression. The well-known difference in behavior between the
fierce, aggressive meat eaters and the timid, readily frightened
herbivores appears to be associated with a difference in production of these two chemicals. In the adrenal medulla of the
lion, noradrenalin predominates; in the adrenal medulla of the
rabbit, adrenalin predominates. As for man, his reactions depend
largely on type. The muscular, athletic mesomorph (to use
Sheldon's terminology) who delights in hunting big game,
assaulting mountains, and generally challenging nature and his
fellow men has a system favoring the production of noradrenalin.
The more rabbitlike ectomorph, timid, retiring, and of slender
physique, will rely in his reactions on flight rather than fight
and possesses a system favoring the production of adrenalin.[25]

The third nerve hormone is called acetylcholine, and the
nerves which operate by the production of this substance are
called cholinergic. All movements of our voluntary muscles
depend on the flashlike production of acetylcholine and on its
no less rapid destruction by the enzyme cholinesterase. Without
both the substance and the enzyme we literally could not move a
muscle. That tragic affliction, *myasthenia gravis,* in which
muscular weakness becomes so great that the sufferer often has
not strength enough even to swallow, is due to some failure in
the production of acetylcholine. This neurohormone is also
responsible for several effects beyond the reach of our will, for

one segment of the autonomic nervous system (parasympathetic) operates by means of acetylcholine rather than adrenalin.

Practically all those manifestations which form the outward and visible signs of our inward emotional lives result from the action of these chemical agents: adrenalin, noradrenalin and acetylcholine. Their effects form a part of the stock in trade of every novelist who, though he may never have heard of them, never wearies of describing their more obvious modes of action. So, when we read that "her heart stopped beating for a moment," we can guess that the vagus has secreted acetylcholine; when the same organ starts "pounding like a sledge hammer," we can safely assume that the "accelerans" nerve has been stimulated and has produced adrenalin. If the heroine goes "pale as a sheet" we can be reasonably sure that contraction of her surface blood vessels has resulted from the production of noradrenalin by her sympathetic nerve endings. If she blushes we can assume that vasodilation instead of constriction has occurred and that the chemical cause is a whiff of acetylcholine, generated this time by nerves of the parasympathetic division.

Thus, underlying the sparkling play of the emotions, the ecstasies of lovers, the fury of foes, we see these three fundamental chemicals playing their roles like the three basic characters in the old harlequinade. It must not be imagined, however, that the display of emotion—its outward expression—is the same thing as the emotion itself. Behind the scenes there takes place a more subtle drama concerning the chemistry of which we know much less. For all our blushings and palings, the speeding or slowing of our hearts, our cold sweats, our tremblings and other outward manifestations are but the expressions, not the emotions themselves. The actual *experience* of emotion takes place, as Papez has shown, within the depths of the "old brain," in the thalamus or hypothalamus.[77] So we can *experience* an emotion we do not express and, if we are any good at acting, can *express* an emotion we do not experience. The chemical processes involved are different and the difference is important. Thus, if an actor in a highly emotional drama really experiences those emotions which, night after night, he must portray on the stage, there is every probability that he will develop a nervous breakdown. Ability to express without experiencing is the essence of great acting, and the chemistry of the two processes is quite different, the James-Lange theory of emotions notwithstanding.

The Shape of the Future

As we stand at the entrance to the chemopsychiatric era and look toward the future some may feel disposed to cheer and some to shudder. What can we expect from this intrusion of the chemist into the most sacred recesses of the human soul? Some may complain that he is going too far. Cannot this inquisitive analyst leave us in peace to be masters or victims of our fate, to struggle with our difficulties, our depressions, our manias without the aid of pills? We have a hard enough time already to convince ourselves that our souls are our own. Must our very moods be by-products of the contents of a bottle, must the stuff of our lives be fashioned by a chemical formula? Let the chemist stay in the laboratory and make nylons to cover girls' legs or cosmetics to beautify their faces. But let him, for heaven's sake, leave our minds alone and not intrude into our holy of holies, the innermost sanctum of our spiritual being.

To this the chemist may answer that he has no intentions of intruding where he is not wanted. Those who are masters of their souls have no need of psychochemistry. Built into their own machinery they have all that is required to protect them from the whips and scorns of time. They are well buffered, to give a chemical term a psychological meaning. The blows of fate are cushioned by an internal system which knows how to maintain its own equilibrium. Balanced, collected, and inwardly serene, beyond the reach of the storms that blow from the outer world, these fortunate beings carry within them their own snug harbor. For them no oil need be poured on the troubled water in the form of an ataraxic or a sedative. They manage very well without such aids.

It is not for such as these that the modern chemist has plunged into this new and strange domain. Let the well-balanced philosopher steer his own ship where he wishes. Our concern is with the troubled, the unbalanced and the insecure. For these the age of chemopsychiatry offers a smoother road on which to make the journey of life. For these the future prospect seems brighter.

Lucky neurotics! Soon the specter of care will be banished from your world, the burden of anxiety and guilt will be lifted from your souls. The restoration of your primeval innocence, your reentry into the garden of Eden, will now be accomplished through the agency of a pill. Soothed by reserpine, calmed by chlorpromazine, mellowed by "Miltown," elevated by "Meratran," what need you fear from the uncertainties of fortune? Tranquilly, smoothly your days will succeed one another, like the waters of a peaceful river flowing through green pastures in which graze dewy-eyed cows whose state of placid contentment resembles your own. O most fortunate of mortals, whose spiritual defects are made good by the skill of the scientist, whose personal shortcomings are supplemented by a formula. No longer need you struggle with your weaknesses or agonize over your sins. Salvation need not be purchased at the cost of spiritual war. In the chemopsychiatric age you can buy it by the bottle. O brave new world that has such bottles in it!

The prospect of a world so well tranquilized may awaken some protests. Some may maintain that man was not placed on earth to be comfortable, that he should aspire toward something nobler than the placid contentment of a well-pastured cow. One is reminded of the paradoxical irritation of William James after he had spent a week at Chautauqua, that "middle class paradise, without a sin, without a victim, without a blot, without a tear":

> . . . What was my own astonishment, on emerging in to the dark and wicked world again, to catch myself quite unexpectedly and involuntarily saying: "Ouf! What a relief! Now for something primordial and savage, even though it were as bad as an Armenian massacre, to set the balance straight again. This order is too

*tame, this culture too second rate, this goodness too uninspiring.
This human drama without a villain or a pang; this community
so refined that ice-cream soda water is the utmost offering it can
make to the brute animal in man; this city simmering in the tepid
lakeside sun; this atrocious harmlessness of all things—I cannot
abide with them. Let me take my chances again in the big outside
worldly wilderness with all its sins and sufferings. There are the
heights and the depths, the precipices and the steep ideals, the
gleams of the awful and the infinite; and there is more hope and
help a thousand times than in this dead level and quintessence of
every mediocrity.*[46]

This disdain for an excess of tranquillity is echoed by more
recent commentators. Eric Hodgkins, in an article on the tranquilizing drugs (*Life,* October 22, 1956), quotes Dr. James H.
Wall of New York Hospital: "I don't look with any favor on a
society where everybody just floats around in his own tub of
butter. A certain amount of tension and alertness is essential to
keep things straight in life." This reaction is quite understandable.
It is obviously possible to tranquilize a man to the point at which
he loses not only his anxieties but also his ambitions, ideals,
creative urges, everything, in short, that distinguishes him from a
contented cow. That this is undesirable goes without saying.

Our late-twentieth-century world, however, is very far from
being in so tranquil a state. It is crowded, tense, anxious, and
unstable; two huge powers stand ready to blast each other with
thermonuclear devices whose cumulative effects may be destructive enough to wipe out a large part of the globe's terrestrial life.
Under these circumstances we can hardly share William James's
enthusiasm for massacres. Even quite modest massacres have a
way of getting out of hand and at this stage of the world's history
we can hardly afford to indulge in them.

This mechanized, fast-moving, highly explosive culture
balances on wheels as finely poised as the jeweled movements of
a watch. To keep it in equilibrium men are needed who are
equally well balanced. We are already in the situation described

by Aldous Huxley in his futuristic fantasy, *Brave New World:* "Wheels must turn steadily, but cannot turn untended. They must have men to tend them, men as steady as the wheels upon their axles, sane men, obedient men, stable in contentment."[44] It was to obtain this stability that the rulers of the brave new world developed "soma," a drug which combined the properties of an ataraxic with those of a euphoriant and a hallucinogen. "All the advantages of Christianity and alcohol, none of their drawbacks." Soma, in fact, was largely responsible for the stability of that imaginary technocracy and Aldous Huxley, who appreciated, so many years ago, the social potentialities of pharmacology, might well be called the prophet of the chemopsychiatric age. There is no drug known at the moment with the properties of Huxley's "soma," which appears to have combined the more desirable qualities of hashish, mescaline and reserpine. We are, however, only at the beginning of the chemopsychiatric age, and "soma," the perfect euphoriant, may at any time emerge from the test tube of the chemists. If mankind *must* take an occasional holiday from reality it is certainly high time the chemists found a more satisfactory "happiness drug" than that dreary old nerve poison, ethyl alcohol.

Meanwhile the great interest being shown in drugs which affect the mind is a cheering sign, indicating a new realization on the part of scientists of the importance of research into mental processes. The real frontier of research does not lie out in the wastes of interplanetary space; it lies within the small mass of pinkish jelly, the human brain, which Sherrington called the "organ of final cause." By using this organ man rose to a position of dominance among the living things on the planet. By *misusing* this organ man might conceivably destroy not only himself but most other living things as well. Within that "great ravelled knot," with its marvelously complex network of branching fibers, those processes take place which lead to the ultimate choice between good and evil. It is a realm the exploration of which is worthy of the utmost efforts of the serious scientist, a realm in which science, art, religion and philosophy find their natural meeting place. Here we can go beyond our present rather childish preoccupation with rockets, spaceships, and the like and face the supreme task which confronts our age: how to reach spiritual maturity before we destroy ourselves. It is not an exaggeration to say that the future progress, perhaps even the future survival, of man depends on his rate of progress in this field of endeavor.

Bibliography

1. Allen, P. H. "Indians of Southeastern Colombia," *Geographical Review,* 37:567–82, 1947.
2. Alpert, R. (Baba Ram Dass) *Remember: Be Here Now.* San Cristobal, New Mexico: Lama Foundation, 1971.
3. Baudelaire, P. C. *Les Paradis Artificiels.* Paris: Poulet-Malassis, 1860.
4. Beringer, K. *Der Meskalinrausch.* Berlin: Springer-Verlag, 1927.
5. Beyle, C. R. "Letter to the Editor," *The New York Times,* October 30, 1969.
6. Bleuler, M. "The Offspring of Schizophrenics," *Schizophrenia Bulletin,* 8:93–107, 1974.
7. Blood, B. P. *The Anaesthetic Revelation and the Gist of Philosophy.* Amsterdam, New York, 1874.
8. Brand, S. "The Native American Church Meeting," *Psychedelic Review,* 9:21, 1967.
9. Brecher, E. M., ed., *Licit and Illicit Drugs.* Boston: Little, Brown and Co., 1972.
10. Cambell, A. M. G., et al., "Cerebral Atrophy in Young Cannabis Smokers," *Lancet,* 2:1219–24, 1971.
11. Cannon, W. B. *The Wisdom of the Body.* New York: W. W. Norton & Co., 1932.
12. Castaneda, C. *The Teachings of Don Juan.* New York: Ballantine Books, 1969.
13. Castaneda, C. *A Separate Reality.* New York: Simon & Schuster, 1971.
14. Cohen, S. *The Beyond Within.* New York: Atheneum, 1968.
15. Crancer, A. et al. "Comparison of the Effects of Marihuana and Alcohol on Simulated Driving Performance," *Science,* 164:851–54, 1969.
16. Domino, E. E. "Neuropsychopharmacologic Studies of Marijuana:

Some Synthetic and Natural THC Derivatives in Animals and Man," *Marijuana: Chemistry, Pharmacology, and Patterns of Social Use*. Annals of the New York Academy of Sciences, 191:166–91, 1971

17. Dorenbos, N. J. et al. "Cultivation, Extraction and Analysis of Cannabis Sativa L." *Marijuana: Chemistry, Pharmacology, and Patterns of Social Use*. Annals of the New York Academy of Sciences, 191:3–14, 1971.

18. Dumas, A. *The Count of Monte Cristo*.

19. Ellis, H. H. "Mescal, a New Artificial Paradise," *Annual Report of the Smithsonian Institute*, p. 537–48, 1898.

20. Ellis, H. H. "Mescal, a Study of a Divine Plant," *Popular Science Monthly*, 41:52–71, 1902.

21. Eugster, C. H. "Isolation, Structure and Synthesis of Central-Active Compounds from *Amanita Muscaria*," *Ethnopharmacologic Search for Psychoactive Drugs*. U.S. Public Health Service Publication No. 1645, pp. 416–18, 1967.

22. Fabing, H. D. "Frenquel: A Blocking Agent against Experimental LSD–25 and Mescaline Psychosis," *Neurology*, 5:319–32, 1955.

23. Fabing, H. D. "The New Pharmacologic Attack in Psychiatry," *Drug and Cosmetic Industry*, 78:32, 1956.

24. Fabing, H. D., Hawkins, J. R. "Intravenous Bufotenine Injection in the Human Being," *Science*, 123:886–87, 1956.

25. Funkenstein, D. H. "The Physiology of Fear and Anger," *Scientific American*, 192:74–80, 1955.

26. Gajdusek, D. C. "Recent Observations on the Use of Kava in the New Hebrides," *Ethnopharmacologic Search for Psychoactive Drugs*. U.S. Public Health Publication No. 1645, pp. 119–25, 1967.

27. Gautier, T. *Le Club des Hachischins*. Paris: Feuilleton de la Presse Medicale, 10, VII, 1843.

28. Geis, G. "Social and Epidemiological Aspects of Marijuana Use," *The New Social Drug* (Smith, D. E., ed.). Englewood Cliffs, New Jersey: Prentice-Hall, Inc., 1970.

29. Gerard, R. W. "Biological Roots of Psychiatry," *Science*, 122:225–30, 1955.

30. Goldman, D. "Treatment of Psychotic States with Chlorpromazine," *Journal of the American Medical Association*, 157:1274–78, 1955.

31. Goodman, L. S. and Gilman, A. *The Pharmacological Basis of Therapeutics.* New York: Macmillan, 1955.
32. Graften, S., ed., *Addiction and Drug Abuse Report,* Vol. 2, 1971.
33. Halleck, C. W. Testimony in *Comprehensive Narcotic Addiction and Drug Abuse Care and Control Act of 1969.* Washington, D.C.: U.S. Government Printing Office, pp. 105–6, 1969.
34. Hawkins, D. "Orthomolecular Psychiatry: Treatment of Schizophrenia," in *Orthomolecular Psychiatry.* Hawkins, D. and Pauling, L., eds., San Francisco: W. H. Freeman Co., 1973.
35. Hawkins, J. A. *Opium: Addicts and Addictions.* Danville, Va. (author's publication), 1937.
36. Heath, R. G. et al., "Taraxein: Mode of Action" in *Serological Fractions in Schizophrenia* (Heath, R. G., ed.). New York: Harper & Row, 1963.
37. Hentoff, N. *A Doctor among the Addicts.* Chicago: Rand McNally and Co., 1969.
38. Hirsch, J. *The Problem Drinker.* New York: Duell, Sloan and Pearce, 1949.
39. Hollister, L. E. "Antidepressants—A Somewhat Depressing Scene," *Clinical Pharmacology and Therapeutics,* 6:555–59, 1965.
40. Hollister, L. E. "Status Report on Clinical Pharmacology of Marijuana," *Marijuana: Chemistry, Pharmacology, and Patterns of Social Use.* Annals of the New York Academy of Sciences, 191:132–42, 1971.
41. Hollister, L. E. *Clinical Use of Psychotherapeutic Drugs.* Springfield, Illinois: Charles Thomas, 1973.
42. Holmstead, B. and Lindgren, J. E. "Chemical Constituents and Pharmacology of South American Snuffs," *Ethnopharmacologic Search for Psychoactive Drugs.* U.S. Public Health Service Publication No. 1645, pp. 339–73, 1967.
43. Huxley, A. *The Doors of Perception.* New York: Harper and Brothers, 1954.
44. Huxley, A. *Brave New World.* New York: Random House, 1956.
45. Iberico, C. C. "Ayahuasco," *Bol. Museo List nat. Janier Prado* (Lima, Peru), 5:313–21, 1941.
46. James, W. *The Philosophy of William James.* New York: The Modern Library, Random House, 1925, pp. 341–43.

47. James, W. *The Varieties of Religious Experience*. New York, 1902.
48. Johnson, C. E. "Mystical Force of the Nightshade," *International Journal of Neuropsychiatry*, 3:268–72, 1967.
49. Jones, E. *The Life and Work of Sigmund Freud*. New York: Basic Books, 1953.
50. Jones, R. T. "Tetrahydrocannabinol and the Marijuana-induced Social 'High,' or the Effects of the Mind on Marijuana," *Marijuana: Chemistry, Pharmacology, and Patterns of Social Use*. Annals of the New York Academy of Sciences, 191:155–65, 1971.
51. Kline, N. S. "Use of *Rauwolfia serpentina* in Neuropsychiatric Conditions," *Annals of the New York Academy of Sciences*, 59:107–32, 1954.
52. Klüver, H. *Mescal: The "Divine" Plant and Its Psychological Effects*. London: Kegan Paul, Trench, Trubner and Co., 1928.
53. Kolansky, H. and Moore, W. T. "Effects of Marijuana on Adolescents and Young Adults," *Journal of the American Medical Association*, 216:486–92, 1971.
54. Kolansky, H. and Moore, W. T. "Toxic Effects of Chronic Marijuana Use," *Journal of the American Medical Association*, 222:35–41, 1972.
55. Kolb, L. "Pleasure and Deterioration from Narcotic Addiction," *Mental Hygiene*, 9:699–724, 1925.
56. Kramer, J. C. "Introduction to Amphetamine Abuse," *Journal of Psychedelic Drugs* 2 no. 2, 1969.
57. LaBarre, W. et al., "Statement on Peyote," *Science*. 114:582–83, 1951.
58. Lasagna, L. von Felsinger, and Beecher, J. M. "Drug-induced Mood Changes in Man." *Journal of the American Medical Association*, 157:1006–20, 1955.
59. Leary, T. *The Politics of Ecstasy*. London: Paladin, 1970.
60. Le Dain Commission. *Interim Report of the Commission of Inquiry into the Non-Medical Use of Drugs*. Ottawa: Queen's Printer for Canada, 1970.
61. Lewin, L. *Phantastica—Narcotic and Stimulating Drugs*. New York: E. P. Dutton & Co., 1931.
62. Louria, D. B. *The Drug Scene*. New York: McGraw-Hill, 1968.

63. Ludlow, Fitz Hugh. *The Hasheesh Eater; being passages from the life of a Pythagorean.* New York: Harper and Brothers, 1857.

64. Marriott, A. and Rachlin, C. K. *Peyote.* New York: Thomas Y. Crowell Co., 1971.

65. Masters, R. E. L. and Houston, J. *The Varieties of Psychedelic Experience.* New York: Dell Publishing Co., 1966.

66. Meiers, R. L. "Relative Hypoglycemia in Schizophrenia," *Orthomolecular Psychiatry.* Hawkins, D. and Pauling, L., eds., San Francisco: W. H. Freeman Co., 1973.

67. Mezzrow, M. and Wolfe, B. *Really the Blues.* New York: Random House, 1946.

68. Mikuriya, T. "Historical Aspects of *Cannabis sativa* in Western Medicine," *The New Physician,* 18:902–8, 1969.

69. Mitchell, S. Weir. "The Effects of *Anhalonium Lewinii* (the Mescal Button)," *British Medical Journal,* 2:1625, 1896.

70. Moreau, J. J. *Du Hachisch et de L'alienation Mentale.* Paris: Masson et Cie., 1845.

71. Nahas, G. G. *Marihuana—Deceptive Weed.* New York: Raven Press, 1973.

72. Naranjo, C. "Psychotropic Properties of the Harmala Alkaloids." *Ethnopharmacologic Search for Psychoactive Drugs.* U.S. Public Health Service Publication No. 1645, pp. 385–91.

73. Okakura-Kakuzo. *The Book of Tea.* Edinburgh: T. N. Foulis, 1919.

74. Olds, J. "Pleasure Centers in the Brain," *Scientific American,* 195:105–18, 1956.

75. Osmond, H. Postscript in *In Search of Sanity* by Gregory Stefan. New Hyde Park, New York: University Books, 1966.

76. Osmond, H. and Smythies, J. "Schizophrenia—A New Approach," *Journal of Mental Science.* 98:309–15, 1952.

77. Papez, J. W. "A Proposed Mechanism of Emotion," *Archives of Neurology and Psychiatry,* 38:725–43, 1937.

78. Parsons, E. C. *Mitla—Town of Souls.* Chicago, 1926.

79. Pauling, L. "Orthomolecular Psychiatry," *Science,* 160:265–71, 1968.

80. "Report of the Committee on Legislative Activities," *Journal of the American Medical Association,* 108:2214–15, 1937.

81. Rinkel, M. et al. "Experimental Psychoses," *Scientific American,* 192:34–39, 1955.

82. Rouhier, A. *Le Peyotl*. Paris: Doin et Cie., 1927.
83. Schultes, R. E. "The Identification of Teonanacatl, a Narcotic Basidiomycete of the Aztecs," *Botanical Museum Leaflets,* 7:37–56, 1939.
84. Schultes, R. E. "The Place of Ethnobotany in the Ethnopharmacologic Search for Psychotomimetic Drugs," in *Ethnopharmacologic Search for Psychoactive Drugs*. U.S. Public Health Service Publication no. 1645, pp. 33–58, 1967.
85. Sheldon, W. H. and Stevens, S. S. *The Varieties of Temperament*. New York: Harper and Brothers, 1942.
86. Sherrington, C. S. *Man on His Nature*. London: Cambridge University Press, 1940.
87. Shulgin, A. T. et al. "The Psychotomimetic Properties of 3,4,5-trimethoxyamphetamine," *Nature,* 189:1011–12, 1961.
88. Smith, D. E. and Mehl, C. "An Analysis of Marijuana Toxicity," in *The New Social Drug,* Smith, D. E. ed., Englewood Cliffs, N.J.: Prentice-Hall, 1970, pp. 75–76.
89. Stefan, G. *In Search of Sanity*. New Hyde Park, N.Y.: University Books, 1966.
90. Stein, L. and Wise, C. D. "Possible Etiology of Schizophrenia: Progressive Damage to the Noradrenergic Reward System by 6-hydroxydopamine," *Science,* 171:1032–36, 1971.
91. Stockings, G. T. "Clinical Study of the Mescaline Psychosis with Special Reference to the Mechanism of the Genesis of Schizophrenic and other Psychotic states," *Journal of Mental Science,* 86:29–47, 1940.
92. Stoll, W. A. "Ein neues, in sehr kleinen Mengen wirksames Phantasticum," *Schweizerische Archiv von Neurologie,* 64:483, 1949.
93. Stromberg, V. L. "The Isolation of Bufotenine from *Piptadenia Perigrina*," *Journal of the American Chemical Society,* 76:1707, 1954.
94. Sturtevant, F. M. and Drill, V. A. "Effects of Mescaline in Laboratory Animals and the Influence of Ataraxics on Mescaline Response," *Proceedings of the Society of Experimental Biology and Medicine,* 92:383–86, 1956.
95. Tart, C. T. *On Being Stoned: A Psychological Study of Marijuana Intoxication*. Palo Alto: Science and Behavior Books, 1971.

96. Taylor, N. *Flight from Reality*. New York: Duell, Sloan and Pearce, 1949.

97. Waser, P. G. "The Pharmacology of *Amanita Muscaria*," *Ethnopharmacologic Search for Psychoactive Drugs*. U.S. Public Health Service Publication no. 1645, pp. 419–39, 1967.

98. Wasson, R. G. "Fly agaric and Man," *Ethnopharmacologic Search for Psychoactive Drugs*. U.S. Public Health Service Publication no. 1645, pp. 405–14.

99. Weil, A. "Nutmeg as a Psychoactive Drug," *Ethnopharmacologic Search for Psychoactive Drugs*. U.S. Public Health Service Publication no. 1645, pp. 188–201, 1967.

100. Weil, A. *The Natural Mind*. Boston: Houghton Mifflin Co., 1972.

101. Weil, A. et al. "Clinical and Psychological Effects of Marijuana in Man," *Science,* 162: 1234–42, 1968.

102. Wilkins, R. W., Judson, W. E. "The use of Rauwolfia serpentina in hypertensive patients," *New England Journal of Medicine,* 248:48–53, 1953.

Index